Acclaim for Benjamin Buchholz's
One Hundred and One Nights

"*One Hundred and One Nights* is a fearless and seductive piece of ventriloquism by a storyteller in full command of his craft. Written in spare, lyrical prose from the point of view of an Iraqi doctor haunted by violence, this first novel is a spike in the heart, a powerful testimony to the insanity of war and the undeniable demands of love."

— Hillary Jordan, author of *Mudbound* and
When She Woke

"Benjamin Buchholz's brilliant debut offers a powerful look at life in war-torn Iraq. Stocked with finely drawn characters and political intrigue, *One Hundred and One Nights* blows down the highway with all the furious momentum of an army convoy while delivering its real prize: a heart-wrenching story of love and loss and redemption."

—Zoë Ferraris, author of *City of Veils*

One Hundred and One Nights

مئة ليلة وليلى

A novel

Benjamin Buchholz

BACK BAY BOOKS

Little, Brown and Company

New York Boston London

Back Bay Books / Little, Brown and Company
Hachette Book Group
237 Park Avenue, New York, NY 10017
www.hachettebookgroup.com

First edition, December 2011

Back Bay Books is an imprint of Little, Brown and Company. The Back Bay Books
name and logo are trademarks of Hachette Book Group, Inc.

The characters and events in this book are fictitious. Any similarity to real persons,
living or dead, is coincidental and not intended by the author. Any references to the
United States military or policy are not endorsed by the United States military.

The publisher is not responsible for websites (or their content) that are not owned by
the publisher.

The author is grateful for permission to reprint the excerpt from "…Baby One More
Time." Words and music by Max Martin. Copyright © 1998 by Grantsville
Publishing Ltd. All rights in the United States administered by Universal Music–Z
Tunes LLC. International copyright secured. All rights reserved. Reprinted by
permission of Hal Leonard Corporation.

Excerpts from the Holy Quran are based on the translations of Yusuf Ali and M. M.
Pickthall.

Library of Congress Cataloging-in-Publication Data
Buchholz, Benjamin.
    One hundred and one nights : a novel / Benjamin Buchholz.
    p. cm.
    ISBN 978-0-316-13377-7
    1. Safwan (Iraq) — Social conditions — Fiction. 2. Families — Iraq — Fiction.
3. Friendship—Iraq — Fiction. I. Title.
    PS3602.U2535O54 2012
    813'.6—dc22   2010044935

10 9 8 7 6 5 4 3 2 1

RRD-C

Printed in the United States of America

To my wife, Angie, for abiding my absences,
both physically during war
and mentally, when the writing overfills me.

يقولون ليْلى بالْعِراقِ مَريضة   فَمَا لَكَ لا تَضْنَى وأنْتَ صَديقُ

سقى الله مرضى بالعراق   فإنني على كل مرضى بالعراق شفيقُ

فإنْ تَكُ لَيْلَى بالْعِراقِ مَريضَة   فإني في بحر الحتوف غريقُ

أهِيم بأقْطارِ البلادِ وعَرْضِهَا   ومالي إلى ليلى الغداة طريقُ

~قيس ابن الملوح

They say Layla of Iraq is ill
And ask, "Why, if she's yours, don't you care?"
Allah succours the frail of Iraq
So, too, must I feel for each of the ailing.
For, if Layla's unwell I drown in a sea of the lost
Wandering the land's width and breadth
Without knowing the way to her.

— Qays ibn al-Mulawwah

One Hundred and One Nights

1

الإثنين
Monday

LAYLA FIRST VISITS TODAY, in the evening, like most evenings
hereafter. She stands in shadow under the awning of my
little store, my shack, as a golden sunset reflects its light
against the overpass where the highway from Basra to
Kuwait and the even larger highway from the port of Umm
Qasr to Baghdad intersect. Here, the American convoys
pass around the outskirts of the little town of Safwan, crossing the border between Iraq and Kuwait. They pass north
and south and I count them as they pass, a hobby, a private
game, relieving the boredom of work in my store. This girl
Layla is, I guess, ten years old. Or something like that. A
girl. A small girl. Her appearance coincides with the closing
echo of the evening call to prayer, so that among the kneeling, quieted people, she is the only object seemingly alive.

Today is not only the first day of Layla's visitations but

also the nineteenth day of business for me since I moved to Safwan. A good day. I received a shipment of used and new mobile phones to sell, so now it is not just phone cards with minutes for the people to buy, but also actual merchandise.

As the sun dips lower, I see on the edge of the road above me the guard for the overpass leaning back on his three-legged chair. He smokes a cigarette with deep concentration while his Kalashnikov rests against the tent behind him. The day has been a windless one. A trail of smoke from the guard's cigarette rises through the sunset, mirroring plumes from oil fields behind him, where gas by-products burn above the scattered derricks and refineries of the Rumailah oil fields, staining the sky.

Layla arrives from the direction of the guard, as if emerging from the smoke of the oil field. Gradually her apparition then mingles with and breaks free from the thinner smoke of the guard's cigarette. This distortion wafts over a patch of scrubby, littered desert toward the market, toward me. The guard is a lazy man, letting a little girl cross the highway unnoticed and without reprimand. I tell myself to remember to speak to Sheikh Seyyed Abdullah about his laziness.

Layla wanders into the market and eventually comes to my store. Eventually, but not immediately. Having seen her cross the road, picking her way between prostrate figures of men kneeling on prayer rugs, I watch her. She talks to Jaber, who sells whole plucked chickens or kebabs of chicken from a shop even smaller, more pathetic, than mine. Jaber shoos her away as he rolls up his prayer rug. She runs a stick along a row of empty propane tanks at the tank exchange point, skipping to the rhythmic hollow-shell sound. She passes my stand, heading into town, then passes more stands lining the way between my store and the town gate: Rabeer's used-car lot fenced with barbed wire; the lot where some of the Shareefi cousins, Maney'a and Ibrahim, sell parts of houses, doors, sinks, siding; a concrete vendor, Wael, whose bags of powdery mixture lie in the open, stacked on weathered wooden pallets. Layla blends with the trash that fills all the space between and around our shops—faded plastic bottles, napkins, bits of paper and plaster and mortar and clothing. She steps on, over, through these items. As she passes each shop, the vendors or their hired thugs stare through her even as they look at her. She is a part of the landscape, a rag doll in dirty clothes amid dirt and dust, debris and decay. The guards pay her no more attention than they pay to the roving mongrel dogs.

At the town gate Layla stops beneath a poster of Muqtada al-Sadr recently plastered over a mosaic of his father, Grand Ayatollah Mohammad bin Mohammad Sadeq al-Sadr, whom Saddam Hussein killed just before the American war. The gate is a relic of more prosperous years, twenty feet tall, its two solid pillars tiled in beautiful blue-and-gold faience with the ayatollah's white turban luminous in the center. In the poster, as in all his posters, Muqtada al-Sadr includes his father, the two of them standing nearly side by side, the son hoping thereby to share some of the aura of his father's respect and eminence. The mosaic beneath had been made in days when workmen took pride in their art. It evidences patience, the piecing of so many little fragments into a whole. It evidences care. As I think about it, I find it suddenly comical that the mural should be covered with the poster's ridiculousness, its flimflam politics jockeying for attention, the two images of the ayatollah juxtaposed in faience and in flimflam. But neither the poster nor the mosaic is really in accord with Islam. They are idols: art, advertising, politics—pictures of men serving only to distract from the contemplation of the Compassion and Mercy of Allah. A trail of little machine-gun holes peppers the mural, breaking through the luster to reveal plain, skin-colored adobe. The holes brutally underscore my point about impiety while also providing a flavor of the history of this town.

Layla looks up from the mosaic, back across the market. Perhaps she has heard my involuntary sigh of disdain over the poster's symbolism. When she sees me, some hundred feet away, and when our gazes meet, she moves steadily toward me, shop to shop, retracing her footsteps. Her approach can mean no good for me, nor can it mean anything good for my business. I begin to close my store, putting away mobile phones I've unpackaged, returning phone cards to their plastic cases. I step out the side door and look into the shade under the awning, expecting to find the girl there, frowning with an expression of practiced piteousness. I do not see her, and I breathe a sigh of relief. One less beggar to fend away. As any good man does, I pay *zakat,* the yearly religious alms that go to support the poor and the needy. Perhaps this girl's father and mother already have benefited from my money. Anyway, I need not tithe every beggar girl or boy who chances into the market.

I reach up, under the awning, and unfasten the corrugated tin cover I have made for my shop window. It swings down, and I lock it in place with a padlock. I run my hand over the front of my *dishdasha* to return the key for the padlock to my breast pocket. But I miss the pocket with my hand, and the key falls to the ground. Bending to retrieve it,

I see the girl standing very close in front of me. First I see her bare feet, then blue jeans that end in tatters just below the hem of her flowing caftan. There, where the jeans end, I notice a length of yarn with bird bones and little dollhouse keys tied around her left ankle.

"I have no handouts for street children," I say.

"I don't want handouts," she says.

This should end the conversation but for some reason it does not. Layla stands still, as if sprung freshly from the ground. I put my shop-window key into my pocket, patting it for extra certainty. I feel a touch of remorse for having spoken harshly, for having assumed the girl would ask me for *baksheesh* — money or food or water or some little trinket.

"My name is Layla," she says.

"Mine is Abu Saheeh," I say.

If this were a business deal between men, we would clasp hands, kiss cheeks. But I know of no rules to govern a meeting between a forward little urchin of a girl and an old man like me. Or no rules I wish to follow. Doubtless she is a street child, but I can't bring myself to speak the harsh words that would send her on her way to beg from the next stall in the market, to steal from the next unwary businessman. Instead, I stand there, looking odd, my stomach anxious for me to begin my walk into Safwan, where I will go to my favorite café and order tea and hummus and falafel.

"Have you been to America?" she asks. "I haven't," she says, "but I watch TV, and I talk to the soldiers sometimes, and my favorite is Arnold Schwarzenegger."

"He is not a real soldier," I say.

"I know," she says.

Again, this should end it. I stand a little straighter, look past her toward the gate and its mosaic of the ayatollah, past the mosaic toward the town, the café, my dinner.

"Do you believe in robots?" she says. "Arnold Schwarzenegger is a robot."

"Only in the movie," I say.

I wonder why I am arguing with her about robots, about movies, about American actors.

"So you don't believe in them?"

"No. How silly."

"But the Americans have them; the British, too. I've seen them blow up a bomb with a robot near the az-Zubayr al-Awwam Mosque up near Basra. I think the Americans are robots and the British are becoming robots. I think they have skin over their metal, and they send their old robots that aren't shaped right for skin coverings to blow up the bombs, to do the dirty work."

She leans closer to me. She puts a hand to her mouth as if to shield her words, her secret words, from being overheard by others in the market. She whispers, "I think it is a conspiracy of robots, anyone, everyone. I think they all might be robots except for you and for me."

"I think you're funny," I say.

She laughs, a snorting little falsetto laugh. I notice that the tendons of her neck are tight, nervous.

"I like you," she says. "I will come back tomorrow evening."

At that, as quickly as she had come, Layla leaves. I lock the side door to my shop. When I close the door it emits a deep thump that reminds me of the sound a hand makes when slapping an empty oil drum, an empty shell. The wind, absent all day, gusts in from the north, across the oil fields, bringing with it the stink of burning crude and causing my corrugated window covering to rattle so that the shop continues to resound, tinny clanging over a deep and fearsomely sad undertone of emptiness.

I shrug, look up toward the road, to where the guard still lounges on his three-legged chair. I take my time walking through the gateway that has the mosaic of the ayatollah on it, and as I pass under it, I touch one of the blue fragments of mosaic tile. It is cool and rough along its edge.

When I arrive at the café in the main downtown market of Safwan—a place owned by a man named Bashar, a friend of mine from university—I am greeted with a handshake and a kiss on each cheek and a handwritten menu. I read the menu for a while but I order only tea and hummus and falafel, my usual dinner. The evening is warm and pleasant and empty around me, even though it is filled with myriad voices, people everywhere, people passing in the street, haggling, ordering food from the café. The noise washes over me like an outgoing wave, while beneath it I hear a darker undertone, a shell of a town, perfect for me, resonating yet hollow.

2

الثلاثاء

Tuesday

LAYLA VISITS IN THE EVENING, this second evening, just as
she said she would. She stands in shadow under the awning
of my little store, my shack, as a golden sunset reflects its
light against the overpass where the highway from Basra
to Kuwait and the even larger highway from the port of
Umm Qasr to Baghdad intersect. As always, the American convoys pass around the outskirts of the little town
of Safwan, wreathing it with the commerce of war, so
much merchandise, so many things required to maintain
the American troops and the Iraqis who work for them.
The convoys head north, and I see them filled: everything
ranging from low and sinister M1 Abrams tanks loaded on
big green flatbed trailers to butter and Gatorade in plain
white civilian refrigerator trucks. These same convoys return south after a week or two, their trailers and flatbeds

empty, except sometimes for damaged items, things exploded in the main battlegrounds far to the north of this sleepy little border town. I count the convoys as they pass, a hobby, a private game, relieving the boredom of work in my store. Eighteen of them go north today. Twenty-one return southbound. A normal day, about a thousand vehicles in all, thirty per convoy.

Today marks the second day of Layla's visitations. Also the twentieth day of business for me since I moved to Safwan. A good day. I sold the first mobile phone from the shipment received yesterday. The more mobile phones I sell, the more customers I will have for mobile-phone cards. At this rate of increase, I will soon be as wealthy as a Saudi.

As the sun dips lower, I see on the overpass the flaps of the guard's tent closed firmly against both wind and sun. The guard has already gone into his tent and has been asleep for at least an hour. Will he wake for evening tea? A meal? Will he wake for the call to prayer? Did he have company on his lonesome cot last night, making him weary and moonstruck today? I tell myself to remember to speak to Sheikh Seyyed Abdullah about him, for his habits are not conducive to good order and safety in the market or on the overpass he has been assigned to guard. I, as a merchant, should be concerned about such things.

After I rise from my prayers and roll and store my rug on an upper shelf in my shop, I start to put away my wares, turning my back to my shop window. I count phone cards. I slip them into plastic jackets to preserve them from the desert dust. I count phones, returning them to their boxes and sealing the boxes with clear strips of tape. I arrange everything on the shelves and then stand back, wistfully, to admire the neatness, the simplicity, the order I have imposed on at least one little section of the world.

"If you don't believe in robots," Layla says, "what do you believe in?"

Not having seen her coming, I spin around. She notices the surprise on my face.

"What?" she says. "Don't look afraid. I told you I'd come back this evening."

"Does your mother know you are here?" I ask.

Layla leans inward over the sill of my shop window. She shrugs off my question about her mother by continuing with her thoughts.

"Do you believe in genies? Do you believe in aliens? Do you believe in rock-and-roll music? Birth control? Do you think animals can talk to each other?"

"You have a lot of questions!"

"Yes, I suppose."

I think about her questions one at a time. She watches me, scrutinizes me.

After a moment, I say: "I believe in Allah, but His ways are many and often unknowable. I believe in rock-and-roll music because I have heard it so I know it is real, but I don't like it; instead, I prefer Umm Kulthum, the classics. No, I don't believe in birth control; it's immoral, humans making such decisions. And, yes, I suppose animals do talk, in their own way."

"*Alhumdu l-Allah!*" she says. "You only forgot about the aliens."

"Alas, you should have no great expectations of a poor mobile-phone salesman like me. How could I possibly remember them all, so many questions? And anyway, what silly things to talk about, genies and aliens, robots and rock and roll!"

"You are a mobile-phone salesman?" she asks, looking at the phones and phone cards. "That's not what you are. Not really. Aren't you something better? Something more romantic? A soldier? A pirate? An Internet hacker? A singer or a dancer or an acrobat?"

"Well," I say, "what self-respecting Iraqi cannot sing a song or two, do a dance or three?" I puff my chest out good-naturedly. The conversation has no logic to it, no rules, no reason that I must be particularly polite, particularly stoic, particularly friendly, or even particularly truthful. No reason other than the fact that this girl, this Layla, entertains me. And, because she entertains me, I am somehow predisposed to be kind to her in return, to engage in this sort of small talk with her. She makes me laugh inside myself.

"I will sing you a song," she says, "but it must be rock and roll. I listen to pop music and stuff like that, not Umm Kulthum or fuzzy grandfather songs. Britney Spears is my favorite."

"Okay," I say. I *do* want to hear her sing.

She growls a first note and then launches into the song:

> *Oh baby baby, how was I supposed to know*
> *That somethin' wasn't right here*
> *Oh baby baby, I shouldn't have let you go*
> *And now you're outta sight, yeah*
> *Show me how you want it to be*
> *Tell me baby because I need to know now, oh*
> *   because*
> *My loneliness is killin' me*

I must confess I still believe
When I'm not with you I lose my mind
Give me a sign, hit me baby one more time.

"That is good," I say. "Very good! I like the little dance move at the end the most."

"You believe in dance moves?"

"Yes, definitely."

"You believe in mobile phones?"

"Why not? Of course I do. They work. I sell them. They provide money so I can live. What's not to believe?"

"I believe in mobile phones and dance moves and pop music," she says. "I believe in almost anything. My mother says I dream too much and believe in things too much. My mother doesn't like me hanging around with the American patrols because she says they give me ideas."

"You should listen to your mother," I say.

"Bah," she says. "The Americans are interesting. They *all* live next to Sharon Stone. They have in-ground swimming pools. Each American is a prince."

"I thought they were robots," I say.

"Robot princes," she says.

She should laugh as she says it, a nice little joke, tying up all her bits of scattered philosophy in one neat bundle. I smile but when I look at her I see she is not joking. She speaks in earnest, her teeth clamped shut. Her eyes, I notice, are blue rather than the usual shades of brown and sometimes green common to the people of southern Iraq. The blue pierces through the dust-streaked and darkly tanned skin of her face like a desert wind piercing a traveler at night, a traveler exposed at the top of a dune ridge.

I realize Layla stares at me. She knows I have drifted away. To cover my lapse, I start to ask her for another song or dance, or both if she knows more, even if it must be pop music. But, as if she has heard a sound in the distance, a call for her to come home, she turns and says over her shoulder: "I'll come see you tomorrow evening once again."

Then she runs toward the north, across the road into the desert on the far side of the highway overpass.

I finish shutting my shop and I walk into Safwan. I mention Layla to my friend Bashar when I reach his café. He laughs, sits at the table with me for a moment, clasping my hand.

"Do you believe in genies?" he asks, one eyebrow raised.

"She's no genie, Bashar."

"Perhaps you need a companion tonight. I know any number of widows in town. So many widows now. Many have been eyeing you from afar—an eligible, educated man like you makes quite a catch."

I smile, pick up the menu, scan it to the bottom, and order tea and hummus and falafel. When he brings my food, only a few minutes later, the image of Layla's pop-music dance disappears from the forefront of my mind. I eat, enjoying the noise of the crowd in the evening and the passing of cars and carts and scooters and bicycles on the main street. The heat of the day dissipates into the night sky, rising above the noise of the town, passing through the tangle of electrical wires and clothes-drying lines that loop and arch over the street, freeing itself at last to journey up to the empty and quavering stars.

Somewhere a few doors away, from a balcony overlooking the street, a man sings in a fine gravelly old-fashioned tenor. It's something sad, filled with longing and distance and loss, but I can't quite place the words. Farsi perhaps, a Persian song. Too much of that language slipping into the dialect used by these far-southern Iraqis. Certainly it isn't a sacred song, or I would hear somewhere in it the warbled and elongated sound of the name of Allah, the Gracious, the Merciful, Praise Be Unto Him.

3

الأربـعاء

Wednesday

LAYLA VISITS IN THE EVENING, this evening, just as she promised. She stands in shadow under the awning of my little store, my shack, as a golden sunset reflects its light against the overpass where the highway from Basra to Kuwait and the even larger highway from the port of Umm Qasr to Baghdad intersect. The convoys do not rest today. Just as always, they slow as they approach the off-ramps and the on-ramps between the north-south highway and the military bypass around the western edge of Safwan. Three Humvees accompany each convoy: one in the front, one in the middle, one to bring up the rear. From my store in the market, at the next highway intersection southeast from the American bypass, I can actually see the faces of the American soldiers in their vehicles. They wear dark sunglasses and helmets. They stare into the desert and into the town as they turn the corner away from me, heading north to Baghdad or south to Kuwait. Each Humvee has a big machine gun and small machine gun mounted on a turret on its roof, manned by one of the soldiers whose body protrudes through the turret opening. Some of these soldiers I name in my imagination, a little game I play with myself to take my mind off the boredom of my work. However, I quickly run out of suitable American names, so I have Dave and then I also have Dave Junior and also Dave-Who-Is-Shorter-Than-Dave-Junior and additionally several Patricks, a Robert or two, a Winston. Maybe Winston is more of a British name? I wonder.

My feelings toward the Americans are mixed. I don't hate them. I feel sorry for them, exposed and prominent as they are, noticeable as they are. Giving them names makes them seem more real to me, more human. I know that naming them is something I shouldn't do. It will only increase my feelings of guilt. I should cling to the various jihadist slogans—Evil Empire, Great Satan, etc. But my mind, so lulled by the rhythm of the days in this market, cannot help but indulge in this name-giving diversion.

Today marks the third day of Layla's visitations. Also the twenty-first day of business for me since I moved to Safwan. A good day. I sold four mobile phones and fifteen mobile-phone cards with a hundred minutes apiece on them. One man, a Shareefi, inquired about purchasing a satellite dish for his niece's home. The inquiry calls to mind certain hints that Sheikh Seyyed Abdullah has made, to the effect that I could easily expand my business to sell satellite dishes and other electronics. The extra profit from such sales would be most welcome. The conversation with the man from the

Shareefi family seems promising. I resolve to order some satellite-dish sales brochures.

The guard for the overpass goes into his tent for tea. He is not as tired today as he seemed yesterday and he has spent most of his time pacing from his tent across the intersection and back. At the farthest point in his patrol he is only about fifty meters from my shop. His tent is much nearer, maybe only fifteen meters, perched like the nest of a roc on a little flat space between the precipice of the overpass embankment and the road itself.

The guard at last ceases pacing. He enters his tent to make tea. As he fools with his tea set, a British patrol approaches, four dun-colored Land Rovers brimming with soldiers. The British bring more soldiers with them than the Americans, wherever they go. The Americans have more stuff; the British bring more people—different styles of war. Maybe all the British are actually robots, which would mean they have the same amount of stuff as the Americans, just more cleverly disguised so that they might fool a simple mobile-phone merchant into considering them people. Meaningless speculation, robots and whatnot. I chide myself and bring my mind back into focus. The patrol moves off the road from Basra into Safwan, taking the exit ramp that passes just behind my shop. I guess they are on their way to a meeting with the town council down near Bashar's café in the city center. The guard on the overpass does not even notice the vehicles as they turn in succession before him. After all the pacing and watchfulness today, he does not notice. He just continues making his tea with his back turned toward the patrol. I can hardly believe it. It fits with all the other negative things I must report to Sheikh Seyyed Abdullah.

When the British patrol clears through the market and passes beneath the blue-tiled arch into Safwan, it disappears from my view. I look down. Layla stands in front of my shop.

"Hello, girl," I say. "*Masah il-kheir.* A fine evening!"

"It is," she says. "Do you have a son?"

"No," I say. "Why?"

"The honorific," she says. "I am calling you father of someone. Who is this *Saheeh* you speak of when you tell me Abu Saheeh is your name?"

"No son," I say. "Just a joke."

Layla looks disappointed but she does not reply. She merely turns her head to the side as if examining me. I come out the side door of my shop. Expecting her in the shade under the awning, I find nothing there.

I turn around and look back into the stall, where the shelves now display several styles of phones and headsets, stacks of brochures for calling plans, and new phone cards in their plastic sleeves. A Shasta orange soda on the storefront sill attracts a swarm of bluebottle flies. Layla has vaulted through the window and over the counter. She stands inside the shack. Brushing flies away from the soda, she picks up the can and shakes it. Some liquid remains in the bottom. She looks at me and I nod to let her know she may drink.

"What will we talk about today?" I ask. I lean in through the sill as though I am the customer and she the owner of the store. "More stories of America and Americans? How about the soldiers you've met? Let's talk about them."

She shakes her head no as she drinks.

"TV stars?" I say. "Arnold Schwarzenegger?"

"No," she says, wiping the corner of a lip now colored brighter orange than any henna. "No. Not Americans. Not TV. Not movies or aliens."

"Then what?"

She puts the can on the dirt floor, raises a small bare and calloused foot above it. I notice the same circlet of bird bones and dollhouse keys around her ankle as I had seen the first day we met. Maybe my initial guess at her age was wrong. She is older than ten. Maybe twelve, maybe even thirteen or fourteen. Too old for a street urchin. Too old to run wild. Nearly ready for the *hijab*. Nearly ready for marriage. She is just small-boned. Malnourished. A waif. It makes me feel uncomfortable to see her up close, and to better comprehend her true age, this nearness to womanhood.

With her bare foot Layla crushes the can, retrieves it from the dust, and stashes it into an inside pocket of her caftan.

"I want to talk about you," she says. "About Abu Saheeh. About Father Truth."

"Me? You think I am more interesting than Americans? More interesting than Arnold Schwarzenegger?"

"Yes," she says. "I think you're a spy."

I laugh, heartily. More heartily than I have laughed for months.

"Like Peter Sellers?" I ask.

"Who?"

"The Pink Panther."

She frowns, doesn't get it, hasn't seen the movie. Probably hasn't seen the cartoon, either. Not in vogue for the youth now. Certainly not shown on our local broadcast TV, the Egyptian station Nile Drama. She waits until I have finished laughing and wiping my eyes. I feel young for laughing, still suppressing giggles that threaten to surge from belly to throat. But I feel old for thinking of Peter Sellers. I am forty-two. I vaguely remember that a new *Pink Panther* movie has come out from America, a remake. I wonder who stars in it? Arnold Schwarzenegger? I try to think of the names of other, more modern actors. Tom Cruise? Jack Black? Rufus Wainwright?

"Peter Sellers is an actor," I say. "I've always thought I look a bit like him, the mustache. Or maybe he looks a little bit like an Iraqi. But he's no Schwarzenegger, no Tom Cruise. Not handsome. Not someone you'd like."

Suddenly a little angry, Layla strikes a pose far too mature for her, hip thrust forward, chin high. It reinforces my opinion that she is likely older than I had supposed. Is it fourteen? Just a frail, bird-boned fourteen-year-old? Her mother should be ashamed, letting her out of the house at such an age and dressed in nothing more than rags! Rags, when she should be veiled to preserve her family's honor!

A ray of sunlight catches Layla's face, the last of the day, now long and trembling as it passes on an almost impossibly flat and honey-colored route over the crest of distant Jebel Sanam, the Camel's Hump Mountain, then between the western buildings of Safwan. The ray enters the market. It flows around hastily strung electric wires, antennas for the shops, it aches and yearns and tunnels and breathes and darts this way and that way until at last it pierces through my open shop door to perform its final and glorious mission: outlining Layla in gold.

She's beautiful, more beautiful than anything I've seen for months. Not a warm beauty. Not a beauty that makes the heart melt. Hers is, instead, a cold calamitous tragedy of beauty. I sober in the presence of her, my good humor irradiated as if the belly laugh I gave myself had met its opposite in her slightly troubled and impious gaze. She is not tall; shoulder height for me. She is not yet shaped like a woman; no womanly curves. She hasn't eaten enough to suitably fatten herself. In fact, she may never have curves. From afar she seems the very avatar of the Iraqi street urchin I initially thought her to be: gangly, dirty, barefoot, wearing frayed blue jeans and an even dirtier greenish knee-length caftan. An accent of blue trapunto stitching on the hem of the caftan shows that it was nicely made, most likely an import from Kuwait, one of the many that flow across the civilian border station to the east of the American military crossing point. Layla has a small sharp nose set between rounded cheeks. Her face, darkly bronzed from sun and dust, merges into a mass of curly hair bleached from brown to the same hennaed honey-gold the sunset casts into the market. Most striking, though, as I noticed before, shining through that grubby facade, are those blue iceberg eyes.

I wonder if she might be the bastard girl child of an American soldier from their first war here. Not impossible. The war ended with a treaty of peace signed just outside this very town. Not impossible for an American soldier to have met and to have known her mother in that way. But impossible to ask, impossible for me to determine; rude, even, to mention the idea of her foreign eyes in this conservative and hierarchical society.

"I am no spy," I say at last, breaking the spell.

"But what if you were?" she says. "What would you spy on?"

"Not a market like this. Not a town Allah has forsaken

like this, three wars in two decades. No men my age left, except those who were wise enough to flee to Iran during the latest troubles. I am a commodity here."

"A what?"

"So many widows," I say, remembering Bashar's hint.

"Ah," she says.

She doesn't blush or turn away. Like every girl, she has grown up around the conversation of women, around the jokes and veiled references. She knows what I mean.

"You're looking for a wife."

"I don't know," I say. "I don't know what I'm looking for. I don't know if I'm looking for anything at all, other than customers for these mobile phones. I know it is time for me to shut shop, though. And time for me to get my dinner. And time for you to run home."

At that, as quickly as she had come, Layla leaves. I reach under the awning and unfasten the tin shutter. It swings down and clicks into place over the window. I lock the side door and the tin shutter. Then I take my time walking the few hundred meters of road from the market into Safwan proper. I reach Bashar's café, order tea and a flatbread with tomato and *shawarma* and hummus and oil, and sit among people who enjoy the coming night and the noise of the streets and the same song of a hot summer wind, though tonight without the meditations of that lonesome Persian song.

* * *

Later that night, I lift the bottle to my lips.

Memories from the very earliest days of my life churn and boil in the blissful vapidity that soon overwhelms me, flowing out-

ward from the heat of the drink. These are sensory impressions: polished mahogany woodwork; the aroma of cigars and my father's narjeela, *his water pipe, in his private rooms, his salon, his study; arguments or laughter piercing outward into the silence of the other chambers of our big old house, places where I played amid warm shafts of light, rooms where I hid and spied and tried my best to orbit my father in the nearest possible ellipse.*

This was Baghdad in the 1960s.

Vaguely and strangely, among the earliest of my memories I recall bits and pieces of discussions far too political to belong among a young boy's formative remembrances: the names of the leaders of the coup of 1968—General Ahmed Hassan al-Bakr, Salah Omar al-Ali, and Saddam Hussein; hot words about a nationalist movement to unite all Arab lands under a single banner; varied expressions of hope and dismay over the possibility that the Baathist party's control of Iraq might ensure all Sunni Muslims continuing prosperity in a land where the less affluent Shia formed the vast majority.

More clearly than these things, I remember myself a year or two later, dressed in a starched school uniform: white shirt, pressed slacks, thin straight necktie. I remember that I was a good student, not from any particular award received from school itself, but from the impression my older brother, Yasin, left on me.

Many nights after school he would be summoned into my father's bedroom, upstairs on the colonnaded second floor of our big empty house, and my father would beat him with a cane or a belt or with his hand. School wasn't Yasin's best subject. At fifteen years of age, he failed his entrance exams for secondary school, a shame on our family.

On the night Yasin brought home the news of this failure, my governess, Fatima, sent me upstairs to wait outside my father's room with a warm rag so that I might apply it to Yasin's back. The beating lasted five minutes, maybe ten, but it seemed like an eternity to me as I listened in the darkness of the hallway from behind the locked bedroom door. I was amazed that Yasin did not cry.

I knew I would have.

When the door at last opened, before Yasin came out, I heard my father say to him, "Allah's blessing that I do not have two such failures as you to scourge my name. Your brother, praise be, has no such handicap."

Yasin exited the room, back bowed. I offered him the warm towel but he stiffened, gazed directly into my eyes with his flat black expression, and spat on the floor before walking away from me.

He didn't take the towel.

4

الخميس

Thursday

LAYLA VISITS IN THE EVENING, again this evening, as is becoming quite usual. She stands in shadow under the awning of my little store, my shack, as a golden sunset reflects its light against the overpass where the highway from Basra to Kuwait and the even larger highway from the port of Umm Qasr to Baghdad intersect. As always, the American convoys pass north, pass south, just far enough away from me that they shimmer from the heat. The wheels of the lumbering vehicles disappear in this mirage so that their chain of chassis looks like a snake gliding over the road. The noise from the convoys reaches me through the mirage, distant and rumbling. Twenty go north. Sixteen return south. One convoy passes over the bridge of my intersection, much closer to me than the bypass. It heads southeast toward Umm Qasr and the big American prison called Camp

Bucca that is located just off the road between Safwan and Umm Qasr. The convoy is made up of buses rather than semis. The buses are guarded by the normal three Humvees, one in back, one in the middle, one in front. A short convoy, four buses in total, compared to the normal thirty-plus semis. A different sort of convoy. I make a little notch on the doorpost of my shop, the fifth such notch since I arrived here and began my game of convoy counting.

. Today marks the fourth day of Layla's visits. Also the twenty-second day of business for me since I moved to Safwan. A good day. The toughs from Hezbollah have stopped at my shop, as they have at every shop in the new market here on the north side of town. They are a gang of youths with green headbands, though their leader, Hussein, is close to my own age, maybe forty. He has a hawklike face, the classic Semitic hooked nose, and deep-set eyes under-scored with purplish semicircles. He is a short man, though wiry, and the young men in his gang are all short and wiry as well. It seems to me that Hussein has collected a half dozen imperfect copies of himself.

Hezbollah performs three functions in the market and in the town. The first of these functions I applaud: providing a sort of social welfare, distributing assistance to the poor, setting up some services—like vaccinations—that neither the Iraqi government nor the American or British military regularly provide. But the other two functions I deplore: coercing merchants and citizens to pay for their protection and conducting a campaign of moral policing.

The Hezbollah gang's arrival could easily become an ugly scene for me, for I neither want, nor feel like paying for, their protection. And, as a new man in town, my moral qualities are—I am sure—still somewhat suspect in their eyes. Fortunately, they do not bully me very much, Allah in His Mercy be praised.

"It is your first month," Hussein tells me, eyeing my mobile phones. "We like to encourage new businesses, so no fees for you yet."

I give him a phone to try for a week or two. He repeats his line about the importance of protection for businessmen in the Safwan markets, especially in this newer market, where, if I haven't noticed, I am inside the on-ramp loop of an overpass, ground that is officially government property. Hussein doesn't go so far as to call it a black market, as some townsfolk do. Nor does he tell me that I have taken up my place in the market illegally. And I do not go so far as to tell him that I have already made special arrangements with Sheikh Seyyed Abdullah for the privilege of the location and for the privilege of better protection than his band of scrubby youths could ever hope to provide. I want to say, "Seyyed Abdullah guarantees my business." I want to say that very much. But I remain perfectly cordial with the man.

As the *muezzin* wail of the call to prayer dies in the evening air, the guard for the overpass wanders along the edge of the quarry on the far side of the road. It is an abandoned quarry, a place where the local people dump their household trash. The guard can see the bridge from his position, so he hasn't completely abandoned his post. He prods at mounds of garbage, stoops to pick up objects from wind-tattered black trash bags. Goats and a crow graze through the refuse behind him, more closely inspecting what he has overturned and discarded.

"My mother asked me to check on the tomatoes in the market today," Layla says.

"Tomatoes?" I say.

I don't want to look startled at her abrupt arrival this fourth day, so I keep watching the guard in the trash pit at the edge of the quarry. I should not be surprised at her anymore, at her sudden appearances and her sudden departures. I should be at ease around her. I am a man of business. I am a man. I should be unflappable, stoic, a model of sobriety and confidence. I should not panic.

Layla steps in front of me, making sure I do not ignore her.

"Yeah," she says. "You know…red, round, squishy inside. Tomatoes."

"Is she making a salad?"

"No. She doesn't eat salads. We don't eat salads."

"What?!" I say. "All mothers like salads. Or is she a robot or something? Maybe an alien?"

I laugh at my joke, this theme of robots and aliens and genies. I expect Layla to laugh. She does not.

She says, "We farm tomatoes. She wanted to know the price for when we go to sell them. I saw *Close Encounters of the Third Kind*. I wonder that Nile Drama TV allows such a thing, such a show to air, where the U.S. isn't destroyed by aliens at the end, like in the movie *Independence Day*. Such a movie the imams certainly approve! *Independence Day*! I like to see the U.S. destroyed, the White House being exploded by death rays from the sky."

"I have not seen this film," I say. "I do not pay much attention to the cinema."

"You don't? *Alhumdu l-Allah!*" she says. "I love movies."

"They are idolatry," I say, but only halfheartedly, as I ponder again my list of movie stars: Tom Cruise, Schwarzenegger, Jack Black. Maybe Rufus Wainwright doesn't belong in the same list...I take him off the list but I add Fred Astaire and Cary Grant and Gary Oldman, who played a splendid Beethoven. I admit to myself that I know a lot about American movies, certainly more than a mobile-phone merchant should.

Layla's words continue over mine, drowning my objection on the grounds of idolatry in a fine flow of enthusiasm: "He's drawn out to the desert, Neary, the hero in *Close Encounters* who confronts the aliens, like Muhammad is drawn to the desert when he says he has seen the breaking of the light of dawn. It is the same. They climb a mountain of light, Jebel an-Nur. He has visions. He is persecuted by the men of his tribe but escapes. Just like the hero Neary in the movie. Then he hears the voice of Allah."

"But Allah is no alien," I say.

I begin to take offense at her comments. I tell myself I should visit this girl's father. I tell myself that the man must be convinced to use whatever means necessary to banish such wild thoughts from her. They will not do, such thoughts, such travesties. They will not.

"And Muhammad, Peace Be Upon Him," I say, "Muhammad hears the voice of Angel Gabriel when he is on the mountain, not the voice of Allah, not the voice of aliens."

"It is one and the same," she says.

This is blasphemy for sure.

I anger and say, "Girl, you should not speak in such terms!"

As if bowled over by the force of my irritation, Layla closes her eyes and sits cross-legged on the ground in the dust in front of my shack, positioning herself as an unmovable object. She puts her hands to either side of her body, bracing herself. In the street behind her, cars pass, honking and screeching and rumbling as always, the nearest lane only a few feet from where she sits. The drivers do not notice her. A bit of tissue paper—colored, like the wrapping of a present—tumbles along the road in a draft of air behind a truck. Layla sways back and forth and then starts to hum. Between the notes of humming I hear bits of words, snatches of sound, like the distant lonesome Persian song I had heard from my seat outside Bashar's café, yet even less comprehensible, even more elusive, more wonderfully foreign.

I cannot make out the words beneath and between the humming. Perhaps they are Quranic. Holy. Perhaps they are the talk of devils or of genies who have taken possession of her body and possession of her voice. I come out of my shack. I mean to shake some sense into her. Instead, my arms go out to her. I mean to grab her but I am incapacitated by the sound of her voice, by the shield of her voice spreading around her, and I never truly touch her. I kneel, first one knee and then the next, holding my arms toward her like a supplicant in some Eastern religion who has prostrated himself before an idol or before a fasting holy man in the shade of a thorn tree.

"What are you singing?" I ask.

She doesn't reply. She just keeps singing. From the shop beside mine, where Sadeq sells oils and lubricants for cars and machines, a few men emerge, grubby men. They stand around me as I kneel. More men come from other shops, shopkeepers and their guards and people browsing through the market.

"It's beautiful," I say.

She sings, then stops, then sings and hums and speaks between the humming and singing, words that aren't words at all. I can feel it in my bones, the high fluting resonance of her voice conducting a call-and-response with something I cannot pretend to hear, cannot pretend to know, something distant and angelic. The sheer beauty of it banishes the idea in my mind that she might be possessed by evil, by the Devil. But I'm convinced, utterly convinced, that she is possessed by something.

"The music," I say again. "Beautiful."

The group around me grows larger: an old veiled woman with a basket over her arm; a gaggle of schoolchildren in buttoned vests, pants, and dresses; two traffic policemen in blue shirts with white gloves and batons holstered at their sides. I try not to notice them. I focus on Layla.

Layla strikes a last long note, the loudest of all, then looks up at the sky and stops. She stands and looms above me. Her shadow crosses the ground in front of me. I am shaken.

"Abu Saheeh," she says, "that is the music the aliens sing when they come to the mountain. That is everything I remember of the song Neary hears as he watches the alien ship descend. He communicates with the aliens by singing back to them and making mountain shapes in his mashed potatoes."

Her voice returns to normal and she asks: "Do you believe in aliens?"

"It is beautiful," I say again. *"Alhumdu l-Allah."*

Layla reaches down and touches my forehead, lifting me from the dust where I have bowed down. When I am on my knees, we are more closely the same height. She looks at me directly, her blue eyes searching and holding mine. Then she releases me.

"I must check on the tomatoes," she says.

At that, as quickly as she had come, Layla leaves, running to the south, toward the vegetable market at the center of town, just past the town hall behind Bashar's café. I realize I am facing Mecca as I kneel. I say a prayer, touch my head to the dust once more, as if to atone for any blasphemy I may have unwittingly committed in kneeling to the song of a girl rather than to the song Allah has put in my heart. I know they must be different, the two songs, the spiritual God-reflecting song and the song of a little beggar child, stolen from an American movie. But do not all things reflect the majesty of Allah? And, maybe, sometimes some of those things reflect His majesty and wonder more perfectly, more clearly, more purely. Perhaps worship in any form leads the mind and the spirit toward Allah in His Oneness. Perhaps that is so. Or perhaps I am an old fool of a man, an old fool of a *kafir*.

When at last I rise, the men from Sadeq's shop and the others who have gathered still look at me.

"You have had a vision?" one asks.

"Yes," I say.

I am not blaspheming in answering them with this answer. The vision, and her voice, the song of the mountain, have gone, not into the wilderness, but into town on a common pathetic errand to find tomatoes. I look up. I look around me. Through the crowd I see the guard on the lip of the quarry using his Kalashnikov as a crutch or a staff, prodding at the body of a dead goat decaying in the mounds of trash beneath his feet. If he were Moses, the prodding of his staff might cause a spring to gush from the earth. The guard, however, has no such luck. He picks his way from mound to mound, looking up at the overpass only every once in a while.

Tonight I do not go to the café of my friend Bashar. I go, instead, to the mosque, where the silence inside allows me to hear more clearly in my mind the remembered notes sung by Layla's aliens. I stay there, in the mosque, through the last of the day's calls to prayer, the fifth call. Yet, all that while, and despite my best efforts to both exactly remember and completely forget, the song Layla sings never wholly returns to me.

* * *

My brother, Yasin, continued to live in our father's house for several years after his expulsion from school, up until the time I reached twelve years of age.

"Maggot," he would call me, daily, like a term of endearment, as he descended the back staircase into the kitchen, bleary-eyed, tired, just catching me on my way out the door to my school. "You look like a maggot in that prissy shirt."

I tried to ignore him, but from the very start he knew the most cutting words to say, the most hurtful things to do to me. I was happy when he started spending most of his evenings out on the town with a band of friends he was smart enough never to bring within my father's sight.

My father's friend Abdel Khaleq as-Samara'i was among

the important men who sometimes visited our house. He would give his coat to the doorman and then he and my father would seclude themselves in my father's parlor, smoking and talking.

Sometimes Abdel Khaleq brought his daughter, Nadia, and her nursemaid with him. Nadia's nursemaid and Fatima would cook for the men and talk to each other as they boiled tea and made pastries in the kitchen. No one paid attention to Nadia and me. We were free to roam where we wanted. I was happy, very happy, to spend the evening with a companion, even a girl. I was happy to have a friend of any sort, especially one less cruel than Yasin.

I remember Nadia as a roly-poly button-faced child, shorter than me by more than a head, a thing that was natural enough, since I was twelve and she eight. We had been engaged to marry when she was born, my father hoping to cement his place in the Baath party by tying our family to the family of as-Samara'i, who was one of Salah Omar al-Ali's close associates. I thought nothing of it at the time, the idea that at such an age my future bride had already been chosen for me. We knew no other way.

These nights of her father's visits, Nadia always wanted to play house, to pretend we had already gotten married. I wanted to climb trees in the walled pavilion behind our kitchen or to make forts in the garage, where my father kept his cars. Usually my ideas won, and I persuaded her to play my games. But usually, also, she changed the rules just enough to accommodate her plans.

When I suggested that we make a fort, Nadia agreed but said, "Only if I can set up tea inside the princess part of your fort."

So we slipped into the garage through an open side window and crawled down from the window over the workbench, where my father's chauffeur oiled and retooled various parts of the cars. We slid from the workbench onto the earthen floor of the garage and fumbled around in the dark until, reaching for the pull-cord attached to a light above my head, I found Nadia standing on tiptoe just in front of me, the smell of her breath warm against my face.

"Kiss me," she said.

Quickly, as quickly as I could, I turned my face away from her, saying, "No, that's disgusting."

"All married people kiss," she said.

"But you're like my sister."

"I'm your fiancée."

The statement was true enough. I had no recourse. So I kissed her, though I didn't want to. A small peck of a first kiss, our lips brushing against each other and our hands stiff at our sides, unsure where we should put them.

5

Friday

IF LAYLA VISITS IN THE EVENING, as she has on most evenings,
I am not there to see her. She may stand in shadow under
the awning of my little store, but I do not know.

Today would mark the fifth day of such visits. Also the
twenty-third day of business for my shop. A Friday, the
day of prayer. So leaving the shop shuttered and locked is
natural, though my piety in this instance feels most unnat-
ural, most unlike what I normally think of as godliness.
I hear, but do not see, the continued ever-present movement of the American convoys bypassing Safwan. I am
not offended that they continue their passage on a holy
day like today. They are ignorant, sure. But only annoy-
ing, not offensive. I imagine that my hearing is as good at
the game of counting convoys as is my sight, but such is
not true. I can only guess at the number of convoys today.

Same as usual: twenty or so heading north, twenty or so south.

I do not know what the guard on the overpass does today. I'm not sure I care. I imagine he sleeps. Or leans on his chair. Or watches the cars and trucks pass in an endless rhythm along the highway toward destinations far from his little outpost. He remains as effective a guard as always. I do not care what the Hezbollah thugs do in town today, harassing someone other than we merchants, all of us with our shops closed for the day of prayer and rest. It crosses my mind that their leader, Hussein, is the only man in town, other than myself, who is both unmarried and of marriageable age. I tell myself to remember to speak to Sheikh Seyyed Abdullah about this man Hussein and about the guard on the overpass.

At noon I go to the house of my friend Bashar and knock on the wrought-iron front gate. I have not visited him at his new home in Safwan, though often we have walked past the gate of his house when returning together from his café at the close of the evening. I live far on the western edge of Safwan, across the north-south military road and the special border-crossing point for America's military convoys. I can see Kuwait from the top windows of my house, more of the same empty, dusty scrubland, but with electric lights on gray metal light poles all along the big highway. The poles have not been stolen for scrap metal, as they have been on our side of the border. From my house I cannot see the yellow-and-black pipe that stretches far to the east and west or, just in front of that pipe, the big antitank ditches, three meters deep and ten across, that mark the no-man's-land created after the first U.S. war. But I know those obstacles exist, hidden behind other buildings and fences and trenches. What I can most clearly see is the place where the line of light poles ends, the place where Kuwait ends, the place where Iraq begins.

On the far side of the military road, a few new houses have gone up on the western fringe of sand among an old dusty orchard of date palms. My house is one of these, a building too large for my bachelor needs. In contrast, Bashar told me he lived above his café when first he moved to Safwan, his six children and wife in two meager rooms. My idea of his new home, hidden behind a wall and gate, is not much better. A separate space, but no palace. I am, therefore, surprised when he opens the courtyard door.

At the gate we shake hands, clasp each other close, kiss on each cheek.

"Hello and welcome, my friend. Your presence pleases us," he says, ushering me inside.

"May Allah's peace and blessings be upon you and upon your family," I say.

From outside the cracked and decaying plaster wall, the scribbles of political graffiti and the tattered limbs of Russian olives shielding the courtyard present an image of poverty: foreboding, glum, not worth a burglar's time or effort. From within, though, the wall is clean, brick with a veiling cascade of purple flowers. The olive trees have been pruned on their undersides. They form a small arch over the center of the yard, a leafy cloister, beneath which a fountain burbles beside a curved concrete bench. A cobblestone path winds from the door to the fountain, spreads around the fountain in a ring three meters wide, and separates toward the two doors of Bashar's home. One door opens onto the family quarters, where I hear Bashar's children playing. The other opens onto the *diwaniya,* Bashar's private den, where children and women are forbidden and Bashar may entertain guests like me in relative peace.

I ask after his children, how they are growing, the health of the family. He promises to bring them out later to see me. I don't ask after his wife. Such a direct question is wholly inappropriate, even for old friends like us. I imagine her in a flurry of activity at this unexpected visit: scrubbing feet and hands and hair; finding clean caftans for the girls and clean pants, maybe school uniforms, for the boys, the starched white shirts. I try to remember if it is three boys and three girls. I decide it is actually four boys and two girls, although a girl is the eldest of the brood, somewhere in her midteens. Bashar and his wife have been fertile, productive. He will grow old in comfort with his family settled around him in this town. I wonder if he teaches them specially in the sciences, which he learned during our days together at university—anatomy, chemistry—or if he is content to let the schools and the normal way of life inform them, mold them, save them from knowing too much of the world. It was his excuse when he left Baghdad that he wanted safety for his family above anything else. But with too much safety comes ignorance.

Better for them to grow up safe and dumb or world-weary and wise? I wonder.

As Bashar and I walk toward the door of his *diwaniya,* I scan covertly each window of the house that looks upon us, thinking that I might see his wife. I shouldn't even look for her, but the lure of a forbidden thing is too tough for me to resist. However, I do not see her face in any of the windows.

When we enter the *diwaniya* we sit on cushions. Bashar lights a water pipe that burbles softly as it warms, the scent of *bukhoor* wafting from it. He smokes flavored tobacco. I do not smoke. If I do, I do so only when occasion demands, social niceties. A small silver radio in the corner of the room tinkles with the sound of a Lebanese singer, perhaps Carole Samaha? More modern than my taste, but pleasant. Not Britney Spears.

"The house is very nice," I say.

"Better than above my shop. Still nothing like the old days," Bashar says.

I nod. I remember his house in Baghdad, the sound of water sprinklers on the lawn in front, beneath the palm-lined driveway, such a luxurious waste, that free-flowing water, such a westernized existence in our gated and guarded secure little community of diplomats and recon-structionists.

However, I say only: "I can't remember the old days."

Bashar offers me a sad smile. He serves tea in delicate *fin-jan* glasses, a lump of sugar dissolving in each. We discuss the weather, the crops, the American and British occupation, their soldiers, the smell of their breath at close quarters—cow's milk and meat, sugary soda and hot minty chewing tobacco—a different smell on them from the smell of diplomats and politicians with pressed suits and cologne. We discuss the coming elections, Muqtada al-Sadr's effect on the various parties, whether the Sunni minority will get any seats in the Council of Representatives, whether there is a Kurdish conspiracy to steal northern oil. Our conversation winds through these topics with no real feeling, just formality. This takes time, half an hour, almost an hour. I am in no rush, but I can tell that Bashar wants to know the reason for my visit.

"Is it about women?" he asks at last. "I meant what I said the other day. I know people here in Safwan now. Saddam killed most of the men after the southern tribes rose in support of the Americans the first time. And now this war means more have been killed. There are plenty of eligible widows for your big new house. Ulayya bint Ali ash-Shareefi, for instance. An alliance with that family would do your business good. You would sell a million mobile phones."

He mentions the number and the business, but secretly carves the shape of an hourglass in the air between us to show me that Ulayya is also a comely woman.

"No," I say. "Not women. That's not why I visit today. Nor business, mobile phones, or whatever."

Bashar sits straighter on his cushion. He looks taken aback. His mind must have been filled with such plotting. He appears to wipe his thoughts clean, not without some effort, a crinkling of lines on his narrow forehead and between his eyes. Then he leans more comfortably on one elbow and waits for me to explain.

It is hot in his *diwaniya*. The *bukhoor* smoke causes the walls to feel close and the air to feel raspy, like the voice of Carole Samaha.

I take a moment to compose my thoughts. I have mentioned Layla already to Bashar. I do not want him to think I have any marital or sacrilegious intentions regarding the girl. None whatsoever. Nothing so simple as that. Two mentions of her in as many days might give him the wrong notion, would almost certainly give him the wrong notion.

So I approach the subject carefully, in a roundabout way. I decide not to talk about Layla at all.

I ask, "Have you seen the movie *Close Encounters of the Third Kind*? It's an American movie...released back when we were at university, I think."

"Why, no," he says. "No, I haven't."

"Do you know whether anyone here owns a DVD of it?"

"Was it a popular film?"

"Yes, perhaps. I think it played on Nile Drama TV a few nights ago. A rerun."

"You want to watch it?" he asks.

Something obviously doesn't make sense to him. Why would I pay a visit, a formal visit of this sort, to discuss a movie?

"A friend of mine compared it to the time Muhammad, Peace Be Upon Him, spent meditating on Jebel an-Nur. I wish to watch the movie in that regard, to see if the friend has spoken a blasphemy. Most of all I want to hear the music of the aliens because the friend, my friend, likened it to the sound of the voice of Angel Gabriel."

"Certain blasphemy," Bashar says.

He stands. He is filled with anger, perhaps a mocking show of anger. His face turns red. He pulls at his thin, clipped mustache with the fingers of one hand. He is unsure how I feel about blasphemy and he wants to err on the safe side.

"Is this friend Shia or Sunni? We should ban this movie, write a protest to Nile Drama TV. We should have the imam issue a decree, a *fatwa,* against such a..."

"We should watch the movie first," I say.

Bashar sits. He composes himself. He is happy to hear

that I am rational, not full of indignation. But he is confused and flustered.

"I will make inquiries," he answers after a moment of unbroken eye contact between us. He can tell it is important to me but he doesn't understand why. He wants to ask me why it is so important as to merit a visit like this. If I am not necessarily condemning it as blasphemy, then what? I can see the words of various questions forming on his lips, reforming as he searches for the right phrases.

Just then his eldest son, Saleem, enters the *diwaniya*. The boy is about ten years of age, taller than Layla already but younger and cleaner. He has a blunt little snub of a nose and a roly-poly face.

"Mama asks if we should present ourselves."

"Around the fountain," says Bashar. "Abu Saheeh and I will finish here in a moment."

Saleem leaves. I hear him, under his breath, repeat my name, "Abu Saheeh...Father Truth." The boy laughs. He has his father's sense of humor, a short, under-the-breath laugh followed by the silent repetition of the joke, mouthing the words as if he will be called upon to repeat the joke later, afraid that he might fail.

I hear Bashar's children lining up outside, hear little Saleem pipe up over his older sister, putting them all in order. Saleem, or one of the other children, whistles like a bird, somewhat secretively. With that, Bashar stands.

"I will let you know if I can find the movie," he says as he takes me out into the courtyard again. "And you let me know if you change your mind about Ulayya bint Ali ash Shareefi or another woman, any other woman. I tell you, you will have your pick of them, my friend."

"I'm not interested in women," I tell him. "I'm not here to settle down."

"Then what? What are you here for?"

"The market."

"Lofty new ambitions as a mobile-phone salesman? I don't get it. A man like you!"

"It's the view," I say, which makes him laugh.

The children smile and stand straight as Bashar and I inspect them. Bashar ruffles Saleem's hair. He raises an eyebrow at the youngest girl's sandals, unbuckled and clinging to her feet in a most slipshod fashion. I don't say anything. The children don't say anything, either, but they giggle a little as Bashar and I pass them. I hear Saleem whisper "Father Truth" to the sister nearest him. Despite several glances I cast at the in-facing courtyard windows, I still do not see their mother. This is traditional society now. This is her role—cloistered, separated. She won't break the pattern, now that it has settled over her, even for the sake of an old friend like me. Though I don't see her, I feel her watching us, watching me. I feel her intensity and it takes all my willpower not to ask Bashar about her specifically and directly.

After saying good-bye to Bashar at the gate, kissing each cheek, shaking hands, I walk the few hundred meters from his home to mine. Out in the noonday sun, without the protection of the shade of my shack, I feel my age more pointedly, sweating with the minor exertion of a walk across town. I stop in the shadow of a ruined building along the road where the U.S. convoys pass. There are no convoys in sight at this moment; no traffic from Iraqi vehicles, either. The gate, the border crossing, is just visible to the south: a

Kuwaiti guard sitting on a chair on the far side with the door of an air-conditioned booth splayed open behind him. Such a waste. Such a waste of energy. Such a waste for Iraq and Kuwait to be separated in this way. Such a waste to have had this war, these wars. Such a waste to have light poles and an abundance of electrical power that end at an antitank ditch and a painted pipeline and a series of guard towers strung out in the desert like a barbed necklace.

I cross the road and walk to my house, where I spend the rest of the day and most of the evening thinking about Bashar's family, his beautiful growing little family. And I think about how tribes have been split as men draw lines across the desert.

* * *

The day when Nadia and I built our fort in my father's garage, I began my construction by searching in the loft for scrap materials. When I returned with my first armload I expected Nadia would already have arranged some of the chauffeur's disassembled engine parts—headlight reflectors for cups, an oil pan for a teapot—on the upside-down cardboard box that would serve as our tea table. I expected she would already have tea ready and that, upon returning to her with my sheet of rusted tin, she would force me to sit for a while and pretend to drink. I would have to make small talk with her. I would maybe even have to kiss her again.

So when I returned to find the tea set abandoned, I dropped my building materials and rushed to find her. My first thought was that Yasin had come into the garage and done something to her, tied her up, hidden her from me. I searched the corners of the chauffeur's workshop. I opened the back door of the garage to see if Yasin had taken her out by the chicken coops. I returned into the garage and ran down the line of shining black parked cars. I found her on her hands and knees, peering under the wheel of one of the cars. I watched her for a moment, her head cocked to the side, her body trembling, but still. I approached her as quietly as I could and knelt beside her.

"Do you hear it?" she asked.

"Yes," I said.

I reached up, inside the wheel well, as deep into the engine compartment as I could angle my arm, and pulled a small crying kitten free from the tangle of wires and sprockets into which it had wedged itself. It was a mangy thing, emaciated and losing tufts of its white and orange fur. Blood caked its stomach, oozing from a spot where it had licked its belly bare, licked and bit and nibbled at a long cut slicing from the inside of its right hind leg nearly to the start of its rib cage.

Nadia put her hands to her mouth at the sight of the kitten's blood. I cupped the little animal in the crook of my arm and took it over to the chauffeur's workbench. There I turned on the overhead light and examined the wound. It was clean. It hadn't yet started to fester. The kitten had done well licking itself, but I knew already then, at the age of twelve, that a wound so deep and long would not heal, not on its own.

"Go into the house," I told Nadia. "In the room to the side of the kitchen, the little room where Fatima keeps her sewing things. Get me thread and a needle, also a candle and some rags."

When she returned a few minutes later I had already lashed the kitten's limbs to the table so that it could not bat at me with its sharp little claws. I made Nadia hold its head so that it could not bite me, even though she turned her own head away from the sight of the open belly, the green and blue glistening intestines, the matted fur, the mealy-white skin.

I lit the candle and ran the flame up and down the length of the needle, sterilizing it as best I could. Then I threaded the needle, doubled the thread over on itself, and pierced the kitten's skin, first on one side of the wound, then on the next, knotting the end, drawing the suture tight. The two sides of the torn flesh puckered toward each other. I cleaned the needle on a rag, held it to the candle once again, and repeated the process of piercing and knotting for a second stitch and a third stitch. Untying the kitten's limbs, I reused the lengths of rope to bind a clean rag around the site of the wound, wrapping it tightly and completely so that the creature, meaning to clean the area with its tongue, could not accidentally reopen the wound.

Then, satisfied, I took Nadia's tea table box, tipped it upright, filled it with some shredded rags, put the kitten in it, and carried it up the ladder to the loft. There I stowed it in a corner behind a discarded portmanteau.

"That was very brave of you," Nadia said as we returned to the house to get milk and a saucer.

"Very brave of you as well," I said to her, and I took her hand in mine.

6

السبت

Saturday

LAYLA VISITS IN THE EVENING, like most evenings, this evening no exception even after the passing of a day apart, this yesterday, the day my shop and every other shop closed for the Friday prayers. She stands in shadow under the awning of my little store, my shack, as a golden sunset reflects its light against the overpass where the road from Basra to Kuwait and the even larger road from the port of Umm Qasr to Baghdad intersect. The convoys flow north and south on this main road, as they do every day. I see a crane on the back of one flatbed truck, an army-green crane. I imagine it hoisting barricades into place in the streets of Baghdad as the elections near. I imagine it returning south on the back of a different flatbed truck, damaged, exploded, sabotaged, a shell of iron barely recognizable for what it had been. Where does all the waste from this war go? Is it deposited in the gulf, dumped overboard from hulking trash barges to make new reefs and new coral for the fishes? Is it left in the desert, buried, to rust and decay? Is it shot to the moon?

Today marks the sixth day of Layla's visitations. Also the twenty-fourth day of business for me since I moved to Safwan. A good day, though a strange one. The Shareefi clan spent several hours at the shop, various cousins and uncles looking through my brochures on Nilesat, the satellite TV I can obtain for them, which has the sports, the drama, Dream TV, the news as reported in Egypt and Lebanon and Dubai.

The guard for the overpass leans on his three-legged chair as usual. He hasn't moved since three or four o'clock this afternoon. The flaps of his tent are closed tight. Maybe he hides someone inside. A night visitor? A lover? Earlier, I started walking up to him to see if he was awake, alert, alive. I thought, perhaps, that I would scold him into doing his duty more passionately. But just then another group from the Shareefi family approached my shop and I put the need to correct the guard to the back of my mind. Perhaps I stall in scheduling an appointment with the sheikh on purpose. I do dread the visit a little, the formality, the bustle of people around him, the chance that I might mistakenly offend him. Any of a hundred little things could go wrong. I don't know if it is worth a visit just to report on this guard's bad behavior.

These particular Shareefi who visit me, from among the many today who have found a reason to inspect my satellite brochures and my mobile phones and my other wares, are the women of the clan, including Ulayya bint Ali ash-

Shareefi herself, daughter of the head of the clan. She has been widowed but not very recently, perhaps five years ago. Although she wears black, as do all the others—black robes, black *burqa*—she definitely appears no longer to be in mourning. She has managed to convey to me, even with several of her escorts chattering at a respectful distance, that she hasn't lost her firm figure and that the two daughters left behind by Zayed, her first husband, are both well provided for, with dowries enough to ensure good marriages and stipends for their day-to-day expenses in the meanwhile. As she talks to me, Ulayya's eyes gleam brightly, dancing black jewels deep within the slit of her *burqa*. Not altogether unattractive. I imagine myself in her company. I imagine her in my home. I imagine her in my bed. The image is an odd one, she clothed in black throughout all the imagining, though in truth she would shed the *hijab* behind the doors of any house we might share.

This woman, Ulayya, has a basket of tomatoes over one arm. I think for a second that I might ask her how much they have cost, just to make pleasant talk and to have some information for Layla if her mother once again sends her into town to spy on prices. Ulayya holds one of my satellite brochures in her free hand. Everything is proper: a widow shopping for a satellite. But also she is putting herself on display. I laugh a little at the absurdity of these things and at my inability to picture her in normal clothes or even to picture her naked. I can't bring myself to imagine what she looks like, despite years of such practice. When I try to see her naked, in my mind I see nothing, a void, as though an explosion occurred in my imagination and left only a vaguely woman-shaped infinity of emptiness, black cloth and black dancing eyes and nothing deeper than that. The void, the inability to focus or to force my imagination to-ward this woman, makes my head hurt. I think, very briefly and guiltily, about shutting my shop early, returning home, and having an early drink to help wipe away the blackness.

Though my head spins in this way and though my stom-ach also tells me it is time for dinner, Ulayya continues with a description of the house where the satellite dish will be placed, if her father does indeed decide to purchase the equipment and the plan from me.

"It is a nice house," she says, "with a big garden—two gardens, actually. One for the growing of vegetables. One for pleasure, to sit under date fronds in the evening. To hear music playing softly in the background. To be in pleasant company, to have pleasant conversation…"

I look up from her and see behind her Hussein, the leader of the Hezbollah, lounging in the shade of the store directly across the street from me. Some of his gang members stroll from store to store but Hussein does not. He watches his subordinates as they collect money from other shops along the sides of the road. He watches them as they warn Rabeer's employees, playing cards in their shop as usual, against the vices of gambling. He watches them as they dole out a quick lashing on the calves of a woman whose *abaya* does not reach all the way to the ground, leaving her sandaled feet showing. He watches his men, but he also watches Ulayya from his partially concealed place beneath the awning of the store.

I think about calling to Ulayya's attention the fact that she has an admirer. I wonder how she might react. But be-fore I have a chance to do this, behind Hussein I see another thing. Little Layla runs toward me. Hussein sees that I look beyond him. He turns to look at Layla but doesn't seem to understand what I see: he must be blind to Layla just as the other store owners and guards and helpers in the market seem to be. To them she is only another street rat, nothing of concern, as invisible as Ulayya's body under her cloaks. Ulayya also notices where I glance. What is more, she must also notice something about the quality of my glance, the way it lingers, the way it lights up, the way it focuses, for she does not dismiss Layla's rapid approach without comment.

"What a horrid little creature," she says. "How could any mother let a daughter out of the house looking like that!"

Indeed, as Layla pulls to a halt in front of my shop, I see that she is especially dirty this evening, her face nearly black, her strange blue eyes flashing through the soot or mud or oil that covers her. I sing a little song in my head, one I remember from my schoolchild days: *aini zarqa tubruq biruq*. It means something along the lines of "my blue eyes shine like lightning."

"Abu Saheeh," she shouts, still from the far side of the street, where she has paused to let the traffic pass. "I have found a geyser. Black gold."

"Obviously," I say.

Ulayya looks at me.

"You know this girl?" she whispers.

"She visits the shop," I say. "She is funny. She dances, she sings, she begs."

I regret this last epithet, for Layla has never begged, not from me.

I let my gaze return, flickering back to Layla. She runs across the road, through the last bit of the market. Ulayya is obviously offended by our familiarity. The posse of Ulayya's escorting aunts and female cousins also shows its displeasure. They gather together more closely, as if Layla were a tiny little lioness and they a herd of water buffalo, all horns pointed outward. Layla appears not to care. In fact, she smiles as she stops in front of the venerable aunties and does a small bit of her Britney Spears routine, possibly the most inappropriate part, with a thrust of her bony hips in the direction of Ulayya herself.

Ulayya stands her ground.

Ignoring Layla, she says, "I will discuss the satellite with my father."

Then she and the cousins and the aunts and the great-aunts and the friends of the great-aunts gather their long *abayas* about them and waft back into Safwan, from whence they originally came. Behind them, at a moderate distance, Hussein's patrol of Hezbollah follows. As he leaves his shaded spot, Hussein takes from the front breast pocket of his *dishdasha* the mobile phone I lent him when he first visited my store. He touches it to his forehead, a little salute. I wave back at him, being friendly, but he does not smile.

When they all have gone, Layla's voice assumes a tone similar in its huskiness to Ulayya's way of speaking. She says, "I will discuss the satellite with my father."

"You should be more respectful of your elders," I say. "And more respectful of Allah. Your stories disturb me. I still wish, as I said when we last met, for you not to compare American movies to a messenger from Allah!"

For just an instant Layla looks at me as if I have said something strange, or funny, or inappropriate. Then she moves closer to my shack, leans on the sill, and says, "Jed

Clampett and his whole family moved to Beverly Hills because he shot the ground accidentally and black gold came up. I borrowed the guard's Kalashnikov and shot the pipe on the far side of the road. I thought it would have water for our tomatoes but it has oil, not water. Useless oil."

"You shot the Kalashnikov?" I ask. "How'd you get it from the guard?"

I look up, see the man fast asleep on his stool. My question seems suddenly silly. The rifle rests an arm's length away from him, leaning against his tent.

"He has only one bullet, you know," she says. "So returning the gun isn't as difficult as taking it."

"You need a bath," I say.

"I look like the black soldiers in the American Humvees."

"But stickier," I say.

I run a finger through the smear of oil her elbows leave on the front counter of my shack. I picture Bashar's daughters, fuller, heavier, fleshier than Layla. And cleaner. The difference between them, though, is the difference between the sand and the sandstorm. I think of asking Layla to sing again, to sing the *Close Encounters* song. But I can't imagine the semidivine sound of that song coming from a face so covered in filth. I can't imagine any sort of saintly presence emanating from a girl so happily dirty.

"Is the oil still leaking?" I ask.

I look up again, under the overpass, toward the pipeline and toward what I imagine must be Layla's home, her family's tomato farm. It's a rundown shack half hidden behind the far embankment of the overpass. Like every other Iraqi farm, it is dun-colored, low-slung, thick-walled, with a scruffy palm tree sprouting on the edge of the hole in the earth that serves as an irrigation well. I see a flurry of activity nearby, just beyond the house: U.S. Humvees and British Land Rovers gathered around the leaking pipe.

"You're a terrorist," I say. "You've ruined the economy."

"I'm a jihadist," she replies. "And I'm moving to Beverly Hills tomorrow! Do you want to come? You would make a fine butler for me!"

I take a swipe at her, as if to hit her in reprimand, but she skips away. I am glad for it. My *dishdasha* would have been hopelessly soiled by the dripping crude oil she wears. I shake my head and my fist at her instead. I decide to speak no more to her, at least not this evening. I send her away, quite forcefully, telling her she had better wash herself and look presentable if she should wish to visit me again, telling her she had better treat her elders with more respect. I think I go so far as to call her a little urchin or maybe even a little devil but perhaps that is just the voice in my head, my conscience, as compared to the words I actually spoke.

Whatever I have said, Layla leaves, as quickly as she had come, running and sliding back under the overpass and keeping a wide expanse of desert between her, the broken pipeline, and the assembled multitude of U.S. and British vehicles.

I shut and lock my shop and walk into Safwan.

Bashar asks me about the oil on my finger and whether I had any interesting visitors today. I tell him about the broken pipeline and the hullabaloo it caused. I do not gratify him by mentioning Ulayya's visit, but I order my tea and my falafel and ask him why he does not call himself Abu Saleem in honor of his healthy, smart little son. I know it is because he has a girl as his firstborn. His feelings are delicate about the matter and he pretends not to hear me, touching his mustache once, nervously, and then flitting away to help another customer.

***

A few mornings after Nadia and I found the kitten, Yasin thumped down the back stairs into our kitchen to give me his typical surly good-bye. He didn't look as bleary-eyed as usual. He didn't look as if he had only gone to sleep a few hours earlier. In fact, his face glowed with what I took to be excitement. The idea crossed my mind that he might offer to walk me to school. I felt in my pockets for spare change in case the opportunity presented itself to buy us daheen *cakes from a street vendor.*

Yasin waited in the corner of the kitchen until my governess, Fatima, left with a plate of breakfast for our father.

"I see you found my little experiment," he said.

From behind his back he revealed the kitten, my kitten. Holding it by the scruff of its neck, he seemed to offer it to me across Fatima's big butcher-block chopping table. I reached for it.

"Give it to me," I said.

He pulled it away. Stepping back but still holding the kitten high in the air, he brought his other hand up to the kitten's belly. Before I could rush around the table, he untied the cords holding the safety rag around the kitten's midsection. Then, as the kitten frantically clawed the air, all four paws in furious motion, he dug into the gash. Sawing upward, inserting one, then two, then all four of his fingers, he further tore the wound. He pulled my stitches free. The kitten's intestines spilled out in a long, coiling mass.

When at last he handed the little animal over to me, its heart had already stopped beating.

7

الأحد

Sunday

LAYLA DOES NOT VISIT THIS EVENING. Perhaps the dirt and oil could not be scrubbed off in time for her to visit. Perhaps she is afraid of my wrath, as well she might be, if she doesn't heed my warning from yesterday and show up clean and with a reformed attitude toward Allah. As the sun sets behind the overpass, I watch for her, unwilling to be surprised at her arrival. In addition to the convoys today, I notice a British patrol moving about the desert near the bypass road's intersection. This is the first time I have noticed a patrol near the convoys, something other than the normal three Humvees the Americans use to guard their vehicles. Maybe they are concerned about the pipeline still. Maybe they hunt for a jihadist.

Today marks the seventh day since Layla's visitations began. Also the twenty-fifth day of business for me since I moved to Safwan. A good day. I did not sell much of anything but, after the repeated visits from the Shareefi clan yesterday, I do not feel much like talking about satellites or mobile phones. I do not feel much like haggling over prices and plans.

The guard for the overpass brings out his tea set and arranges it on an overturned box beside his three-legged chair. I watch him make tea for himself, the lukewarm water he had left in a tarnished tin pot under the sun all afternoon, the sachet of chai dipped over the edge of the pot, two small tin cups ready to receive the brew.

Seeing no sign of Layla, I begin to walk down the road into Safwan. I try to think of Ulayya and of other Safwan women, but I discover I am thinking of Layla's story, of Jed Clampett finding oil. I picture myself as a butler. I picture Layla in Beverly Hills, among mansions and swimming pools and robot actors. I picture Layla with a corncob pipe in her mouth like Jed Clampett, riding through town on a flatbed jalopy with a gun laid across her lap. I remember Layla stealing the guard's gun. I turn around and look up at the guard. He has poured one cup of tea for himself. He drinks from this cup but the other cup sits on the tray unused. He apparently does not have a visitor, no one to drink from the second cup.

I change course, walk back across the market, past Rabeer's used-car lot, past Maney'a and Ibrahim's stacks of doors, door frames, sinks, knobs, and fixtures, past Wael's dusty gray bags of concrete, past my own shop. I stop at Jaber's stand and purchase two kebabs of chicken. These I take with me as I walk up the gradual curve of the cloverleaf on-ramp to the place where the guard's tent perches in the last of the day's long light.

"Masah il-kheir," I say. "Fine evening!"

The guard snaps to attention. I am happy to have caught him unaware, lazing. I feel like a genie or an alien arriving unannounced. I feel like a nosy butler. I want to put on a fake Austrian accent and say "I'll be back," but I don't think I have the necessary talent for voices. I am, nevertheless, proud of my stealth, and my pride erases most of the self-loathing I had felt for my previous thoughts about him. I do not put the young man at his ease. It is good that he should be deferential to me. I must be twenty years his senior, maybe twenty-five.

The guard looks at the kebabs, one in each of my hands. They are oily, cooked to a perfect golden brown and flavored with fenugreek, caraway, cumin.

"Would you like one?" I say.

"Thank you, but no thank you," he says, the polite thing.

"Please," I say. "Please. It's my honor."

Again the guard refuses, but only after darting a glance at the kebab nearest to him.

"No," he says. "No."

I thrust the kebab in his direction, making it hard for him to avoid the gift.

"I insist," I say.

He takes longer than I expect to reach his hand out for the food. During the pause, the delay, he looks past me, quickly, up over my shoulder across the market toward town. I follow his gaze and see a slim-bodied boy standing beneath the ayatollah's arch. This boy looks at the guard and then at me. For a second time he looks at the guard before turning and running back through the arch into Safwan. I recognize this boy: one of the waiters or busboys from Bashar's café. Perhaps he was bringing the guard some food for dinner. No matter. I have food.

"By Allah, yes," the guard says at last, snapping his eyes back to me, back to the kebab. He is still standing straight, at attention, as if I am his commanding officer or some such thing.

I release the kebab into his grip. At the same time I glance at his teapot and his spare cup. The man has no manners. I glance at the cup again, more pointedly, and almost nod my head in its direction.

He gets the hint at last.

"Please, please," he says, "please, sir, sit. Do share of my tea if you are in the mood to share with a humble man such as me."

"I am just a vendor in the market, a humble man myself," I say. "No need to be so formal. We are like brothers, men who work for a living. Not princes. Not politicians with stuffed-up shirts."

This at last puts the man somewhat back into balance, though he twitters around me, arranging space for me among his things on the little flat space around his tent, arranging his tea set, his box table, his chair to make more room for us both. Throughout this dance he steals looks whenever possible across the market toward the spot where the boy from Bashar's café had stood. After a moment he finally manages to pour a cup of tea for me while still holding the kebab I gave him. I look around for a chair to sit on. There isn't one. The guard offers me his, pulling it away from its spot beside the telephone pole and placing it nearer to his tea set. Before I sit, I introduce myself more completely.

"Abu Saheeh is my name," I say. "I own a shop below."

"My name is Mahmoud, sir," he says.

We try to shake hands but the kebabs baffle us, both in our right hands, both of us unwilling to touch the food or each other with the impure left hand. I wave my kebab in the air to show Mahmoud that the handshake doesn't matter, not now. I am glad not to have to complete our introduction with the customary clasp and kiss. The man is unshaven like most men, but he has also been a long while without a bath. He likely has vermin in his patchy beard. I sit on his chair. He opens the front flap of his tent and pulls his cot from within. He sits on an edge of the cot as it teeters and adjusts to his weight. We eat the kebabs chunk by chunk, chicken and onion and tomato, sliding the pieces from the skewers into our mouths. I drink a little of his tea, poor thin stuff, bitter.

When I finish eating, I say, "You have a marvelous view."

"Nearly the whole city."

"And up the road quite a distance."

"And that way." He points. "Down toward Umm Qasr, too."

"Quite a responsibility!"

"A start, for me. A start," he says. "I hope to become a member of the Safwan police soon, or even maybe the special police from Basra, when I have the money to pay the deputy his bit."

"You have to pay to become a policeman?"

"To pass the test," he says. "Just a little *baksheesh* goes a long way. That, or family. Or both."

"How much do they ask?"

Mahmoud blushes.

"Come, come," I say. "I am a merchant. Money is just money. I am accustomed to such things. And maybe I can help you."

"I could never repay—"

"We can work something out," I say, not at all certain why I am offering him my patronage. In fact, the next thing I say is nothing but a bald lie: "I watch you working diligently up here. You are here every day, yes?"

"All day," he says. "Except for Fridays, when the deputy relieves me so I can visit my father and attend prayer. They bring me food, water. I sleep here."

He thumps his hand on the edge of the cot to emphasize the place where he sleeps. He points out his prayer rug, too, to show me he completes his daily observations even when not allowed to go to the mosque. I see his Kalashnikov leaning against the side of the tent.

"Are you a good shot?" I ask.

"I don't know," he says. "They never let me shoot."

"Why don't you shoot that can?" I point to a paint can overturned on the edge of the on-ramp embankment about thirty meters down the road.

"I have no spare bullets," Mahmoud says. "What will I do if I use the bullet they have given me?"

"What purpose will one bullet serve, anyway?"

"I am to use it to signal the police."

"Then ask the police for a new one. Tell them you used it for practice. Or tell them you used it to scare away the dogs. Or that you shot an American or something."

"It will come out of my pay. I cannot afford—"

"Hah," I say. Without rising from my chair, I reach back toward the tent, pick up his gun, shoulder it, aim at the can, and pull the trigger. I brace for the kick the gun should make, but it doesn't kick at all. There is no bullet in the chamber. Layla's story is true. I am disappointed at the weapon not firing, having had in mind a remembrance of the smell of sulfur and saltpeter, the sweet acrid hot deathly smell that should have filled the air after the click of the trigger.

I play dumb.

"It must be broken," I say. "See if you can fix it for me."

Mahmoud is standing. His mouth is open, aghast that I have touched his Kalashnikov, the mark of his limited authority. He is a little man, not much taller than me even as I sit. His uniform, dark blue, sags from his shoulders and bunches at his waist, where he has belted it with a length of rope.

I hand him the weapon so that he can open the chamber and inspect it. He grabs it from me, pulls the bolt back, and looks inside.

"There's no bullet," he says after a long puzzled moment.

The thought crosses my mind to seal some sort of deal with the man: offer him help with his police examinations, with the bribes, offer to bring him some additional bullets for the gun. Yet I'm not sure enough of myself. Not sure how this man, Mahmoud, fits with my plans. I need to watch him more. I need to study him more. I need to play a game of "Watch Mahmoud," similar to my game of convoy counting, though *game* is probably the wrong word for such an activity, too soft by far, whereas *spying*—as Layla calls it—sounds far too indirect.

"I'll bring you a bullet," I say, a small concession on my part. "Maybe a few bullets. What good is a guard without bullets?"

"Thank you," he says.

The conversation ends on a down note, like that. It had been building toward something, toward a partnership, an odd sort of uneven partnership. Do I need him to watch over my store, my shack, when Sheikh Seyyed Abdullah guarantees it? No. I'm at a loss. I stand. I see the city of Safwan spreading beneath me into the distance to the south, with the overpass high enough above the flat desert to command a view for miles in every direction. I take longer than I should, standing there, observing everything, turning my head to and fro.

We've finished our kebabs. I've got nothing left to say. I see him, Mahmoud, secretly looking toward the town, toward the arch, maybe in the hope that the boy from Bashar's café will return. He cleans up the tea set. He shuffles around me. Like me, he has nothing to say. Yet all the while, he glances uncomfortably toward the arch.

I think of Layla in the market, there beneath the arch, and for just a second a very different image from how I usually see her flashes through my mind. In this vision she is covered with blood. She is shot through with bullet holes. She scurries from place to place, from shop to shop, trying to pick up pieces of herself that have come apart, that have spilled from her body like the intestines of a dying kitten. The vision brings with it a pounding sensation in my head. I blink. I put one hand out to the side as if I am about to stagger. Mahmoud moves toward me, concerned. He is about to touch me but I shake my head, rather vigorously, and the vision of blackness disappears.

"One more thing," I say to Mahmoud, my voice ringing falsely, almost angrily, in my ears. "Who do you work for?"

Mahmoud has sensed the shift in my disposition. He looks troubled. The muscles of his face tighten.

"No one," he says.

"No one?"

"The police—"

"The police?"

I spit to show my disapproval of police in general and also my disbelief in his statement. He *must* work for someone. The police don't initiate the sort of man-to-man, tribe-to-tribe relationships on which real work depends.

However, Mahmoud insists it is the police, only the police.

I ask him twice more, just to be sure.

"The police," he insists. He shows me the stamp of the Ministry of the Interior on the butt of his Kalashnikov.

I give up, thinking: perhaps he has no master, no one to whom he is bound. The thought causes me to change course once again, to establish my authority over the man in a way even more complex than I had originally thought possible—with a carrot and with a stick.

"Maybe I *should* talk to the police," I say. "I don't want to see you sleeping on the job anymore."

With that, the matter is concluded. He had been waiting for it all along. The pleasantries of eating together, sharing tea, small talk, all of them had been building toward some sort of official message. Mahmoud had been expecting it. His posture immediately stiffens. He thinks he has been inspected, checked on, tested.

"You're Hezbollah?" he says. "You work for Hussein?"

"No," I say. I slap him. He winces but tries to hide it. "Don't say that again. I work for no one. But I'm watching you, and I don't want to see you sleeping anymore."

I hold Mahmoud's gaze for a moment. To his credit, he does not flinch. Then, as quickly as I had come, I leave him and head on my way, not toward the center of the city, to Bashar's café, where I would normally dine, but along the outskirts, the outer road, which leads more directly to my house.

Tonight, the kebab has filled my need for food. I do not wish to talk about Ulayya with Bashar, as he certainly will wish. I wonder whether it is wise for me to have antagonized the guard. It was clumsy. I had no clear plan when I approached, and he knew the visit from an older man like me could not be attributed to anything purely social. Yet it wasn't all a waste. Mahmoud fears me a little now: an unknown force in town, not Hezbollah. He will watch me and watch my store as well, which is worth a little even with the protection of Sheikh Seyyed Abdullah overarching everything.

What's more, lazy and inattentive as Mahmoud is, he can see all four ramps of the overpass from where he leans and idles on his camp chair. He can see my store. And I've checked with my own eyes just how far in each direction—up the road toward Baghdad and down the road toward Umm Qasr—the view extends, a vantage of many miles, a great length of important road.

* * *

The year 1980 was a glorious year for Iraq, to be followed quickly by seven years of ignominy. Saddam Hussein launched his surprise attack on Iran in September of 1980 and, at first, Iraq's armies trampled over unaware Iran like a second blitzkrieg. I had just turned seventeen. I wanted to go to war. I wanted to join Saddam's Republican Guard. I wanted to be among the first of our conquering armies to set foot in Tehran.

My father offered Yasin his blessing when Yasin signed up for Saddam's army. I think he felt ashamed that Yasin had not yet found a calling in life. At least this would be something, a career, a chance to distinguish himself, something better than spending his nights on the town, wasting his money in idleness. My father allowed Yasin to join, but he forbade me.

"You are meant to do better things," he said. "And Yasin is a man now, old enough to make his own decisions."

When Yasin came home on leave after military training, when he came home clothed in pressed military fatigues with a body and a face hardened from the rigors of military discipline and physical training, I nearly cried with envy. He stood straighter when he walked. He spoke more clearly and more decidedly. And when he looked at my father, he looked less like a beaten child and more like the grown man my father said he had become.

"The war will be over in three weeks," Yasin boasted.

"Don't be so sure," my father replied.

"We have the latest Soviet tanks on the ground, the latest MiGs in the sky," said Yasin.

"But they have religion," my father said, a thing I didn't understand at all until our initial gains, trumpeted in the headlines of every Iraqi newspaper—capturing the Shatt al-Arab in Basra and Qasr-e Shirin in the north, entering Khuzestan and Abadan and Ahvaz, laying siege to Kermanshah deep in Iranian territory—until these gains were repulsed by Iran's human-wave tactics. Our papers said nothing about the turning of the

tide at the end of 1980, but rumor spoke of the fearlessness of Iranian martyrs who came to the front lines with death shrouds wrapped around their shoulders, ready, joyfully ready to enter heaven. These martyrs would walk into our machine-gun fire until our machine guns ran out of ammunition.

After Yasin left for the war, we did not hear from him, not by letter, not by phone, not by telegram. For all I know, my father may have received notice of his death or capture through some private channel. He may even have had some communication with Yasin. If so, he kept his information to himself.

He never again spoke Yasin's name in my presence.

8

الإثنين

Monday

I WATCH FOR LAYLA'S VISIT this evening, as I do most evenings. As the sun sets behind the overpass, I wonder if she will return tonight, appear magically when I least expect her. Or, alternatively, I wonder if our customary meeting has been halted by my harsh words, like the breaking of a charm, or halted by Ulayya's intrusion, like the freezing of time under the influence of a curse. I lose track of the convoys, at least superficially. They become something more like background noise. My little game of counting their comings and goings has been supplanted by other games, reminiscences, and my wandering mind cannot be controlled from thinking about Layla, about Layla, about Layla and Ulayya.

Today marks the eighth day since Layla's visitations began. Also the twenty-sixth day of business for me since I moved to Safwan. A good day. A normal day. I sold a few items. I chatted with a few customers. I held off my impatience for the setting of the sun and the shutting of my shop by watching the guard, Mahmoud, as he watched me, watched my shop, pointedly walking down the overpass bridge at hourly and semihourly intervals to see behind my shack, to crane his neck this way and that, demonstrating, with astounding subtlety, his diligence. I am a new factor in town. I'm starting to show a little authority. I don't belong to Hezbollah. Need he know anything more? I brought him a box of ammunition this morning, but it is, of course, the good word with the police he really craves, the potential that I might even pay the bribe required to get him on the police force.

As if to prove his loyalty, Mahmoud again rises from his stool and walks the length of the bridge, checking on me, checking on my store, though I am in the store myself. Could the man truly be so thick-witted? Could he think I mean for him to watch over the store while I inhabit it? I question myself for having struck any sort of deal with him. Yet he can see all four ramps of the overpass from where he sits, a much better view than the view from my shop, looking up from the market.

Mahmoud doesn't look at me. He never looks at me directly. He is trying to be sneaky about his attention to me. He now shoulders his Kalashnikov instead of leaving it at his tent or carrying it listlessly at his side. He walks back and forth with it like a tin soldier on parade. As he returns to his tent, an American convoy approaches the overpass from the north. It is Monday, just at sunset. I note the time, seven forty-two. Three gun trucks, Humvees, topped with .50-caliber machine guns in turrets operated by gunners with dark face-shielding sunglasses. Robots, all these Davids and Patricks and Winstons. That's more like it: robots. Less human. Less need for me to feel any sort of remorse, watching them, watching their movements, recording their habits.

The vehicles of this convoy shepherd four coach buses. I observe the convoy as it passes. The buses have opaque windows with blinds drawn tight. I let my eyes linger on the vehicles until they are out of sight to the south, heading toward Umm Qasr and Camp Bucca, just ten kilometers farther down the road. After I can no longer see the convoy, I can still hear it, even above the sounds of the market, above the braying of goats, the clucking of chickens, the banter of men, the passing of automobiles, the sigh of the wind. The diesel rumble of Humvees: a distinctive, marrow-numbing sound. I make a notch on the door frame of my store, the sixth such notch.

A group of schoolgirls in black uniforms passes my shop. They all have backpacks. They all have hair tied modestly with modest-colored ribbons. The eldest cover their heads—some cover even their faces—with plain, modest scarves. In the countryside, here in the south, where the old traditions prevail, girls of such age are considered old enough to marry. I avoid looking at them directly. They wait under the bridge of the overpass, where their families, mostly from outlying tomato farms, pick them up.

I imagine Layla among them, cleaned, looking proper, looking, perhaps, contrite after a good stern lecture from her father about religion and blasphemy and cleanliness and robots. The imaginary Layla shyly waves at me from amid the group.

A little Toyota truck arrives under the bridge. The schoolgirls jump into the back, onto the open, sand-swept bed of the truck. The truck turns a half circle in the middle of the road without coming deeper into the market, without coming closer to me. I watch it disappear. Unlike the sounds of the convoy, the sound of its small engine is soon overwhelmed by the noise around me.

Does Layla attend school? I don't know the answer. I picture her years from now, that spark of creativity gone, maybe with the sound of an American movie from a little black-and-white TV droning unheeded on a kitchen shelf above her as she completes her house chores, a good wife but nothing like the sparkling thing she is now. What a shame to think ahead on the life she must lead.

I shut and lock my shop for the night.

I walk into Safwan and eat dinner with Bashar. He does not mention Ulayya directly. But as he sits with me he shows me a list of other names, potential brides, women I should meet. It is a new tactic for him. I notice how pointedly he avoids mentioning Ulayya. She is an absence in his recommendations. He wants me to notice the absence and mention her myself.

"Let us not talk of women," I say instead. "Have you found the movie?"

"Yes," he says, looking disappointed. "A friend's cousin from Kufa has a copy on disk and will bring it down tomorrow. Will you come to my house to watch it?"

"I will be delighted to watch the movie at your house. I have no DVD player."

I tip him an extra thousand dinar, which is just a few dollars now that Iraqi currency is so much inflated. He takes away my empty teacup and, with it, the remains of my dinner.

After Bashar has gone, as well as all through the time he and I spoke, I keep my eyes open for some hint of the boy who works for him, the boy who visits Mahmoud on the bridge. But I do not see this boy tonight in Bashar's café.

* * *

I don't talk about the war with Iran.

I refrain from thinking about it if possible. My father kept me from going to the war for as long as he could by obtaining an exemption for college study. I would have preferred to join the army immediately, like Yasin. I itched to join. But my father's word was law. He sent me to Al-Mustansiriya University in Baghdad and I took a bachelor's degree.

When, after I graduated in 1984, my draft notice arrived at our house, my father did not immediately share it with me.

He called Abdel Khaleq.

And Abdel Khaleq told Nadia.

And Nadia was the first to inform me.

"There's nothing my father can do about it," she said after rushing to my house with the news.

She had just turned seventeen and her roly-poly face with its button nose now graced a figure dark and willowy. She wore American-style blue jeans, a T-shirt splattered with paint, and an assortment of golden bangles on her wrists. Iraqi culture, like its army, had become a secular place, a more westernized place, especially for wealthy families like ours. All the girls at that time dressed like Cyndi Lauper, all the boys like Tom Selleck in the role of Magnum—Ray-Bans and Hawaiian-print shirts. Thick mascara bled onto Nadia's cheeks from eyes wept red and swollen.

When I didn't respond, Nadia added, "Father says every young man must serve."

I wanted to share her feeling of disappointment, though truly—not yet knowing the horror of war—I felt no sort of disappointment at all. Quite the opposite. I pictured myself wearing a pressed uniform like Yasin's. I pictured myself beside Yasin as we turned back the Iranian hordes, turned them back to the very gates of Tehran.

I didn't want to reveal my excitement, so I sadly said: "This will delay our wedding."

"Yes," she said. "Father told me it will be two years until we can reschedule."

9

الثلاثاء

Tuesday

LAYLA VISITS IN THE EVENING, like most evenings, this evening once again. And this evening I am at least a little glad, I admit, to see her. After two days of her absence I had begun to doubt whether she would ever return and whether I would ever hear the song again, the alien song. She stands in shadow under the awning of my little store, my shack, as the sun sets behind Jebel Sanam and casts its light against the overpass where the road from Basra to Kuwait and the even larger road from the port of Umm Qasr to Baghdad intersect.

Before her arrival, I concentrated sincerely on the convoys, focused my mind on them. In the greater resolution of this focus, each of the soldiers in the Humvees looked less robotic, more alive, more real. I counted my Dave and my Dave Junior and my Dave-Who-Is-Shorter-Than-

Dave-Junior. I saw one of my Patricks. I noticed that Winston was not wearing his sunglasses. The color of his eyes appeared darker than I expected: brown rather than the American blue all Americans supposedly have. I think about Layla's blue eyes, rare in the south of Iraq but not wholly unknown. What freak of nature made them blue? How strong was the gene in her, the gene of blue eyes, to overcome generations of brown, brown upon brown, like the clouds of a sandstorm parting at last to reveal the far-above sky? Are they naturally blue, bred from the depths of some ancient Assyrian lineage? Are they a carryover from the days the British fought here in Basra province during the world wars, some intermingling of fair British genes? Or, as I first thought, might she be a mistake, the result of a moment's lust during the Americans' first war here? Her age would be just about correct, thirteen, maybe fourteen years.

Today marks the ninth day since Layla's visitations began. Also the twenty-seventh day of business for me since I moved to Safwan. A long day. A weary day. The bottle lay beside me when I woke and, ever since, this whole morning, I have felt leaden. I am happy, if happy is the right word, to only perform the work of an immobile seller of mobile phones. I can handle such work on days like this, sitting with a thick head while I keep an eye on the roads.

My convoy counting and my naming of the American soldiers helps me pass the time and today I have additional reason to scrutinize each car. I do not know what Bashar's friend from Kufa who has the *Close Encounters* disk might look like. I cannot, of course, expect that he will be holding his copy of the movie against the window of his car to advertise his presence, the sun casting reflected rays from the

DVD in a halo of self-proclamation. But somehow I think I might know the man. I think some slight signal, some glint in the eye, might cue me that he isn't just a normal shopper come south to our little market for bargains on the latest Kuwaiti imports, legal or smuggled. Or, inversely, perhaps I think that I might later recall his arrival when Bashar introduces us.

"Ah," I could say. "You were the man in the Volkswagen."

Or the Toyota pickup.

Or the Yukon with the shaded windows and nice shiny hubcaps.

But I see nothing out of the ordinary among the multitudes who pass through the market, north to south, south to north.

The idiot Mahmoud on the overpass waves to me. I make a point of not waving back. I feel foolish. He clearly wishes to speak to me but I don't care to have a conversation with him. I begin shutting my shop.

Layla speaks to me before I see her.

"Are you angry with me, Abu Saheeh?"

"That depends," I say. "Are you clean?"

"Yes."

"Are you going to blaspheme Allah's name? Muhammad's name, Peace Be Upon Him?"

"No," she says. "I do not mean to…I did not mean to…I never do. I am sorry."

I can tell she sincerely regrets it. I can tell she is somewhat upset. She won't look directly at me. I speak over her protestations: "Don't worry. Don't worry. I am not angry with you."

Then I look around. I had heard her, but she wasn't nearby. Behind another shop? Behind a stack of tires in Rabeer's used-car lot? I spin in a circle and then look back into my shop.

"Where are you?"

"Behind the store. I see you through this crack in the wall."

"Hiding?"

"Why does the guard on the overpass look behind your shop now?" she asks. "Every day for the last few days he looks behind your shop. Many times every day. I'm hiding here until he next walks along the bridge, just to prove he is blind. He looks behind your shop but he doesn't see me, so what is he looking for?"

"I threatened him in order to—" I stop speaking; it would be foolish to tell her such things. She doesn't care anyway, it seems. She leaps to her next question, her mind skipping like a rock on the surface of a glassy pond.

"Can *you* see me?" she asks.

I go out the door and look for her. She has leaned a section of sliding door, probably stolen or discarded from Rabeer and Maney'a's lot, against the back wall. The bottom of the door props against the base of the shack behind mine, where the men from the propane filling station play cards and listen to music during the day. The top of the door rests against my tin roof. The space in which she hides is not large, a foot and a half across, not large enough for an adult. She crouches under the door. I pretend not to see her although she is plainly visible, her eyes wide open, glinting in the shadows.

"I can't see you," I say, pretending.

"You can't?"

"No."

"I thought not," she says.

She comes out from under the door. She walks around me in a slow circle. I keep squinting at the door, at the place from where I last heard her voice.

"Still can't see me?" she asks.

I startle as she speaks from beside me. She laughs.

"No," I say. "Are you walking around? Are you a ghost?"

"Ooooh," she says as eerily as she can while still stalking around me. "Ooooh."

I stick my hands straight in front of me, like a man sleepwalking. I try to feel around the space where she had just stood. I find nothing.

"Show yourself!" I say. "Show yourself, you fiend!"

She ducks back under the sliding door.

"Show yourself!" I say again, and louder.

The propane filling station men break from their game and look through their side window. They can see me but they can't see Layla. I notice that I'm making a fool of myself. I stand straight, put my arms down at my sides. I smooth the front of my *dishdasha* over my legs.

"Masah il-kheir," I say to the men, a little too formally.

They wave their cards and focus on their game again, dismissing my episode as just a touch of craziness, nothing worth watching, nothing worth mentioning. Or so I hope.

I wait until they are no longer interested. I bend. I look under the sliding door.

Layla has gone.

Later that evening, after falafel and tea at the café; after smoking a little *bukhoor* with Bashar in his *diwaniya;* after all the pleasant conversation, the preliminaries; after seeing his children once again paraded before me; after feeling again the gaze of Bashar's wife upon me, lurking out of sight behind the shadowed lattice of one of the courtyard windows—after all this, Bashar at last produces the DVD.

"I am sorry my friend could not remain in Safwan long enough to meet you, Abu Saheeh," Bashar says. "But he left the movie for you, for us."

I imagine the black-tinted windows of a GMC Yukon rolling down as the vehicle of Bashar's friend stops in the alleyway behind Bashar's house. The friend, in sunglasses, hands the DVD through the window, drop-and-go, fast-food style. Bashar blesses him, wishing him a safe journey back to Kufa. The friend waves, noncommittally, and then squeals his tires as he drives away over the trash and spliced electric lines, the open sewer and piles of goat manure in the alley. Any man who owns DVDs of old American movies would have more important things to attend to, surely. It is a wonder to me that Bashar knows someone who possesses the movie at all, and that he has influence enough to get the movie delivered. But then it seems Bashar knows everyone, a benefit stemming either from his new career as a restaurateur or from his old career, our old careers, in Baghdad.

Bashar has placed a TV on the far end of the *diwaniya,* away from the windows. We move our pillows toward it and sit in front of it. I recline on my side, propping my head with my arm. Bashar puts the movie into his DVD player. He moves his *narjeela* between us as the credits roll. We watch the movie and smoke. When, partway through the movie, I take a small handheld tape recorder from my pocket and set it on the ground in front of me, Bashar looks at it and then at me, questioningly.

"I bought this in the market today. Amazing the things you can buy! I want to record the song, you see," I say.

Yet the tape recorder remains unused for most of the movie. It is much as Layla said: aliens, various alien sightings, science fiction, as the man Neary, who is the hero, fights his way through the American secret military and onto the American secret base. Thinking about it more deeply than I would have otherwise done, I suppose the plot does exhibit certain parallels with the experience of the Prophet Muhammad, Peace Be Upon Him, when he first appeared with his message before the merchants and old families of Mecca. They fought him. They tried to detain him and hinder him before his escape north to Medina. They were unbelieving, some of them, until the events and miracles and words of Angel Gabriel conveyed through Muhammad showed clear proof of the Message and Messenger of Allah.

At the climactic moment in the movie, I turn on my cassette recorder. It hisses as the tape winds forward to capture the sound from the television. The alien ship sings to the assembled scientists. All of them stand together in awe on the mountain platform specially prepared for the occasion. The aliens sing. The American scientists play their own song in return. The two sides communicate through music. And just as Neary is about to meet the aliens, just as he walks out from his hiding place among the rocks to meet the aliens at the gangway of their ship, at that moment Bashar stops the movie.

"This is what you want to see?" he says.

"No," I say. "I've seen enough already."

"It disgusts you?"

"Yes," I say. "Blasphemy."

I turn off the tape recorder and slip it into my pocket. Blasphemy, I say. But in my heart I think something altogether different. The song the aliens sing in the movie, although having similar notes to the melody Layla sang, isn't at all the same. It is something different entirely. Heard through her, amplified through her, resonating through her, the song changed. That change made me think of Muhammad again, reminded me more of the true miracle of the Prophet, Peace Be Upon Him, than did any part of the movie's plot: how the supposedly illiterate Muhammad heard the words of Angel Gabriel and spoke them, recited them, read them so that they would be known to the minds of men. The change Layla wrought in the music reminded me of the way that the spoken sound of the Quran is itself hypnotic and sacred. Had Layla done something similar? Was her voice, singing alien songs or songs of rock and roll, somehow influenced by a godly power? Was she touched, divine? Were her mixed-up tales of Beverly Hillbillies and Arnold Schwarzenegger an index to something, when taken in aggregate, infinitely more precious?

While I ponder these things, Bashar continues speaking. I catch the end of his thoughts: "...this person who asserts these blasphemies. I will have his name! Abu Saheeh, you will give the man's name to me and I will tell Hussein from the Hezbollah and then: woe unto this blasphemer, this *kafir!*"

The TV, with the DVD still paused at the aliens descending the gangway of the ship onto the mountain platform, flickers with static.

"No, Bashar. No," I say.

But he is frantic. Whether to calm him or whether due to some deeper, more human impulse, I change the topic. He sits immediately.

"Let us talk of Ulayya bint Ali ash-Shareefi again, my friend," I say, dropping her name on him like a bomb. "And let us forget this movie entirely, though I wish you to give my devoted thanks to your cousin's friend for driving from Kufa with the DVD."

We spend the rest of that fine evening talking of Ulayya and of women in general. The TV flickers with the suspended moment of alien contact. The tape recorder in my lumpy breast pocket is heavy, feeling heavier because it is full. I waste time with Bashar, but the waste isn't something unpleasant. Time slips easily past me here. I see myself changing, mellowing a little. It is as if the shell of me, the exterior, has begun to cool and harden. And perhaps that is why Layla bothers me so much. Each time she comes to my store, the cooling shell, the part of me that most easily molds itself to this town and this life and the possibility of marrying again, each time she comes, the shell feels more like a shell, the inside feels more like an emptiness, a shiftiness, a pool that churns and churns under the surface, though with less force each and every day. I worry that my soul will callus completely.

At the end of the night, when we are parting at his front gate, just after Bashar and I kiss each other's cheeks, I think of Mahmoud, the guardian of the bridge. I should probably not be reminded of Mahmoud by this kiss, this formal and customary kiss between men, yet Bashar and I are the type of close friends for whom the kiss is a mark of deep endearment, kinship, almost, that is as binding as, and maybe more enduring than, any passionate love.

I should not think of Mahmoud, but I do. I think of him and I think of his night visitor, whom I suspect to be Bashar's own employee.

"The boy in your café," I say, "the one with the big white teeth and the slim face."

"His name is Michele," says Bashar.

The two of us hold each other by the shoulders, our faces near together. I can smell the sweetness of pear-flavored *narjeela* smoke on his breath.

"What do you think of homosexual relations?" I ask.

Immediately as I say the words I realize that they have come out wrong. Bashar drops his hands from my shoulders.

"No, no," I say quickly. "You've got me wrong. Not me. I'm not interested in him! I'm a confirmed lover of women, my friend. Like I said, maybe this woman Ulayya. The thing is...I suspect the boy, your employee Michele. I think he visits the guard on the overpass in his tent at night."

I've approached the subject wrong. Bashar's eyebrows furrow into a frown. Perhaps he, too, feels the kiss we exchanged was oddly uncomfortable. Perhaps he feels even now the same emotion that made the image of Mahmoud and his night visitor come unbidden to my mind. And perhaps Bashar feels embarrassed about his feeling for me. Whatever it is, he is suddenly cold, formal.

"I don't think about private relationships between men," he says after a moment of hesitation. "I'm sure it happens. But..."

"Never mind," I say. "Never mind. Just a random thought; forget about it, please. Forget about it."

Bashar slaps my shoulder with his hand, trying to be jovial, but he doesn't embrace me again before we part. He promises to disregard my remarks. The gate of his outer courtyard, open behind him, creaks as a gust of wind swirls. He shuts it, looking at me through the iron scrollwork, an effective divider.

"Allah's blessing for your walk home," he says.

"And upon your family as well," I say.

It is close to midnight when I leave him. The gusty wind blows from the west, having shifted during the time I spent watching the alien movie. It is a dry wind, the *simoom,* scorched by its passage over the wastes of Saudi Arabia, a wind bearing aloft thickening clouds of dust and sand. I put my face to the sleeve of my *dishdasha* to keep the particles from entering my lungs, but I force myself to look upward at the sky, where the stars are smudged by thickening dust so that only the brightest few remain. I know in my heart and in my bones that a storm will blow.

* * *

I wrote to Nadia as I promised.

In the beginning I wrote to her. But my letters stopped after only the first few months of my time on the front lines. I couldn't convey what I had seen and smelled and heard. How could I have done justice to the sight of one of our many machine-gun battlements firing into the pacing bodies of massed Iranian martyrs, firing until no more bullets remained, then waiting until the hordes overwhelmed and ripped apart the men behind the silenced weapon? How could I have told Nadia what odor burned flesh emitted, burned hair, the sweet harsh wafts of poi-

sonous chemicals pooled in low places, like bomb craters, all over the battlefield? How could I have adequately described the sound of a man's scream or a man's prayer in the strangled moment when he realizes he must die?

When the letters seemed hollow and false and when, at the same time, the words wouldn't come to me—then I stopped writing.

Nadia's father and my father hadn't prevented me from being drafted. But they ensured my service would be as a medic, rather than as an infantryman or a tanker, the more dangerous jobs. The work suited me. Every man I treated was another kitten, another chance to show Yasin that he hadn't really defeated me.

I won an award, a decoration. I don't really know why, for everywhere on the battlefield men undertook heroic or foolhardy deeds and most of the time these deeds were impossible to distinguish one from the other, impossible to assign value to, impossible to quantify as worthy of notice. At the time, the award felt misplaced. I recounted a hundred events I had witnessed that far surpassed my action in terms of daring, in terms of impact, in terms of compassion.

When my father heard of the award he quickly sent me the following telegram:

You've served well enough and long enough. I've used the most recent example of your valor to persuade certain people to send you for further medical training. You will be recalled to Baghdad.

I did not argue as I had once before argued, when I had imagined myself among the conquerors of Tehran.

The summons came.

I went home.

10

الأربعاء

Wednesday

NOTHING MOVES IN SAFWAN today. I stay in my house. Where the wind finds chinks in the construction, around the bases of the doors and windows, the ventilation, I place wads of paper towel or rags. These turn tawny brown as fine particles of dust clog their fibers. It is as if each towel ages before my eyes, withering and yellowing. Better to stop the dust there, at the chinks and creases, than to let it into the house. Or better to stop at least some of the dust before it enters. Plenty more finds its way. The air is thick and stale. My teeth feel dry and they grind whenever I close my mouth, a film of fine grit coating them.

The bypass for the American convoys, so close to my house, remains quiet all day. Allah's storm stops them. I picture convoys in their staging areas, so much material destined to move north now backlogged in dust-choked parking lots, so many semis to return south and refill. How vast is the might of America, this far from its own sovereign soil, to bring the power of one thousand semis a day north and south, south and north, day in and day out, except for a day such as this, when the force of nature, Allah willing, halts them in the dusts.

Inside my house I keep the lighting low, just one or two bulbs burning in case the sky darkens completely. Everything takes on a color similar to bruised flesh: cinder-block walls, most of which I have not painted; the kitchen, with its unfinished floor tiles heaped like counted coins among bags of powdered grout; the refrigerator, which is empty and unplugged. Perhaps most disturbing, the only item lending a true splash of color to my house is a small child's toy, an old-fashioned crank-operated jack-in-the-box that came with me from Baghdad. Its home is now one of the bare shelves in my kitchen. The jack-in-the-box is sprung. Its face leans and leers at me across the intervening space between my kitchen and the place where I sit at a small table in my big, empty dining room. When the wind of the storm blows hard, the house itself, though made mostly of concrete, shakes. Then the head of the jack-in-the-box bobs on its spring.

The house is barely habitable, but it is all I need right now. Just a few rooms and the promise they offer of being, someday, complete. Bashar tells me I should hire a crew to finish the house more quickly, but I am happy enough with the slow progress I make in the evenings. What else do I have to distract me? What else should I do today but slowly and meditatively place tiles in simple crosshatch patterns on the kitchen floor? What else except string wires to bedrooms, install plumbing in the bathroom, in the hope, Allah willing, that electricity will one day soon be made available for more than a few hours each day; in the hope, Allah willing, that the water tower in the town square, burst open by a helicopter rocket at the beginning of this latest war, will once again be whole and provide enough pressure for water to reach my toilet and my bath? I will have crown moldings to set off the joinery between the ceilings and the walls. I will paint the rooms by hand with bright and lively colors, blues and reds and golds. I will have wallpaper, pillows, dark satin-finished wood trim and a library, Allah willing, a library. I will, one day, cover the bare cinder block and the bare floors. I will make these things according to the speed and the skill of my own hands.

But the house will be as empty as was my father's big old house if it is only me, only my voice and my thoughts and my work and my play to fill the rooms. Because of this, I am in no hurry to rush the gilding, to superficially alter a thing that must retain its essence of emptiness until the time comes for it to be empty no longer.

Because everything is written, happens as it will, according to the unknowable plans of Allah, and because I am in no rush—after I fill, with my rags and towels, all the spaces where the wind and sand and dust penetrate, and after taking the little tape recorder from my pocket—I begin to drink. I am in no hurry. I drink: whiskey from a bottle that came to me in a sheath of sawdust hidden beneath one of my shipments of mobile phones from Kuwait. When I finish that bottle, a bottle I had sipped slowly for the last few days, I open another and I drink most of it. I drink without the benefit of a cup. I do not own a cup. The glass lip of the bottle is cool when it presses against my lips. I listen to the wind outside, shivering in tune with the bass note the gusts strike against my hollow-drum house. I look at the tape recorder where it sits, noiselessly, on the table in front of me. I drink. Then I walk through each room: bedroom, bedroom, bedroom, empty bedroom, balcony swept with sand, piling with sand, a balcony that overlooks the town but is not used by anyone for the act of overlooking. I walk down the stairs again, into the hall, front room, sitting room, empty sitting room, half-tiled kitchen, washroom, courtyard, *diwaniya*. A big house. A shell house.

I lie on my bed, a mattress only, no bed frame, just a mattress placed haphazardly, diagonal on the bare living-room floor. I have been watching the market for the right bed frame. Oak or mahogany. Beech or maple. Carved but not with figures of men, no blasphemy in my house. I'd like ivy, a European dream, rivulets of ivy and acorns and cascading leaves in lustrous oak or mahogany. Mahogany or oak. Or teak. Well-oiled. Old. Old like me. But just the right age for a widow like Ulayya, who has retained her womanly figure. I picture the frame of the bed encompassing the bare mattress on which I now lie. In the air above me I outline the frame of the bed with my hands, a big four-poster. I hold the tape recorder, which has come with me from room to room, and as I outline the shape of the imaginary bedposts in the air, the tape recorder waves, swishes, cuts through the greenish gloom. Its weight makes my hand feel heavy. I let it rest, setting it down on my belly.

I think of Mahmoud and Michele. I try to picture them together, perhaps sharing the cot in Mahmoud's tent. Perhaps they kiss, Mahmoud's beard coming close to, then touching Michele's hairless face. I shake my head, shiver, forcing the image away. I grope for something else to think of. My brother, my brother, Yasin, appears in my mind, his dark but depthless gaze staring at me and through me and beyond me like the gemmed eyes of a funerary god. I shake my head again, more vigorously. He disappears, but in his place I am surrounded by the faces of the American soldiers, the Davids, the Patricks, the Winstons. They clamber on my shadowed ceiling like cherubs in a baroque fantasy. They parade before me, each with sunglasses, Kevlar helmet, clean white teeth. They point fingers at me. They mouth words of accusation, each of them with a belly split open, flaccid drooping intestines like living coils of rope gathered and bunched in bloody, mucus-covered hands.

I feel for them. I feel bad for them. I try to apologize to them. I try to apologize in advance. "It's not you," I whisper toward the impersonal and undecorated ceiling of my room. "You're just in the way. You and your good intentions. You and your noble ideas of justice."

I pull these phantom soldiers down from the rafters of the room, one at a time, and I make motions in the air with my hands, needle and thread, scissors and clamps, sewing them, making them whole, doing what I can to fix them. Poor little kittens, lifeless things.

When at last I sleep, I do not dream. But I wake with the recollection of things that were like dreams, nearer to me, more precise yet elusive, too, as if I have read the labels of manufacture on gifts I have purchased, like jack-in-the-boxes, or new little red dresses, or windup toy soldiers, remote-control boats, robots. As if I have read the labels on the gifts but cannot account for the make or the model of the things I have purchased. I wake full of little useless details, the times when convoys roll over the bridge from north to south, south to north; the times Mahmoud the lover comes and goes, sleeps and wakes, takes tea, checks on my shop; the times when British and American patrols enter Safwan, regular as clockwork, for meetings with the Safwan police, with the Safwan town council. I am full of details but completely empty of association between each detail, a string of savant facts flowing from the mouth of a man who can no longer speak the names of the things he has seen.

At last, having slept most of a day, having roamed in and out of dreams, and having eaten nothing, for I have nothing in my house to eat, I get restless. Fully awake, I realize the daylight that remains has perceptibly brightened, the storm has nearly blown itself out. So I dress myself in a clean white *dishdasha,* my best, find a cloth to hold over my face so that I do not inhale a devastating amount of dust, and go to the house of Sheikh Seyyed Abdullah, where I know I will be welcome to a plate of food, a fresh drink, and some news of the world.

* * *

Forty-two men and eight women received scholarships from Saddam's government in 1984 to attend medical programs in the United States or Europe. My father, with Abdel Khaleq's assistance, reserved one of these scholarships for me.

All fifty award winners appeared together for a photograph session and a press briefing. I had my picture taken with Saddam Hussein. He put his arm around my shoulders for a moment. Then all the scholarship winners boarded a flight from Baghdad headed to Zurich, each of us taking connecting flights to the countries where we had been assigned to study.

"Where are you assigned?" asked the man in the seat next to me as our plane taxied onto the Baghdad tarmac.

"I don't know," I said. "Somewhere not in Iraq."

"Alhumdu l-Allah!" said my neighbor, a fine-boned man about my age dressed in penny loafers and a soft woolen sport coat. A wire-thin mustache decorated his upper lip. His eyes were a lively light brown, his fingers slim, his disposition cloyingly cheerful. He held his hand out to me in the Western style, offering it to me to shake.

"My name's Bashar Dulaimi," he said. "My father's the minister of—"

"I know," I said, cutting him off rather abruptly. "I was in his army."

"The army? You?" he asked, seeming puzzled.

He pulled his unshaken hand away from me as if I might contain traces of poison gas. Then he looked at me slowly, carefully—my good shoes, my well-tailored suit coat. He breathed in the lavender scent that still clung to me from Fatima's freshly pressed towels and sheets. These things didn't add up in his mind to the idea of a soldier. He looked at my face and saw, set deeply in it, eyes that still retained a vacancy despite the pampering and luxury I enjoyed since my return from the war.

He must have seen this because he coughed a little and then said: "Didn't your father buy you an exemption?"

A stupid question, a self-evident answer. I didn't bother to reply.

"I'm sorry," I told him, turning away to look out the little fogged window of the airplane. "I'm sorry but I just said good-bye to my fiancée, and I've never flown before. I'm not feeling quite well."

He shrugged and left me alone, but only for a little while.

When the wheels of the plane lifted off the ground, he turned to me again and said, "Was she pretty?"

"Who?"

"Your fiancée."

"Very."

"You don't speak much."

"Don't have much to say."

At this he wrinkled his nose and closed his eyes tightly so that crow's-feet appeared around their edges. He tugged at one corner of his mustache.

"It's going to be a long flight," he said. "A long couple years, actually. Let me start over with this conversation. I know where you're going. We're going to the same place, you and me: Chicago. Northwestern University. I had my father specifically request that I be allowed to sit on the plane next to whomever shared—"

"If you mention your father one more time during this flight I will specifically request a new school," I said.

"Okay, then," he said huffily.

He raised his hand. When the stewardess came down the aisle to check on him, he slipped her a hundred-dinar note and got himself moved to a new seat closer to the front of the plane.

I put the armrest between our seats into its upright position and curled my legs beneath me, happy to have both spaces to myself.

11

مساء الأربعاء

Wednesday Evening

SEYYED ABDULLAH'S HOUSE IS not far from my own. It looks
toward the border of Kuwait, toward the American military crossing point on the border, just as my house does. Yet
his house is on the far side of the military road, in the older,
original part of the town, and it is surrounded by the wind-
ing type of alleyway and the mud-brick sort of hovels that
make old movies about Baghdad or Damascus or Cairo pic-
turesque. His house, like mine, is also a two-story affair. But
that is where the similarity ends. Whereas mine is empty
as a tomb, his is as peopled as a bazaar. Whereas mine is
bare—bare rooms, bare ground, bare walls—his is clothed
with the trappings of a well-established man. Whereas mine
is without family, his teems with family. He has taken a
third wife recently and he dotes upon her, making it gener-
ally known in town that the pick of new jewelry smuggled

from Kuwait should be hers; likewise the pick of perfumes and of flowers harvested by children from the banks of the Shatt al-Arab canal near Umm Qasr. His children from his first two marriages play underfoot. They stream from the gutters and over the railings of balconies that look inward on his bowered courtyard. They are like living rain or handfuls of sand tumbling along a dune face. Most pointedly, whereas my house lacks visitors, his visitors queue outside his *diwaniya* even on, or especially on, a shut-in stormy evening such as this.

I hold back the image of my brother from the forefront of my mind as Seyyed Abdullah approaches to greet me. The resemblance between them is close, uncanny: tall, dark, smilingly feral. I almost pull back from Safwan's sheikh when he puts his hands on my shoulders, as we exchange our greeting kisses.

"I am sorry to have kept you so long," he tells me as he leads me inside his *diwaniya,* takes me from the group of anxious supplicants as though he is the embodiment of a saving angel. The others, those not fortunate enough to merit his personal greeting, these others huddle under the half-shelter of the courtyard, rags to their mouths to keep the last wisps of the gritty sandstorm from their lungs.

"I am sorry to have kept you so long," he says again, "but I have so much business, so many people to see."

"You must not apologize to a simple mobile-phone salesman," I say.

He laughs at this, a good-natured laugh. Despite his position of authority in town, despite his autocracy, Seyyed Abdullah is a good-natured man. In fact, his humor and disposition support his authority rather than detract from it. He is the type of man who makes the best of companions and the worst of enemies. I feel the humor radiating from him. It contradicts the resemblance to my brother that clings to him in my mind. No man fears to come to Seyyed Abdullah with problems. His effectiveness as a mediator is both academic—he knows the law and the traditions and the histories that exist between the families and tribes of his town—and personal: he pronounces judgment and reward with candor, goodwill, and very little in the way of personal pride, though he is proud and wealthy and educated.

As we enter his *diwaniya* through a massive set of green-painted double doors, we must indeed appear to those within the room to be brothers, our features so similar, our arms linked together. As my eyes adjust to the light of the room, I see on the couches lining the walls several other men, most of them in *dishdashas,* different from Seyyed Abdullah's neat, dark, silken suit and coat. The men smoke from two big *narjeelas* that dominate the middle of the room, braided glittering rubber pipes extending from the central hookahs like tentacles. The men talk among themselves. They are relaxed and friendly, though they all look at their sheikh when he enters.

"Come, come," Seyyed Abdullah says.

"Really," I say, "no special favors. Nothing."

"As you wish," he says. "You know everyone here?"

I nod in affirmation, although in truth I do not know one of the men, a fat policeman who does not wear his uniform shirt but betrays his occupation by his shined black shoes and his flat blue polyester pleated pants, the cuffs of which show under his *dishdasha.* Seyyed Abdullah notices my glance at this man and he shrugs, as if to tell me not to worry. I exchange some mild pleasantries with the seated men. The nearest of them rises to his feet, intent on shaking my hand. I motion to him that it is not necessary for him to stand, but I take his hand anyway. We embrace, and he sits, and I sit next to him.

"Will you take food?" the man asks me.

"No," I say, though I am almost painfully hungry after the day of unexpected fasting.

"Smoke?"

"No," I say.

"Are you sure you will not take food with us?" Seyyed Abdullah says, still hovering over me until he is certain of my comfort and my reception. "We have platters and platters coming, albeit slowly. It will be a fine evening."

As if this were his cue, a young man steps into the *diwaniya* with a tray. I want to eat very much, having eaten nothing all day, but to seem too eager would be poor manners. The food is only partly the reason I visit, should be none of the reason at all if I were visiting purely for the sake of business and not because the sandstorm had caught me without food in my house. I shake my head no at this second offer of food, but I do not shake it very emphatically. Seyyed Abdullah waves the boy with the tray into the room and the boy sets the food in front of me. The man with whom I sit selects a sticky sugared date and then settles back onto the couch. He arranges his *dishdasha* over his knees, plucking at it, and listens as Seyyed Abdullah and I talk. I notice that the serving boy wears a pistol on the belt of his blue jeans. He thinks the blousing of his T-shirt hides the weapon but its hilt shows plainly, a hard angular outline of gunmetal under cloth. Seyyed Abdullah notices me looking at the outline of the gun.

"These are difficult times," he says. "One in my position cannot be too careful."

"The Wild West," I say. I think of Jed Clampett and black gold. I think of Mahmoud, the sleeping guardian of the overpass. "Do you know the boy who guards the overpass?"

"Small in size, although maybe twenty years of age?" asks Seyyed Abdullah. "From the family of al-Jorani? His uncle on his mother's side owns a farm north toward Az Zubayr."

"Yes," I say. "He has been given no bullets from the police. How is he to guard the overpass without bullets?"

True, I have bought him a package of ammunition, but I'd rather fix the problem, have the police themselves provide the bullets.

"Must a guard be seen to be a guard?" says the man sitting beside me.

Seyyed Abdullah turns away, rather too quickly, as the man beside me says this. I understand the idea of invisible guards, the true way to have something stay guarded. What worries me is the very visible presence of this guard and the possible reasons why he is not better supplied. It is not just a matter of a lack of money for bullets. I want to ask why they bother posting a guard on the bridge at all, if there are truly invisible guards for the market and for the overpass. But I know the Americans like to see guards. Are these town leaders embarrassed to have given the Americans such a simple thing, embarrassed to let the Americans feel like they are protected? And if a guard like Mahmoud is to be seen and to be uniformed, why not equip him with bullets anyway? Might he mistakenly interfere with the real guards or with the business, legal or otherwise, these town leaders undertake in the markets and on the highways? Have they purposefully selected Mahmoud for this job, knowing he will conduct his duties in a slipshod and inattentive fashion? I ask none of these questions. Instead, I take a small sesame-crusted pastry from the tray and lean back on the couch. I feel like I have embarked on business too quickly by asking about Mahmoud's situation. I tell myself to enjoy the food, to enjoy a smoke with the men, to enjoy the evening. The time for questions will come. Or it won't come. Either way, as Allah wills.

As I eat, Seyyed Abdullah moves farther away from me, makes a trip around the room, seeing to his guests. There are five other men in total: the mayor, who sits against the far wall and has loosened the tie of his Western-style suit beneath his over-draping *ghalabia;* the fat unnamed police-man, who pretends not to have heard my remark about Mahmoud's bullets; the manager of the electric utility, who has but one leg; a prominent farmer from the north of town, upon whose lands most of the little farmers like Mahmoud's uncle and probably also Layla's family work their living; and, last, my companion. All these men are older than me, each in his sixth or even seventh decade. They represent the generation too old to have been intimately involved in the rising against Saddam at the end of the first American war. They were spared the cleansing afterward, the cleans-ing that must have claimed their sons and nephews and younger brothers. The man sitting with me is the eldest of the group, white-haired, with a lined but smiling face.

"You are from the Shareefi clan?" I ask him, though I know it to be true. My couch mate, as if by providence, or as if by the quick and artful arrangement of Seyyed Abdullah, is the head of the Shareefi clan, Ali al-Hajj ash-Shareefi, who is a trader with connections in Riyadh, Tehran, Port Said, Kuwait City. An influential man. Head of the family of that woman, Ulayya, who has made herself known to me.

"Yes," he says. He looks at me for a long while and then exhales from the tube of the *narjeela* that he has plucked from the low table holding our food. "You are the new mobile-phone and satellite merchant in the north bazaar?"

"The only such merchant in either bazaar, actually."

"You are not from Safwan? Not from Basra Province?"

"No," I say.

"You are Shia?"

"Yes, from Kufa originally, though Baghdad was my home for the recent past. I am from the family of ash-Shumari, but from the more southern, Shia branch."

This is a lie, of course. No sense, though, causing him alarm. I tell the lie well, quickly, nonchalantly. Our tribe, ash-Shumari, is well known to be split in half. Such things happen: families on each side of the war, families divided by antitank ditches etched in the desert.

Al-Hajj ash-Shareefi puts the *narjeela* tube into his mouth again and then inhales. I think our interview has concluded. I pick up another pastry and eat it. I think about introducing myself to the policeman: perhaps a more direct appeal to the police to fix the situation with Mahmoud would work best, although I am sure Seyyed Abdullah understood me about the bullets and I am sure he will take some sort of action. I expect, almost, to be introduced to the person responsible for the silent guardianship of the market and the overpass. Perhaps that person will stop at my store tomorrow, make himself known to me in order to restore my confidence in Seyyed Abdullah's patronage. I decide not to talk to the policeman directly. The time will come for that, I'm sure. Mentally, I walk around the room, thinking about what I might say to the others if the chance were to arise. There is business to be done with the electric-utility manager, especially if we are to have satellite dishes in town and other electrical appliances that work. There is business to be done with the mayor. He wants very badly to tax merchants like me in the highway market, but we are all squatters on land supposedly owned by the Ministry of Transport, by the government in Basra Province and in Baghdad, not on land owned by the town. So how can he tax us? I should speak with the farmer, too, just to know him better, since his lands come so near to the market. An opportunity, there, for him to lease space as the market grows to the north along the road to Basra. Already I have noticed shops springing up on the far side of the interchange. Why doesn't he parcel his nearby lands and allow the market to spread onto them, each tenant paying him a small fee?

I think of the important things these men control, the public and private functions each of them oversees, things upon which the future of this little town depends. But before I make any attempt to speak to these others, before I even finish eating, Ali al-Hajj ash-Shareefi speaks privately to me again.

He tugs my sleeve and leans very close. I smell *narjeela* smoke on his breath, sweetened with a little apple scent, *bukhoor.* "You have met my daughter in the souk?"

"As Allah willed, I believe that I have indeed been so fortunate. It was a meeting between a merchant and a buyer, though, nothing inappropriate…"

I start to ramble, a little embarrassed. But the old man waves his hand in the air to show me he is unconcerned.

"She is widowed," he says.

This brings the real issue immediately to the forefront of our conversation.

I take a second to reply, then carefully say: "So I understand."

"She is a good girl, a good Muslim. Shia, of course."

"These things, too, I understand."

"And did you look upon her?"

"Only when she asked about purchasing a satellite connection for her house. She was quite discreet in her questioning of me." This is something of a lie, and I think back to the meeting, how Ulayya did everything possible within the limits of her black draping clothes and veiling *hijab* to show me the contours of her body and the beauty of her face. "She seemed interested in buying a satellite dish for her house," I say.

"It is a big house," he says. "An empty house now, too."

"Empty like my own," I say after surprisingly little hesitation, the words slipping from me before I even realize what I am saying.

Al-Hajj sets his *narjeela* pipe down again and, using the hand that had held it, the same hand I had shaken and held earlier, he clasps me again, then folds his other hand over both of our hands so that I am caught in his weathered but solid grasp.

* * *

At the start of my fifth school year in America, September of 1990, the most beautiful woman I have ever seen entered the emergency room of Northwestern Memorial Hospital. Bashar and I were on night shift together, having drawn the worst duties during the first year of our medical residency.

This woman stepped into the ER through the automatic double doors—the same doors through which paramedics usually rushed gurneys into curtained rooms. She took two strides into the center of the shining waxed floor and then stood still, looking around her, apparently dazed. From the elbows down, blood sheathed her arms.

I was too stunned to react, not by the blood but by her: tall—taller than me—wearing roan-colored knee-high boots that perfectly matched the chestnut color of her hair. Her skin had a luster of translucence to it, like bone-thin porcelain. And though her eyes were absent of sparkle, they were wide-set and liquid and framed in a face seemingly stolen from a cinema poster—Grace Kelly, Audrey Hepburn. I hesitated but Bashar leaped from our shared desk at the nurses' station and rushed to help her.

Nurses joined him. They swept back the curtains of an examination room, threw back the thin blankets of a bed, readied bandages and towels. Bashar took the woman's hands, heedless of the blood, and ushered her behind the partition. Then he shut the curtain.

I hadn't even stood up. I doubt whether I even breathed from the moment this woman entered until the moment Bashar closed the curtain.

12

ليلة الأربعاء

Wednesday Night

I LEAVE SHEIKH SEYYED Abdullah's house with a package under my arm, not, avowedly, the main purpose for my visit but something I knew I would receive. Seyyed Abdullah and I have not spoken of the package all evening. But, as I prepare to leave, he motions to his serving boy, the boy with the half-hidden pistol. I know what is coming when the boy quickly exits the *diwaniya* and when Seyyed Abdullah rises to escort me to the door. Just beyond the *diwaniya,* outside and a few paces out of earshot from us, I see the remaining visitors who wait for their audience. Seyyed Abdullah looks at them but pulls me close. The serving boy reappears behind him with the package.

"So much business to do," he says.

"I don't envy your position," I say.

"Sometimes I think of doing what you're doing," he says.

"Starting over, being unknown. Having my time to myself once again."

"It has its advantages," I say, but then I think of his house, his many children, his wives. "But, too often, loneliness is my companion. For that reason I thank you most sincerely for your hospitality tonight. I have felt welcome here, and happy."

We exchange these words directly into each other's ears, like conspirators in a crime, and then we kiss, the customary farewell. I feel nothing when I kiss him, nothing but a slight revulsion that still fills me from the similarity I've inadvertently noticed between him and my brother. When we have finished embracing, the serving boy comes even closer and hands the package to me. It is of medium size, not something unnoticeable but certainly something unmentionable. It's a box wrapped in plain brown paper and string, like a cut of meat from a butcher shop.

"Mahmoud needs no bullets," Seyyed Abdullah says. "Not with you."

"I know," I say. "I am watching, will be watching."

"Soon it will be more than just a single bottle of whiskey. Soon more important things will come."

He taps the box.

"Yes," I say. "No problem."

He shifts his eyes away from me for a moment and then back to me, looking directly at me. The tone of his voice shifts, too, softer yet equally authoritative. "Do you want to marry Ulayya bint Ali ash-Shareefi? Her father, Ali, with whom you just sat, mentioned the thing to me this evening before your arrival. He seems to favor you as a match for her."

"Does he know me for something other than a merchant?"

"I have said nothing," Seyyed Abdullah says, and I can tell by the continued unflinching directness of his gaze that he speaks in earnest.

I wonder if my friend Bashar has let something slip. Perhaps I should tell Seyyed Abdullah about Bashar. Perhaps I should tell Seyyed Abdullah that at least one other person in town has been taken into my confidence, that one other person in town knows my history both recent and long past, and that at least one other person in town seems to have guessed at my reasons for moving here.

I say, "Not only does Ali al-Hajj ash-Shareefi want me, a seemingly poor merchant with no family, for his daughter's husband, but he also asked me if I was Shia or Sunni. It led me to suspect—"

"It's the Baghdad accent in your voice. From so far north. It calls the question to mind, especially in these times, when we kill each other like curs."

"Indeed, how do your townsfolk reconcile the idea of a northerner come so far south to live among them? This has always bothered me about our plan."

"I told you that you would be noticed."

"I know. But what do they think I am?"

"Wounded."

"That's all?"

"They don't want to ask the other questions. They make assumptions. You pray as a Shia. You go to mosque with the people. But you haven't been overly open or friendly with them. Perhaps they think you were a fighter. *Mujahideen.*"

"For whom would I fight?" I ask, somewhat laughingly.

"That is the big question, isn't it?"

"Marrying into a Shia family might be necessary," I say. "The people will suspect an eligible bachelor who shows no interest in marriage."

Seyyed Abdullah nods to show his agreement just at the moment when Ali al-Hajj approaches us, looming in the shadowed interior of the room. Ali looks at the package in my hands. Then he looks at Seyyed Abdullah. He touches his forehead in a salute, not at all similar to the mocking, military-style salute Hussein gave me with his mobile phone in the market as he followed Ali's daughter into town. Ash-Shareefi is a tall, thin man when standing, perhaps only a little shy of six feet. On the couch he had seemed smaller, with his white hair like a flame in the charged darkness of the room. His height now gives me the feeling that he had been folded up, neat as a message in a bottle, when he sat.

"Ya fendem," he says to Seyyed Abdullah. "It is time an old man like me returns home for the night. May I trouble your guest, my new friend Abu Saheeh ash-Shumari, to walk with me across town to my house?"

"These are difficult times," says Seyyed Abdullah, a phrase he has come to repeat quite often, his mantra, perhaps. "Allah willing, Abu Saheeh ash-Shumari will indeed see you home safely."

Seyyed Abdullah emphasizes my family name, questioningly.

"Yes," I try to silently convey to Seyyed Abdullah with my own fretful expression. "Yes, I told Ali al-Hajj my real family name. It was only proper, with him offering his daughter in marriage. He should know to whom he allies himself."

Aloud I say that I will enjoy walking my esteemed new friend home. Putting my wrapped package under one arm, I take Ali al-Hajj's hand and leave the doorway of Seyyed Abdullah's *diwaniya,* crossing his open courtyard and proceeding through the gate of the house into the sand-strewn alley, into the last of the dusty maelstrom. Only when I am outside do I remember I had meant also to ask Seyyed Abdullah about Hussein from the Hezbollah. Was he truly competition? What was his history? Was Ali al-Hajj's offer of marrying his daughter to me inspired by a desire to avoid union with the likes of Hussein?

These questions mirror in my mind the swaying shadows of Russian olive trees that arch over the alleyway. Bits of paper, a black plastic bag, a tin can rattle and flee, circle in whirling eddies where the alleyway walls angle and the wind churns. We step around these things, Ali and I, over them, arm in arm. I help him when proper, but for the most part he does not rely on me. He is strong and wiry for an old man. He seems not so much ashamed of my help as hesitant about accepting it, as if leaning on me becomes by extension symbolic, part of our relationship. He is hesitant about letting me help him but he does accept my help, up small flights of stairs in the alleyways, across rough patches of ground. This leaning and supporting and assisting mirror the process of becoming a member of a town, of a community, of gaining family. It involves finding allies, making enemies, spending hard-earned money and respect in pursuit of something infinitely more difficult to quantify: trust. And for one like me, the idea of being trusted, relied upon, might be the scariest thing to have occurred so far since starting my life anew.

"You will see Ulayya's home a few streets from here," says Ali.

He is tiring from the walk, leaning on me more and more, even over small obstacles, even when there is no obstacle. Our arms are more comfortable where they link together.

"Ulayya's brother, my youngest son, Shakr, lives with her as a matter of propriety until the time comes when I find her a new husband. Shakr is only thirteen, though, and Ulayya quite effectively rules her house. I offered her a place in my own home and so, too, did her dead husband's family. But she pleaded that she would rather have her husband's things—his house, his memory—around her as she mourned. A lie, of course. She is fully finished with her mourning, though I am sure she is lonely and misses Zayed. The truth is, she likes her independence, at least for as long as it takes me to find her a new husband."

I raise an eyebrow. "A dominant woman?"

"Certain of herself, but pliable."

"I am flattered that you consider me suitable for your daughter," I say, bringing the matter fully into the open.

Al-Hajj nods as I say this.

We pass through a small gateway and out of the tangled maze of alleys that surrounds Seyyed Abdullah's home, in the old part of town, into the open central town square, which was once graced by the fountain-statue of a mermaid in blue tile, the same blue tile as in the mosaic of Muqtada al-Sadr's father. All that remains of the fountain is half the catch-pool wall and the torso of the mermaid, her broken arms ending in masses of rebar and chicken wire, which had once strengthened and supported the weight of her destroyed concrete body. The mermaid no longer spouts water. The ground around her bears a countenance as pitted and dusty as the face of a beggar. Stalls for vegetable and fish vendors keep a respectful distance, as if she were a tombstone. But the smell of the food market, rotten cabbage and fish, hangs thickly in the midnight air.

I hear children running in the alleyways. At midnight? Why? Are they stalking us? Chasing the old man and the new mobile-phone vendor from the market? Are they spies? Matadors? I think of Layla. I imagine her in a pith helmet carrying Mahmoud's gun. I imagine she has come to revenge the destruction of this mermaid. I imagine she has come with stolen bullets and sweet misconceptions of life to paint the statue of the mermaid shimmering blue again.

I stop as I listen to the voices. I glance behind me, where echoes from the walls of the alleys and the houses ring as though they were caught in glass jars.

Al-Hajj turns to face me, a step ahead, and he asks me, "Is something wrong?"

"No," I say.

We stand a few feet apart for another moment, there in the dark town square. The voices do not return. Quickly, taking a single big step, I close the gap between the place where Ulayya's father stands and where I have been standing. I catch his arm in mine.

"This marriage, how does it benefit your clan?" I ask. "I am no one compared to you and to yours."

"Ulayya wants it," says al-Hajj. "She is too old now for a young husband, too wise for a fool, too beautiful for an old man, too rich for a poor man. She is unsuitable for the men I know in this town. Your arrival here is like providence to her. She is lonely. She has her children, yes, my grandchildren, but there is a hole in her like the hole in the water tower above us, and her soul grows dust."

He waves good-bye to the mermaid.

The gate to Ulayya's house stands before us. We stop. He fiddles with the latch. The door creaks open. He motions for me to follow him into the yard. With a mockery of stealth we enter through the gate and find a seat in Ulayya's blooming garden. It does not appear to me that she grows dust. Fronds of date palm sway above us. Trickles of sand from the storm snake around the fountain Ulayya herself had earlier described to me, a fountain with real water but with no mermaid at all. The pathway, crisscrossed by these trails of sand in the moonlight, looks like a miniature desert, dunes upon dunes from the thin grit and sand of the sandstorm. I notice a layer of dust on the petal of a flower, filmy as milk in the moonlight.

Ali ash-Shareefi has given me a nice speech about the rationale for wanting this marriage, I admit, but I am not wholly convinced. I think he must know something more or suspect something more. His eyes did not really light up when I gave him my family name. How could he not know ash-Shumari? How could he not be impressed? How could he not wonder whether I am part of that same family of ash-Shumari that is now at the forefront of the new government, trying to find a way to make the country work again, to bring Sunni and Shia together? The only explanation for this would be that he either really did not know the name Shumari, or that he already knew and already had made his decision to ally himself to my clan with the full knowledge, the premeditated knowledge, of who I am and what sort of failure I must represent, fleeing as I have from Baghdad.

I ask no further questions, though, but agree with the old man as he points out the many fine aspects of Ulayya's house: the trellis of climbing jasmine, the stonework, the fine beveled glass in the windows. The house is quiet at this hour, now in darkness, and when the light in a window above the courtyard turns on, Ali al-Hajj ash-Shareefi whispers up toward its source: "Just me, my daughter, just your old father sitting under the jasmine."

From above I hear Ulayya's sleepy reply, trusting and warm: "I love you, Papa."

Then a smaller voice, high and piping, shrill almost, speaks from a balcony jutting from the opposite wing of the house. For a moment I think it is Layla, stalking me in her pith helmet, ready to accuse me of manufacturing androids or of hoarding all the secret Cracker Jack decoder rings. But the voice coming from the room is only the voice of one of Ali's granddaughters, one of Ulayya's children. Ulayya says something soothing, something soft and birdlike. The two lights in the balcony windows go dark. The women of the house speak no more. Ali stands, his sandaled feet rubbing the groomed gravel pathway with a sound like the grating of teeth.

"Good night," he says to me.

"Good night, Father," I say as we embrace. Then I leave the courtyard and head home.

A few feet outside the gate I fill with water, like a merman planted haphazardly in a town-square fountain, a merman who sees the replica of something he has lost, like a water tower rocketed in war but patched again, the replica of a thing but not the thing itself.

In the distance I hear the American convoys revving up, once more starting their journeys north after the storm. The return of their noise, the ever-present diesel engine rumble, reverberates around the town.

A reminder, a constant reminder.

* * *

When I entered the ER examination room, the beautiful woman with the bloody arms was sitting on the edge of the bed with one nylon-clad leg crossed over the other. Her hands she held out straight at her sides, as if the blood—already mostly dry—might drip and stain her clothes. She stared at the empty cinder-block wall of the exam room to the left of the place where I parted the screening curtain. She didn't look toward me at all as I entered, but said, "I told you already that I killed him. What more do you need to know? I killed him and I'm not sorry at all. The asshole."

"Bashar has gone to get the police," I said to her, my voice faltering, sounding dumb in my ears. I felt helpless.

"Who's Bashar?"

"The other doctor."

"Oh, shit," she said, turning to look at me. "You're a different guy. You look the same."

"We get that a lot. We're both Iraqi."

Her eyes lit up. In perfect Arabic—high Quranic-sounding Fus'ha—she said, "I grew up in Saudi. Father worked for Saudi Aramco."

"I am amazed," I said, switching to Arabic as well. "I would never have thought—"

But she interrupted me: "Caught him with the babysitter."

"Who?"

"My husband."

"Damn," I said.

"Damn what? He deserved it."

"Damn, you're beautiful."

This stopped her for just a moment in her rage. She looked at me.

And she blushed.

13

الخميس

Thursday

LAYLA VISITS IN THE EVENING, like most evenings, this evening once again. It has been only a day since I last saw her but such a day indeed—a long, lonely day despite the people who surrounded me at Sheikh Seyyed Abdullah's house, despite my tacit agreement to become part of the family of Ali al-Hajj ash-Shareefi. Absurdly, I feel as though I should announce to Layla the news of my impending marriage to Ulayya. I should tell Layla as a matter of conscience, as a matter of good form. But telling her would place her on the same plane of consideration as Ulayya. And that would be absurd.

I see Layla now. I see her before me in flesh and blood. She stands as if nothing has happened. How can she know that anything happened? She can't know! But her mere presence, her nonchalance, makes me watchful, wary, nervous. So much has happened and I may tell her none of it. She must guess. And she hasn't yet guessed.

So, just as she does every day on her visits, today she stands in that same shadow under the awning of my little store, my shack, as the sun sets behind her, where the road from Basra to Kuwait and the even larger road from the port of Umm Qasr to Baghdad intersect. Twenty-nine convoys have gone north, a new record. The Americans push the supplies hard today. After delays from the sandstorm they must be running low on all the various things hauled from Kuwait up to Baghdad and Ramadi and Najaf and Mosul. Only twelve convoys come south. I imagine them bottlenecked, held back at bases farther north, where the sandstorm still churns. All the soldiers guarding those convoys, the Davids and Patricks and Winstons in their buttoned-up Humvees, all of them must be homesick, must be road-weary. And the convoy of buses for Camp Bucca, it is late as well. Due every fourth day, usually on schedule, it didn't come yesterday. Nothing moved on the roads. Nor have the buses come today. I watch for them and I look at the notched marks on the post of my store's door frame: six notches; should be seven now. Maybe tomorrow, resuming their regularity.

Today marks the eleventh day since Layla's visitations began. Also the twenty-ninth day of business for me since I moved to Safwan. An exhausting day. A day with no buyers. Like me, everyone deals with the sand. Sand has seeped under the door of my shack. Sand has seeped between the stacked boxes of mobile phones on my shelves, forming ridges and pyramids in the spaces where it came to rest. It has wormed into the boxes themselves. When I open one such box I find the phone inside packed tightly in sand. I find even within the wrapped plastic that a fine powdering of dust coats my merchandise. I spend the morning opening each phone, plugging it in, charging it, testing it. All but one works. I can afford the loss of a single phone. Likewise, I think to myself, I can afford the loss of a little market rat if the news—when she discovers it—of my engagement to Ulayya should scare her away.

As the sun dips lower, Mahmoud shovels sand off the overpass. I see his tea tray arranged outside his tent and I see the boy Michele with food from Bashar's café. Mahmoud shovels sand. Michele tends to food and tea. It's a division of labor between them like that of man and wife. While Michele waits, Mahmoud continues to shovel. The sand from his labor puffs and drifts in a cloud where it has landed on the scree of the embankment below him. It looks, in its feathery drifting, as if it is snow, so white and airy and bothersome. My mind strays to a memory of snow, of children playing in snow. I want to discuss snow with someone, a man who might understand. But I know none of these townsfolk around me in the market have ever seen the stuff. I want to go sledding. To throw snowballs. To make a snowman, a snow angel. I wonder what Seyyed Abdullah knows about snow. I tell myself I should mention snow to him. I begin with snow on the top of my mental list for our next meeting, though deep down I know I will not bring it up. I think he might grasp the idea of what I really want to talk about if I ask him about snow. He might connect the thought to America and he might think I am starting to get cold feet about our plan.

Layla stands in front of my shack, there in the shadow,

and she asks me: "Abu Saheeh, how did you weather the storm?"

She means, of course, the sandstorm. But with my mind wandering I think of blizzards instead of the *simoom*. I think of snowdrifts instead of sand dunes. I look tired, she tells me. I tell her I have shoveled all day. I tell her that I have unpacked sand from packages where it should not have penetrated. I tell her that I have swept sand from my porch, brushed the dust of sand from my clothes, swallowed sand with my tea, rubbed sand in my eyes. I tell her that there have been no customers because of the storm and because of the cleanup, which is the storm's aftereffect. I tell her all the windows of my house have frozen shut from the blizzard, iced up, the water pipes have burst and the fire hydrants all down the block have come alive with fountains of ice, feathers of ice, sculptures of mermen and blasted-apart blue-tiled ladies of the sea. I don't really tell her that last little bit. I think about it, though: the farcical idea of this town even having fire hydrants or blizzards. I think about people wandering the streets wrapped in parkas and mittens and earmuffs. I think about frozen pipes and a new sport we might participate in, Layla and I, in which we go from house to house to shoot frozen pipes with Mahmoud's gun, spewing ice crystals into the air.

I hear Layla's voice, far away, her conversation droning a little. I have trouble focusing on her. I think about Ulayya, which is a change. An image appears in my mind's eye of Ulayya immersed in the middle of a giant snowball, rolling downhill, with her hands and legs flapping wildly. She caws like a bird. Perhaps she is naked inside the snowball. I can't tell. The *hijab* blocks everything from my imagination.

"Have you ever seen snow?" I ask Layla.

This makes her pause, but only for a second.

"I was with the Americans during the storm yesterday," she says.

I am jolted back to the present. Turn for turn, I try to get ahead of her, asking her about snow, sharing with her a bit of my private language without giving her the secret key to the Cracker Jack decoder ring. Her response, flitting from fact to non sequitur, disturbs me on many levels: Why was she with the Americans? Why does she answer my question with something that isn't an answer at all? Does she ever hear the words I speak? Does she guess at the idea of America that was coded into my question about snow?

At last, quite profoundly, I say, "What?"

"The American lieutenant took me into his Humvee for a ride. He found me on the side of the road and it is a good thing he found me because I came into town, to your house, to check on you. I was worried about you with the storm raging and everything. And I got confused by the sameness of the sky and the desert. I got lost. I found my way back to the road after an hour or two of wandering, and I sat there on the roadside until the American Humvees came. They gave me some water and a Gatorade and some chicken from their MREs. It tasted like sugared cardboard. Then they took me into their base with them. I stayed there for the night in a big empty tent, where the wind beat against the tent flaps and made them sound like the wings of a giant bird."

"The base in Umm Qasr?" I ask. "The base called Bucca?"

I am incredulous. Such a thing is nearly impossible. No

Iraqis get into American bases and then come back out again, not after only one day. Not without looking at least a little scared.

"No," she says. "Across the border. The Safwan base, not the Umm Qasr base, where the prisoners are kept. The Americans call their base across the border Navistar, which sounds like science fiction, a place Darth Vader might—"

For once, I interrupt her: "That is in Kuwait!"

I am in even greater disbelief. No Iraqis ever, ever go across the border to Kuwait. Not anymore. Not since the invasion of Saddam's forces in 1990 to regain Kuwait as an Iraqi province. Nowadays, even when the ministers from Baghdad go into Kuwait it is with much wrangling, much hassle, much bowing and hand shaking and signing of official letters of cooperation and love. When they go into Kuwait it is a matter of national attention, news, acclaim. No girl from Safwan would be let across the border, simply given a ride in a Humvee into the American base.

"I bet that next you'll want to tell me they have robots and Arnold Schwarzenegger and genies on their base, too," I say.

"No," she says. "But they have delicious food. Nothing cardboardy like the MRE. I had a hot dog and a slice of pizza and a root beer and three scoops of ice cream, one vanilla, one strawberry, one chocolate, all in the same bowl. My stomach still feels full today! They like my stories. I speak to their interpreter and he tells the stories to the lieutenant and the lieutenant laughs and when he laughs all the soldiers sitting at the table with us laugh, too."

I do not know what to say to this. I lean forward over the counter of my shop. I put my weight on my elbows to bring myself closer to her height. I stare at her. My mouth falls open. I do not realize it is open until Layla touches me, touches my chin, pushes my jaw to close my mouth. Her fingers are warm and thin. I do not expect them to be warm. In my imagination, her otherworldliness, her singing and her magical appearances and disappearances, makes her seem as if she would not share such a tangible thing as warmth with the rest of humankind. She should be cold. She should be aloof. She should be more terrible, sprung from the mind of Zeus, as the Greeks imagined Athena to be, rather than from the heated flesh of man. Such a being should not help an old merchant mind his manners by closing his mouth with slim, warm, living fingers.

"Can you tell me about Chicago?" she asks.

"Chicago?"

"Yeah, a city in America, I think. They tease the lieutenant, the American soldiers tease him, because his Chicago team loses the World Series every year or something. Is this baseball they tease him about? The World Series? Is it like the Mondial? The World Series isn't on our television. They tell the lieutenant his city is cursed. It must be a horrible place. And it has snow."

I look around me, at the market in which my little stall stands. And I think: this is the place that is truly cursed—the flying paper, the flying sand, the flies themselves, landing on the chickens hanging in Jaber's kebab stand. This place isn't Chicago. I picture snow angels. I see in my mind a flickering image of the steel-black waters of Lake Michigan where they contrast with the sheet of snow on the shore, snow blanketing a lakeside park over which loom the lights of so many skyscrapers. I see seagulls. I see children playing in snow, little groups of children scattered and at play throughout the park. They all appear safe, happy, warm, living, though I know they are nothing more than a figment of my dreams.

"Yes," I say. "It is baseball that curses Chicago."

"You've seen snow, then," says Layla as she examines my faraway gaze. Perhaps she can see the reflection of snow swirling in my eyes. Perhaps she can see the groups of safe and healthy children who play in my mind.

"Why must you ask me about snow if you have already seen it?" she says. "You should tell the lieutenant from Chicago that you know about Chicago and about snow and about America. He would be interested in swapping stories with you like how he swaps stories with me."

Indeed, she has made the leap into my Cracker Jack code, an astounding leap, an intuition more womanly than waiflike. She stares at me as if she will ask something more specific, something more threateningly close to the truth of the pain and the loneliness that grind like steel-black water at the small harbor sheltered in my heart.

But she only says, "I've brought you a gift. He gave it to me but I thought you would like it and find it more useful, my Abu Saheeh."

She hikes up the hem of her caftan in a way that is certainly neither womanly nor waiflike and takes from a pocket beneath it a folded-up baseball cap. It is blue with a big red English letter *C* on it. I recognize it immediately, the Chicago Cubs, the cursed team. I smell hot dogs. I smell popcorn, Cracker Jack. I hear the sound of wooden bats striking horsehide beneath and behind the sounds of this dusty market, the hollow wind that rattles my tin shack, the squabbling vendors, the brooms and shovels that still ply through the settled sand, the honking of cars, the voice of this girl in front of me. She's given me a mark of the cursed, a baseball cap from Chicago. I wonder if I should even touch it.

"Do you think I'm crazy?" I ask her.

"I think you're a secret," she says. "A secret like those written in the bottom of Turkish teacups. I don't think you're a mobile-phone salesman at all."

A pause occurs in our conversation, a rare thing. Usually Layla skips fluently from one idea to the next. But now she waits for me. She looks at me. I look at her, then past her, through her. On the overpass behind her, I see two American Humvees pull up and stop, one on each side of the road. Lost amid my remembered sounds of baseball, I have failed to hear them coming. I have not picked the sound of their diesel engines from the real and remembered sounds that assault my ears. Now one of the American soldiers speaks with Mahmoud the guard. Now Mahmoud motions toward the market, toward my stall. Tall and tanned, with sunglasses covering the main portion of his face, his eyes, his expression, the soldier looks over Mahmoud's shoulder toward me.

I wave at him. I am friendly. I am nonchalant. I begin to ask Layla if this is her new acquaintance, the lieutenant. But when I look down from the soldiers on the bridge I find Layla nowhere near me. All that remains of her is a smaller version of herself, running away, halfway through the market, heading toward the Americans.

As if suddenly and stupidly possessed, I call out: "I am engaged. I will marry Ulayya."

I am unsure if she hears me but I know others in the market do indeed hear; the men and women around me stop their haggling. One says to me, quite softly, "*Alif mabrouk,* a thousand congratulations."

I do not respond to him.

I see Layla turn to look back at me, as if the sound of my words at last reaches her. She puts her hand to her mouth and kisses it, then blows a kiss to me across her open, flattened palm. I see her disappear over the edge of the highway. I do not know if she has understood the meaning of what I have said. I am to be married. The relationship between us is now *haraam,* has probably always been *haraam,* inappropriate on many levels, an old man and a market-rat of a girl having such conversations. But it will be more than inappropriate when I welcome Ulayya to my house, or she welcomes me to her house. Then I must respect Ulayya. I must be a respectful man, not a man who associates with a girl who sings alien songs and talks about America. Everything will change. But everything will be as Allah wills. Everything is as Allah wills. *La illah ila Allah:* there is no god but Allah and Muhammad is His Prophet, Peace Be Upon Him.

I remove the black rope of my *aqal* and my red-checked *kaffiyeh* and put the Chicago baseball cap where they had been. It fits, but only uncomfortably. It needs time to break in, to form to my head, to become part of me. I know that by wearing this cap I will draw unnecessary attention to myself as I walk into town for dinner but, heedless, I keep the ball cap on, close my shop, and go to Bashar's café for tea and conversation. I am sure he will want to talk about Ulayya. And, for once, I, too, want to talk about Ulayya. Layla's blown kiss, a distant kiss, so fleeting, has done nothing but harden my resolve. The things that are wrong, *haraam,* with such a kiss can be easily remedied with a good dose of self-respect and propriety, things like wanderlust and craziness and the half-formed sense that somehow, through her felicity, part of me has sprung alive.

* * *

The receptionist's voice sounded far away, reaching me as if through water or through a thick layer of golden honey. "Paging Dr. Shumari."

Reluctantly, I excused myself from the woman in the exam room, breaking away from the quick flow of our conversation: places we had each known in the Middle East, chances we may have run into each other, fate, fortune, the strange path that life hobbles along. I excused myself, backed out of the exam room, and took a deep, cool-feeling breath.

I picked up the phone line and said: "This is Dr. Shumari. How may I help you?"

I heard no reply. A long, static-filled interlude worried me as I waited.

"Is this my son?"

"Father?" I said immediately, tensely.

The woman in the exam room did not disappear from my thoughts altogether. I kept a close eye on the thin blue curtains, hoping no other doctor — not even Bashar — would usurp me and begin ministering to her. Part of me listened to my father on the phone. But most of me watched the exam room. Most of me recalled the bits and pieces of this woman that I could not concentrate on during our first moments together: the white sheen of drying sweat, the tear in her dress, a broken finger-nail.

"Yes," my father said. "Yes, it is me. Allah be praised, it is good to get through to you on this telephone connection. I am in the Ministry of Culture building, Baghdad, patched through Syria on a government line."

My father had written to me every month, a rambling series of letters filled with politics and talk of Saddam. And I had faithfully visited Baghdad every summer, returning to see him and to see Nadia. But he had never before called me, and the effort of speaking to him, stuck on a very public phone in the middle of the ER floor, was palpable. I knew he would speak to me in a roundabout way, not only because—outside his own house—he always veiled his words, but also because he wasn't familiar with telephone etiquette or with the costs associated with transatlantic communication.

"You have been following the news?" he asked.

"Yes," I lied.

"It will happen tomorrow."

"Okay," I said, playing along. "Is everything okay?"

"Everything is in the hands of Allah," he answered.

"You can't talk about it?"

"No."

"Then what?"

"Just wanted to hear your voice," he said.

"Okay, Father," I said. "It is nice to hear your voice, too."

I knew there had to be a more definite reason for his call. I had just returned to Chicago no more than three weeks earlier, after spending most of July and August with him.

"Are you sure you're okay?" I asked again.

"We're sending Nadia to you," he said. "Abdel Khaleq is

smuggling her to Damascus and then she will go to Beirut and then to New York and then Chicago. It might take a few months because she doesn't have her papers."

"But she has money?"

"Of course."

"All will be well, insha'Allah,*" I said.*

"All will be as Allah intends," he said.

Then, after a moment, he said, "Good-bye," and the line cut.

14

مساء الخميس

Thursday Evening

As I WALK INTO Safwan, my thoughts turn inward. I forget about the Cubs baseball cap and I do not notice if people stare at me.

I pass through al-Sadr's arch. Among the crowd of people, the noisy cars, the white-gloved traffic police, the old men lounging in what shade they can find, I am lost even as I tread familiar steps toward Bashar's restaurant. Vividly I remember and replay in my mind the first coincidental meeting I had with Bashar in this town, so far away from where we had once known each other. This meeting occurred before any of Layla's visits. It occurred before Layla ever stood in shadow under the awning of my little store, with the big highway behind her and the cars rolling north and south between Baghdad and Umm Qasr. It happened the first day I spent in Safwan, before Sheikh Seyyed Abdullah and I scouted for the particular shack where I have established my shop, before I knew my way around town, before I began counting American convoys.

Without knowing it was Bashar's café, I chose to take my dinner there after having traveled south from Baghdad with Seyyed Abdullah the day before, arriving late in the night and then sleeping and breakfasting as a guest in Seyyed Abdullah's home. Chancing into Bashar's café, I happened to sit in the very same chair, at the very same table on the outside patio, where I habitually sit now every time I visit Bashar. It was as if the seat had been preordained for me, the table laid. Bashar maintains a few such outdoor tables on one side of his building, connected to the main room and the kitchen by a decorated door. The patio is raised, a wooden platform. The platform keeps guests aloof from the street, removed from the filth of the gutters, above the noise of the crowds but connected to the world. An awning covers the group of tables on the platform, bowered by sparkling lights that work intermittently, as electrical power in town allows. The tables are small, black-painted iron.

That first day, I raised the menu to my face as the waiter from the café approached me. He knew I wasn't a resident of the town, and I knew he would have no reason to recognize me, so the gesture of raising the menu, the veiling it provided, I undertook unconsciously and purely as a reflex, a very guilty sort of reflex. I did not mean to hide. But in hiding, I made myself conspicuous.

"What can you recommend?" I asked the waiter.

The waiter did not respond. I said it again, more clearly and with as much of a southern, Persian-influenced inflection as I could muster: "Do you have a recommendation from this menu, my host?"

When the man spoke, his voice cracked at first, failing him. The man was Bashar himself, waiting tables as he often does when short of staff or when he sees one of his particular friends enter the café. Not knowing it was he, I continued to hide behind my menu, strangely scared and off-balance in this new place, this new town.

"Perhaps...perhaps I can recommend some bowling," Bashar said at last. "And, as an aperitif, God willing, maybe you would be so kind as to tell me how you have been these last months, and why you have chosen to visit me here in this wasteland, my dear friend."

I dropped my menu. I recognized him at last. I stood, toppling the little iron table. It caused a commotion among the other diners, but neither Bashar nor I cared. I took my friend in my arms and held him for a long while, a long minute, until he withdrew, straightening his *ghalabia,* and with a hand on each of my shoulders, grasped me at arm's length so that we could more honestly and closely assess the changes, large and small, that life had written on our faces.

"Let me take you to a special table, maybe to my house itself, it is not far from here, a place more fitting, all these people..." His thoughts were not in good order. They tumbled one upon the other.

"Do not mind the people, my friend. This is how I want to be known," I said. I looked at the ground.

"You are undercover? You are trying to blend?"

"No. Not exactly."

"You are what?"

"A businessman. I will start a business here. That is my goal here."

"But your little..."

I put my hands on his shoulders and I squeezed him more forcefully than he expected. I could see in his gaze that he wanted to wince, that he had become a little soft in his restaurant hauteur. I held him steady, though. And he held me steady. And without saying anything, I know he certainly understood what had happened to me. He understood me in a way that was more clear and convincing than any words of mine would ever have been able to communicate. He has never since asked me about it but it worries me, nonetheless, that he knows this particular truth about me. With two men, Bashar and Sheikh Seyyed Abdullah, in a small town such as Safwan holding fast to the secret of a third man, how can that secret not escape? I am sure Seyyed Abdullah has said nothing and will say nothing. He is the soul of discretion. Perhaps Bashar, too, has been discreet in that regard throughout the few weeks I have operated my store here. But perhaps he has said other things unintentionally, bragging and unwittingly bringing about the interest of Ulayya and her father in making a match with me, making a match through me with my clan, ash-Shumari. Certainly they expect great things from me in the future, things that I will not be able to deliver, not anymore. They could not have birthed such expectations of me without some hint, without some loose talking from one of these two men, my friend Bashar or my patron, Seyyed Abdullah.

"What shall I call you," Bashar said then, "if you are not to be known here? Surely you must have a name?"

"Call me Abu Saheeh," I told him, birthing the alias immaculately. "Which will be for me the greatest lie of all."

* * *

What was supposed to be merely a year apart from Nadia—a first year for me to concentrate on my medical studies, establish myself in Chicago, and then return to marry her and bring her back with me to the United States—had become two years, then three years, then four. I returned every summer, sometimes also during the winter break, and we spoke of the subject of marriage each time.

"After this second year I will be finished with my classroom work and then we will better enjoy our time together," I told her.

"This next year, my third year, is the first time I deal with real patients. I must be sharp," I said.

"I am still just a poor student. I can't provide for you the things you deserve. Next year I will be a resident. Then I earn money. We'll be able to buy a real home," I rationalized after delaying the marriage for a third time, though—between her father's fortune and my father's fortune—money wasn't the issue.

"I will wait," Nadia simply said.

Always she took these postponements well. It wasn't ever a matter of if we would marry. It was a matter of when. She could come with me immediately or she could wait. It was one and the same thing. She was still young, not yet twenty-two. She had almost completed a degree herself, a path many young women were able to pursue under Saddam's government.

All of this, all this history, I told to the woman in the ER as we waited for the police. I told her how I had come to America. I told her of the call from my father. I told her about my childhood engagement. I told her that my fiancée, Nadia, was fleeing Iraq at that very moment to join me in America. I told her about my brother, Yasin. I spoke to her about the war with Iran, the things I had witnessed. When speaking to her I found words I could not say or write to Nadia. I don't know why I felt able to speak with her so openly, so freely. Maybe it was the flow of her Arabic, intoxicating layers of Saudi inflection and American liberality. Maybe it was because she didn't know me, hadn't grown up with me and with expectations of me that I might feel unable or unwilling to fulfill. Maybe it was her eyes, so clear as to be innocent but demanding from me more than just the usual superficial explanations. During the time we spent waiting for the police, we said nothing more about her husband at all. She told me nothing about his death. But I told her everything.

After what must have been two or three hours, Bashar opened the curtain of the examination room and said, "The police aren't coming."

The woman held up her hands, the blood on them now quite dry.

"They don't believe I killed him?" she said.

"I didn't call," said Bashar.

After a moment of uncomprehending silence from her and from me, Bashar said to me: "Go on. Get her out of here. Take her somewhere. She's not hurt and the police don't need to know she was ever here. I'll cover the rest of your shift."

He tossed me a warm wet towel. I took one of the woman's hands and then the other into the folds of the towel. I massaged them until most of the blood rubbed away. When her right hand was no longer soiled, she held it out to me.

"Annie," she said. "Annie Dillon."

We shook hands the American way, firmly, quickly. But then I also folded my other hand over our clasp, a more tender embrace than is customary between Americans, and we held hands that way, the Iraqi way, for a long moment.

"Let's go," she said, leading me from the hospital to her home, a little suburban cottage, a whitewashed American romance, complete with a porch swing.

15

مساء الخميس
في مقهى بشار

Thursday Evening at Bashar's Café

WHILE REMEMBERING THIS FIRST night in Safwan, Bashar and I sit and talk to each other in the very same place where we reunited. Yet now we talk about my engagement to Ulayya. I know Bashar brims over with happiness inside himself, though he remains controlled and calm on the outside. He questions me with the voice of a disinterested person but with the intensity and clarity of a man fully involved in the topic.

"No, I don't know where we will have the engagement feast. Nothing has been formalized yet."

"No, I haven't met with Ulayya and the rest of the family of ash-Shareefi, though I intend to do so before long."

"No, I do not plan to sell my house. Maybe we will keep two houses, both houses."

"No, the fact that she has children by another man

doesn't bother me. I am an old man. I have no conflict help-ing her raise them." To which, almost as an afterthought, I mention that I had indeed already seen and heard one of Ulayya's children speaking from the child's balcony room the previous night.

"You have done what?" asks Bashar.

"I was sitting with her father, you fool," I say quickly, in case he thinks I have exchanged my disguise as a practical, middle-aged, respectable businessman for that of a lover, singing beneath windows, reciting poetry, mooning. "Ali ash-Shareefi led me there last night to show me the house. We sat in the garden together after our walk across town from Seyyed Abdullah's home. I think this will be the first real challenge in my marriage to Ulayya, if Allah indeed wills this marriage, for the woman seems quite settled in her house and I am not willing to part with mine. Perhaps we will keep them both, both houses. One house for the family and the other house like a separate *diwaniya,* a place for me alone, when I want to be alone."

"You will lose, brother," says Bashar with a knowing laugh. "A woman is the government when it comes to the house and the home."

"I will have to take your word on that matter," I say.

Mention of homes and of houses makes me think of snow, of Chicago. The snow makes my heart and mind feel still, quiet, blanketed, cloistered. I look away from Bashar and his gaze follows mine, out across the busy street toward the town's finger-thin minaret and the electric loudspeakers af-fixed to its bricked-up, old-fashioned windows. When I look back at Bashar I notice that he focuses on my baseball cap.

"Your hat is drawing a lot of attention," he says. "People

in the street have glanced at it. I've overheard several in the café talking about it. They will tell Hussein, I'm sure, and it will be declared *haraam* from town, forbidden. His Hezbollah will have a real reason to bother you. They'll say you're Western. They'll start to look into your past. They'll find out that you've lived in America, that I've lived in America. Then there will be hell to pay."

"It's just a baseball cap."

"We don't wear baseball caps here, my friend."

"I'm starting a new trend."

"New trends are out of style."

"I know. Call me crazy."

"I think some people are indeed calling you just that," he says. He lets the thought hang.

After a long moment I say: "Ulayya does not remind me of her. She doesn't remind me of her. Not at all."

Quickly Bashar becomes conciliatory, quiet. "I know, it must hurt," he says.

"Every day," I say. "I was swept up by the moment and by the hope of the times we lived in. It was a bad decision to come back. I wish I could return to Chicago."

"It wouldn't be the same," Bashar says.

"No," I say. "No, of course not."

I am crying and I don't even realize it until the tears hit the waxed paper that protects the tin plate on which my *shawarma* had been served. My tears make a crinkling noise as they hit the paper. I pull off the baseball cap and use it to shield my face.

After a moment, as if certifying the idea that I am indeed going insane, I put the baseball cap on my head again and say, "I told her about it."

"Who? What?" he says.

"The engagement," I say.

He waits.

"Who?" he says. "Who did you tell?"

"The girl," I say. "That girl who has been visiting me in the market, Layla. I told her that Ulayya and I are engaged. I don't know why I told her, but I did."

Bashar stands, pushes himself away from the table. He eyes me suspiciously again. "You are indeed going insane. I think this marriage will be good for you, my friend. Maybe the only thing that can help you."

He steps away, turns his back to me as if he is going to leave me. But then he turns around and faces me again.

"I warn you, my friend," he says. "These are difficult times. Hezbollah will crack down on you for something like this. Inappropriate relationships are very much frowned upon these days."

"What do you mean by that?" I say.

The muscles at the sides of his mouth clench. He doesn't intend to say anything more, but neither does he turn from me to flee into his café.

"What do you mean?" I say again, angrily, though I control my voice. "Do you imply that I take advantage of this girl?"

I stand. Bashar and I face each other, almost chest to chest. The hard, partially molded brim of my baseball cap touches his forehead. Sweat from his brow clings to the cloth lip of the cap, a fat quivering droplet suspended just at the place where the focus of my vision blurs.

I am about to say something else. I am about to, maybe, say something I might regret, something to prod Bashar still further in his accusation, something to bring the matter fully into the open. But, at that very moment, the busboy Michele moves toward my table to sweep away my dishes. He must think I have finished eating. He must think Bashar and I have stood because we are done with our conversation. He must think that the table is ready to be cleared. When he approaches and realizes that Bashar and I confront each other in anger, he backs quickly, quickly away from us, off into the shadows of the bowered door. He says nothing. But Bashar darts a guilty glance at him. The words of Bashar's last statement flit through my mind—"inappropriate relationships are very much frowned upon."

I fix my gaze more firmly on my friend and I say to him, very quietly, "You told Hussein."

Bashar does not deny it.

"You told him," I say. "You told him what I thought about the bridge guard."

"He's lazy and incompetent," Bashar says at last. "You said so yourself. And it is good, important for me and for my business. Important for me and for my family to keep on Hussein's good side."

* * *

Bashar and I sat together for coffee in the hospital cafeteria before the start of our shift the next evening.

"You're glowing! You look like a new man!" he said.

"Thank you! I had no idea—"

"You'd never, you know, with Nadia?"

"I told you, she's always been like a sister to me."

"And this murderess, this—"

"*Her name is Annie.*"

"*—this Annie. I guess you felt no similar inhibition?*"

"*Ya Allah,*" I said, *rubbing my eyes with exaggeration to show Bashar I hadn't slept at all.*

"*She'll go to trial. She'll be in prison,*" he said.

"*I'll pay her bail.*"

"*That'll only delay it. Then what?*"

"*I don't know. It's been a strange night, a strange day. I've got to think.*"

"*Don't do anything too crazy,*" he warned me. "*You're a good doctor and you'll do good things in your life. But once you get an idea in your head—*"

"*You know, it was my father who called, all the way from Iraq. It was him on the phone when I had to step out of the room.*"

"*What did he say?*"

"*Good-bye,*" I said. "*He said, 'Good-bye.'*"

"*That's odd. Do you need to go home to him?*"

"*No. He said Abdel Khaleq is finally sending Nadia here to America.*"

"*It'll be a pretty scene when you introduce Nadia to your pretty little murderess of an American mistress.*"

"*I know. I know. My father will disown me,*" I said.

I stood from the cafeteria table, leaving my coffee and my half-eaten plate of dinner, peas and scalloped potatoes and questionably halal *meat loaf. I paced. But only a little. Just two strides away from the table and one stride back toward it. Then I froze. My gaze fixed on Bashar. I grabbed him by the shoulders and looked him squarely in the eye.*

"*I owe you so much already from yesterday,*" I said. "*I hate to even think of asking another favor of you.*"

"Anything," he answered.

I told him my idea, an idea I thought he wouldn't mind: that he would host Nadia — take care of her, show her the town, show her America — while Annie and I ran away.

Bashar agreed. He remembered that I had described Nadia as being pretty. And he knew her family, Abdel Khaleq. He agreed most eagerly and, without delay, we launched into detailed, mischievous planning. So intent were we on our scheme that we did not notice the television in the cafeteria as Brit Hume, the ABC reporter, announced the entrance of Iraq's armies into Kuwait. Only later did we pay attention to Saddam's invasion and the repercussions that would follow.

16

الجمعة

Friday

THIS DAY IS A FRIDAY.

I would omit it from my story, for nothing happens.
The stores are closed. The market is closed. The houses are
closed. The mosque, with its dusty spire, hums with life.

I would omit this day except to do so would be akin
to omitting Allah. I spend the day in contemplation and
surrender. I spend the day in my home, every moment in
prayer, with my concentration distracted only by the sound
of the highway to the north, the cars and trucks rolling
along it, the American convoys with their fitful stops and
starts, air brakes squealing, as they pass through Safwan.

Perhaps the sound of the highway lures me back to the
market that afternoon. I decide there is no harm in stretching my legs. I go to a small hill between my house and
the market, a place where I am at the same height as the

overpass and can see across the roofs of the houses and the shops. I stand there as sunset casts warm colors across the land. I look for the American convoys. I look for Layla. I see Mahmoud's replacement, the man from the police force who gives Mahmoud his weekly Friday respite. He is a fat man. He never stirs from Mahmoud's little three-legged chair for the entire time that I observe him. When the boy from Bashar's café, Michele, brings the evening plate of food, the fat man takes the plate and eats it all while Michele waits. Then the man calls the boy close to him, wipes his greasy fingers on the boy's *dishdasha,* and waves him away. The police send only their best and brightest to guard my overpass.

I leave in disgust, thus ending the twelfth day since Layla's visitations began, the thirtieth day I have owned my shop.

* * *

After my shift I rushed back to Annie Dillon's house to tell her the solution Bashar and I had devised. Yet instead of finding her wrapped in the sheets of her bed where I had left her, instead of finding her waiting for me, I returned to a locked front door, darkened windows, and a folded sheet of plain lined paper taped to one of the two hollow wooden columns that framed her little front porch.

The note wasn't addressed to me by name but the content left no doubt. It said:

I've gone to the police to surrender myself. I think I went mad, out of my mind, those hours between

killing my husband and loving you. It was a good sort of madness. I'm sane again now. Thank you for that.
—Annie

Like any lover, I read, reread, dwelled upon the words, the meanings, the hidden meanings. Though the message seemed a little off-kilter, a little too conditioned, a little too measured, still I extracted from it great pleasure, the words loving you *and* good sort of madness *especially. They seemed to me to contain important promises for a future that I imagined we might spend together. The words did not, in all those many first readings, hint at good-bye.*

I drove directly to the police office nearest to Annie's house.

"Yeah, she's here," the booking officer told me. "She showed up this morning with a little suitcase of clothes and makeup. Just like a flight attendant. Funniest thing."

I reached for my checkbook, spread it open on the counter between the policeman and me.

"I want to pay her bail."

"It hasn't been set. And anyway, she refuses."

"What?"

"She refuses," the sergeant said. "She told us specifically that she would not accept bail if anyone tried to post it."

"What?"

The sergeant whirled his finger in the air next to his forehead and rolled his eyes: crazy. "She said she's guilty and that she's happy to serve her time."

"Can I see her?" I asked.

"No," he said, quite simply, and though I tried to argue, tried to convince him, tried—even—to pay him, bribe him, he could not be moved to change his mind.

I left the police station and, like any lover, I read and reread Annie Dillon's letter. I dwelled on its meanings once again, and the meanings seemed to change, to morph in front of my eyes into ugly, bald dismissals. I could hardly believe it. It could not be. She could not know that I would try to free her, to run away with her, to throw away my life for her. It ruined the plan Bashar and I had developed—he and Nadia getting to know each other, alone in Chicago, while Annie and I went to Greece, Russia, Fiji, Kilimanjaro. Annie needed to play along. She had to come with me. It was impossible, given my feelings toward her, to consider that she would refuse me in such a blanket fashion. It must be wrong. I must have heard wrong. The police sergeant must have misunderstood. After such a night, after such wonders, how could coldness of this sort possibly exist in the world?

17

السبت

Saturday

LAYLA VISITS IN THE EVENING, like most evenings, this evening once again. But before I even open shop, before Layla arrives to stand where the sunset casts its light on her, before then, an important thing happens as I walk to my shop.

Most days I take a circuitous path around the outskirts of town, where the desert most closely approaches the city. I like the possibility of meeting wild things in the early morning, lizards basking on the freshly sun-warmed ground near their burrows, half-domesticated goats, stray dogs sleeping in old bomb craters and tank scrapes, and, if I am lucky, maybe even a falcon turning high in the oil-stained sky. I like to watch the lights in the houses turn off as the sky lightens. I like to hear the silence that descends when the farmers and homesteaders power down their generators one by one and the town gets quieter as a result, a stillness before the noises of the day. I like to watch people begin their routines, men waiting on the roadside for trucks to come and taxi them to their places of work, women softly singing, hidden behind the walls of houses as they hang clothes and knead dough and feed their chickens, children complaining as they get into starchy school uniforms and are fed, tidied up, prepared for the day. I can feel the town come alive around me as I watch it. It pleases me to see the world continue as it has always continued, unshakable despite the shaking and the changing and the pulsing and the tumult.

But today—the day marking the thirteenth day since Layla's visitations began and also the thirty-first day of business for me since I moved to Safwan—today I walk through the middle of town instead of journeying around the desert edge. I come close to the green single spire of the minaret lofting above the empty, quiet market. I hear the tape-recorded *muezzin* call from the loudspeakers. Those who are outside kneel right where they stand in the street to pray in the direction indicated by the *Qibla,* to pray toward Mecca. I, too, pray, facing southwest, at an angle to the street. This is the time of the greatest quiet, all prayer, no business, very little background noise, just the voice of the *muezzin* crier. As the prayer finishes I stand and continue walking. And when I come into the shadow of the mosque itself, I see something that gives me a great deal of concern, something that I think about throughout the rest of the day before Layla arrives at her customary evening hour.

The something that worries me is a small gathering of men, no more than a dozen, standing around the entrance to the mosque. They do not face into the mosque, where one might expect them still to cling to the echoing words of our imam, Safwan's imam. Neither do they face outward from the mosque, as if they were leaving their prayers behind to venture into the daily routines of work and worry and business. Instead they face to the side, where a young man stands on a pile of lettuce crates. I move into the midst of these men and listen, looking up at the youthful speaker as he continues his address to the gathered group.

"…not Baghdad, not Fallujah or Ramadi or Najaf or Mosul. Not even Basra. This town, this very town, is the place to strike. Why? Exactly because it is peaceful here. Exactly because life has returned to something near normal. This is jihad. It is sacrifice. We all must sacrifice so that we each may win a share of glory. Here, in the south, the Americans are weak. Their focus is not here. Their energy is not here. Their weapons are not here, not in the same overwhelming numbers as farther north. Here on your road, around that far side of town, on your road, your city's own street, all the supplies travel north to feed the army that is occupying our lands. This road is the jugular of the beast in all its throbbing vulnerability. By shutting the road we will shut down the American war machine."

The speaker is, as I said, a young man, maybe twenty years of age. He wears a clean white *dishdasha,* a black *aqal*. He has a very finely clipped mustache, no beard, not even the shadow of a beard. Rather than sandals, beneath his *dishdasha* the tips of polished, expensive shoes reveal themselves, oily black leather with a fine sheen of unavoidable dust on them, as though he has only just recently stepped out into the street. I hear the foreign accent in his voice as clearly as all the people must hear my own accent. He is, without a doubt, from somewhere other than here, most likely not even Iraqi. Is he Lebanese? Syrian? Is he Jaish al-Mahdi? Hezbollah? Is he allied to Hussein? If he is Shia from the northern militias, does he know for sure that the Shia clans here will embrace him? Who has sent him? Has he come from Iran? Was he trained there? He has a very carefully folded pair of sunglasses in the breast pocket of his *dishdasha,* new sunglasses, dark and shiny like the ones the American soldiers wear. I wonder where he got them.

I step back out of the crowd. The speaker's gaze locks on me as he sees that he is losing me from his audience. Rallies of this sort have a critical mass. Speech makers and jihad-mongers know this. Those first dozen men, alone, are not enough, though they are a good start, certainly a better start than no listeners at all. Thirteen, me included, becomes something more like a crowd, each body lending legitimacy to the cause, excitement to the speech, a sense that the force and feeling are shared among all. What is more, if one man leaves such a rally others may follow him. I would rather see this boy preaching to dust. I would rather keep the town quiet. And I am sure Sheikh Seyyed Abdullah will feel the same. His goal is to consolidate power, and the presence of a radical speech maker can do nothing but disturb his plans.

Having singled me out, the speaker asks me, "Are you a believer?"

"Of course," I say.

I try not to speak too much. I do not want him to hear the foreignness of my own voice, the northern tones, for if he is indeed an Iraqi he will hear them, he will know he is not alone, not unique as a visitor here. If he is Syrian, Lebanese,

Palestinian, maybe my Baghdad inflection won't sound so wrong. But I keep my sentences short, just in case. I do not want to chance the matter.

"Will you join us?" he asks.

"Perhaps when your voice changes," I say.

I hear the other men laugh and I finish turning away from the warmonger completely. I show him my back just as Bashar showed me his back last night. I think to myself that the boy doesn't know what he asks. He knows nothing at all. It is as if he were fresh from the *madrassa*, given a first assignment somewhere harmless, trumpeting his own importance. Perhaps he should have spoken with Sheikh Seyyed Abdullah before he came here to proselytize on behalf of jihad. Seyyed Abdullah is against war—not fundamentally, but only insofar as it hurts business and stability. Nothing good can come from a trumpeter, a braggart, a boy who needs jihad for his identity rather than for his God. Nothing good can come from this boy's assignment to our town.

This is what I think about all day: the million bad things the speechmonger's presence might lead to. The million bad things his presence *will* lead to. I tell myself, as I begin shutting my shop, that I must speak to Seyyed Abdullah tonight, immediately, maybe even before my dinner. I am sure Seyyed Abdullah will contrive to remove the boy from town, if he hasn't already put things in motion to do so. Perhaps the police are raiding the mosque even now.

With my mind churning over these thoughts, focusing itself on this one thought—how to rid myself of the boy—I am startled (as always, it seems) when Layla arrives.

I do not recognize her at first.

What I see, coming toward me through the ramshackle market, is a tall thin woman in a black *abaya* who appears to be drunk. She wobbles from side to side. She spins around in a circle, nearly falling. Then she rights herself, wobbles on, crashes into a garbage can, frantically reaches out with a hand that seems too short for her body, catches hold of one of the supporting poles of Jaber's kebab stand, disturbs the carcasses of the hanging chickens so that the flies that have landed on the chickens rise up in a cloud, buzz around her, and settle again on the swaying, slapping, hanging chunks of featherless yellow meat.

This drunken woman arrives at my shop, leans against the windowsill of my storefront, looks at me, makes eye contact with me through the slit of her *burqa*. I am bewildered. I do not yet comprehend that this woman is Layla. The height, the wobbliness, they do not connect in my mind with the girl who channels angelic alien voices. Nor does the *abaya,* the black covering robe, connect with my idea of a dirty market rat. What I see of her eyes, from a distance, shaded as they are, shows me only a heavy application of kohl, artificially dark lashes in the shadow of the *burqa*. Beneath the lashes I cannot see the blue of Layla's eyes.

Thinking the woman is drunk, I close the tin shutter of the shop window in her face.

"Business is done today," I say.

She grabs hold of the corner of the shack, peering through the open doorway, and says, with an artificially deep, gruff voice: "You do not recognize me?"

Despite all this camouflage, the sound of her voice, still girlish as she tries to mock Ulayya, betrays her. I do not jump at the recognition. I laugh a little, covering my laughter with a fake cough, then return my voice to the same gruff tones, playing along with her charade. "No, madam. But if you would like to buy a mobile phone, perhaps it would be best for you to return tomorrow, when you are more stable."

"I am not in need of a mobile phone," Layla says. "I have a big empty house and a big empty heart and a big empty purse and I need more than anything in the world to buy a husband today."

She bats her eyelashes at me and continues with her imitation of Ulayya: "Unfortunately, my father, who is able to smuggle everything else into this country, everything from Rolex watches to Mercedes cars, cannot get me the sort of satellite dish I need, not one with diamonds encrusting it, or with pearl hearts forming its center. Do you know anyone who sells satellite dishes so perfectly ornamented?"

"Indeed I do," I say.

"It's me," Layla says at last, lifting the veil of her hijab a little so that I can see her face. "It is me, your friend Layla. Do you like my disguise?"

"Very much," I say. "Are you pretending to be Britney Spears?"

"No, silly," she says. "I'm your sweetheart."

The words hit too close to home. A cloud forms in front of my eyes.

"It was my fault," I say. "My decision."

"What?" Layla asks.

She sways to the side and dismounts from a unicycle hidden under the too-large *abaya* she wears. The black fabric drapes over the ground. She lets the unicycle fall. I should be amazed. I should wonder to myself where a market rat purchases, let alone learns to ride, such a thing. But I merely stare at it, dumb and deaf, my mind drifting away, away.

"Sweetheart," I say.

I see snow, a shroud of snow descending around me, which the Sears Tower pierces like the black spire of an evil mosque rising up and up and up into the Chicago skies. I see drifts of snow, like dunes of sand but lighter and brighter and cold. Upon them I see the pink snowsuit of a little girl. I see her tumbling and laughing and running toward me. These wafting, disconnected memories feel like dreams, are dreams, actually, removed from my current time and place and context. I feel, as they swirl in me, like I am floating, being buoyed and floated by them, weightless. In my mind, my dream, my memory, I grasp for the girl in the pink snowsuit but my arms miss her. I run after her. My hand takes hold of her hand for a short moment. I tug, and the pink mitten she wears comes free from her hand. It falls onto the snow at my feet.

Layla snaps her fingers in my face.

"Yoo-hoo," she says. "Mobile-phone man. Tune in."

I look at Layla again. From up close, the thick lines of kohl around her eyes seem grotesque on her young face.

"I love you," she says, trying to mock Ulayya's voice again, trying to cheer me up.

Her words seem far away: she loves…

She loves me.

I realize I should say something back to her. I should say, "I love you, too." I should say, "I love you right up to the moon and back," just as Nutbrown Hare says to her little bunny. I should tell Layla that no father has ever loved his child to the depths and to the heights and to the distances that I love her. I should say something. I should say, "I love you," but the closest I come to those words is to repeat myself, to say again, "We never should have returned. It was my decision. My decision. It's horror. Horror. I picked your arm from the rubble."

Layla's face contorts. Her brow furrows. She has had enough. This is too crazy even for a girl whose universe includes robots and unicycles and Arnold Schwarzenegger. She veils herself again. She mounts her unicycle. She begins, stiff-backed, to pedal backward away from me. Her *abaya* swells out in front of her as though it is blown on the wind. She rotates on the axis of the single wheel so that I see her back. Then she wobbles away, through the market, her nose up. A few meters down the road she turns her head, thrusting her arms out to her sides for balance. She looks like a giant bird fighting to control the lift of its leathery wings, to balance updrafts of air. Then she drops her flapping arms, leans forward, and—like a ghost hovering over the pitted market street—cycles away, under the bridge, toward the place where her family must maintain its desert tomato farm.

As she passes under the bridge, I see the American convoy from Baghdad to Camp Bucca approach in the northern distance—four buses surrounded by three heavily armed Humvees. I make a notch on the doorpost of my shack: the seventh notch. Two days late due to the sandstorm. I wonder whether they've packed the buses fuller to compensate for lost time. Shutting down Abu Ghraib and moving all the prisoners south takes effort, takes planning, but the Americans, Allah bless them, thrive on effort and planning.

Later that night I see Layla again, between the time I

dine with Ali ash-Shareefi and when I go to speak with Sheikh Seyyed Abdullah about the new speech maker, the new jihadist, who has arrived in Safwan. I see her as she entertains the soldiers of one of the American patrols who sometimes lounge on the overpass bridge. She doesn't look at me, doesn't look for me. She is oblivious to my presence, as I am usually oblivious to her presence in the brief moments before I notice her at my store. She couldn't have known I was watching for her, that I went looking for her. She couldn't have known that I needed to see her.

The unicycle had lodged in my mind that evening. It was absurd, a child in Safwan riding such a thing. The more I thought about it the more unreal it seemed, up to the point where I even doubted the authenticity of everything I had seen, everything I had felt. Why had none of the other merchants or townsfolk paid any attention to such a strange sight—Layla on a unicycle, wearing the *hijab,* wobbling, seemingly drunk?

I had to reassure myself. I had to look at Layla again. I had to see that she is real and not some figment of my imagination, some clinging projection that had come to haunt me. I needed to see her on her own, independent of me, her fire, her liveliness, her spark still lit when not immediately before me. And I did see her. I saw her spinning in a circle with her finger on her nose and her face to the night sky so that the soldiers on that bridge laughed as she ran, crazy-legged, from one side of the overpass to the other. Closing my eyes, I could almost see the tracery of her footsteps burned into the back of my eyelids, like the negative image of fireworks, pion and muon trails, and protons bursting. The capture of her, however fleeting, proved to me at that moment that the girl was created in the world, inhabited the world, worked her strange magic in the world.

I walked away, back to my house, convinced more than ever that Layla was real.

***

I visited Annie every day in that jail while she waited for her trial. Every day I visited her and every day the sergeant told me she refused, once again, to see me.

I didn't tell Bashar.

"When do you two leave for Venezuela?" Bashar asked me.

"I think we've decided on Ireland," I said.

"Aren't you worried that the Irish will arrest her? I think Venezuela will be safer."

"We're going to change our names."

"And say that you've got a really deep Irish suntan?"

I shrugged. "Maybe we'll go to Iraq."

"It will be unsafe for Sunnis. The Americans will topple Saddam after they're done bombing him," Bashar said. We had been watching the buildup of Allied forces in Saudi Arabia, listening to fruitless UN negotiations over Iraq's occupation of Kuwait. We'd been listening to war analysts speculating on options ranging from diplomatic coercion to the use of nuclear weapons.

"Baghdad might not even exist when the Americans are done," Bashar added.

"Maybe we'll go to Canada," I said.

I didn't care about the war. I didn't care about anything other than Annie Dillon.

"Nadia arrives when?" Bashar asked.

"Today, maybe tomorrow. She called from London this

morning. Her plane probably is in the air right now," I said. "You'll tell her I'm gone?"

"It would be better if you were, actually, gone," Bashar said. "You should make it quick."

"They'll set bail for Annie soon," I said.

Not wanting to dwell on it too long, the subject of bail, the subject of my plans with Annie after I bought her freedom from jail, I added, "Nadia won't miss me at all."

18

ليلة السبت
وزيارة منزلي علي الشريفي
و سيد عبد الله

Saturday Night, Visiting the Homes of Ali ash-Shareefi and Seyyed Abdullah

I VISIT ALI ASH-SHAREEFI first, not owing to any sense of propriety or any shadowy, foreboding intuition, but mostly due to mere convenience. His house, his new house on the outskirts of the town, the opposite side of town from the American road, is situated farther from my final destination, my own house, than is Sheikh Seyyed Abdullah's residence. It is a fortunate decision to see Ali al-Hajj first because, after my conversation with Sheikh Seyyed Abdullah, I am sure I would have been in no mood to discuss the arrangement of an engagement feast and a marriage.

The way to ash-Shareefi's home leads me, as does my walk to Bashar's café, through the blue-tiled arch with the poster and the mosaic of al-Sadr. But, at the first intersection, where the headquarters of Hezbollah and, behind it, a children's elementary school are prominent landmarks, and from where the main section of the downtown—the city hall, the police station, the fire station, the civilian border-crossing compound—can all be seen, from there I turn left, away from my own home, away from my dinner and tea at Bashar's café, away from Seyyed Abdullah's house. My stomach is not happy about the change in my schedule, nor is my mind, which continually drifts toward conversations I might instead have been having with Bashar, with Layla, with Layla's father, should I ever be so fortunate as to meet him, drifting toward the remembered taste of falafel, toward the enclosing comfort of the sounds of the market that blanket all such difficult, troubling thoughts in a muffled haze of numb communion.

The road around the outskirts of Safwan passes a makeshift football field, just an open lot with some white-painted cans to mark the goalposts. The boys playing this afternoon are oblivious to my presence. They concentrate on their feet, on the movements of the other players toward the goal, the press of their bodies toward a common objective. After I spend a few long moments contemplating them, and as the sun sets over the desert behind them, they at last notice me. They stop, all of them, spontaneously. One of them picks up the ball, an old thing, worn bare in places and neither perfectly black nor white but a constant dusty brownish gray. They do not wave at me. They do not salute me. They do not smile. They watch me as I walk away, and it isn't until I come to the gate of Ali ash-Shareefi's house, where the road circling the outskirts of the town bends toward the south, that I hear the game resume. What has scared them about me? I have seen men die, men who know they are walking toward their deaths. Men of that sort are not objects of terror but objects of adoration. A kind of calm, a kind of holiness clings to them, wreaths them. Why do these boys turn to look at me in silence when I am about to meet with a man and start my life anew through his graces? To marry and start life anew: this isn't dying, though it is trading one skin for another. The process is holy, but not as holy as dying. It isn't martyrdom. But perhaps the lesser holiness retains some of the same awe as that of a man with death on his head.

When I arrive at Ali's house, I see that he has a man on guard at his gate, not a strange thing for a rich merchant in a town such as this. The guard leans on the hood of a black Mercedes parked in the exterior courtyard. A bank of prismatic new windows looks down from the house's second story over the courtyard and the Mercedes, over the street, back into the heart of the town, like a blind man who turns his face when he feels sun warming his skin.

I tell the guard I am to visit Ali. He doesn't say anything. He just nods to show me he hears me and understands me, the classic tough-guy silence. He goes into the house and a moment later ash-Shareefi returns, with the guard behind him, and unlocks the gate for me himself.

"Come in, my son, come in," he says. "We have been expecting you."

"Thank you," I say. "I shall not stay long."

But I leave after nightfall, having eaten dinner, having smoked the *narjeela* with al-Hajj, having committed to a firm date in one week's time to hold a feast for my engagement to Ali al-Hajj's daughter, Ulayya. His family, his clan, will set up tents in the streets. They will close off several blocks of the city in order to hold a general celebration. They will bring musicians and dancers and foods from Basra, Baghdad, Kuwait City. Of course, his daughter must have a dress. And as to the matter of the dowry, he understands my position, the fact that my business is a new business without an accumulation of capital, without a basis for credit. He tells me he is sure I will thrive in the near future. He is sure of it. And I am more sure of it, too, leaving him at last in the darkness of his courtyard when we part. I am so sure that my business and my life will thrive that I almost forget to visit Seyyed Abdullah on my way home. I almost forget Seyyed Abdullah until I pass the green single spire of the downtown mosque and see the upturned crates where the jihadist had spoken that morning to the villagers.

It is thus, at a late hour and without proper invitation or warning, that I visit Sheikh Seyyed Abdullah to ask him if he knows of a new man in town who has taken to talking publicly of jihad. This question catches my benefactor in a very different frame of mind from our previous meetings, perhaps because my visit comes at a time when he is not expecting to receive me or to face my questions. Or perhaps he feels a little guilty and assumes the rougher attitude as a mask.

"Indeed," he says. "I am the one who invited this boy to Safwan."

"You've done what?"

"Calm yourself, my brother," the sheikh replies. Involuntarily, I shiver as he calls me brother—for I see Yasin superimposed on the split and exploded bodies of U.S. soldiers, like so many kittens. I hope that Seyyed Abdullah does not notice my lapse of attention, my shiver, my loss of concentration.

"The boy is my new wife's nephew," he says, stroking his chin with the fingers of his right hand. "I now consider him part of my family. He is harmless. He will soon be under control."

"Talking like that, gathering a crowd, he isn't harmless at all. He could be a big problem for us. Do you want to rally more people toward Hezbollah?"

"Maybe things with Hezbollah need to be brought to a head."

"With your wife's young nephew as the instigator?"

"You're doing nothing to instigate, as was our agreement."

"I'm getting to it. Give me time."

Seyyed Abdullah stops stroking his chin. He rubs his hands together and passes a flattened palm over his eyes. When he looks at me again, he speaks very plainly, which is a frightening thing.

"These are exactly the reasons why I have invited the boy to Safwan. First: you're taking him on as your protégé. It is time for you to expand your shop. You need an assistant. Mobile phones are getting more popular every day, and I hear that you now sell satellite dishes as well. You will teach him the business and, in addition to the business, I hope you will teach him some restraint."

I am exasperated. That boy as my assistant?

"What will I do with him?" I ask. "Is he tied to Hezbollah, to Hussein, to some other militia? Where did he learn all this speaking and speech making and rhetoric? And, never, never, did I ever agree to take on an assistant."

Seyyed Abdullah raises his voice at me for the first time in our acquaintance. He says: "You need an assistant, I'm certain of it. You are moving too slowly. And my wife's nephew needs a master. Better that master be you than someone else."

"I need no help. And I'm in no frame of mind to mentor the troubled youth of the world," I say, trying to sound as bitter as I can. "And what about Hezbollah? Are they the ones you worry about?"

"I don't worry at all," Seyyed Abdullah says, in such a tone, so icy, that I know even if he does worry it is a worry grounded in patience and preparation. "I want Hussein to seem more closely tied to your activities. If my firebrand nephew leaks our plan to Hezbollah, all the better. We will direct the fury of the Americans toward Hussein and I will have one less problem in town after the Americans deal with him."

I start to say "One less competitor in town," but instead I change my mind and try a different angle, asking him: "Why, suddenly, why must I hurry? I thought I was merely observing until we get word from Baghdad."

"I have had word from Baghdad," he says, calming down, finally lowering his voice. "Abu Ghraib is almost empty now. It will be one of the next few convoys. We'll know for certain the day before it happens. So my nephew will be useful to you. He *will* help you get ready all the more quickly." He emphasizes the word *will* rather than the word *help* to demonstrate that the condition is settled, no longer open to argument. The emphasis comes with some of the anger, some of the gruffness of his earlier tone.

Seyyed Abdullah beckons for his gun-carrying servant to approach. He takes from the servant another plain brown cardboard box, similar to the one in which my smuggled whiskey comes.

"So soon?" I ask. "I'm not finished with the last one."

I shake the box. Amid the muffled sounds of packing tape and plastic wrap I hear the faint jingle of metal against metal. The weight of the package had at first led me to believe it contained liquid, booze. But the jingle isn't that of glass on glass or even of glass on metal. It is metal on metal. I have long expected such a shipment, but now that I am receiving it I'm not sure I want it after all. I'm not sure I want it near me. I'm not sure which of my two selves actually takes the box from Seyyed Abdullah, whether I am at that moment the regenerating man who is starting his life over or the shriveled soul of a man who can no longer think, speak, or reason without his ghosts surrounding him. Is it steel in the box? Steel on steel? Is it copper? A triggering mechanism? Timing components? The device, so long discussed between Seyyed Abdullah and me, rests in this box either in part or in its disassembled entirety. It has reached me easily, disguised by the ruse of the whiskey bottles that the border officials have grown accustomed to passing, with a small bribe, through their offices. Alcohol is forbidden, yes, but for a bit of *baksheesh* the border becomes permeable. And that *baksheesh*, at regular intervals, numbs the border official's mind. He becomes addicted to it, grows accustomed and easy to manipulate, so that the pieces of a bomb, which weigh the same as a bottle of whiskey, cause no comment, no excitement, when passed under the table to Seyyed Abdullah's agent.

Seyyed Abdullah merely smiles, doesn't discuss the contents, even as he reaches toward me, touches the box I hold, and makes its contents jingle again. His smile is a knowing one.

"My wife's nephew Abd al-Rahim will visit you tomorrow in the market," he says.

Then he shows me to the door of his house, kissing me on each cheek and holding me close.

"My town," he whispers. "Though you are welcome to stay here as long as it takes."

"Thank you," I say, which upon reflection is a very weak, an uncharacteristically weak, way for me to voice my sudden disgust. Weaker even upon reflection, since his parting words contain the first hint, not so very deeply veiled, that my presence in town is not to be permanent. Our conversation ruins the feeling of belonging brought to me by my meeting with Ali ash-Shareefi. Any stability I might find here is only temporary, only a clever disguise I must now assume.

I can excuse Seyyed Abdullah's initial brusqueness with me. It is his town, after all. And I am only a mobile-phone salesman with nothing to recommend me, no reason to receive his favor or the hand of Ali ash-Shareefi's widowed daughter. I have nothing to recommend me but what these people guess of my background, though all of them except Seyyed Abdullah guess wrong. None of them knows that I am dead, more than half dead. None of them guesses that I struggle, part of me numb, part of me awakening in the embrace of a new family, awakening to a simple life, here in the south, here as a man of business.

The dead half and the alive half of me fight. And that is why I opt to get very drunk when finally, finally I reach my house this night.

* * *

Every day for a month I visited Annie in that jail. Every day for two months I visited her. Every day for three months. When Nadia came to Chicago, I did not stop visiting Annie, I just disappeared from Bashar's life, from the hospital, from my life, for enough time to let Bashar and Nadia get to know each other. I transferred my residency to a hospital downtown. I rented a new apartment. But I did not stop visiting Annie's jail.

The day the Americans launched their Desert Storm ground offensive, routing Iraq's armies from Kuwait, I visited Annie. The day they stopped pushing north, stopped in Safwan itself, in the shadow of Jebel Sanam, I visited Annie. When the truce was signed, leaving Saddam Hussein and his Baathist party still in power, I visited Annie.

Not once did she appear at the visitation window.

"The trial is in two months," the desk sergeant told me. "Then what'll you do?"

"I will sit in the courtroom every day. I'm looking forward to seeing her."

"You're crazy."

"I know," I said.

"She's crazy," he said.

"I know."

He laughed, saying, "Guess you're perfect for each other."

I skipped visiting Annie just once. Once only.

"You didn't come yesterday," said the desk sergeant when I appeared the following day, regular as usual.

"No," I said. "My brother contacted me from Baghdad to tell me my father is dead. I haven't spoken with my brother in a decade and he calls with such news..."

"That's too bad," said the sergeant.

"Which part?" I asked.

"*All of it,*" *he said.* "*But especially the part about you missing your visit. Your girl, Mrs. Dillon, she has impeccable timing. She was waiting for you, all prettied up in her orange jail suit, and you didn't show.*"

"*What?*"

"*First time in how long—a hundred days? She said she knew you were just like every other man. Said you made a good show of being faithful for a while but in the end, you weren't there. Just like us all, that's what she said,*" *the sergeant said, rolling his eyes.* "*She also said to tell you she thinks it's yours.*"

"*What's mine?*"

"*The child,*" *he said.* "*She's just starting to show.*"

19

ليلة السبت
مع أحلام

Saturday Night with Dreams

LAYLA FIRST VISITS MY dreams tonight, like most dreams hereafter. She takes on two lives for me, the life of the living young earthly rag-clothed girl with her sudden appearances and disappearances, her improprieties, her penetrating questions; and the life of the girl who lives increasingly in my imagination and my dreams. Perhaps these two halves of her correspond to the two halves of me, the dead and the alive, the halves that fight for control of me and drive me to the absolution of my whiskey. Perhaps there is no Layla. Perhaps I just desire her so sharply that I have created all her spark and aura, like a man walking out of a desert who has been so long without water that even the idea of water pains him.

I doubt her.

My doubt settles into me so that, as I stare at my kitchen

wall and drink myself to sleep, I cannot really distinguish what has been real and what has not. From a place of mild euphoric drunkenness I settle into a state of mild euphoric sleep with such ease and such a slight leveling of conscious-ness that sleeping and waking are difficult to tell one from the other. I have on my table in front of me the cassette recorder containing the captured sound of the *Close En-counters* song. I have these two boxes from my last two visits with Seyyed Abdullah. The cassette recorder remains mute. It occupies a space exactly in the middle between the two identical brown boxes: brown paper, brown tape, very little written on the exterior. I arrange them on my bare kitchen table: box one, box two. I move them from side to side. I shift them. I lift box one. I lift box two. I put them down at different angles and at varying distances from the cassette recorder. As I lift them, I imagine they would be of equal weight if I had not already consumed half the bottle from the first box on previous nights.

A fear similar to that which prevents me from playing the tape-recorded song prevents me from opening the second of the two boxes. I don't want to see what is inside. Surely it contains something other than a bottle of whiskey. Surely it hides within it some sort of electronic equipment, stuff whose presence a mobile-phone salesman just might be able to justify, assembled or disassembled, in his home if police forces or the Americans raid him.

I ignore this second box, just as I ignore my doubts about Layla. I leave the box unopened on the table, orbiting the tape recorder at the same respectful distance as the torn-open whiskey box. Then I take down from the shelf above my kitchen sink the jack-in-the-box that has stared at me, so brightly colored, and kept me company through the long nights all this time since I first moved to Safwan. As I remove the toy from its place on my shelf, its head bobs and dances, giving it a moving, lifelike feeling in my hands.

Although the jack-in-the-box is in perfect condition, I spend the remainder of my evening breaking it down into its component parts, screw by screw, spring by spring, lever by lever, wheel by wheel, gear by gear, even stripping from the body of the jack the patched and polka-dotted clothing the wooden clown-faced figure wears. I peel carnival-colored stickers from the outside of the box, leaving a spiderweb pattern of glue over the blue surface of the four sides. I organize the parts in rows and files. I drink a finger of whiskey after each part I disassemble. As the whiskey burns in my throat, I place the parts in what I deem to be the correct astrological relationship to other objects on the table: hidden ellipses and orbits, constellations and zodiacal shapes emerging.

This is how the last half of the bottle from the first box disappears. This is how I put myself to sleep, face falling to rest in the crook of my arm, sprawling on the table, surrounded by a plethora of jack-in-the-box pieces that might mean more in their tea-leaf configuration than ever they had in their finished, assembled whole.

Frequently now, Layla arrives in my dreams by standing in that familiar place outside my shack, the highway behind her, the late sunlight's long shadows crisscrossing the ground around her. I cannot tell, in dream-sight, whether her feet touch the shadowed ground, whether she has feet at all, whether her feet *are* shadow, part of the greater shadow that falls on the silently spinning and aging world. Often she arrives this way, but not tonight, not on the first night of our nights together. This night she comes through the kitchen door. I lift my head from the organized disassembly around me. I look at her. Outside the door—which leads to an interior courtyard, where I have not yet planted any flowers, not yet cultivated any fruit trees, not yet caused a fountain to flow so that it might provide lovely watery music, like the fountain in Ulayya's court—outside this door the sun shines as though it were day. Layla's ghostly body wafts between the sun and the place where I stand, shadowing the light. I think, as on the day of the sandstorm, I have slept a long while. I think I am waking into day-lit reality when, actually, the light of the day is itself nothing more than a dream; around me, in the real world, everything broods darkly and silently, perfect for dreaming.

Layla walks toward me.

Still she has the *abaya* and *hijab* she recently wore in the market, but she has folded and draped them over one of her arms, as if she just removed from herself all marks of womanhood. I look behind her. Against one wall of my empty inner courtyard, I see her unicycle leaning. I can plainly read a set of hieroglyphics embossed on its spokes and pedals. I can read them even from so far away, but I do not know what they say. I fear it is something revelatory: birds' heads and hyenas and feathers, prayers full of snakes and moons and such things as should never have been created under heaven. I see little details of Layla that contradict my idea of ghostliness. For instance, she has been sweating. What ghost sweats? Also, her hair is matted to her head and she appears breathless, winded. I blame her speechlessness on the effort required to recover her breath after her unicycle journey. I am sure she will talk with me very soon. I am sure her stunning quiet is due more to her breathless condition than to any inborn, dream-borne inability to speak.

I wait for her to speak.

I look at her.

She looks at me.

She doesn't speak.

How can a man's mind, in his dreams, give voice to the very randomness of the childlike utterances that make a girl such as Layla magical? It is impossible. It is impossible for my mind to invent such magic and grace and serendipity. But I don't realize the dilemma, not while I dream. And, at last, after holding out as long as I can, I blink.

The blink transfigures my dream. Now I stand on the shore of Lake Michigan, a Chicago night with snow drifting down through cityscape lights. Layla is in the snow with me. She wears her pink snowsuit, her pink mittens, her pink winter hat with the image of her bird-bone anklet embroidered in black thread on the folded brim. She bends, picks up a handful of snow, raises it level with her eyes, and lets it fall from the soft round confines of her mittens. It is fresh snow, light and fluffy, and it billows around her as it falls. Behind her, the skyscraper lights, bluish and bright in the night sky, catch the swirling snow and make it shine like so many weightless and migratory diamonds.

Layla runs toward the water, the black flat surface of the great cold lake. She steps into the water, puts one hand to her face, and, in a gesture far too human for the dream state, plugs her nose with her mittened fingers. Then she kneels, slips under the surface, and disappears from me, ghosting away into the depths like a blue-eyed, black-haired fish. I take off my baseball cap, the Cubs cap, cursed as it is, and hold it over my heart until the ripples from her disappearance themselves disappear.

Yet the dream continues. Again Layla stands in the doorway of my house. Her blue eyes, strange in the southern Iraqi desert, stare into me. She does not approach me but, as she stares at me, I know she sees the parts of the jack-in-the-box scattered in their highly organized symbolic Cracker Jack system. She begins to decrypt the pattern of the disassembled parts. She speaks words as she decodes, but her words come out in hieroglyphics, bird-headed and jackal-headed, feather-light and golden, each surrounded by a cartouche. With staff and rod and wheat and linen they rise up in the air between us. She pleads with me to catch them, corner them, contain them, document them, translate them, understand them. But I am no fool. I know that the mere act of reaching for such things will change them forever. I know that the force of reaching will disrupt them in their flight, ground them, strip them of their marrow. I let them rise and fall and waft where they will until I hear a knocking noise.

I wake.

I look around me, hoping to see Layla still standing in my kitchen. Perhaps she has made me breakfast. Perhaps she has convinced Annie to come to the visitation window when, pathetically, I next go to the jail and wait for her to show herself. Perhaps we can all be together, all three of us—Annie and Layla and me—if only in a dream.

But, awake, I see Layla nowhere around me.

The knocking on my door continues. I rise from the kitchen table, straighten my *dishdasha* over my legs, and go to the door.

* * *

The one day I missed visiting Annie was the day that Yasin called me. Over the echoing long-distance line, the connection between Baghdad and Chicago, he told me to come back to Iraq.

I froze.

I had thought I would never hear from him again. Truthfully, I thought he had died in the war against Iran. My first instinct was that the phone line, like black-magic voodoo, had transported me, linked me, to a world of spirits, to a hell.

Even after I realized it was Yasin, a living man, I still felt uncomfortable about him contacting me, with what seemed like uncanny ease, across half the world—even after I had just moved into a new apartment, even after I had changed my job, even after I had quit my other life so that I might give Bashar and Nadia some space. I certainly didn't feel happy about it, hearing from him.

After a moment I said, "I thought you were dead. We all thought you were dead."

"I'm not. But Father is."

"He called three months ago. I knew from the sound of his voice that he wouldn't live much longer."

"He went out like Abdel Hakim Amer," said my brother.

"Suicide, then?"

My brother's voice took on a hint of menacing secrecy, saying: "Many people have doubts about Abdel Amer."

"And you?"

"I'm alive."

"Alhamdulillah," I said.

"I work for the president."

"Saddam?"

"Yes."

"Doing what?"

"Whatever he wants me to do."

My new apartment, the apartment I chose to hide from Bashar and from Nadia, was a loft midway up a twelve-story renovated factory building in Wrigleyville. From its bank of big plate-glass windows I could see directly into the far upper-deck seats of the baseball park. I paced to within an arm's reach of the window and leaned the weight of my body against my outstretched arm, my hand pressing flat on the cold, thick glass. A ring of frost formed on the outside of the window in a halo around the heat of my fingers so that when, a moment later, I took my hand away, a negative imprint remained. The Cubs weren't playing. It was February, not yet even spring training. Snow covered the field. Snow covered the folded-up stadium seats. The dark amphitheater of the stadium seemed to me like a heroic temple whose god had abandoned it.

"We want you to work for us."

"We who?"

"Iraq."

"Iraq needs a doctor?"

"Saddam needs better information on America."

"No," I said.

"Don't say no. Not yet. Come home for father's funeral next week."

"No," I said again, thinking of Annie in her jail cell.

"Don't say no so quickly," my brother told me. *"I'll call you tomorrow for your answer and then we'll arrange a plane ticket to Baghdad. We'll be able to speak in more detail."*

I said no again but Yasin had already hung up the line.

I couldn't go to the jail to see Annie, to not-see Annie, as was *usual—not after such news, so many things all at once. The well-established order of my world had been rocked: my father was dead, my brother was alive, and Saddam wanted me to spy on America. That's why I skipped that one day out of all those hundred days—the day when, according to the desk sergeant, Annie actually came out from her cell to visit me.*

20

الأَحد

Sunday

TODAY MARKS THE FOURTEENTH day since Layla's visitations began. Also the thirty-second day of business for me since I moved to Safwan. Things move quickly now, too quickly. Suddenly I find I have too many irons in the fire. The life of the last month, spent watching the American convoys on the overpass move north, move south, toward Basra or Umm Qasr, toward Kuwait City or toward Baghdad, is a thing of the past. I still count them, but only in the background of my mind, like a soothing song playing over and over. Sixteen north. Eighteen south. The convoys are an afterthought as I deal with my impending engagement to Ulayya, as I deal with Seyyed Abdullah pushing me forward on a plan I have only half conceived and that I even now only half imagine I will really follow to completion. I deal with my dreams of Layla and I deal with Layla in waking reality, when her dirty, living, street-rat embodiment visits my shack. And now I deal with Abd al-Rahim as well.

The visitor who knocks on my door to wake me in the morning is Abd al-Rahim, the youthful nephew of Seyyed Abdullah's new wife. He is eager and pleasant and not at all the contentious warmonger I expected. He is surprised when he first meets me, recognizing me from the haranguing outside the mosque. Seyyed Abdullah must have spoken well of me, must have threatened his nephew with all sorts of ostracism should he not follow me and obey me with perfect respect. Otherwise I think Abd al-Rahim might have been more difficult.

Nevertheless, I keep the boy busy for most of the morning on this day, which is our first day together. I keep him busy in order to keep him away from me and away from my shop and my life. That way I can pretend, even if just for a little while, that everything has returned to normal, that today will be just one day among many. Despite my best efforts, around noon I can no longer find suitable busywork. By this time I have already watched the idiot Mahmoud make several sweeps along the overpass to guard my shack. By this time I have already sold more mobile phones and equipment than I usually do in a whole week of normal sales, due in part to the huge size of Ali al-Hajj ash-Shareefi's extended family, all of whom seem suddenly to find themselves in great need of mobile phones and satellite dishes. By this time I have already watched the cars come and go and the people come and go and the shadows on the street grow short as the sun rises. I have been stable, watching the world from my shack. But I can no longer think of relevant errands to occupy Abd al-Rahim's time. I can no longer think of a task for an assistant that would keep him far from me.

Thus Abd al-Rahim lounges outside my shack, a moon in close orbit to its mother planet. He retains the fine black shoes he wore when he spoke to the small crowd outside the mosque. He has freshly shaved what small amount of hair his neck and his cheeks produce, as if his new job as a phone salesman requires pristine rose-pink skin. His *dishdasha,* in the summer heat, shows on its white surface nary a blemish. He wears his dark and reflective American sunglasses. He is far too fine, far too well-mannered and well-groomed, to seem like a natural part of the market.

He annoys me.

I am a little hungover from my whiskey, and his pristine healthfulness annoys me.

I plan what I will say to Sheikh Seyyed Abdullah about Abd al-Rahim when I next see him. Of course I cannot bluntly tell Seyyed Abdullah how the boy fails to disguise himself and how he perpetually reminds me, just by his mere presence, of my own foreignness. Neither can I express to Seyyed Abdullah the prickly feelings Abd al-Rahim's manners elicit in me. Both would be poor form, though I can certainly find words that hint at something less than perfect pleasure. Having lost my battle to fend off the boy from me, and having lost it quickly, I now feel obligated to either make the arrangement work to my advantage or, at least, to tell Seyyed Abdullah that the arrangement does indeed work. And that, as the boy is proving to me, will be a complete falsehood: I send him first thing in the morning to get a broom to sweep out the space on the sidewalk in front of the shack, he returns with a garden rake; I send him for screws and a screwdriver to more securely fasten the corrugated shutter that protects my front window, he returns with a hammer, fingers greasy from eating kebabs; I send him to the civilian border-crossing point, where the goods flow in from Kuwait, in order to determine whether any shipments have arrived for my shop, he returns with a fresh brown box from his uncle Seyyed Abdullah's house. I do not want the box anywhere near my store, what with British and American patrols likely to pass through, possibly to stop anytime and peruse the market; and what with Hussein's group of Hezbollah, who would know no limit to their curiosity should they find an item as taboo as whiskey smuggled into town. The boy has been an utter failure at all these tasks.

The day stretches long and busy before me, only a few hours past noon, and I find myself occupied both by planning proper words for the lies I must tell Seyyed Abdullah and by thinking of work for a now-idle Abd al-Rahim, gathering wool outside the shack, commenting on the unhurried flow of people in the market, in contrast to the hurried flow of people in Baghdad; unspoiled, in contrast to the barricaded souks of Baghdad; unpolished, in contrast to Baghdad, completely un-whatever, in contrast to Baghdad. He rambles on at no short length about Baghdad, Baghdad, Baghdad.

At least he keeps away Ali ash-Shareefi's relatives—they don't know him, so they won't approach too closely. Instead they stand across the street and wait, and wait, and wait for me to dispatch him, for me to find him a new task. So I am caught between the desert and the sun. I have no shade and my feet are bare. On the one hand it is Abd al-Rahim, left to idle. On the other hand it is this flock of family from the ash-Shareefi clan, all having been commanded by the head of their family and hurried by their own curiosity to visit me and to buy from me and to ask me as many questions about my past and about my impending engagement as their impertinent minds can invent.

At last I strike upon the perfect solution for this double dose of unwanted attention.

I say to Abd al-Rahim, "Do you know, boy, that I plan to marry?"

"I have heard it spoken of," he says. "But how is that relevant to the larger task?" He emphasizes the word *larger*. He emphasizes the word *task*. I am not allowed to pretend I misunderstand him. He has been dropping hints all day, as though somehow what I do here in the mobile-phone shack leads toward and builds toward a greater purpose. Or, as he would say, a *Greater Purpose*.

"It isn't relevant," I say. "But those people across the street—"

"The group of women?"

"Not just women. They have a man among them, a man I know only vaguely but who is, I suppose, one of the many cousins of the ash-Shareefi clan."

"What of them?"

"They distract me from the Purpose." I emphasize the word *purpose* in the very same way he emphasizes such words, purring it, making it pop.

Abd al-Rahim perks up at this. "Yes?"

"They are all relatives of my soon-to-be fiancée. Nosy people. They are making a nuisance of themselves."

"What do you propose?" As Abd al-Rahim says this, his eyes narrow. He looks as if he would do anything I now ask, anything at all, since whatever task it might be is somehow, if only vaguely, related to the Purpose.

"I think they would make an excellent group of advisers for the engagement presents I must buy, one present for each day from now until the engagement ceremony, which is scheduled for next week."

Abd al-Rahim looks a little deflated at what I have said. But he offers: "I will call to them. I will tell them to give you some advice."

Quickly, trying to keep his spirits up, I say: "No, that will only make matters worse, all of them crowding and blocking my view of the overpass…"

I stop, having said that. I know I have said too much. Abd al-Rahim whirls around, looks at the overpass. He sees Mahmoud the guard, who still walks along the railing with his rifle on his shoulder like a toy soldier. He sees an American convoy in the distance, moving from north to south like so many toy trucks. The lead vehicles of the convoy move off the main highway and onto the bypass, where they will skirt the town on its western edge and go into Kuwait, across the border. He judges the distance from my shack to the convoy's turning point, less than a kilometer. He judges the distance from my shack to Mahmoud's guard tent, ten meters, maybe twenty. And when he turns back to face me, he smiles.

"I will take the relatives of your bride into the market downtown. I will prevent them from obstructing you. How much would you like me to spend on these gifts?" he says.

"Not too much," I say. "But not too little, either. Ali ash-Shareefi's family is wealthy and Ulayya must not feel slighted. Buy on credit. My name is now known a little in this town, it seems. I should have credit on my own and, if not, I am sure that this coming alliance I will make with the town's wealthiest family must be good for the necessities."

With this Abd al-Rahim leaves me, finally, and both he and the family of ash-Shareefi, the hordes of family, the herd of water buffalo, remain absent long enough to give me time at last to collect my thoughts.

I think: I am about to get married.

That thought is followed by a period of silence during which, in the background, I hear my mind churning with all the myriad details of the engagement and the wedding to which I must soon attend: the gifts that Abd al-Rahim is now arranging; the rental of a tent for the engagement party and for the marriage-contract party; the reservation of a band, dancers, food, fees to register the marriage in the town hall; *baksheesh* distributed to anyone with anything approaching an official role in the ceremony; *zakat* and gifts of food for the poor; arrangements with Ali for something more than just a token dowry; deeper legal wrangling over Ulayya's assets, ownership of her house, guardianship of her children, their financial support, and future dowries for the girls born from her first husband, Zayed. I briefly wonder about taking a vacation with Ulayya, a honeymoon, as they call it in America. Perhaps we could go to France. Perhaps to Salalah for the cool rainy season of the *khareef*. Not to America. We won't go there.

I think: I will never see America again.

Yet behind that thought, weaving among the silence as the rays of the sun finally start to dip, finally start to cast their slanting light through the market, in that silence I *do* see America. I see all the places of my memory, all of them at once—the university, Chicago, baseball stadiums, snow. More strangely, in each scene I now see Layla, too. I see her standing with me in the ER, standing in the corner like a ghost. I see her holding my hand as she and I walk out of Wrigley Field amid the throng of fans leaving a ball game. I see her everywhere. It makes the image of America painful and blurry and more difficult to clearly observe.

I expect, any moment, during all this thinking, to hear Layla's voice, to see her suddenly before me with her questions and her songs and her bird-bone anklet. I expect to see her face shining and clouded and troubled and wondering and wondrous. I lean on the sill of my shop, staring into the western desert and waiting for her arrival. I expect to see her but I do not. She does not come.

So it is with a little sadness in my eyes that I greet my friend Bashar when he arrives at my store. I should be surprised, pleased, amused that he has made the trip away from his café to the outskirts of town, where I work. I should be pleased that he comes to talk to me after the angry ending of our last conversation, when I accused him of telling Hezbollah about Mahmoud and Michele. The reversal in our journeys, in our meetings, should please me, he having come to find me and greet me and spend a few moments at my shop. But I am sad and he doesn't expect the sadness he sees in me.

His first comment—"I hear you have been very popular with your mobile phones today, my friend"—falls a little flat, fails to end on the optimistic note of teasing laughter he had intended.

He wants to ask me what it is that bothers me, but I see he cannot find the words.

Instead, he continues, saying, "I have brought you a plate of falafel and I have brought you a cup of the tea you like. I thought you might be too busy today with all of your new in-laws to find time to eat at my café. I wanted to hear all the details of your good news firsthand."

So I tell him of the things agreed between Ali ash-Shareefi and myself. I tell him of the gifts that Abd al-Rahim is now arranging, the errand that Abd al-Rahim is at that very moment in the process of performing in order to distract all the ash-Shareefi aunts and sisters and cousins. I ask Bashar for his recommendation on the rental of a tent for the engagement party and for the marriage-contract party, which will occur a few weeks after the engagement. I ask him which musicians to reserve, which dancers. I ask him to cater the food for the party from his café. He is flattered. He is pleased. He starts to compile lists of various foods and drinks he will provide. I inquire about fees for registering the marriage. He suggests a wedding official, a *qadi,* from the town of Az Zubayr, with its famous mosque, just a few miles up the road. He offers to lend me money for the *mahur,* the dowry, so that I can provide something respectable, a few thousand in American dollars, and he waives the fees for his catering.

"How could a friend like me expect to charge you for the honor of serving the guests at your wedding?" he says.

We close my shop and walk to my house as the sun sets, all without Layla appearing. Much to my shame and discomfort, I hold part of myself aloof, waiting for her, for the duration of our conversation. Bashar and I discuss so many things. We even fantasize about exotic honeymoons: maybe escaping to Dubai, where Ulayya and I could put on earmuffs and jackets and breathe the indoor, artificial winter chill at the Dubai ski slope. But we don't talk about America. And we don't talk about Mahmoud and Michele or Hussein's use of his Hezbollah as moral police. Most certainly we avoid any mention of the song from the *Close Encounters* movie—I wait for him to ask me about it, if he will. My attachment to the song has steadily increased, the melody playing constantly in the background of my mind. I don't want Bashar to know about this attachment, this possible blasphemy. Likewise, I am especially careful not to mention the fact that Layla has begun to infect my dreams, waking and sleeping. The combination of her dream self and her real self forms a layer of truth and beauty through which I now see the roughness and the pollution of the world.

* * *

I knocked on the door. After I stood for a few moments, staring blankly up and down the empty hallway, Bashar opened the door of his apartment, the apartment he and I had shared for close to five years.

"My father is dead," I informed him.

Bashar wore nothing but loose-fitting sirwal *pants and plastic flip-flops. His chest was bare—no shirt, no* ghalabia. *I needed to talk to him. I needed to tell someone about the phone call I had just received.*

"Now is not a good time," Bashar said.

"My father is dead," I said again. "My brother is alive. He wants me to come back to Iraq. He wants me to be a spy—"

Bashar put his hand to my mouth, pushed me out of the doorway of the apartment, and shut the door behind him.

"Some welcome," I said.

"You're supposed to be in Ireland."

"I'm not."

"No bail for your murderess?"

"She won't even see me when I visit."

"Jesus," said Bashar. "That's so pathetically romantic, so majnoon…"

"Can I come in?"

"No," he said.

But I didn't hear him. I pushed past him. I put my hand to the latch of the door but before I even turned it, Nadia opened it from the inside, leaving me grasping at air.

She slapped me.

"There," she said. "There. I hope it hurts a little. But I hope this hurts more: I've decided to marry your friend. You and I are no longer engaged."

Then she shut the door, slammed it.

From behind me Bashar's voice, keyed up a half note from the tension, said: "We'll all be friends again soon. Don't worry. Just give it a little time. It'll be the three of us. The four of us. You and Annie. Me and Nadia. We'll do things together. We'll go bowling…"

With his words echoing behind me, I walked down the hall, away from him, away from Nadia.

I did not see either of them again until thirteen years later, when Bashar sought me out and convinced me to return to Iraq with him after the Americans' second Iraqi war.

We never went bowling together, the three of us, the four of us. But the promise figures in the memories Bashar and I share of America, like a secret password, a code between friends. Bowling—a word to represent things intended but never completed.

21

ليلة الأحد
وصخرة بحجم القلب

Sunday Night with a
Rock the Size of a Heart

AT NIGHT, WHEN I arrive home after walking with Bashar, I find the window to my upstairs bedroom shattered. Someone has thrown a rock through it. Big as a fist, plain brown, rough-edged. It is hard for me to look at the rock as if it were anything more than just a rock, such an obvious thing, so earthen, so devoid of symbol. Yet with the shards of glass glinting around it and with the rock itself the size of a heart, casting a Zen-like shadow on the bare bedroom floor of one of my upstairs rooms, I know it must contain some meaning, some message to me, a violent message. Children do not throw rocks as big as this. Nor do children throw rocks so high as to shatter second-story windows. A baseball, a home run, hit by a great batter, the champion among the children, maybe, just maybe, could be excused in this context. I would go into the street, find the child who hit it, scold him, and then secretly put the ball on a shelf in my house beside my Cubs hat. It would be a trophy, a monument to the skill of some forlorn child whose talent the world of baseball will never know. But rocks are not toys. And children do not hit rocks with baseball bats, not in Safwan. Children play football, European football. And when children throw rocks, they do so in jest. They throw pebbles, clods of earth, nothing more. It takes a man to throw a rock as big as a heart through an upstairs bedroom window.

I wonder: whom have I angered? Is it Hussein? I think he might really be intent on courting Ulayya. Maybe my wearing the baseball cap gives him justification to harm me or to threaten harm. I can picture him doing something as impersonal and aggressive as throwing a rock through my window. But maybe it isn't Hussein. It could be anyone.

The warning this rock contains within it leads me to imagine men with faces wrapped, townsfolk whose eyes I know but whose expressions are turned away from me due to guilt and conflict within their hearts. I imagine them as they come for me in the night to take me, half-struggling, from my house. They blindfold me. They put me in the trunk of a car. We travel up a paved highway, one of the big roads north or northeast toward Baghdad or toward Basra. But after a few miles we leave the smooth surface of the roadway. I am rocked and bruised as the car bumps and struggles over rutted country roads, up *wadis* and down, turning to the left and to the right as my shoulders ache from the bindings that fasten my arms, ache from ropes they have wrapped around me, ache where cords bite into the flesh of my wrists to keep my hands tied behind my back. My legs cramp from the confines of the small trunk. I push with my calves against the metal of the trunk's interior, but I cannot escape the awkward fetal position for the entire duration of the journey.

I imagine all of this. I imagine all of it right up to the point where the car stops at some dusty shack far from anywhere, a place with one light run by a diesel generator chugging in the near distance. Banditos with hats pulled low over their eyes gather under the single light, bad men. I am manhandled by them from the trunk and I am set on the ground. That is where the image ends. After this point I cannot picture what happens next. I cannot bring my imagination to complete the scene, though I have heard stories of what might occur, though I have seen pictures of what might occur. And what might occur occurs now all too often in the name of Allah the Compassionate, the Merciful. May He forgive us.

I lift the rock from my bedroom floor. I feel the weight of it in my hand, heavier than a baseball, rougher than a baseball. Through the shattered pane of glass I hear the noise of the American bypass outside my house, a sound usually muffled and insulated from me by the barrier of the glass. The sound comes through the hole in the window like blood squirting from a severed artery, pulsing, truck after truck, the labor of diesel engines and air brakes, the rumble of heavy-duty tires, the singing of metal rubbed against metal as wheels and axles turn.

With the rock in my hand I wind up, deliberately cock my arm like a baseball pitcher, lift my front leg, turn my hip, and pitch a perfectly flat beeline back through the window. I am no ballplayer. The throw is a little high, a little outside the strike zone, but it is moving fast. The rock nicks a jagged edge of the glass that remains in the window frame. The broken glass fractures completely. More shards scatter, this time outward. Now the snow of shattered glass glitters outside the house as well as on the floor beneath my feet. I hear the rock thump in the dust somewhere in the moon-shadowed orchard of date palms that surrounds my new little Safwan neighborhood.

The convoy has passed. I only faintly detect the sound of its many engines in the distance north of town. The town has grown quiet. My house feels more vacant than ever before, now that it has this opening, this puncture, this wound that exposes it to the noises of the world.

I go downstairs, open the first brown package, sit at my table, where the parts of the jack-in-the-box are still scattered. This time, to ward away the silence, I let the tape recorder play. I listen to the song of the aliens, deep and fluting but never quite imbued with the same meaning and importance and resonance as when I first heard it sung by Layla. I listen to the song over and over again, rewinding the tape, playing it, rewinding it as I drink myself to sleep for the second night in a row and hope to hear again the similarity, the echo, the collusion that exists between that song and heaven.

* * *

I laugh at myself—Father Truth.

Thirteen years, my last years in America, are an emptiness, a vast blackness in my memory.

I know the shape of this void.

I know it well.

It isn't the shape of Annie Dillon. I have never forgotten her. How could I? But life came between us. She got her prison time. She refused to consider defending herself, each time stating to the court her bald and unremorseful opinion: "He deserved it." And, although at first I visited her, gradually, ever so gradually, the space between visits grew until I made the two-hour drive south to the women's penitentiary in Dwight, Illinois, only once or twice a year.

I know the shape of the void.

It isn't Bashar. Nor is it Nadia. Nor my father.

I can look into it, the emptiness, the thirteen-year expanse of nothing, and I can see the outline of it the way astronomers infer the existence of a black hole from the bending its gravity exerts against starlight. As with starlight, I can see things on the edges of the void, collected around it, aggravated by it, in close orbit. But I cannot see into the thing itself, despite so many nights spent staring at it through the bottom of my whiskey bottle.

Maybe it is in aggregate, in that periphery of memory, where the best image exists for me, seeing the thing in its outline as a means to draw myself closer to the missing substance. Whereas the void itself is cold, callous, and silent, the objects, the memories orbiting it, are sometimes loud, sometimes warm, oftentimes trivial, occasionally brilliant, and gut-wrenchingly real.

I see myself, for instance, working in my clinic in Chicago. I see any number of my former patients. I see their wounds, their maladies, their complaints, their whitely aged ankles with folds of skin drooping over old bones.

I see Annie's house, her little whitewashed house. I bought it from her and nailed a black Quaker-style mailbox over the place on the hollow porch column where she had taped her farewell letter for me. I see a snow-dusted holiday wreath on the front door of the house. I see a Christmas tree lit in its living-room window.

I see myself praying, unrolling my prayer rug in the morning from the shelf in my bedroom closet, during the day in the break room of my clinic, on Fridays kneeling in Al-Fatir Mosque on Woodlawn Avenue.

In the periphery I watch movies. I watch TV. The Terminator *and* I Love Lucy *and* Stand By Me *and* Beverly Hills Cop *and* Encino Man. *Also* Sesame Street, Steamboat Willie, Home Alone 1, 2, 3, *and* 4, Cinderella *at least four hundred times,* The Goonies, *and god-awful* Barney.

I see Cubs games, Cracker Jack, popcorn, corn dogs, Pepsi-Cola, the windows of my former loft staring down at me from the twelfth story of that nearby apartment building.

I see a girl's mittens discarded in a drifted snowbank, pink mittens.

I feel fishing line spooling out from under my thumb as I cast and reel and lounge with my feet propped on the railing of a gently rocking pontoon boat. A bobber drifts behind the boat. A loon calls from the far tree-lined shore.

These memories aren't empty. They aren't cold. They aren't lonely. They aren't upset. They are peaceful, radiant, loving, open, and detailed.

And they stand in stark juxtaposition against the thing into which I stare and cannot, cannot name. It's a space of thirteen years into which I stare. It's a space of thirteen years that is completely invisible to me.

22

الإثـنين

Monday

WHERE LAYLA HAS BEEN these last few days, I do not know. But when she visits me at last today, this fifteenth day of our acquaintance, I am like a lamp that has been stored in a closet or an attic, a lamp uncovered at last and into which a spark is fired, finding its oil still flammable, finding its light suddenly grown large and hungry, finding itself transfigured from mere spark into solid, voluminous flame.

Yes, the convoys move north and south. Yes, Mahmoud paces on the bridge. Yes, Abd al-Rahim annoys me. I find work for him as I must, a morning's worth of work. But by the time Ali ash-Shareefi himself, my new friend, my new father-in-law, visits my shop, Abd al-Rahim has assumed his lounging attitude. I introduce Abd al-Rahim to the head of the ash-Shareefi family. And I must admit that the city boy has manners—too-fine manners, perhaps. He removes his sunglasses so that he does not hide his eyes and his soul from the old man. He bows. He addresses ash-Shareefi respectfully. He calls him al-Hajj without even having been told that ash-Shareefi is one of the few in this town who have indeed made the Holy Pilgrimage to Mecca, one of the few who deserve the title that is so blithely applied in our current age. It is a good introduction between them, and I notice that Abd al-Rahim's attitude of perfect attention reflects well on me. He is my assistant and his conduct is my responsibility. Ash-Shareefi's eyes have a look of wonder in them, knowing as he must that Abd al-Rahim is not a local boy. I am sure that Ali, like the others in this town, expects great things of me, and I suspect that having an assistant with shined leather shoes and American sunglasses is merely confirmation of the honor they already imagine I will bring them.

My father-in-law leaves only after purchasing a satellite dish and a subscription to Nilesat. He does not haggle with me and his expenditure is an astounding sum of money, more than I had thought to charge. All of it he pays in actual U.S. dollars. It seems more like an outright gift than a purchase. And it will certainly make things easier for me in arranging my wedding to Ulayya. Purchases on credit are normal for such an occasion as a wedding and I had planned to buy almost everything on credit, hoping my name and reputation might bear the burden. But even a few purchases in cash, or down payments of cash, open the gates of trust and fine service anywhere, not just here in Safwan.

Halfway down the street on his way home, ash-Shareefi turns and says to me, "Excuse an old man for his poor memory, my son. In talking of the satellite dish I forgot the main point of my visit today. I would like you to please do me the honor of dining at my house again tonight."

It is an invitation I gladly accept.

So when she does arrive—Layla, my little friend—it is with much confusion that Abd al-Rahim watches me. He must wonder: how can a man soon to be the son-in-law of al-Hajj ash-Shareefi acknowledge such a girl as Layla? How can he have these conflicting bits of personality: ascending social aspirations yet also easy familiarity with the dregs of the earth?

Layla is not on her unicycle when she arrives, a thing for which I am thankful. She is not covered with oil. She hasn't just shot Mahmoud's Kalashnikov and returned it to him empty. She is not singing alien songs or dancing Britney Spears's hip-thrusting dances. She is a little girl, just a little girl. As she walks down the street she extends her hands for alms, for *baksheesh,* on the chance that one of our merchants or one of our shoppers might feel pity today. She could be anyone, though I notice her ankle with its bird bones and yarn, white in the glancing rays of the sun.

Abd al-Rahim tries to shoo her away when he first sees her standing in the shadow of my shop. She emerges from the shadow with her hand out, palm up, her face turned toward me, smudged and open-eyed, pitiful, not grinning with any familiarity at all. Abd al-Rahim sees her, sees the reality of her, her physical presence. I am glad he sees her, because I had half convinced myself that Layla was all along nothing more than a mirage, a genie, a bit of flotsam cast loose from my imagination.

Abd al-Rahim sees her and brushes her away from the shack with a look and a gesture that would surely scare away any other beggar child. His eyebrows crease into a frown. He glares. Yet he remains aloof, too, as if to say, "Your life and your death matter not at all to me. It would be a little thing to me, nothing at all, really, to toss you out of a moving car somewhere deep in the desert."

Thinking he has shooed her away, Abd al-Rahim leans over the counter of my shack, looking from the outside in. I lean on the counter, too, on the opposite side, under the cover of the shade of the tin roof. Between us we have spread the engagement gifts, little trinkets, really. Each of them I will wrap and then have Abd al-Rahim deliver to Ulayya's house on the days between now and the engagement party. One for each day, as is the custom in this far southern part of the country.

Abd al-Rahim refocuses his attention on the gifts, points to one of them, a length of blue silk. Then he notices that I no longer focus on the silks, the linens, the rolls of wrapping paper and bright bows. He looks at me and then he looks back over his shoulder at Layla, who has not fled at his first withering glance. Abd al-Rahim straightens, turns, and takes a step toward Layla with his hand raised as if to do her at least a little bodily harm. What does he care? What is she to him?

"Stop," I say.

Abd al-Rahim does not expect this from me. He does not expect my interference. He hesitates.

Poised on the curb of the road, they stare at each other, Layla and Abd al-Rahim, a lioness and her prey. Layla looks at me, looks at me for approval. I shake my head at her. Whereas Abd al-Rahim's earlier gaze did nothing to her, my disapproval affects her much more noticeably. First she frowns. The sunlight disappears from her face. Then she drops a little package from her hands into the dust. She stands there, a shadow falling on the package. She hovers over it and looks from me to Abd al-Rahim and back to me again. I see one of the corners of Abd al-Rahim's mouth slowly turn up, a feral half smile. He has measured her, judged her age perhaps more accurately than I at first judged, weighing her on a scale of his own shameless appetites.

The change in his look, from one of utter dismissal to intense yet impersonal interest, breaks Layla's will, breaks her ability to stand firm in the dust in front of my store under the combined intensity of my disapproval and his desire. She turns around and runs back into the market toward the north, through the narrow tented alleys between the shops. And so she disappears. She has said nothing. Her visit isn't as remarkable as most, except for the fact that she has come and has been seen by someone other than me and has left me what appears to be a gift, a gift wrapped in plain brown paper with a little silken blue bow under which the stem of a single orange flower is lodged, a desert flower.

Abd al-Rahim takes the package in his hands and lifts it carelessly from the ground.

"That was strange," he says with leering intensity still coloring his features. His voice has a slightly snarling sound to it, higher pitched, as if his throat has constricted. Yet he speaks without alluding to the change. He speaks as if to cover, to hide from me the change that has overtaken him, saying: "What a strange sort of beggar child to leave behind a gift! Most of them take, take, take, hands out, pouting faces, poor little children. I am sick of them, sick of them all. But this one shies away at the last moment and leaves us whatever this is. Do you think we should open it?"

He begins to finger the blue bow and the seams of the brown wrapping paper that cover the package. He lifts it toward his face and smells the flower.

"I know her," I say. "The girl visits me every now and again."

Abd al-Rahim raises an eyebrow at this.

"Visits me here at my shop," I say quickly, lest he—like Bashar—get the entirely wrong idea about the relationship between Layla and me.

I hold out my hand for the package. Abd al-Rahim gives it to me but looks at it as if he expects me to open it in front of him. I don't give him the pleasure. I put it in a pocket under my robe. I will open it later, after I close the shop, after I go to dine again at Ali ash-Shareefi's house. I will open it after the day is done and when I am at last alone with my disassembled jack-in-the-box, my tape recorder, and my bottle of whiskey.

I look down at the wedding gifts arrayed in front of me. Abd al-Rahim and I have spoken about them all at length. We have consulted Bashar about them: the silk, the cotton, the linen, the jewelry, the crystal cups, the clothes, the package of henna to adorn Ulayya's feet and hands. Bashar approves of them, of course. He approves of me adding someone new and real to my empty shell of a life. He approves of me starting over, starting anew, putting the past behind me. He approves of these things, I think, because of Nadia.

Abd al-Rahim and I have done all the consulting, talked all the talk, completed every minute examination I can think of with regard to these gifts, their symbolism, which to give Ulayya first, which last. The topic has been thoroughly exhausted. There is nothing new to say about any of these things, nothing that will take Abd al-Rahim's attention away from the other gift, the new little package Layla left on the ground for me.

Worried about what Abd al-Rahim might ask me in regard to my relationship with Layla and having nothing else of substance to distract him from the package, I say out of desperation: "Meet me at my house tonight, maybe ten in the evening, maybe later. You will know when the sounds of revelry from ash-Shareefi's house go quiet. Then I will be on my way home. We will work late, so please bring tea for keeping your mind sharp and candles for lighting our work when, like most nights, the electricity fails."

Abd al-Rahim nods to show me he understands and agrees. He does so very slowly and precisely, not wanting to ruin the moment of trust between us with any sort of spoken words or any sort of overt display of excitement. Then together we close the shop, one of us on either side of the corrugated tin shutter, letting it fall slowly so that it doesn't disturb the screws Abd al-Rahim has finally fixed, first with his hammer and then later with a proper screwdriver. We let the shutter fall slowly so that it doesn't scratch the fresh coat of paint he has applied to the exterior of the shack. We let it fall slowly so that it doesn't tear the temporary sign he has made of paper letters and glued to the front face of the shop, a sign that proclaims MOBILE PHONE SALES. Below those big letters is a line of smaller script spelling out the name of the proprietor, me, Abu Saheeh, Father Truth.

* * *

In Baghdad my friendship with Bashar flowered anew. He con-
vinced me to return, to take a job working for him in the
Ministry of Health, helping patch together our countrymen and
our country after the Americans at last overthrew Saddam in
2003.

Our days were filled with important meetings, planning ses-
sions with generals and ambassadors, delegations of visiting sen-
ators and members of Parliament. Bashar and I asked for and
received many millions of dollars to rebuild hospitals, to hire
doctors, to reinvigorate vaccination programs, to treat our fel-
low citizens who had suffered either directly from the war or
indirectly from the long period of sanctions against Iraq.

I was sewing up the bellies of many thousands of ripped-apart
kittens, helping many thousands of Iraqis. And the evenings
were filled with wonderful parties in our gated and guarded lit-
tle diplomatic community on the island of Umm al-Khanzeer,
an island on which Saddam had built houses for his ministers,
an island accessible to the rest of Baghdad only by a small bridge
that connected it to the west bank of the Tigris River. There, on
plush lawns, amid the clink of wineglasses and the rush of ram-
bunctious children around us, Bashar and I toasted the success
we thought nearly within our grasp: a new Iraq, a place where
a family like mine, split into Shia and Sunni branches, need not
fear subjugation by one sect or another, a new democratic Iraq
where power might be shared among the Kurdish peoples, the
Shia, and the Sunni.

Thinking back on it, I remember that I became very fond of
one of Bashar's several young daughters, a tenderness of the sort
I might have felt had the girl been my own child. I played catch

with her in our fenced backyard under the high whitewashed walls of our home, lulled by the shifting shadows of tall watered date palms, charmed by the scents of climbing jasmine and bougainvillea. I remember putting a ball cap on the girl's head, a Cubs cap, of course, fitting the adjustable strap to her small head. I remember her smiling at me, even giving me a shy but warm kiss on my cheek.

I remember all this about Bashar's daughter but I find myself unable to remember her name. I rack my brain to think of her name but it does not exist in my mind. I hear her voice in my memory, but each time I speak to her in those memories I call her something sweet, some little pet name or another: "my bird," "my pet," "my dear."

And often, very often, I call her "sweetheart."

It troubles me even more that I can't seem to remember having seen this girl among the children Bashar and Nadia presented to me in their new home here in Safwan. Was she older than Saleem, his eldest boy? Was she younger? I am amazed at the quality of the memories that surround her, the warmth, the happiness. But I am also amazed that I cannot recall her name.

Tragic things have happened to many, many children in Iraq. I think about asking Bashar what has become of the girl, but quickly I put the idea to the back of my mind. It would be the height of bad manners for me to mention such a thing as a dead child if the child's father hasn't been open in his grief. Truly, I think that Bashar is just the sort of man who might pretend or might even convince himself, in his sorrow, that the child herself had never even existed.

It might be, for Bashar, the only way to deal with such haunting despair.

23

ليلة الإثنين
وعشاء في منزل الشريفي

Monday Night Dinner at the House of ash-Shareefi

LAYLA'S PACKAGE, HER GIFT, burns against my ribs as if it were on fire during the whole length of the dinner at the house of my soon-to-be father-in-law. It is small enough not to cause my *dishdasha* to fold awkwardly over it, about as big as a book of poems. With me, to the dinner, I bring the first of my own gifts to Ulayya, which I set on the table in front of Ali al-Hajj ash-Shareefi so that he might present it to his daughter. Of course it is only men at the dinner, for, as at all such traditional gatherings, the women have their own area of the house in which to congregate and celebrate, secluded from the eyes of the male guests.

I am seated this evening at the right hand of the head of the ash-Shareefi family. By arranging the seats in this fashion, Ali proclaims me not only one of his own, but also ranks me as the man second only to him in the order of the affairs of his family. Ali has no surviving sons, and Ulayya is the eldest of the daughters. Since I am to be her husband, my position is such that I become something more like the eldest son of the family, the man who will continue ash-Shareefi's legacy. This makes my rank greater than that of the uncles and cousins and various other men, business associates and honored townsfolk, who have been invited to the first of many parties that will build toward the marriage feast.

I discover from my conversations during the course of the evening that Ali had two sons, both of them older than Ulayya, and both of them tragically killed in the first war against the Americans.

"One of them fought for Saddam," says the man on my right, the closest of the many ash-Shareefi cousins. "This man was like an uncle to me. His journey led him down into the heart of Kuwait when Iraq invaded. Of course history has denied Iraq the possession of Kuwait. America and its henchmen in Europe and the rest of the world fight even now to keep Kuwait separate from Iraq. Otherwise, why would there be a fence, guards, UN sanctions? The Kuwaiti princes hold a strange power over the West."

"Oil," I say.

Ali ash-Shareefi makes the circuit of the room, talking individually with each of his guests, sitting with them for long or short periods of time as their particular issues and concerns and words of congratulation merit. This leaves the seat to my left, Ali's seat, empty for a long while. I am stuck listening to the cousin on my right. He tells me that ash-Shareefi learned from the survivors of the Iraqi retreat from Kuwait City that his eldest son was among those killed, exposed among the many tanks and trucks and other vehicles jammed on the road leading back from Kuwait City to Iraq, all of them nothing more than sitting ducks for the strafing and bombing of the American warplanes.

From this point the cousin's narrative delves into the gruesome details of that strafing and bombing: the traffic jam that the big highway became, the blood that ran in the gutters of the roadway, soaking into the sand, the scream- ing, the explosions that could be heard outside town, the screeching sound of jet engines as planes passed over Safwan, circling in the Iraqi skies to return into Kuwait, to make a second or third pass over the backlogged highway.

"When the Americans finished," he says, "the Kuwaitis had to bulldoze the charred hulks of our vehicles to the edges of the road."

The man's fascination with the slaughter disturbs me. His speech bothers me, physically bothers me. My stomach churns. I excuse myself from the dinner. I go outside, into the courtyard. I cross the courtyard to the bathroom.

When I emerge I am greeted by the black sunglasses— wearing guard at the front gate, the man who said nothing to me on the first day of our acquaintance. He still says nothing. But he nods at me in a friendly way, and he takes from his pocket a red pack of Marlboros, a rarity in Iraq, American cigarettes. He offers me one. I don't want to smoke but I accept. It is a matter of contract, of good form, of doing the right thing. I smoke the cigarette. Between shallow puffs I take my wallet from a pocket under my *dish- dasha* and I show the man the previous year's Cubs schedule, a glossy card with fine metallic blue English print on it. The man admires the artifact, so I give it to him, which seems to make him happy. Yet he doesn't speak a word. I wonder if he is mute. Nevertheless, I enjoy the silence of standing in the courtyard with him, such a contrast with the overwhelming volume of noise and banter inside Ali's *diwaniya*. I enjoy the warm blanket of the night sky, a few stars visible through the smog of oil smoke that covers our town.

When I return to my seat in the *diwaniya,* the cousin starts his story once again. Now, at least, he has returned to his first point, the history of Ali's two sons.

He says, "And then, the real tragedy was Ali's other son, his younger son, who also served as a soldier during the first American war."

Here the cousin pauses a little. He is feeling emotional, I can tell. I reach out, put my hand on his arm. This steadies him.

"The elder son was like an uncle to me," he says. "But the younger son, named after Ali himself, was like a brother to me, that is how close we were. And you, here, sitting in the place that should be his seat, you make me think of him very much."

Again, the cousin pauses. His jaw clenches before he launches back into his story. "Ali the Younger was a soldier, too. However, he left Saddam's forces before entering Kuwait during the war's first days. He deserted, stealing back here to Safwan in the middle of the night. Ali hid him, kept him hidden by moving him from home to home as Saddam's soldiers barracked in our town. Young Ali was our consolation during the time when news of so many deaths reached us: at least one boy had lived. Feelings ran high among us here in the south. The American forces would overthrow Saddam with our help, with Shia help.

Then the Shia people would hold power for the first time in many centuries. The euphoria spread and the younger son joined the Shia resistance. Ali the Younger helped sabotage Saddam's forces. He helped organize resistance and I helped him. I was his message boy. I was his cupbearer, his flag bearer. I was there beside him throughout all the resistance. But I was young, too young to do anything too dangerous.

"So when the American forces stopped in Safwan itself, having killed ash-Shareefi's first son on the road south of town, when they signed a peace treaty with Saddam that left the dictator still in charge of our country, these glorious expectations of our resistance forces were shattered and we were left without any support. The Americans retreated into Kuwait and into Saudi Arabia. We Shia who plotted against Saddam continued our fight but without the warplanes of the Americans, without American tanks, without American soldiers to cover us. Saddam waited, but not very long. Soon the purge began. Saddam's Republican Guard came into Safwan and into many of the other southern Shia towns. They cleaned out every man between maybe sixteen and forty years of age. Among them, Ali the Younger was lost. If it had been a matter of a trial or a stay in jail, I am sure Ali al-Hajj would have been able to use his influence to save his second son. But they took him and all our men of fighting age away that same night. We were no match for the soldiers. We never saw them again. Their bones must rest somewhere in the nameless desert west of here. What could we do? We were left with nothing more than old men and women and children.

"I went running into the street hoping to save them. I

was the eldest and most experienced of the children of the resistance who remained. But my own father rushed after me. He grabbed me around the waist. He lifted me on his old shoulders with a strength I didn't know he possessed, he being maybe sixty-five years of age then. He lifted me and took me, kicking, from the street so that I would not get in the way of the truck onto which they had loaded our men. And he beat me, my father, he beat me with a belt and a stick all the rest of that evening so that I could not walk, could not run, could not chase after my heroes into the desert. It was for my own good, that beating, though I didn't know it at the time. I would not be alive otherwise."

The cousin then lifts the back of his *dishdasha* and with it the back of the white undershirt he wears. His bare flesh is revealed to me in the soft light of the *diwaniya*. I see on him the permanent marks from that beating, savage puckering lines of scar tissue. The cousin notices my interest. He proceeds to describe the beating in more and more gruesome detail. I grow sick again at the thought of the gore. I force my attention away from him.

I think to myself: where do these paired tragedies leave Ali al-Hajj ash-Shareefi? Sons killed on each side of the war. Does he love the Americans less than he hates Saddam? Did he support them during their second war, when they fulfilled the promise of the first war and finally overthrew the Baathists?

During the remainder of the dinner, once he has returned to his seat next to me, I want to ask Ali these things, questions more important to me than any planning of engagement feasts or wedding parties, questions deeper and with more specific future consequences than the things that are asked of me by the others in the room.

Who is my family?

What jobs have I held?

What do I think are the prospects for mobile-phone and satellite-dish sales in Safwan?

What do I plan for the *mahar* and the *shabka,* the dowry and engagement gifts?

I lie profusely and wantonly. I don't know what to say to these things and it seems more important to tell them what they want to hear than to tell them any sort of truth, especially when it comes to my past. I speak glibly, but beneath my laughter, beneath the little jokes I tell, I think continually about Ali al-Hajj's relationship with the Americans. Where does he stand? I imagine he has chosen a very careful balance, a path between full support and full antagonism. He is a family leader at the height of his consummate skill, a man facing a real issue that has already claimed two of his sons, whereas I am somewhat new to this necessary sort of dithering and waiting and making-no-firm-commitments.

In the center of the three tables arrayed in Ali's *diwaniya,* a single musician has been playing, a well-known man from Basra City hired by Ali for tonight's feast. He has a gruff but pleasant voice, a deepness that contrasts with the sweet love songs he has been commissioned to sing. He plays an *aoud,* strumming it sparingly as an accent between the graveled ululations of his voice. Ali looks at me during a pause between the man's songs.

"The packages," he says. "The packages arranged through Sheikh Seyyed Abdullah…"

He does not finish the statement. The room is too quiet, everyone watching us, everyone trying to overhear what we say. The cousin on my right leans especially close, feeling that he has been excluded from this bit of the conversation. Ali wants me to respond to his half-formed question, but I feign misunderstanding. Ali tenses his mouth, forming additional words of clarification, but he waits to speak again until the music resumes, until the music provides cover. In a very short time, the awkward pause ends. The singer intones deeply, like the rumble of a distant convoy heading north, a song of love newly awakened after a long time asleep, a song like a fairy tale. The man's voice contains the presence of cobwebs, the brittleness of spiders, the thorns of brambles grown up around a slumbering castle. I let my hand float up in front of me. I let my fingers sway in the air and I snap them together in cadence. I show the crowd of men at the tables around me that I am enjoying myself.

While I do this Ali leans toward me. I try to focus on the dancing movements of my hands and arms. I try to ignore him. I don't want to discuss what Seyyed Abdullah's packages contain. The cover of the music is enough, yes, to disguise our conversation, but the men in the room will read the conspiracy on our faces as surely as if we were speaking to them aloud.

But Ali leans close, speaks directly into my ear, saying: "I can order the same items for you that Seyyed Abdullah obtains."

This is too much. He is too close. I have no recourse but to confess to him the truth, to let him in on the plan Seyyed Abdullah and I undertake. Ali has let me come so near to him. I feel guilty that I haven't told him my truths. I mumble something. I start to say, "Bombs…"

But Ali hushes me, saying: "We are men here, all men. In the circle of men such things are not forbidden. Better, I say, to enjoy your whiskey with dear companions and good food and the *sheesha* than to drink and to smoke alone."

At this he laughs and produces a silver flask, highly ornamented with the same inlaid patterns and jewels that decorate the *khanjars,* the daggers worn by southern Gulf peoples. He unscrews the lid of his flask and passes it to me. Gratefully, I drink. Gratefully, I feel my load lighten both from the burning of the alcohol and from being absolved from any sort of confession. Ali guesses at only the least harmful part of the contents of Sheikh Seyyed Abdullah's packages, the whiskey, the smuggled whiskey.

"I accept your offer," I say, my face regaining some of its color and warmth. "I need some for my house, some for my friends. How can a man host men in his home without the trappings a good host must provide? And these things are so difficult to obtain for any but the most well connected of hosts, impossible for a man like me, who has no connections whatsoever!"

He laughs, Ali, suspecting me to be anything but unconnected. He knows that he and Seyyed Abdullah are most connected among the citizens of Safwan. But he must guess that the two of them are only temporarily more connected than me. Once I get myself grounded, once I reestablish myself, he thinks I will begin calling in favors from all the friends of a former life.

I could make those connections if I wanted. These men know of my education abroad. They know my past jobs in Iraq. If Bashar has indeed spoken of the days in the Green Zone after the first successes, the heady successes of the

Americans' second invasion, then they know I can move in circles at the very center of power. I was here on a dream and with something that was, truly, a Greater Purpose: to make a new and better Iraq. Nor would Bashar have forgotten to tell them of the Chicago where he and I studied and worked together. Bashar, you secret-keeper! They suspect a grand design here, a grand design from a man whose biggest design has failed amid the divisive conflicts of our new civil war.

Indeed, I could reopen the connections if I wanted. I could reopen them in service of an idea more worthwhile to these townsfolk than the abstract concepts of peace and national rebirth. I could reopen my contacts in the pursuit of profit, a life of profit, a life spent making myself and Ali's daughter obscenely rich, a life smuggling, sneaking things of value into Iraq. Such an idea would fit perfectly with Ali ash-Shareefi's own businesses. I presume he intends for us to merge commercial forces; mobile-phone sales are just a preliminary to an empire of sales and smuggling. We will be poised at the forefront when the economy recovers, when Baghdad and Basra and Mosul become metropolitan once more and desire shipment through the border of Kuwait all the electronics and all the comforts the rest of the world now possesses.

Ali then speaks again, this time to all the assembled cousins and uncles.

"A man from the north, this soon-to-be son-in-law of mine, he will not mind viewing his bride a little more openly," he says.

Not waiting for my response, he claps his hands together. Ulayya immediately enters from the women's quarters, bringing with her a tray of *halwa* and tea. She sets the tray in front of her father. Ali has partaken of enough liquor from his silver flask to color his thin face red, to make him chuckle proudly at the sight of his daughter before him. He allows me to look at Ulayya for a moment, though she is veiled in a colorful gauze headpiece, blue and red and gold, and though she keeps her eyes modestly averted through the long moment of her time in the room. She knows I am present and she knows where at the table I sit, though she is careful not to look at me directly.

Ali nudges my present, my little *shabka,* toward Ulayya across the low table.

"A gift from your betrothed," he says to her.

She takes the package and leaves the room, smiling just a little as she steps through the sheathing curtains of the doorway and returns with her prize to the gathering of women in the rooms adjacent to Ali's *diwaniya.*

I am afraid I will disappoint Ali ash-Shareefi by bringing the war here to this almost-quiet town, to his almost-quiet family, which still mourns the loss of two sons and the loss of Ulayya's first husband, among the many men Safwan lost. I am afraid I will disappoint them, yet I am also intensely interested to know how Ulayya receives her gift. It has been a long while since I courted a woman. Her presence in the room has left my head feeling light and my heart feeling heavy.

* * *

Often during those evening parties in Baghdad, whether on the lawns of our houses or in more formal settings—dinners, banquets, balls—I saw Nadia with Bashar. Like Ulayya, despite the effects of children, Nadia retained a beautiful figure, slim and curvingly elegant. The liberation of Western clothing, Western style, suited her. She wore low-cut evening dresses. She wore stiletto heels. She wore diamonds—faux or real, I never could tell—in her hair and on her fingers and around her neck. The only element of style she retained from her upbringing in Baghdad was a preference for the heavy application of kohl around her eyes. This, combined with her darkness—the raw-honey color of her skin, the obsidian shimmer of her hair—contrasted markedly with the few other women in attendance at these parties, most of them female British and American officers or ambassadorial staff.

Nadia flaunted this beauty in front of me as if to say, "See what you have thrown away."

I was immune to her hints at first.

It was natural, I thought, for her to gravitate toward me during these parties when Bashar found himself occupied by some deep and laborious discussion, expounding upon plans to accredit Baghdad Medical City as a research institute, plans to build factories for pharmaceuticals in some city or another, plans to start a medical scholarship program similar to the one that had launched his career and mine.

Nadia and I knew each other better than we knew the other people at those parties. What was more natural for her than to seek my company when Bashar wasn't available? Thirteen years had passed since she slapped me in the doorway of Bashar's apartment, thirteen years for her to forget her anger.

24

ليلة الإثنين
وأحلام ليلى

Monday Night with
Dreams of Layla

LAYLA VISITS ME IN my dreams tonight, like most nights now. I drink a little from my bottle when, at last, I am alone. But I'm weary. By drinking I only mean to relax myself so that my face-down sleep on the bare dining-room table comes quickly and easily. The passage from wakefulness to sleep and from sleep to dream happens almost reflexively.

Just as my dreams begin, Layla appears.

She stands in shadow under the awning of my little store, my shack, as the golden sunset reflects against the pillars of the overpass where the highway from Basra to Kuwait and the even larger highway from the port of Umm Qasr to Baghdad intersect. She is wearing the gift she gave me. She is wearing it as if in the moment I opened her little boxed and flowered present—quickly, between the time when I first arrived home after Ali's party and when Abd al-Rahim knocked on my door—I somehow gave the gift back to her, reflected it onto her in the odd logic of a dream. It is a length of blue silk, exactly like the length of silk Abd al-Rahim bought for Ulayya on my behalf, exactly the same thing as my first gift to Ulayya. Layla wears it wrapped around her head, as a scarf. In the dream it shimmers like water. It *is* water, flowing, blue, ebbing, encircling her head. It is a river, a lake, a sky, a field of budding blue lavender rippled by breezes. It is all these things in rapid succession, shifting and shimmering.

Layla spins in a slow circle as the watersilk on her head ripples with her movement. Not far from her, perhaps three meters away, Abd al-Rahim also enters the dream. He does not understand me when I tell him to remove the sky from Layla's head so that I might see her more clearly. I don't want any shimmering distractions. Abd al-Rahim does not understand. He doesn't have any distractions. Maybe he doesn't have any shimmering, either. Maybe that is why he wears polished shoes and fancy clothes and dark sunglasses: to hide the fact that he doesn't shimmer.

"Remove it," I say to him. "Remove that slice of fallen sky, that shimmer. Unwrap it, untie it. Use something other than a hammer. Use something other than a garden rake."

But despite my protests, Abd al-Rahim will come no closer to Layla. He is, in fact, located on the very edge of the steel-black lake. He keeps his hands folded in front of him, looking very steadfast. He comes no closer to Layla, and I find myself irritated with him, irritated at his optimism, the way he smiles behind his impossible sunglasses, his snazzy shoes.

I say, "War isn't something distant and oblivious and political."

The words feel like a statement of genius. I tell myself to remember them when I wake, as if the morphing, thrown-together statement of a dream will have even the most superficial resemblance to the grammar of living. I know I am saying something important, inventing something important, so I pay very close attention to myself as I lecture Abd al-Rahim and the spinning shining image of Layla, who stands between us.

"War really isn't news," I say. "Nothing is news. Nothing is rhinoceros big and quicksandy and compelling, as the newspapers will have you believe. At all levels, everything, really, incidents famous or infamous, they all resolve like chocolate into a warm windowsill until they are just nuts and nougat and a wrapper fluttering in the broken air-conditioner vent. Nuts and nougats with real lives, jobs, loves, loving the caramel especially, especially when it sticks to the teeth and tongue, hobbies, quirks, fascinations. War is not big speeches and credos. It is man and man and woman and woman and child, oblivious to everything except the basics of joy and hunger and thirst and inquiry, oblivious to everything except nougat. These things can hurt, death and love and loss, but they aren't political until someone uses them politically."

That is my speech. Begins well, ends well. I'm not sure why all the candy enters the middle, the muddy part. Maybe I am getting hungry in my sleep. Maybe this is just my waking mind now, trying to capture both the order and the entropy of such a dream. What, anyway, does Abd al-Rahim know of war? Why does he stand on the lakeshore with his hands folded, when the sky in Layla's hair needs rearranging? A pigtail, perhaps, fastened in the back by jack-in-the-box springs. I pluck one as I sleep from the spiraling snow between where I stand and the skyscraper lights that loom over the black lake water. I pluck a spring or a gear or a disassembled ticktock and use it to tie the scarf of the silken sky to Layla's hair.

When, earlier tonight, I returned from Ali's dinner, Abd al-Rahim wasn't yet at my house. I expected him there, waiting like a dog on my doorstep, a dog who has found his way home. He shows up only five minutes later, so that I have but a minute or two to settle into my house, remove my *ghalabia,* wet my throat to tamp down the dust of the journey across town, and unwrap Layla's present. When he knocks I shove Layla's gift into one of the unfinished cabinets in the kitchen. I have those five minutes alone. Then, when he leaves, I drink my exhausted mind into this dream. In between, during the several hours of our time together, Abd al-Rahim and I begin our work building bombs.

"Put it together," I say to him after I am done showing him the various empty rooms of my house.

He had indeed noticed the chaos in my dining room the first time he passed it, but we've moved quickly from room to room until, at last, we return to the table. He raises an eyebrow at me, questioning the significance of the brightly colored bits of jack-in-the-box.

"Put it together," I say once more.

"Put what together?" he says.

"It's a jack-in-the-box."

With my forearm sweeping the table, I shove the parts toward him. I pass him a screwdriver, a hammer, forceps, a retractor, some glue, a blowtorch. Everything he should need.

"I don't understand," he says. "A jack-in-the-box?"

"Show me—*wax on, wax off,*" I say, a reference so foreign to Abd al-Rahim that he stares at me until I take a menacing half step toward him with a pair of pliers raised in my hand. I am surprised at my action. I haven't done anything physically threatening or even physically spirited since leaving Baghdad, nothing except for the anticlimactic firing of Mahmoud's ammunitionless Kalashnikov.

Likewise, I am surprised at how Abd al-Rahim reacts. A young man like him should hold his ground. He should challenge me, but he doesn't. There is a moment of hesitation, as though he gathers his strength or his will to attack me. I brace myself. But then I see him change his mind. His shoulders slump. He sits, very quickly, hands folded in front of him. After another moment passes, as I glower above him with my raised and clicking pliers, he begins pushing the various pieces of jack-in-the-box around the table, trying to determine for himself which piece to select first in his effort at reassembly.

I watch him for a long while. I watch him struggle. I watch him choose the wrong piece, the wrong spring, the wrong ratchet or lever. I see him forget things. I notice him disassembling what he has already assembled, fixing it time and again until it is closer and closer to correct. It is a good exercise for him.

But eventually, I tire of watching him.

The jack-in-the-box is usually my cure for boredom. I tear it apart. I build it anew. I tear it apart again. But now I have no such recourse. Abd al-Rahim must have it all to himself. He must practice upon it. I am forced, at last, to open the new brown-paper package. I cut the tape, lift the flaps, and look at the contents from afar before positioning everything in neat rows in front of me. I inspect the items. I turn them this way and that way, feeling their heft and shine and danger. Then I begin to put them together. For the next two or three hours a bit of competition emerges between Abd al-Rahim and me. Both of us seem to need the screwdriver at the very same instant, then the shears at the very same instant, then the spool of wire, the tape, the glue. Our hands reach, our eyes meet, we scrabble over the table to be the first to lay hands on each necessary item. We use our hard-won tools longer than required, just to goad the other into an anger of impatience. When we are at last done, a vaguely jack-in-the-box-shaped object rests on his end of the table, and, on my end, there is a fully assembled bomb.

Abd al-Rahim adjusts the jack-in-the-box on the table so that it faces me. He turns the crank. The gears connect, the springs groan, the jack-in-the-box emerges, but only slowly and only lopsidedly, as though it is drugged. It does not spring forth. Abd al-Rahim shrugs.

"Not bad," he says. "Not bad for a first try."

I do not turn the crank on my bomb.

***

The day Bashar and his family fled Baghdad, he left me a note on official ministerial letterhead. It read:

The vendors of Al-Kindi Street have closed their shops. The parks we thought would fill with musicians and lovers contain only roving bands of teenagers who pretend their crimes are justified by jihad. This is no life for my family. We are leaving. Perhaps somewhere far from here I will open a restaurant or a bowling alley! I wish you and yours the best of luck here. You are braver than me to persevere.

Politically, this message was something I expected. Bashar had begun transferring more and more of his job responsibilities to me and, with the incoming cabinet, newly formed after Iraq's first free elections, we saw our duties decreasing. Ministers from Sunni families like ours were pushed aside, despite our skills and knowledge. The Shia ruled in the government and on the streets of Baghdad, both by virtue of their numbers and through violence, neighborhood against neighborhood, with the result that most Sunni families left the capital for Anbar Province to the west.

Nor was Bashar's sudden departure emotionally unexpected. Nadia had become more and more daring in her temptations. She would wait for Bashar to step away from us. She would wait for him to leave, and then she would approach me, pretend to make conversation with me, but really only say unmentionable things, forbidden words and ideas, fantasies. She might blow softly in my ear. She might lick or nip at my neck. She might, when no one was watching, step behind some semiprivate barrier—a hedge on one of the manicured lawns, a half wall in a restaurant, an open car door in a parking lot—and lift the gauzy lengths of her skirt, quickly and flirtatiously, to show me her smooth dark skin and the plain silken panties hiding her sex.

She was full of suggestions:

"If you return home for your lunch today, I will be happy for your visit."

"Bashar is traveling to Nasiriyah for two days. I would like you to come help me move some furniture in our living room."

"*Perhaps you should give me a key to your house so that I can make sure you are safe at night.*"

I don't think such lewdness came naturally to her. I think it was partially a product of her experiences in Chicago, soap-opera ideas of infidelity and drama. I also think it was partially, and more importantly, a cover, a way to prevent us from discussing the really hurtful matter that lay between us.

She tried to broach this subject once, one such moment, saying, "What is it about her, this Annie, that I don't have?"

I thought about it for a bit before answering her. It was nothing I could express well, but I tried my best.

"You're normal," I said.

She just frowned and went back to her previous method of attack, keeping me on edge, frustrated, painfully aware of her desire for me. Bashar surely suspected her. She was only partially discreet. But what could he do? Nothing, except to uproot his family once again and restart his life somewhere quiet, somewhere safe, somewhere more traditional. Somewhere like Safwan.

25

الثلاثاء وليلى غائبة

Tuesday and Layla Is Absent

LAYLA SHIES AWAY FROM her habitual evening visits. When she is absent I look for her always. I look for her standing in the shadow of my store, appearing there suddenly, magically. I listen for her whispering voice behind me, trying to surprise me. I wait for her to come rolling into town on a unicycle or zooming toward me at some inopportune moment wearing a harlequin mask and roller skates.

She does not come.

I count convoys passing. I wait for the special convoy of buses that is sent south to Camp Bucca every four days. Perhaps it will come today, a day early, because of the possibility that the sandstorm created a backlog of prisoners destined to travel south, a backlog the Americans might fill by sending an extra convoy outside the normal schedule. That extra convoy would be big news, a big problem I would need to discuss with Sheikh Seyyed Abdullah. It would change the flow, the expectation we have developed: one convoy every four days, four buses in each, for a total of about two hundred prisoners. But no such additional, provisional convoy passes me. And Layla never appears in the shadow of my little shack, here on the outskirts of Safwan in the illegal market.

She does not come to visit me for our habitual evening talk, and I think it is Abd al-Rahim's hovering presence that scares her. She has not shied away from me except maybe for a day or two, when I have been angry at her blasphemous ways. Then she has returned with a freshness and a vigor that make me wonder whether there had indeed ever been a break in our visits, an absence in my new life hollowed out into the exact shape of her small and sparkling self.

I think she shies away because she has felt the feral lingering of Abd al-Rahim's gaze, his unhealthy, unholy fascination coupled with his disregard for her. He has measured her with his keen, quick gaze, and she must know she will become utterly disposable once he has used her for the purposes I suppose he contemplates. I hate to think of her fortune should she encounter Abd al-Rahim alone.

That is how I rationalize the fact that she does not visit as usual, does not come to see me in the open, in the evenings, when the town has begun to cool and the people have begun to return to their homes from the market.

Though she does not visit in the evenings, when I arrive this morning—long before Abd al-Rahim has had time to don his clean *dishdasha,* shine his shoes, and trim his mustache—I find the mark of her presence outside my store:

little footprints circling the building. I see them and I follow them so that I, too, circle the shop. With each step I take, my feet trample the traces of her that are left in the fine, dusty earth. Because of this, it seems, after my second revolution, that no such prints, no such evidence, ever existed. I check for her where she had once hidden, under the lean-to door against the back face of my shop, pretending wholeheartedly to be invisible. She is not hidden there. I look closely around the base of the door at the side of the shack. The last of her footprints stop there, two marks that are deeper, more indelible than all the others. These prints face the door directly, capturing a moment of long and earnest contemplation.

Before I open the door I think to myself that Mahmoud on the bridge may have witnessed something, if indeed Layla has circled the shack and paused here, at the door, dreaming of a way to get inside. Mahmoud's task, our personal contract, would seem to require him to note such a thing as a young girl staring at the door of my shop in the thieving hours before morning. Yet as the sun rises across the market, its warm light chasing the shadow of the previous evening down the light poles, down the roadway railings, down the edge of the embankment toward Mahmoud's tent, he only now is wakening. He stretches. He emerges sleepily from his cot into the fresh day. He sees me and salutes. He watches me nervously for a moment. Then he begins to make himself tea.

Of course, I think, he has seen nothing. I wonder if Layla was tempted to steal his Kalashnikov again, sneaking into his tent as she has snuck into the market — without so much as a single glance from any living creature.

I unlock and open the side door. The footprints do not continue inside the shack. I look closely. The wooden floor might not show the prints as easily as the ground outside, but the floor is not perfectly clean, and unless she blew dust from her palm to cover her tracks on the way out, she truly did not step inside. The prints stop at the threshold. Though she left no mark of her presence in the shack, I see another little gift, a package very similar to yesterday's gift: a plain box with a blue silk ribbon and an orange desert flower. The box rests squarely in the middle of my store, farther from the side door than Layla could reach, even if the doorway had been open for her to enter. Perhaps, I think, she grew wings, lifted so softly, so gently in the air as to not have disturbed the delicate dust prints she left outside. Perhaps she hovered for a moment in the middle of the shop. Somehow, she got in.

I enter the shop and pick up the present. Then I look outside the door again, quickly, guiltily. Abd al-Rahim is nowhere to be seen. Only a few other shops have opened, owners and their hired men sliding shuttered windows apart, arranging chairs and tables and cushions under canopies where potential customers will sit in shelter from the heat, and hanging freshly plucked chickens from wires on the roof of Jaber's open-air butcher shop just down the road. Among these industrious people Abd al-Rahim is nowhere to be seen. He will not arrive for at least an hour, certain as the rising and setting of the sun. This I know even after only a few days employing him. He is no early riser.

I duck into my shack again. I haven't opened my front window. That corrugated sheet remains firmly locked in place. Through the chinks around its edges the morning sun now shines, casting nearly horizontal rays that light the swimming dust I have disturbed in my motions about the room. As I open the package, I think about the last gift Layla left me, the blue silk that became in my dream a flowing scarf of water wreathing and haloing her dream form. I almost expect, by extending the illogic of the dream, that this package might contain water, nothing more than water, beaded up into a single teardrop of quicksilver, self-contained and animated.

The present, when I open it, is mundane in the extreme. Another length of cloth. Cotton, this time. White, finely woven Egyptian cotton. Good-quality stuff. I wonder briefly before I fold it and return it to its box and hide the box behind some mobile phones on the upper shelf of the store, I wonder where Layla obtained the money for these gifts. I wonder how she could afford such luxuries. I make no connection with my own gifts for Ulayya until very much later that day. Then, suddenly, I say to Abd al-Rahim, "Have you already delivered my second gift to the house of Ali ash-Shareefi?"

"Certainly," he says. "Just as you ordered."

"What was in it?" I ask.

He looks puzzled. We've discussed the gifts so many times, how could I possibly forget the contents?

"The cotton," he says. "Just as we agreed: silk, cotton, linen, jewelry, crystal, clothes, and henna. The seven gifts I purchased on your behalf. One for each day. This being the second day, it is the cotton."

"And you're sure that the gift was, indeed, delivered to the ash-Shareefi house? It wasn't left lying about? It wasn't accidentally forgotten? It wasn't stolen? You didn't rely on someone else to deliver the package, did you?"

"I put it into the hands of the guard at the gate of the house myself. I did nothing between the time when you handed me the box," he says, looking defensive, "and when I turned the box over to the care of the guard."

My relationship with Abd al-Rahim has taken a big step toward its proper form now. I continue to despise him while still seeing enough of myself in him to make me painfully aware of my own faults and failures, to make me aware of the pathways in my life I have left untaken. This is the proper attitude for a mentor, the type of mentor Sheikh Seyyed Abdullah expected I would become for this nephew of his. And now that Abd al-Rahim's will has been bent by my pliers, my threatening pliers, he has assumed the necessary deference toward me that an apprentice should exhibit. All along, his efforts have been adequate, if not exactly skilled, but his conduct has been aloof, slouching, too cool by far, and casting a sneer of disapproval over everything pastoral, over everything here that in any way might be deemed inferior to Baghdad. Trust and blind obedience—from fear at first and then from the promise of material gain—that is the proper attitude for an apprentice of the type Seyyed Abdullah intends me to use to speed and ease my work.

Indeed, the many things I must do this week will be impossible without an assistant. Most important, I must let nothing interrupt the rhythm of my life, my store's life, my observations, my camouflage. So all the details of the wedding, and now also the execution of the minutiae associated with our planned bombing, all these details require an assistant.

"We go to Bashar's café for dinner tonight," I tell Abd al-

Rahim as the sun nears the point, low in the sky, where it is when habitually I close shop, where it is when habitually Layla makes her visits.

Abd al-Rahim does not reply for some moments. He is busy sweeping the ground at the front of the shack, the sides of the shack, behind the shack. I mentioned the dust to him merely because it was on my mind, Layla's footprints outside, the lack of her footprints inside. I said nothing to him about those footprints. I did not want to clue him in to the idea that she might visit this place alone, in the early morning darkness, a time when she would be defenseless against him. I merely mentioned the dust, and the reference gave me cause to daydream. Yet Abd al-Rahim, in his new deferential attitude, took the words as a reproach. He began cleaning, sweeping.

After a few swishes of his broom, he asks, "Together?"

"Yes," I say. "That is the meaning of the word *we*. We will dine together at Bashar's."

I can't tell if he wants to dine with me or not. I can't tell if the idea pleases him or if I have interrupted some other plans he may have made for the evening.

To whet his appetite I add, "Before I finish my meal, when the evening has grown truly dark, you will leave the restaurant, go to my home, and retrieve the jack-in-the-box."

I hear him stop sweeping. He leans his broom against the wall of the shack with a soft tap, the wooden handle butting against the thin, cheap plywood wall.

"Tonight already?" he asks.

"Why not? No better time to start than now." I discover that I am anxious, excited, like a child at play. I wait another moment for him to respond. He offers no advice, provides no commentary on the great and metropolitan methods of bombing and its associated martyrdom as practiced in Baghdad, Baghdad, Baghdad.

"That okay with you?" I ask when he neither responds nor appears in person to look at me with the proper awe, wonder, approval, and worship. A few more moments pass. Still he does not reply. I wonder if he has gotten cold feet. I try again: "I want the jack. In truth, it is the jack that I want for tonight. The one you built, not mine."

Still no response. Annoyed, I turn around from my work arranging and rearranging the merchandise on my store shelves, being sure to keep the box containing Layla's latest gift of cotton well hidden. I turn around and lean out over the counter at the front of the shack.

"I want the jack," I say once again, this time louder and with a note of aggravation in my voice, just in case he needs a reminder of my capacity to get violent with him. I wish I had the pliers or the wire cutter from last night, a nice prop for the raised, threatening hand. "The jack, I say!"

"What's 'the jack'?" says a new voice.

I lean even farther over the edge of my counter and look around the side of my shop in the direction of downtown Safwan. I am startled at what I see: an interpreter who works for the Americans stands in the shadow just where Layla usually appears. Behind him I see several soldiers in a small group, fanning out in positions around my shop. The interpreter is a Kuwaiti man all of us merchants and towns-folk know, at least a little, for he has worked in Safwan since the beginning of this second American war. He has worked for lieutenant after lieutenant as the American units cycle home every few months to be replaced by new troops. He is their continuity in Safwan.

Irritatingly, this man insists in speaking Fus'ha, the high Arabic of newscasts and professors. I think it makes him feel superior to us. To me, the sound of his voice recalls a particular professor from my time at Al-Mustansiriya University, before I went to America. That man had a long gray mustache, a drooping mouth, and perfect diction. His words came out in discrete little packages, like gunfire, like clear glass baubles floating in an aquarium. No living language sounds so clean. Yet that is the sound the voice of this Kuwaiti man recalls to my mind: glass baubles, droopy mustaches.

The American lieutenant stands only a few feet away from his interpreter. After a moment, when he has seen to the dispersion of his troops, he, too, approaches me. Like all the soldiers and like the Kuwaiti interpreter, he wears a bulletproof vest, a helmet, and dark and shiny Oakley sunglasses. Two Humvees idle on either side of the road some distance from us. I marvel that I did not hear their engines, their approach.

I look about me to see where Abd al-Rahim has gone, to determine why Abd al-Rahim hasn't warned me. I see him at last, quite far off, walking away as quickly as he can through the blue-tiled arch and into the maze of streets in the older part of Safwan. He has lifted a fold of his *dishdasha* to partially conceal his face. He has fled. He has deserted me. Cold feet or too hot a situation, I cannot tell.

"Surprised?" asks the interpreter. "We came from the town hall meeting and the lieutenant wanted to stop to see you. We've been watching you."

I have nothing to say to the man. He hasn't even greeted

me or wished me a good afternoon as is customary and proper. I turn back to the mobile phones on my shelf. I show him the same respect he shows me.

"What did you mean when you said 'the jack'?" he asks me again.

I try to ignore him, but in my mind I fumble for an explanation:

It is harmless...

It is nothing...

A toy, a game...

A little entertainment for my nights alone...

It's just something I take apart and put back together, a neurosis...

I try to find something harmless to say, but everything seems like a lie. Everything is a lie. The blood drains from my face as I feel the interpreter's gaze fixed on the back of my head.

Just then, though, the lieutenant pulls the interpreter aside. They have a short conversation together. I look around my store, hoping there might be some way to gracefully run away. A moment later their talk ends. Together they approach my store and lean even more casually over the counter. Their two heads are shaded by the canopy of my tin roof.

The lieutenant speaks to me with the sort of slow exaggeration usually reserved for the aged and hard of hearing.

"Dear Merchant, I Want To Ask You Something," he says, looking at me and then motioning for the Kuwaiti to translate his English words into Arabic.

The Kuwaiti says only: "Storekeeper, I want to know what this 'jack' you speak of is."

I have understood the lieutenant perfectly well. Most Iraqis know at least some English, so perhaps my slight startle of a reaction, when I hear the interpreter purposely ignore the words he was supposed to translate, is excusable.

"My Problem Is Kind Of Difficult," the lieutenant says. Again, he motions for the Kuwaiti to translate for me.

"You will pretend," says the interpreter, "that I translate correctly. That way you and I can have a real conversation while this American says whatever silly thoughts have inspired him to come here into your godforsaken market. If you don't pretend well enough, if you don't play along like a nice little boy, I have influence enough on the Kuwaiti side of the border to shut down your business and the businesses of your future father-in-law."

I nod to show that I understand. I look at the lieutenant and smile. He smiles back at me. His teeth are white. I wonder if they are fake. I wonder if they are robot teeth. I want to tap them with a chisel to see if the white enamel reveals a Terminator metallic alloy underneath. He is too clean-faced, too fair-haired, though he's sweating a little so that his cheeks flush pink. His dark sunglasses seem like a shield for his youth and he holds himself in such a way that he seems to be compensating for his age, for his good looks, for his cleanliness— chest out, chin high, a wad of chewing tobacco protruding from his lower lip.

The Kuwaiti approves of my conduct, my appearance of unworried greeting. He, too, smiles at me, an imperious smile. We all smile at each other.

The lieutenant speaks again, at last more naturally, the smiles relaxing him: "I am sorry. Introductions before we go any further. My name is Boyer. I am in charge of the

American patrols on the road to the west of Safwan. All the convoys that go north and south, my men protect them."

"Nod and smile in return," says the interpreter, "and tell me a little about yourself. You are new here and different from the other store owners. You carry yourself differently. Are you from Basra Province?"

"*Tah-sharafna,*" I say to the lieutenant. "Pleased to meet you." And, to the interpreter, I say, "I sell mobile phones and subscriptions to satellite TV."

"Your name?" asks the interpreter.

His question catches me off guard, the subtlety of it. I have forgotten in the days since I began my work here the importance of names. Everyone in Safwan accepts me as Abu Saheeh, an honorary name, a joking title, maybe, enough to be known and to do business in an illegal market without causing too much commotion, especially since my real name has at least some connection with the Shia and the southern people. But the name Abu Saheeh won't work for this conversation. Presenting it would seem too glib and informal. The interpreter wants my family name. I put my hand over my heart again. I bow a little. I try to buy time as I scroll through a mental list, people I know, families I know. Something convincing. The interpreter has worked in Safwan a long while, so he knows all the families. He knows I am not ash-Shareefi. He knows I am not a member of Sheikh Seyyed Abdullah's clan. He will also know my own clan, ash-Shumari, a name I will not give him. Perhaps the Americans, and through them this Kuwaiti interpreter, are concerned that one of their government officials has gone missing. Perhaps there has been a bulletin on me, a wanted man, throughout the country.

On the other hand, perhaps they are lazy, careless, unaware, uninformed. Perhaps I am safe. Either way, I will not take the chance.

I say, at last, "Bashar."

"That's a first name," says the interpreter. "Family name?"

The lieutenant interrupts again, somewhat annoyed with the Kuwaiti. "If you're done making friends with him already, can we get to business?"

I steel myself for the tough questions that will follow. The interpreter knows I am getting married. He knows the business I run and the businesses Ali ash-Shareefi runs. What else does he know? The brown packages? The items smuggled across the border? Has he seen me with Layla?

The lieutenant and the interpreter talk to each other again. They argue. I can't give them Bashar's actual family name: Dulaimi, the former defense minister's family. Though it is a big tribe, the name would be suspicious here. A Baathist name. I like the idea of a big tribe, though, the anonymity of it, the countless number of men named Ali or Kareem or Muhammad or Bashar within the ranks of such a tribe. I think of other large families. I think of Layla. Suddenly, spontaneously, a name occurs to me. I blurt it out, interrupting the conversation between the interpreter and his boss.

"Al-Mulawwah," I say.

"Bashar al-Mulawwah," says the interpreter to his boss.

"Now we're getting somewhere," says the lieutenant, an aside to the interpreter.

Facing me again, the lieutenant puts a sheaf of about five papers on the counter in front of me.

"I need you to sign these," he says. "I want to adopt the little girl who told us stories in our mess hall during the night of the sandstorm. She told us you are her guardian, the only person responsible for her, and I need your permission to bring her back with me to the United States. She'll go to a good school and have all the advantages of life in the USA. What do you think?"

This further confuses me. My mind whirls. The Kuwaiti continues to ask me difficult questions as I ponder the paperwork the lieutenant has placed in front of me. I answer him somewhat at random. I look through the papers somewhat at random.

Layla? Adopted? America?

"Why do you talk to yourself?"

Layla to become the daughter of this American man, this lieutenant?

"I am married," the lieutenant says. "I have a good family back in Illinois, which is a state in the very middle of the United States. The big city of Chicago. You may have heard of it?"

"To which part of the family of al-Mulawwah do you belong? From which city? Are you Yemeni? Who are your relatives? Why have you moved here to Safwan?"

"We need your signatures for the adoption."

"What's this 'jack' of which you have spoken? Is it a code word?"

"It will be a few weeks, a few weeks for the paperwork to clear after you sign. Then she can come home with me when I am done with my duties here in Iraq."

Be glad for her. Be glad.

A convoy draws near the western bypass, slows as it begins its turn off the highway and onto the smaller road that leads to the Kuwaiti border. Instinctively, we all turn our heads to watch it. The noise of it is distant but penetrating. When it has passed I take the papers from the counter in front of me, fold them, and put them in the inside pocket of my *ghalabia*.

"I will think about it," I say to the interpreter in Arabic—the low Arabic of the market, the low Arabic of the southern marshes. "You will have an answer from me in a few days' time."

* * *

I first saw Sheikh Seyyed Abdullah at one of the many interminable meetings at the headquarters of the American forces in the Baghdad Green Zone. Bashar was not there. So it must have occurred after he and his family fled, though I'm not quite sure.

"And now Dr. ash-Shumari will brief you on the status of the health-care system," said the American officer in charge of that particular briefing.

Around the horseshoe-shaped table in the bare-walled conference room sat various military personnel as well as members of the elected governing councils from some of the regions of Iraq, cliques of men, each faction with a seat at the table.

"At last we have ironed out a system to ensure the flow of medicine to northern hospitals," I said, starting my briefing. "The supplies will, at least temporarily, come through with American military transports from Kuwait. This is the only way to ensure that critical items reach their destinations."

I noticed one of the well-dressed, fine-suited men in the room lean forward from his place along the side wall of the room. He whispered in the ear of the deputy governor for Basra Province. The deputy governor then raised his hand.

"Yes?" I asked. "What may my honored colleague be pleased to know?"

"Will the Americans still pay customs at the border crossing in Safwan?"

"If they come across on the American convoys, through the American military's own crossing point, customs won't be necessary," said one of the American officers at the table. "It would be like paying the government to pay itself."

As the officer said this I watched the man by the wall. His face was impassive. But the face of the deputy governor for Basra flushed red.

"This will decrease Basra's revenues," the man said.

"It will make medicines cheaper and more available throughout Iraq," said the officer.

I was glad not to have to argue the point. I knew what was happening. It wasn't Basra's revenues that would suffer. It was baksheesh charged by officials at the civilian border crossing that would decline.

I noted, again, the passivity of the well-dressed man. He was really the man in charge of the Basra faction. It was his revenues the new plan endangered. Yet he seemed content to let the Basra deputy conduct the futile argument with the American officer.

I thought to myself that if Bashar were here, he would know this man's name.

I filed the incident away in my mind for future reference, labeling the well-dressed man as the true power holder on the Kuwaiti border. The Americans would be wise to make a friend of him.

26

مساء الثلاثاء

Tuesday Evening

ABD AL-RAHIM DOES NOT come to dine with me at Bashar's café this evening, as I instructed him to do. I eat alone as usual. In fact, I am even more alone than usual. Bashar does not visit my table. I am unsure of his whereabouts until one of his employees tells me he has gone to Basra to make arrangements for an engagement feast he plans to cater. Of course it is my engagement feast, but the employee does not know this. I wave the man away from me. I eat my falafel slowly, dipping little bits of it in hummus with my fingers.

I spread the lieutenant's adoption papers in front of me and stare at them. I read all the fine print. I look thoughtfully at the several places where my signature is required: adoption, naturalization, a waiver of any legal rights I might have with regard to Layla's future, a waiver of my visitation rights so that no problem arises, no future requests for seeing her that might facilitate my emigration from Iraq. I am not part of the deal, beyond the necessary permissions. I wonder what name I will use when I sign each block. Bashar al-Mulawwah. What a dumb-sounding name!

The cord that connects me to Layla will be cut.

I try to guess whether Layla knows anything of this matter. I wonder if the American lieutenant has asked her if she wishes such a thing. I do not doubt what her opinion will be, what her decision must be. I hear her voice in my mind ringing with enthusiasms, speculations, newly birthed associations. She will live next to Sharon Stone. She will ride in Arnold Schwarzenegger's motorcade. She will throw a shoe at George Bush. Surely the lieutenant has come under her spell in the same way that I have. And his solution is better than any I have pondered. It will be no easy thing for him to navigate the extradition and adoption laws, but still better than any future Iraq could possibly offer Layla, unless I were to adopt her myself, unless I were to leave this place with her and return to America or establish a new life somewhere else, France or Australia, Sweden or Fiji.

As Bashar and I sat together one previous night, he brought up another idea, an easier idea, an idea that was like an elephant in the room, too big and too obvious for either of us to ignore.

"Of course, you could simply marry her, if you're so concerned about this market girl," he said.

I shivered a little, inwardly, but didn't say anything in response.

"It's the traditional way to resolve such a situation," he said. "We're in the countryside now. Things are different here. No one will find fault with you for marrying a girl her age. It is what Muhammad himself, Peace Be Upon Him, advocated for the widowed wives and daughters of those men who fought in the great opening of the world at the beginning of Islam. It is one of the reasons he permitted a man to marry more than one woman, so that they might have shelter and protection."

"I'm too American now to consider such a thing," I answered.

This put an end to the conversation. It put an end to Bashar's suggestion. But as I walk across town to my house, I think about it. It's not just the concept of marrying someone so young that bothers me. It's Layla herself. I think of her too much as a daughter to truly contemplate the idea of marriage. She might think about marriage, but I do not. Bashar might think about marriage, but I will not.

I stop walking before I reach the military road, a few hundred feet from the house, and watch from the shifting shadows of an alleyway as a convoy passes northward in the night. Truck after truck, diesel fumes and dust cut by swaths of jouncing headlights, some sulfur yellow, some halogen bright. The drivers in them are fresh, wide-eyed, heading north into the war zone from the safety of their homes and workplaces in Kuwait. How many similar trips have they made? How many rolls of the dice have they taken on these dangerous roads? So far they've won each roll. They live to drive northward. Each trip, they have escaped—narrowly or maybe even blindly, blithely—a fate following them closely. But for how long will their luck hold?

These truck drivers are not Americans. They are contracted Indians, Pakistanis, Sri Lankans, Bangladeshis, Laotians. They speak a thousand languages and are herded north, north, north, always north, by Humvees nipping at their heels. Those Humvees are the only place where actual Americans work on convoy duty: the Winstons, the Davids, the Patricks. The American soldiers don't expose themselves in the thin-skinned semis. They are cocooned beneath layers of Humvee steel.

The rumble of this convoy's passage lasts five minutes, ten minutes. I don't time it exactly. I just stand and watch. When they are gone and when the dust has settled, I cross the road and disappear from the floodlit area of the American occupation into the shadows that surround the cluster of newer homes where my own house is located.

I enter my front gate. To my surprise, the light in my kitchen glows. I see it from the gate and it makes me pause, makes me stop in my barren courtyard to consider. I try to remember if I left it lit when I went to the shop this morning. I have no clear recollection of turning it on or of turning it off, yet I never by habit leave it on. Each day I check off my morning list of chores and habits as regularly as I check off my list of daily observances at work. It is a more mundane checklist by far, but regular: lift head from table; wave once or twice to ward away the spirits and smokes of the dream from the space above and behind my head; listen for the ticking of the clock, the crowing of roosters; listen for the rumble of convoys, that ever-present background noise without which I would feel hollow; wash face, hands, neck, arms; unroll prayer rug and perform the morning *salaam;* prepare coffee, just one cup, an American thing, coffee in the morning, and then a flatbread, jam;

robe myself; clean my teeth; stare at the organized chaos on my kitchen table, how it grows, changes, modifies itself each night as my hands wander over it. Then I leave for the shop, turning off the lights, shutting the blinds, locking the doors. That is the routine, sometimes varied in time, waking before morning light, waking at first appearance of the light, waking somewhat after the sun has risen, but always those same steps.

No, I didn't fail to turn off the lights this morning. I followed every step. I remember them all now, clearly, all the steps, even to the point of feeling again in the first fingertip of my right hand the smooth cold nub of the light switch as I backed out the front door and flicked it down to darken the room.

The glow from the window spills flat and orange on the ground to one side of my courtyard, a pool of lit dust. Rather than enter through my front door, I first step around the bright patch, sneak toward the window, use my arms to pull myself to the height of the iron-barred pane of glass. I look inside. To my relief, I see only Abd al-Rahim there. He has a screwdriver in one hand, a roll of duct tape at the ready on the table in front of him. His back is bent over the table, over my jack-in-the-box. He is working, a study of concentration, and though he squarely faces the window, he does not shift his focus from the work, does not notice me spying on him. The door between the kitchen and the main entryway, the hallway, remains open behind him, as if he entered in haste and did not care to hide his presence. He is at work on the project I assigned him, and I get the feeling he works so as to appease me, an unspoken apology for fleeing from the Americans this morning. My heart warms for him, doing this little thing for me. I imagine that he will apologize in words, grand, eloquent, rhetorical words, when I enter. I will pretend to scold him, but in truth I will be drawing him nearer to me. I will reject the improvements he has made to the jack-in-the-box. I will reprimand him. But I can't truly fault him for his excess of caution in the moment when the Americans approached us.

The muscles of my forearms begin burning from the effort of supporting myself a foot or two above the ground. I release both hands and let myself fall. The short drop produces a muffled thud, just enough to draw Abd al-Rahim's attention. I hear him put down the jack-in-the-box and the screwdriver.

"Who's there?" he says.

I am about to reply when I hear another voice, a woman's voice, from inside my house.

"Just me," the voice says. "Your dear old friend."

Quickly I lift myself to the window again, grabbing the same iron bars. I look inside. Abd al-Rahim has spun to face the door on the opposite side of the room. He holds a gun low at his waist, a sleek black pistol pointed in the direction of the female intruder, but hidden from her, too, hidden behind a fold of his draping *dishdasha*. I can see it plainly from the window because he does not attempt to hide it from behind, a direction from which he expects no interference.

I see no woman. I look from corner to corner of the room. I see no woman, but neither does Abd al-Rahim. He says, "Show yourself."

I am surprised, but only momentarily, to hear how well he imitates my voice. "Show yourself," he renders in a tone twenty years older than his own, a deeper, gruffer, more firmly controlled voice. He is clever enough to hide himself as long as he can, even while the voice of this woman, the voice he and I have heard, seems more seductive than threatening. He is cautious. Abd al-Rahim is far more cautious than I would have thought.

"To one like me who has visited America and who has partaken in its culture of decadence, the words *show yourself* could have many meanings," the female voice, still hidden, says in heavy tones.

I recognize the voice now: Nadia.

Abd al-Rahim lowers his pistol. He secretly lifts the fabric at the back of his *dishdasha* and slides the barrel of the weapon into the waistband of his pants. He looks down, straightens the folds of the overgarment to make it look normal. He does a better job hiding the weapon than Seyyed Abdullah's bodyguard does. He has been trained, and the inadvertent display of this training gives me a moment's pause: the rhetoric in front of the mosque, the training. Who sent him here to Safwan? Is he an agent of Iran? I know Seyyed Abdullah has connections that point toward Iran, as do most successful Shia. For example, it is known that Seyyed Abdullah studied at Qom for a period. He is a man of the book, a minor religious figure. It would be natural to accept one of Iran's undercover Revolutionary Guard into this town, *his* town. Such a simple thing, hiding a weapon. But to do it well requires training, and Abd al-Rahim has done it with deftness, speed, and fluency while keeping his eyes focused in front of him where he expects Nadia soon to reveal herself.

The soft sound his hands make passing over and arranging the fabric of his *dishdasha* is matched, echoed, by a slightly more voluminous but similarly soothing whoosh of cloth from Nadia's direction. Abd al-Rahim stands straight and puts his hands in front of him, forcibly relaxed.

The next moment, Nadia steps into the doorway opposite the place where I watch. I can see her over Abd al-Rahim's shoulder. She has unclothed herself and she stands naked and unashamed in the place where the light of my kitchen first touches the dark safety of my hallway. A shadow snakes over her sensuous middle and divides her body, one half lit, one half hidden.

"God bless America," Abd al-Rahim says in his own, higher-pitched voice as he advances toward Nadia like a man walking in his sleep.

He no longer pretends to be me. His body eclipses Nadia, passing directly in front of me, between the spot where I watch and the place where she has undressed. He continues walking. Her face and her nakedness emerge from behind the blockage of his body, bit by bit, as he proceeds.

I have never seen her completely unclothed. She is lovely, a full woman, no girl. Her hands are on her hips, swelling hips that have been changed by childbirth, made fuller and glassier, rounded and whitened from lack of daylight, marked by their forbiddenness and made more alluring because of the shocking difference between that which had been secret and that which is made suddenly and wholly bare. Above her hips, her belly slims like a tapering candle but neither so suddenly nor so deeply as to show at its top the outline of her ribs. There is a layer of smoothness, fat and fullness and cushion, even before the swell of her breast shadows her lovely waist.

I am guilty, my gaze lingers too long. I notice too late that

Nadia does not concentrate on the figure of Abd al-Rahim gliding toward her. She stares past him. She looks at the window from which I watch her. Slowly her openness and her unabashedness dissolve. One of her hands covers the black center of her pubis, while the other whips across her breasts to push them tight against her. White flesh bulges on either side of her pressing arm. Her eyes widen. They flicker away from me, glancing at Abd al-Rahim to confirm that he is indeed not the man she had expected to find in my kitchen. She looks at him and fear touches her face, a black shadow that leaves the counterfeit blackness of the kohl around her eyes looking false and frivolous. She does not recognize Abd al-Rahim at all.

Abd al-Rahim does not notice her fear. He is focused now. He is unthinking. He is animal. He sees her before him, but his preoccupation with her physical self obscures from him her fright, her withdrawal, all symptoms deeper than the skin. Or maybe the fright and withdrawal themselves are alluring to him. When he reaches her, he pulls her to him and forces her arms and hands from sheltering her shame. She resists, but only slightly, squirming and striking him softly on the chest and on the shoulders in ways that only serve to increase his desire.

All throughout this Nadia looks at me until finally, when Abd al-Rahim pauses to remove his clothes, she mouths the single word *help* in the direction of the window from which I watch.

I drop to the ground just as I hear the heavy thud of Abd al-Rahim's pistol hitting my kitchen floor amid the general discard of his clothes. He has forgotten it, forgotten the place where he stowed it before Nadia showed herself to him. I crouch for a second beneath the window and listen. Abd al-Rahim groans as he falls upon her, but she remains deerlike, noiseless. I can't determine, by listening, whether they grope on the floor together or whether they remain standing. It does not matter. He will take her. He controls her already. She does not resist, does not scream. She does not give away the fact that she might have a rescuer near at hand. She will submit, and he will enjoy her submission.

I enter the front door of my house. I move stealthily. In the darkness I see again Nadia's naked form replayed in my mind, the silhouette of it, the curving hourglass. I feel myself stir, not only from pure and painful animal longing, the likes of which Abd al-Rahim now feels, but also from a sharper and deeper place. I ignored her in America. I ignored her, as best I could, in Baghdad. I ignored her when I felt her watching me from the bowered windows of Bashar's new Safwan home. But I don't ignore her now. I can't ignore her now. She is standing on tiptoe in my memory, waiting for me to kiss her in the garage of my father's mansion. We are children again in my mind, with all the sweetness and promise of life stretching before us.

Nadia, like Abd al-Rahim, begins moaning, though, unlike Abd al-Rahim, her moan is not of pleasure. It's closer to a grunt, containing all the pressure of holding back, of preventing herself from calling out for me to save her. I take another step into the hallway. I hear Nadia shudder. She verges on screaming; her exhalations become intense. I rush forward down the hallway and then stop just at the doorway of the kitchen. I wait in the last bit of shadow before the kitchen light. There I see Abd al-Rahim standing over her. He has already put on his *dishdasha*. He is refastening his pants under the folds of cloth. He picks up his oiled pistol from the floor and puts it back into his belt, hidden again. He has finished with her already. She lays spread wide and breathing heavily on the floor of the kitchen, open to me in all the carnal emptiness a body possesses when it ceases to dazzle. I stop and I watch her for a moment and then, when Abd al-Rahim goes back to the table to work on the jack-in-the-box, leaving Nadia to gather her clothes, I quickly turn and walk from the house, back out the front door and into the darkness of the streets outside.

When the cool night air hits my face, the flush of heat evaporates from me and my thoughts calm. For a moment I don't know what to do and I don't know what to think about what I have seen and what I have done. I want to think that it was more than just cowardice that kept me from intervening. I would have had to kill Abd al-Rahim and I'm not sure I would have succeeded. More than that, I would have had to flee Safwan afterward, for Seyyed Abdullah's loyalty must lie with his family first and must supersede any bonds he and I have forged. It would have been the ruin of everything I have built here, the shop, the coming marriage to Ulayya, my friendship with Layla.

I want to think I am not a coward of this sort, to think first of the things I might lose and then, only second, of Nadia's pain. I begin to justify my actions, telling myself that leaving was, actually, the correct thing to do in order to preserve Nadia's honor. She can be silent. She can return to her family, her shame a private thing, a secret. Had she encountered me alone, as was her intent, the secret would have remained between us, regardless of whether I took advantage of her or not. But had I rescued her from Abd al-

Rahim there would necessarily have ensued a hue and a cry from which her honor could not possibly have emerged intact.

I do not know whether the course I have chosen, through my inaction, was correct. But what has happened is finished already. I cannot go back. I would change so many things, but I cannot go back.

Forgive me, Nadia.

* * *

One particular day as I returned to Umm al-Khanzeer from the Green Zone in Baghdad, I met my brother, Yasin. He approached me in front of one of Saddam's barricaded palaces, a place the American military leadership occupied as their headquarters, surrounded by American tents and American dining halls and American gymnasiums. I carried my briefcase full of papers. I wore a business suit, black, and I had loosened my shirt collar to let heat escape from my chest on the sunny walk home.

"Greetings, brother," Yasin said to me.

I knew it was him. Immediately, even before I saw him, I knew it was him. I tried to ignore him. I tried to walk past him, but he wouldn't let me continue on my walk without acknowledging him. He wouldn't let me pass without stopping, for a moment, right there in the middle of the day in front of all the military might America had brought to our country.

He wore a dishdasha, *leather sandals. Though we looked similar, tall and dark and broad-shouldered, we were differentiated by our costumes and our stances, I straight-backed and hurrying, he easing out from under the shade of a date palm to stand in front of me.*

"You may still join us," he said.

"I have nothing to say to you," I answered.

He put his hands on my shoulders and drew me close as if to kiss me on each cheek, but I turned my face from him.

"Look at you," he said. "All fancied up in your American suit. Have you become a Jew?"

I gave him no satisfaction by replying.

"Certainly you're a Zionist, an occupier, a traitor," he said. "But we know you really want to help Iraq. I've been sent to give you another chance, maybe a last chance."

These words of his did not bother me. He could call me what he wanted. I knew of the strife occurring in the rest of Baghdad, the rest of Iraq, the cleansing of mixed Shia and Sunni neighborhoods, the foothold al-Qaeda had made in our disenfranchised, dissatisfied Sunni former ruling classes. I had long expected a threat like this. I expected, even, to hear the threat delivered from someone close to me. I had thought it might be Nadia's father, Abdel Khaleq, who came to persuade me, a far more difficult man to deny than my brother. Hope remained in my heart if good Sunni men like Abdel Khaleq still resisted al-Qaeda, still strove to make Iraq a better place. Such hope helped me continue my work with the Americans. Such hope helped me deny Yasin.

I ignored Yasin, gritting my teeth and letting him insult me. But he had one deeper, more cutting threat to deliver.

"We've heard of your kafir wife in prison and your half-American, half-Iraqi little—" he said.

This was too much for me.

I launched myself at Yasin. With all my weight, I stepped inside his widespread embracing arms and leveled my shoulder into his chest. The blow sent him sprawling to the ground. He looked at me, there, for a long, hate-filled moment.

"You will regret this," he said.

Then he reached into the front of his dishdasha. *I thought he might take from it a gun or a knife. I thought he might kill me, right then and there. I braced for him to rise. I even lifted my briefcase in front of me, my only weapon. But before he picked himself up from the ground he looked around at the domes and turrets of Saddam's palace, at the weapon-toting troops on the sides of the roads, at the dark-windowed bulletproof SUVs and armored Humvees policing the gated, dusty roads.*

Yasin retracted his hand, empty of any weapon, from the folds of his dishdasha, *picked himself up from the ground, and brushed himself off. Then he walked away from me along a road of dusty American tents and out a side exit, a pedestrian exit. After passing through this fence he disappeared into the Baghdad throng.*

27

الأربعاء ويبتسم ميشيل

Wednesday, Michele Smiles

LAYLA DOES NOT VISIT today, not in the daylight, not face-to-face. Her method has changed. I receive from her the gift as surely as I send, through my emissary, Abd al-Rahim, my own gift to Ulayya. So her presence remains strong with me here, here in my shop, though she no longer stands in shadow under the awning of my little store in the lovely slanting sunshine. Her gifts continue and they continue to match exactly the gifts I provide to Ulayya: today it is linen, fine linen, finely woven, enough to make sheets for the nuptial bed, as is the custom, though I am sure Ulayya's sheets will be silk, imported from Paris, the finest available, at least after our traditional first night together.

Today is not only the seventeenth day since the beginning of Layla's visitations, it is also the thirty-fifth day of business for me since I moved to Safwan. What is more, today is the last normal, uneventful day of my time here. I feel it in my bones now, as the day unfolds. I feel it in the slow and timeless way that the sunlight passes from morning, at its nadir, into its evening goldenness. After a busy week, the calm comes as a relief. I use the lull to think. I luxuriate in the lack of pressing details, the fact that I need not arrange anything, for everything important is already in motion. I need not attend to anything, for the correct patterns are well established. I need not watch the road so closely, or the Americans, or the town, because they have begun to ebb and flow in me and I would sense any disruption as I would sense a quickening of my own heartbeat. The only concern I have is Layla, for she is the wild card, the lightning that might strike me any moment, the unexpected arrival, the thing that could cause me to turn from my decided path. She does not come to me in person, does not visit. And I am glad, almost, not to see her. At a safe distance from me, her presence is like the tickling lift of fine hair on arms and on neck when a thunderstorm passes near, the reminder of lightning without the danger of its shock.

My eyes refocus on the present time and place, and I see on the edge of the road above me Mahmoud once again lounging on his three-legged chair, just exactly as I saw him the first time I noticed him. Indeed, he smokes his cigarette with the same deep concentration while his Kalashnikov rests lazily against the tent behind him. So, too, the men in the shop behind mine play cards the same way they play cards every day. So, too, the chickens are hung in Jaber's store from the same hooks as always. The same flies swarm their carcasses, or at least descendants of the original flies, who repeat an inherited and stable pattern of chicken swarming. This is the way here: centuries, millennia, shifts of time and person and government make only a slight impact. People in this land between the two rivers, Tigris and Euphrates, do what they have done every year, every decade, every lifetime. The set cycle may ripple under the interrupting influence of war. The set cycle may change, slow as geology, wearing away glacially, the language no longer Assyrian, Babylonian, the religion no longer centered on the idolatry of the gods of Baal, but the same people, the same lives, the same skies and rivers and deserts and dreams. Things never change suddenly here. They never leap into robots and American movies. For that reason I feel it keenly: the sense that the tingle at the base of my neck will leave me when Layla leaves, when Layla goes to America to start her life anew with the American lieutenant. I will be like the Ziggurat of Ur, left to crumble in the stillness of time.

When Abd al-Rahim at last arrives at the shop, standing there in the slanting light, he is contrite. Quickly I replay the image of him in my mind, the swift sure stowing of his pistol under the folds of his *dishdasha*. I think of one word to perfectly describe him: *overqualified*. He is overqualified to work and to live in a town such as Safwan. The place is too small for him. Yet when he arrives at my shop he does a good job acting like he wants to learn, like he at least wants to make the effort to blend in. He has brought the repaired jack-in-the-box with him. He offers it to me.

"Not tonight," I say. "I am tired tonight and the pace of the world is such that one day, one night, one moment will not matter."

Abd al-Rahim nods in agreement. He says nothing to me. I wonder if he feels that he will betray himself, betray the liaison he and Nadia experienced, if he speaks too much, too quickly, too loudly. He does not know that I have seen him in the act. He does not know that I already am aware of his transgression. I watch him for signs of overattentiveness and overcompensation. Truly he must fear he will expose himself, yet he is natural. He acts naturally. He has been well taught in the means of disguise, emotional as well as physical. He hides his emotions as well as he hides his pistol.

Finally, as we are closing the shop, Abd al-Rahim says, "I am sorry I fled from the Americans."

I accept his apology, saying, "A young man like you, with all your life ahead, *insha'Allah,* you must be careful, prudent."

"Must be careful," he says, echoing me.

As he turns to walk into town ahead of me I watch for the shadowed outline of his pistol. I want to know if he wears it all the time, or if he only put it on to visit me last night. It isn't odd for a man to wear a pistol here, or a knife. As his uncle Seyyed Abdullah says, "These are dangerous times, lawless times." Nothing strange in wearing a weapon, just strange to wear it so well.

I watch for the outline of the pistol as we walk into town and I do not see it until he plants his right foot and turns, stepping down from the curb into the street. The fabric of his *dishdasha* flows over the hilt of the weapon, catching on it and leaving a minuscule bulge, as if his hip bone projects farther on the right side than on the left. I have not noticed that shadow before. But now I see it. I see it every time he steps. I try not to pay too much attention or to be too joking, too easy, too serious, too harsh. I make myself into a swarm of flies, ubiquitous and everlasting. I hide my knowledge as though in a jack-in-the-box: I am noisy, rancorous, in a great mood, expansive. I tell him stories about Baghdad and America. I reveal myself but I do so only to camouflage the fact that my mind has wrapped itself around him more completely than he knows.

"When I returned to Iraq from America," I tell him, turning toward him and walking half sidewise, crablike, down the road toward Bashar's café, "the first thing I remember when I returned was the smell. It is funny how the body's senses grow immune to such things. America doesn't have strong smells like open-air markets, the rotting vegetables, the rotting fish, sewers flowing uncovered in the streets. Everything is so clean there, so antiseptic."

"So fake," Abd al-Rahim says.

"My bags came off the plane," I say, pretending not to hear him, "and I remember looking at them and feeling like opening them in Iraq would be like opening Iraq to everything American."

Abd al-Rahim spits on the ground. "America," he says. "America is nothing but greed, cowardice, and Israel."

"America is freedom," I say. "America is a torch for the world."

Abd al-Rahim stops walking. Right in the middle of the street he turns to face me. He keeps his expression blank, eyes not meeting mine. He's trying to remain submissive. I watch his right hand, the one closest to his gun, because as he stops walking he uses it to smooth the slight creasing of his clothes over his gun's hilt. It's a telltale sign. His mind drifted to the gun, briefly, at my mention of America, and his hand unconsciously drifted that way, too.

"We're not ready for freedom here," he says, very softly, still submissively. "The people need strong leadership. They need to be ruled."

The thumb of Abd al-Rahim's hand remains relaxed. When he goes for the gun the thumb will open away from his fingers before his hand moves in order to better slide through the slit at the waist of his *dishdasha* and then over the hilt of the weapon hidden underneath. I am sure, if he goes for the gun, he will do so smoothly and quickly. So I watch for his thumb to indicate his intentions. The thumb does not move, but it is ready.

"I have some strange opinions of America," I say. "Especially for a jihadist."

"My uncle cautioned me about this," Abd al-Rahim says.

I smile. It is enough of a confession. I know, from it, why Abd al-Rahim works for me. I know why the sheikh assigned him to me. Abd al-Rahim isn't here to help me. He is Seyyed Abdullah's insurance policy on me, my ticket out of town when I've finished my work. He is overqualified as an apprentice, but perhaps not so overqualified as an insurance policy.

I think of ending that possibility, here, now, in the American way: confronting him immediately in the street, like a gunfight in a spaghetti western, except I don't have Clint Eastwood's steely blue gaze or grizzled chin. Nor do I have a gun. The idea fades. The moment passes. Being gunless at a gunfight is a bad idea. I opt for my rancorous approach once more—pulling Abd al-Rahim closer to me, grabbing him by his shoulder. I drape my arm over him, throwing him off-balance, and I lean on him a little as we continue through the crowded market street toward Bashar's café.

We walk that way, shoulder to shoulder, parting the crowd, until we pass Bashar's busboy Michele heading the opposite way, hurrying toward the overpass bridge with the nightly platter of food for Mahmoud.

Michele smiles when he sees me, recognizing me from Bashar's café and perhaps also from his times passing through the market on the way to Mahmoud's tent. His thin face is washed clean and shining. He averts his gaze from me until I say, "Hello. *Masah il-kheir,* fine evening."

To which, in reply, he touches his right hand to his smooth forehead and says, "Good evening to you. Good evening to you both, gentlemen."

Michele sees Abd al-Rahim. He notices Abd al-Rahim's cosmopolitan dress, the clean clothes, the fine shave, the shined shoes, the folded sunglasses stowed with care in the front breast pocket of his *dishdasha*. He notices how I have thrown my arm around Abd al-Rahim, warmly and trustingly. He finishes his quick examination of us and smiles again, more brightly, aiming the smile at Abd al-Rahim. Abd al-Rahim refuses to say anything. He does not even look directly at Michele.

We part ways, heading in opposite directions.

Abd al-Rahim spits again, and perhaps begins to curse the sort of freedoms Michele represents, saying something like, "In Baghdad this would never—"

Yet before he finishes his sentence a scream silences the crowd around us, continuing and even building in intensity, shrill and loud and shocked, as a ripple of fear causes the people, all of us, to freeze. A smell reaches us, sweet and sickeningly hot. Abd al-Rahim and I turn toward each other.

My mind goes blank for a moment, a sweaty, black moment, and I find that I am holding my brother, Yasin, by the shoulders. I am holding him and shaking him and pounding at him with my hands, clawing at him with my fingers, stabbing at him with a whirling assortment of knives, clean lancets and saws, dirty garden tools. I want to kill him. In my mind I destroy him, pulling him apart limb by limb. I spit on the pieces of him as I toss them from his deteriorating body into the gutter, where the *wadi* dogs come running to fight over his remains.

I blink. I discover I am holding Abd al-Rahim by both shoulders. He isn't Yasin, but I am shaking him, trying to push past him. He won't let me pass.

"Let me go," he says.

I realize where I am. I realize what I am doing. I hear the piercing shriek not far down the street from us. I see my fingers knotted in the fabric of Abd al-Rahim's *ghalabia*. I release my grip. I brush Abd al-Rahim's shoulders, a little clumsily, by way of apology. He shakes himself free of me and runs toward the sound of the scream. He runs back the way we came, back down the street, and after a moment, I, too, run. I follow Abd al-Rahim.

We run toward Michele.

28

الأربعاء والحمض

Wednesday, Acid

ABD AL-RAHIM DOESN'T TAKE his gun out, but I notice that he touches it twice as he pushes ahead of me through the unmoving crowd in the street. When we reach Michele no one from among the mass of people surrounding him has begun doing anything useful. Some of them scream, though their screams are drowned in a scream more intense than anything they could produce themselves. Some of them stare with mouths agape. Most of them simply turn their faces away. One of them falls to his knees and vomits. Yet no one approaches Michele. An empty space, three meters wide, rings the boy.

I see in the open center of the circle Michele's tray of food spilled on the ground. I see shreds of his clothes with vapor rising from them, wafts of curling and hissing smoke, sweetly scented, burningly sweet. I see the boy himself, somehow still upright on one knee. The ground is blackened with moisture around him, maybe his blood, though a stomach-churning steam rises from the damp ground just as it does from his body and from his clothes. He is turned three-quarters away from me so that I see his back, his shirtless back, with a few scraps of white *dishdasha* still clinging to the seared red flesh. He clutches his face with his hands. He scratches his face with clawing fingers. He screams and then, suddenly, his screaming stops. A gurgling, pitched almost as high as his scream, emanates from his face, from his throat, muted in a waterfall of blood. Through it all he remains half-standing, half-kneeling, miraculously though foolishly upright.

I rip off my *dishdasha* and spread it over my arms. I push into the center of the ring of useless observers, panicked observers, and even before I throw my *dishdasha* over Michele's body, even before I push him to the ground, protecting myself with the cloth, I begin giving directions to the people around me.

"You there, water! Buckets of water. Get me water and ice if you can. The boy with the wheelbarrow full of ice should be near."

"You there, get bags of concrete from the market. Wael's shop is not too far from here. The powder will ease the burning."

"You, clean rags. Take off your *dishdashas,* all of you. I need them. Tear them into strips. Clean rags to bandage him."

Yet nobody moves. Nobody. They are as silent and as actionless as I was in the moments I watched Abd al-Rahim rape Nadia.

I spread the weight of my body on Michele's jerking and cramping body, pinning his arms to his sides in order to prevent him from doing additional damage to his face, flattening him to expand his chest and to increase the air capacity of his lungs, rolling him to brush away any residues of acid not yet absorbed into his clothes or his body. That is the sweet smell, the hot, burning, sweet smell: acid.

The boy still breathes. Most of the skin has been eaten from his face. What the acid hasn't destroyed his fingers have decimated. His eyes and mouth are burned away, gaping holes. The flesh and muscle of his right cheek, up to the suborbital ridge, are absent. Slick sinew and the bones of his teeth and jaw protrude. The tissue in the back of his throat, a mass of red, swells and congeals, emitting thick bubbles of blood and gore that drool through the split cheek with each exhalation. I realize I will have to perform a makeshift tracheotomy before he drowns in his own fluids.

"Abd al-Rahim," I yell. "Get me a pipe. A plastic pipe."

I get no response from Abd al-Rahim. I yell for him again. I continue yelling for him.

I yell, "Abd al-Rahim!"

"Abd al-Rahim!" I say. "Where are you?"

But he does not respond. I pump at Michele's chest. I put my fingers in Michele's mouth to try to clear the blockage from his throat. The swollen tissue collapses, swallows my hand, engulfs it. Nothing solid remains for me to clear from the path of his breath. I put my mouth to the place where Michele's mouth had been. I try to breathe for him but I cannot form a seal on his skinless, slippery face. The acid, now diluted in spit and blood and phlegm, still has power enough to burn my lips. I feel the chafed surfaces of them, dry and burning. I push my breath into the cavity where Michele's mouth had been, but the breath will not penetrate. His mouth fills, blood gushes from it, but none of my precious oxygen enters his lungs.

When at last I stand to look for Abd al-Rahim, Michele has stopped breathing. He is dead. I am surrounded by staring, useless townsfolk.

"Where is Abd al-Rahim?" I ask the people.

I speak quietly but my voice sounds loud now that the worst of the chaos is finished. No one answers me. The street has grown suddenly silent.

I am about to condemn Abd al-Rahim in my mind. He has fled twice while I have been in danger, in need of his help, his protection. I tell myself that Abd al-Rahim is truly no servant of mine. He is only Seyyed Abdullah's spy. I am about to condemn Abd al-Rahim in my mind, about to tell myself it will be his death or mine next time we meet. I am about to condemn him when he returns, running, huffing, with a twelve-foot section of plastic tubing—totally useless for a tracheotomy—in his hands. He waves it about as though it were the trunk of an elephant.

"He's dead already," I say, again sounding loud, too loud, as though my voice explodes inside my head. "Probably better that way, dead. It would have been no life after this, no life worth living."

At last one of the townsfolk speaks, saying: "They said anyone who tried to help would suffer."

"Who?" I ask. "Who?"

The villager doesn't reply. No one replies. They look at one another and gradually they depart, drift away, sneak away, ashamed. I do not rage against them. They are not guilty of anything. They are cautious. They are smart. They have survived a hundred thousand harshnesses in this land of Cain and Abel.

Abd al-Rahim and I lift Michele's body and carry him to the overpass, to Mahmoud's tent. I don't know what else to do with the body. I can't leave Michele in the street, where no one will dispose of him until the dogs and the crows have begun their work. I think of bringing him to Bashar's café, which in hindsight probably would have been a smarter thing to do. I decide that Bashar is responsible, indirectly, for having alerted Hussein. But if that is the case then I am responsible, too, maybe more responsible than anyone. It was my suspicion. I told Bashar what I suspected of the relationship between Michele and Mahmoud. Maybe he told Hussein. Michele's death is on my head, despite my effort to save him.

By the time we put Michele on Mahmoud's fragile cot, the residue of acid dripping from him has burned into the sleeves of my undershirt. Abd al-Rahim's white *dishdasha* is red and brown at its cuffs. Blood runs from my nose, singed from the vapors. Blood runs from my lips, blistered by the acid that remained on Michele's face when I tried to resuscitate him. I haven't been able to wipe my own blood clean while carrying the boy, so Mahmoud wipes it for me. Then he tries to wipe the blood from Abd al-Rahim, but Abd al-Rahim backs away.

After a moment Abd al-Rahim apologizes to Mahmoud. He says he is sorry for having backed away. He says he is sorry for Mahmoud's loss. The words are heartfelt yet Mahmoud doesn't hear Abd al-Rahim at all.

Mahmoud tries to light a cigarette, tries to take a cigarette from the pack in the front pocket of his police uniform. His hands shake too badly to open the pack. I help him. I take the cigarette out. Abd al-Rahim strikes a match and holds the flame to the cigarette's unfiltered end. I put the cigarette between Mahmoud's lips. He puffs at it and then shuts his eyes.

When we leave, Mahmoud still wipes at Michele's body, repetitively, meditatively. He rocks slowly from side to side as he wipes and wipes again at the blood, as if cleanliness might mean life. I try to explain what happened, Abd al-Rahim tries to explain, but Mahmoud raises his hand. He prefers silence. He knows what happened. He cries a little, but quietly. I take Mahmoud's Kalashnikov with me when I leave the tent, though only to prevent the boy from doing himself harm.

29

الأربعاء ووفاة ميشيل

Wednesday, After Michele Dies

"I WILL NOT SLEEP tonight," I tell Abd al-Rahim as we pass my shuttered shop.

"Likely the same for me," he says.

"Before this horror occurred it was the wrong night," I say, "the wrong night to practice our bombing. It was a day of relaxation. A day of nothingness."

"Not so much now," he says.

"No," I say. "Now I will not sleep and the day has changed for me. It is now a day for action."

Together we open the side door of the shop. I undo the lock and then Abd al-Rahim holds the door wide.

I crouch, using Mahmoud's Kalashnikov for support. I take the jack-in-the-box from beneath the counter, where I stowed it when Abd al-Rahim brought it as his peace offering. Peace has now been made. An image of Abd al-

Rahim flashes in front of my eyes, ridiculous, with the too-long, too-wide length of drainpipe held over Michele's life-less body. I think about how I had almost resolved, in that moment, to confront him. The scene is macabre. I might scream, rage, or cry over the futility of it. Instead, I laugh.

"What?" he asks.

"You aren't very mechanically inclined."

He realizes that I laugh at him. He stiffens a little, straightens his back. The lights on the highway overpass, which work only intermittently, flash alive, bathing the interior of my shack with a slice of sulfurous, orange illumination. I place Mahmoud's Kalashnikov flat on the ground under the counter and watch Abd al-Rahim's shadow as it plays over the surface of the rifle, losing its stiffness and curling forward. He might be drawing his pistol, ready to shoot me should Sheikh Seyyed Abdullah have ordered it. But the gentle quavering of his shadow tells me he either cries or laughs with me. I turn to face him and I see it is true. He has both his hands on his belly and he is shaking with a wheezing, almost sobbing sort of laugh.

It's good, our laughter, our shared laughter: a natural release after such tensions and horrors pass, though we keep it soft in order to avoid disturbing Mahmoud's vigil on the bridge.

"You brought a rake to sweep sand away from the shack," I say.

"Yeah," he says between chortles. His laugh is higher-pitched than mine, feminine.

"You brought a hammer to screw together the shutter."

"Yeah," he says again, wincing.

I keep up the commentary, or else the laughs will relapse,

fade, turn into real crying. We can distract ourselves or we can give in to the horror and the shame of the nearness, the inevitability of death.

"You brought a twelve-foot section of drainpipe for a tracheotomy."

"That's really morbid," he says, laughing and groaning amid the laughter as every sense of propriety in him fights against the idea that he might find himself laughing over such a situation.

"Ya Allah," I say.

I slap him on the side of his thigh. I grab the hem of his *dishdasha* and use it to pull myself up from my kneeling position. And while I do that, bumbling with my hands aflutter amid his robes, I lift his pistol from his belt, pull it free, and spin it in my grip so that I hold it by its barrel and offer the hilt of it back to him when I stand.

Abd al-Rahim is no amateur. He realizes what I have done.

"Don't screw with me," I say. "Bringing a hammer to fix a shutter is one thing. But you're no idiot with a weapon. Don't pretend to be absent next time I need you. If you must be gone for a while to report something to Seyyed Abdullah, just tell me. I'll be more than happy to let you go."

I return Abd al-Rahim's gun. Then, without saying anything else, I place the jack-in-the-box into a paper bag, shut the door of the shop, lock it, and walk ahead to a spot under the highway overpass. Abd al-Rahim still laughs. He's not angry or sulky at the fact that I was able to steal the weapon.

"That was good," he says. "Real good."

From under the bridge we hear Mahmoud talking to the dead body of his friend Michele. We can't hear his words clearly, just the sound of his voice, the soothing sound, as though he is comforting Michele. After a short while Abd al-Rahim and I hitch a ride in the back of an open pickup truck heading north from our market to the town of Az Zubayr, some twenty kilometers distant. With the wind from the moving vehicle whipping around us, we are alone.

"Why did you do it?" he asks, shouting over the wind.

"Do what?"

"Try to save him, the boy."

"I'm a doctor. That's what we do."

"My uncle didn't tell me that. He said you were a scientist, an engineer or something. He said you know how to make bombs."

"I do."

"That's not normal for a doctor."

"I was in Saddam's army."

"As a maker of bombs?"

"No, as a medic, before I went to university. It is not so much different, sewing up bodies, wiring up bombs."

After a moment, Abd al-Rahim says, "What do you think he'll do with the body?"

"That's trivial," I say. "More important to wonder what he'll do with himself…"

"I don't know," he says. "You took his gun."

"Just until he cools off."

"Will he want revenge?"

"That's the way here. Clan on clan. Feud on feud."

"No," says Abd al-Rahim. "I mean personal revenge. Will he try to go after Hussein?"

"If so, he won't succeed."

Abd al-Rahim looks out over the dusty farms, each with a

single glowing overhead light, a courtyard fenced with woven reeds, a mud-brick building or two, maybe a tractor or a plow or a rusty implement of some sort mingled with the hulks of cars and trucks left to sit in the dust. He looks up at the sky, scans it from horizon to horizon, a warm darkness through which, only a few miles from the glow of Safwan's lights and from the haze of the oil fields, star upon star bursts forth, a frost of stars, a bath of stars.

"My uncle wants to clean Hezbollah out of town."

"I know," I say. "But the Americans are the answer to that, not Mahmoud."

For a moment this reply of mine seems serious because it follows the track of Abd al-Rahim's thoughts and because my voice utters the words in the same serious star-scarching tone of conspiracy Abd al-Rahim had assumed. But then both of us, at the same time, look at each other. We must see the same thing in our minds: Mahmoud with his old Kalashnikov and his too-big police pants assaulting Hezbollah's local headquarters in their two-story barbed-wire-fortified building downtown. The image is evil. It is vile. But, Allah save me, it is funny. We burst into laughter anew and we barely have regained control of ourselves when our pickup truck drops us at our destination, an interchange several miles north of Safwan.

30

الأربعاء وانفجار قنبلة

Wednesday, a Bomb Explodes

ABD AL-RAHIM AND I plant the jack-in-the-box in the middle of the road, where no convoy can possibly avoid it. I unwind the mechanism. As the spring-loaded door opens and the head rises, one of the arms jams. I am forced to pry it loose. The fabric of the sleeve tears. The arm pops free from the body of the jack. I try to refit the arm to the jack but I can't fasten it, not without suitable tools, not without suitable time. I shrug and put the detached arm into the breast pocket of my *dishdasha*.

We retreat to a mound of rubble on the edge of a quarry about one hundred meters from the road. Behind us, the abyss of the open mine provides an escape route should the Americans pursue. No Humvee can traverse the narrow goat paths down the inner wall of a quarry. Nor will the Americans have time to dismount and chase us on foot before we disappear into shadows. We wait for the approach of a convoy, the lights of which will be visible, strung out for miles like a necklace in the northern desert.

"My turn now," I say. "Why do you do it?"

"Do what?"

"Fight."

"I am but your apprentice," he says, rather facetiously.

He laughs again. We've established our true relationship, more like equals than like master and apprentice, despite our ages, despite our nominal daytime roles.

"A man your age," I say, "perhaps he goes looking for war just as a hobby. Perhaps he wants glory. Perhaps he wants to do something interesting."

"None of these things," he says, and I can hear in the tone of his voice that he does want to talk.

"Of course not," I say. "It is never that, never such a thing. Boys might pretend to fight, might dream of it, but none of them goes so long, goes through as much training as you have undergone, without having a reason, a good reason."

"It's not the Americans," he says.

"Yet here we are preparing ourselves to kill them."

"My uncle says they will just be collateral damage. He says you are doing something more important than killing a few Americans."

"Maybe more important. Maybe not," I say. "Certainly an older and more respected reason for war than blind jihad."

"I don't understand," he says. "What's older? What's more respected?"

"Family," I say.

But Abd al-Rahim only looks at me with a blank expression, his face pale and flat in the darkness. I don't know that I can explain it to him any better, not until I know the reasons that commit him to fighting, the reasons he risks his life.

"Family?" I ask, saying the word again but with different inflection so that it points toward a different meaning. "Is it also family that makes you fight? Did Saddam kill your family?"

"No," he says. "We fled to Ahvaz during the war, across from Basra on the Iranian side. They live there still—my mother, father, brothers, sisters, all of them. Even some cousins."

"Then what?"

"There was a boy in my hometown in Iran, Abadan," he says. "That was where we lived before we moved farther north to Ahvaz. The boy was a few years older than me, a blind boy. As a child, I would sit and listen to him sing outside the mosque. Most days a crowd gathered around him because of the purity of his voice, the sweet way that the Holy Suras lifted from his tongue. Other children would play ball in the square or run wild in the streets, but often I would sit and listen, adults around me on all sides, just talking quietly and listening to the boy."

Abd al-Rahim pauses. He wets his lips with his tongue. Then he says, "They killed him."

"So I guessed," I say. "You don't have to tell me. I saw many similar things."

Yet Abd al-Rahim continues. "Saddam's soldiers came into Abadan during the war. A great victory, they called it, retaking Al-Faw and some land from the Iranians. I tell you what I called it: slaughter. There were no Iranian troops in town. Just old men, just old women, just blind boys singing in front of the mosque."

"There is no such thing as a great victory," I say.

A convoy appears. It wends its way slowly toward us, heading south on the Baghdad road along a great sickle curve that shows each vehicle, each set of lights, spaced evenly, rolling smoothly, moving inexorably closer to our jack-in-the-box.

"We watch now," I say. "Take notes in your mind. I think the things that the Humvees do in response to a bomb will be something new for you."

"Yes," he says.

The convoy comes nearer. For a moment it had been silent, just distant gliding lights. But soon we hear the rumble of engines and the hum of a turning multitude of tires.

"They killed him for sport," Abd al-Rahim says when the convoy is only a kilometer or two away. He hisses the word *sport* from his mouth, loudly, with venom, as if the noise of the approaching convoy covers his emotion, makes his emotion somehow permissible. "They toyed with him. Tapped him on the shoulder so that he turned around. Tapped him again, so that he turned around once more. He knew they were there. He sensed the silence around him after the fleeing of his crowd. He kept singing until the silence came. He sang as Saddam's tanks pulled into the square. He sang as they revved their engines, turned their turrets toward our mosque, our Shia mosque, and leveled it with a few well-aimed shots. He sang through the noise of the collapse and through the silence after it, when he could hear no more due to the ringing in his ears."

The lead Humvee in the convoy sees the jack-in-the-box. It screeches to a halt, skidding sideways toward the jack, almost rolling over. Behind it the semis pile up, jackknifed and peeling away along the embankments. All of them stop as quickly as they can, great clouds of dust rising from beneath their wheels. The lead Humvee is only a few feet from the jack-in-the-box. The face of the jack stares into the headlights of the Humvee as if it were under interrogation. I start counting in my mind, slowly, one…two …three …

"They tapped on his shoulder, turned him around, turned him around again. And then one of the men seized the boy and cut his tongue from his mouth."

A light from the lead Humvee shines into the desert. We duck behind our pile of rubble. Shadows jump and scatter as the light shifts from side to side, sweeping back and forth. I continue counting…ten …eleven …twelve …

"They won't leave the road," I say. "That is the first thing to know. You might think they will come out here. But they won't leave the road."

Abd al-Rahim whispers, "They cut his tongue. I remember one of them holding it in the air to the cheers of the others as the boy sank to the ground. I remember blood flowing from his mouth. It was like the boy in the market today."

The light from the Humvee stops passing to and fro over us. It concentrates on an outcrop of stones and rock on the other side of the roadway. I look over the top of our protective mound.

"They have night vision," I say. "They can see even when the spotlight is gone. So don't show yourself. But watch. Watch just a little now."

Abd al-Rahim rolls over, worms forward and up the rubble mound on his belly. My count continues, aloud but softly, under my breath: "…twenty-eight…twenty-nine…thirty…"

One of the American soldiers dismounts the lead Humvee. A second Humvee, the middle guardian of the convoy, rolls forward and stops next to him. I cease counting. Thirty-eight seconds. About what I had expected.

Voices from the two nearest Humvees carry clearly to the spot where we watch.

"If we continue whispering, they can't hear us," I say. "The noise of their engines is too close to them. But their voices cut through the noise to reach us, the deep growl underneath and the higher voices above. Can you hear them speaking?"

I turn toward Abd al-Rahim to see how he is doing. His hands are white, clenched tight. He nods to show me he understands.

"It's just a joke," one of the Americans says. "It's a kid's toy. A creepy joke."

"Maybe a bomb?" says the other, more nervous about it. "Maybe a disguised bomb?"

"Too obvious," says the first. "If they disguise the bombs they make them look like rocks or like garbage. And they don't place them right here, in the middle of the highway. They put them on the sides of the road, under railings, against telephone poles. Someone wanted us to find it. I'm sure they're watching."

At this, the soldiers scan the debris heaps at the side of the road again. I motion to Abd al-Rahim and he follows me slowly, on hands and knees, staying in the shadow cast by the pile of rubble until we reach the edge of the quarry and lower ourselves down into the safety of the big pit's impassable terrain. We walk slowly, then, slowly away from the highway toward a side road, where we plan to hitch a ride south.

Everything goes perfectly well. Our reconnaissance mission provides the information I need, confirming the convoy security element's response time. Abd al-Rahim and I walk away from our mock bombing uninjured. We've established a little more trust in each other. Everything goes according to plan, at least until the soldiers demolish my jack-in-the-box with a burst from one of their machine guns.

I jump then, the noise. A shiver courses along all the bones of my body. I find myself standing over the shredded remains of a patient—car accident, coal-mine blast, a fall into a corn-harvesting combine's grinding gears, something of that sort. Sanitary, glaring lights in a remembered American operating room blind me. I reach for a hand. I reach for a foot. I lay them on the table at the places where they should be reattached. I reach into the patient's open chest cavity, bristling with clamps and tubes. I pull from the wet disordered organs a necklace of bird bones and dollhouse keys. It emerges slowly. I coax it out gently and steadily, like a segmented worm reluctant to leave the blood on which it has gorged.

"Thirty-eight seconds," Abd al-Rahim says. "Is it enough for whatever you plan?"

I mean to tell him of the plan. I mean to confide in him. I know now that he can be trusted because he is fighting for something more meaningful than just himself.

But before I tell him that thirty-eight seconds should be sufficient, Layla interrupts me.

"If you are invisible, then thirty-eight seconds will be enough," she says.

She stands beside me as I walk with Abd al-Rahim up

the path on the far edge of the quarry. She tries to take my hand, to hold my hand, to offer me a little support, a shield against the darkness that plays at the corners of my vision. But I brush her away as though she were completely insubstantial.

"Did you hear me?" Abd al-Rahim asks.

I look at my hands to see if they are bloody from the operating room. I expect to find them sheathed in sterile blue latex. I expect to see myself carrying a little girl's arm. I am surprised to find my hands empty and clean.

"I heard you," I say. "I heard you. *Insha'Allah,* thirty-eight seconds should be enough."

I feel fortunate that Layla leaves me alone for the rest of the trip as Abd al-Rahim and I return to Safwan. Other than noticing the quick spasmodic shake of my left arm, which causes Layla to flee, to disappear, to dissolve into the sparkling nothingness where she truly belongs, Abd al-Rahim pays her no attention whatsoever.

※ ※ ※

Father Truth!

I smash my emptied whiskey bottle against the far kitchen wall. The shards of glass scatter across the floor to cover the ground where Abd al-Rahim raped my Nadia. I spit. The glob strikes the bare concrete wall at head height and flattens into an octopus shape, its arms drooling down the wall for several seconds before the concrete and the hot night air win their battle against gravity. The spittle stops. It begins to dry and evaporate, losing shimmer, solidifying.

Father Truth!

After my confrontation with Yasin that day in front of the Baghdad palace, I bought my jack-in-the-box. Walking home to Umm al-Khanzeer, I was thinking of family, of things I had done wrong, of ways to make amends. I was thinking of Bashar leaving Baghdad. I was thinking of safety. I wasn't looking at the outside world at all until a store window caught my eye. Sun reflected from the big plate glass of its display, somehow miraculously intact despite the recent violence.

"Masah il-kheir," *I said to the shopkeeper.* "Good evening. May peace be upon you."

"And upon you," *said the shopkeeper as I approached.*

"I see you are shutting your store for the night. A toy store?"

The shopkeeper looked at me very carefully: my Western suit, my wingtip shoes, my crisply starched shirt. He noticed my hand in my pocket as it caused a handful of coins to jingle.

"Not at all, sir," *the shopkeeper said.* "The store is open for you."

It was a matter of serendipity to find a toy store open in Baghdad. Also a matter of serendipity that I bought a jack-in-the-box.

A jack-in-the-box!

A thing intended for children far younger than any I knew. Maybe I was thinking of Bashar's young family, though they had already left town. Maybe I bought it for myself. Maybe I thought I might hear the few remaining neighborhood children laugh, startled and jumping, as the thing burst in their arms. Maybe it had been too long since I'd heard such laughter.

A jack-in-the-box!

I walked across the street with it wrapped in a brown paper bag. I walked with it away from the toy store down the length of Zawra Park along Al-Kindi Street. As Bashar's note had said, vendors no longer lined Sharia al-Kindi, selling hot kebabs and shawarma. *No musicians played in the park. I heard across the expanse of the silent street the shopkeeper roll down his overhead security door, protecting the store window. The sound of the rolling door, grating and harsh, flew through the park, across the Tigris, bouncing back from the far shore. A group of birds rose from the bank, circled, and landed again on stilted legs. They gathered around and bent over a carcass in the river mud, picking at it. The* muezzin *call from the Sheikh Ma'aruf minaret began. I set my package with the jack-in-the-box on the grass beside me, knelt facing Mecca to the south and a little to the west, and prayed for the duration of the* salaam.

When the muezzin *ceased wailing, with the air seeming clearer and cleaner between all the towers of the city, I stood, brushed the knees of my pants clean, and walked toward Tigris Bridge. As I summited the bridge, the view of Umm al-Khanzeer spread before me: Saddam's white-stucco ministerial houses nestled amid green-shaded streets, sprinklers whisking back and forth in the jeweled evening, a paradise.*

I looked at the paradise for a long while, not thinking of my brother at all. I forgot about the disagreement he and I had, the blow I gave him. I just looked and looked across the city. Calmness penetrated my mind. I thought clearly for a moment, and the thought that occurred to me was this: it had been a mistake, my mistake, to return so soon to Iraq. It had been a mistake to return at all.

I crossed the bridge and the cloud of foreboding finally lifted from me. I decided that I would admit that I was wrong. I'd tell her that we would soon be leaving. I'd apologize to her for bringing her to Iraq. I'd apologize for staying in Baghdad even after Bashar and all his children, all her friends, had left. I'd give her the jack-in-the-box and I'd hear her laughter again and everything would be good. Everything would be fine.

Father Truth!

Maybe I'd even call Annie to share the news that we would soon return to America and would soon get to be together as a family again, if only through the prison visitation window.

My step lightened.

By habit, I took my identification card from my pocket as I approached the gate on the island side of the bridge, holding my wallet in one hand, the card in the other.

"Late this evening, Doctor?" asked the guard.

"Yes," I said.

I handed him my identification, a formality. We knew each other well after so many comings and goings. The guard opened the pedestrian entrance. Imbued with the sense that everything, everything in the world, would be better once I left Baghdad, I felt lighthearted. I tarried at the guard post for a moment, making small talk.

"Yes, yes," I said. "Late tonight. I stopped at a toy shop…"

It was then, in mentioning the toy shop, that I realized I had forgotten the jack on the other side of the river, in the grass of Zawra Park, where I had knelt to pray.

I took my identification card from the guard and returned across the bridge. As I approached the jack-in-the-box—still wrapped in its brown bag—a terrible vibrating thump shattered the stillness of the evening, shattered the air behind me. The sound was all too familiar, occurring all too often those days. I did not jump. I did not startle. But I turned and looked across the bridge. In the distance the slums of ath-Thawra, Sadr City, glowered, a haze of heat and smog rising from dull brown rooftops. But the thump came from a place closer to me than the slum. In the distance sirens blared, moving toward the sound of the bomb. Smoke curled over Umm al-Khanzeer itself. Smoke on the protected island. Smoke near my home.

Uncertain, panicking, I turned again toward the jack-in-the-box. Then I turned toward the island. Then I turned toward the jack-in-the-box, spinning, the world spinning. At last I chose my direction, toward the south, toward Mecca, away from Umm al-Khanzeer. I knelt again, knelt in the direction indicated by the Qibla, *but I could not pray. I could not pray! I could do nothing other than look at the jack-in-the-box, my jack-in-the-box.*

It had sprung.

31

ليلة الأربعاء
Wednesday Night

FATHER TRUTH!

At one point, I'm not sure when—sometime after I open another whiskey bottle and drink a good deal of it—I crawl to the spot where my spit dried into a dull shellac on the wall. I crawl across the glass pieces on the kitchen floor, hearing them break and screech as they catch in my skin and drag across the tile floor, but I feel no pain in the flesh of my body. I crawl to the wall beneath my spittle and I turn myself around, propping myself upright with my back against the wall so that I stare at the empty space on the shelf behind my kitchen table, where my jack-in-the-box had so long been preserved.

I sit that way for a long while.

At some point that night, while I sit there, I vomit. When I wake the next morning, chunks of food and mucus float in my half-full whiskey bottle. A rancid, sticky coating covers my left hand, clings to my unshaven cheek and my bare chest, soils my pants. Blood from my knees, hands, and shins has also dried on the floor, a smeared brown trail that begins, faintly at first, where the farthest piece of the broken glass glitters in the morning sun. The trail of blood ends where I sit. When I pick the biggest pieces of glass from my legs and hands, the wounds open anew and fresh red blood oozes from me, coating the duller brown.

There is no aspirin in the house. No orange juice. No raw-egg-and-Tabasco-sauce hangover cure. No way for me to easily pull myself together. I look at my whiskey bottle for a long time, with my own acids and greases coagulated on the surface of the sweet brown liquid.

Thirteen years of emptiness, void, and denial.

Father Truth.

I raise the whiskey to my lips and drink, pulling from the bottle like a suckling calf. The taste of it is horrible. *Father Truth.* I drink again. *Thirteen years.* I drink until I cannot sit upright and then, at last, I sleep.

I do not dream, not when I sleep. I am thankful for the absence of dream. The void is imploding. I do not want to look at it any closer than I must, but when I am awake, neither can I bear reality. As a refuge, then, in my waking hours, I dream. I drink and I dream and I sleep when I can, day or night.

Father Truth.

I talk to her, too, as I dream. I talk to her as I walk about and do the real-world things I must do. I talk to Layla, or at least to the image of Layla that haunts my dreams. I am aware of the strangeness of this. Maybe it is like a mark of henna on me, painting me as a bride would be painted, a celebration and a bereavement both, a setting aside of myself, making myself *haraam* from the world. When I talk to Layla I see the questioning looks on those who pass me in the streets, those who pass my store. During such times, as often as I can, I send Abd al-Rahim away from me. I send him on errand after errand, pointless errands, now not so much because he annoys me but because I do not want him to interrupt my conversations with Layla. He has caught me speaking to her, little words, whispers and hushes and laughs and gestures.

I know, now, that she's not there. I know she is just a figment of my imagination, Layla popping up at such inopportune moments. My dreams cling to me as I witness the most real realities, as I endure the most mundane moments. Keeping her with me in my dreams like this provides a little respite for me, a breath in a bubble as I drown, a charmed muon burning her spiral on the CRT screen of my life.

Abd al-Rahim catches me talking to her. Others notice that I talk to her. I don't care.

When Mahmoud leaves with Michele's family to bury Michele's body in one of the cemeteries of the holy city of Kufa, my drunkenness imposes a layer of dream over the reality. I see Michele's family depart with Michele's plain wooden coffin lashed to the roof of their car. But I see, too, an apparition of Layla lying on top of the coffin. She crosses her hands over her chest and has fastened black-painted cutout cardboard *X*s over her tightly shut eyes. She plays at death in order to make me laugh.

Likewise, after I go to the tailor to be fitted for a suit of clothes respectable enough for my wedding, my drunkenness converts reality into dream. I take the clothes home and hang them from a bare nail on the wall opposite my kitchen table. Nothing too odd there. But the suit broods, on the wall, dark and formal, and I think that I will not get along well with it until it says, at last, "Drink! Drink! Don't let my silence disturb you."

We share the rest of that night's bottle of whiskey together, sip for sip, shot glass slammed down against shot glass. We sing merry songs. Layla plays the banjo. We clasp arms and totter down alleyways—my new suit of clothes, Layla, and me—as though the alleyways are a yellow brick road. Layla and the suit will ask Oz for new bodies. I will ask him for a soul.

And when the Kuwaiti interpreter and his lieutenant return to my store, they find me drunk and befuddled by a dream in which Abd al-Rahim, Layla, and I swim together, with Seyyed Abdullah occasionally jumping in for a skinny-dip. Whenever Abd al-Rahim fins too near to Layla, she morphs into a school of goldfish, several hundred goldfish, and they slide apart, around, over Abd al-Rahim in the same way that a shimmering school of sardines first envelops and then scatters away from the onrushing shadow of a shark. Layla falls apart and then re-forms nearer to me, as if I can in some way protect her. She is wrong, though. I have no special powers. I am no superhero. I am only distantly related to goldfish.

I gurgle and the words I form float from my mouth in hieroglyphics, shiny-bubble, jackal-headed, demon words. From somewhere far away, beyond the veil of my drunken dreams, I hear the Kuwaiti interpreter as he says: "A funny noise, that gurgle."

The waters of my dream shatter around him as he steps through parting waves. He wipes his shoes on the curb of the Safwan street to keep them from getting muddy.

"I am drowning," I tell him. "A pleasant feeling, really, once you stop struggling."

"Sa-Bah Al-Chair," says the lieutenant, trying out a little phrase-book Arabic.

"You move like a robot," Layla tells the lieutenant, teasingly, though the lieutenant can't understand the hieroglyphics used by us goldfish as we speak.

Abd al-Rahim does the backstroke several meters away from me, out in the middle of the market road, floating in the image of the dream as though he were a genie or a hovercraft or a hot-air balloon, his body superimposed about three meters above the surface of the road.

"He'll turn around and come for you again," I whisper to Layla. "He looks like he is gone but he is, in truth, afraid of the really deep water. He still needs to stay close. He relies on you."

"My opinion of him exactly," says the interpreter, pointing covertly to the lieutenant at his side. I am surprised for a second. He understands what I am saying! He is a friend, a companion, a goldfish whisperer! He doesn't know that I really speak to Layla. He doesn't know that we talk about Abd al-Rahim. The Kuwaiti thinks I refer to his boss, but what does it matter? I'm happy to have his company, happy to talk to him, happy to have him as a pal. I take his hand in my hand and begin to shake it.

"He's young," I say.

"Yes," says the Kuwaiti.

"But really not robotic."

I'm surprised to find myself defending Abd al-Rahim. Layla looks at me as if I am a traitor, as if I am confused, hopelessly undertrained, and never truly able to be taught the mystic understanding of robots.

"Does he have the papers?" asks the lieutenant.

The lieutenant's face is clean and pink. His hands are scrubbed and hairless. His nails are trimmed and without oil or dirt beneath their white and pearl-like cuticles. He smells like milk and talcum powder and I have to choke down the bile rising in my throat as I remember the curdled taste of the first drink of my defiled whiskey.

"You know that one of our convoys found a jack-in-the-box in the middle of the road near Az Zubayr, don't you?" asks the interpreter, saying nothing about the papers that the lieutenant wants and needs. I still hold his hand.

I think about getting the adoption papers down from the shelf behind me, but I can't do anything with them until the Kuwaiti makes his first reference to them. The lieutenant can say all he wants in English, but I can't let the Kuwaiti know I understand that language. He would surely, then, suspect me despite our shared appreciation of hieroglyphics. So the interrogation continues until the Kuwaiti can no longer resist his master's insistence. He is free to ask me anything he wants.

He is free.

But I am, too.

I have a defense now. I am crazy and I am drunk and I am ruthless and I am beautiful. As I realize this newfound freedom, I itch to demonstrate its powers.

In the middle of the interpreter's next rabid bit of questioning I say, apropos of nothing: "Indeed it is a dangerously powerful thing, this appearance and disappearance of goldfish, the school of them dissolving when the shark comes. And—*ya Allah!* —such gossamer wings."

This makes the interpreter pause. He doesn't know that I am crazy. I see his lips move. He repeats the words for *fish* and for *gold* in high Arabic: *samak, thahab.* He says "gossamer." He recites the word *shark,* which is *qirsh.* This word has meaning for him. He looks over his shoulder at the Humvees stationed along the sides of the road, arrayed like huge finning fish.

I continue, still drawing power and code-meaning from my dream: "When she moves she dissolves and reconstitutes herself. She is near me now, then far from me the next moment, then nearer again before I am even aware."

"She? The network?" asks the Kuwaiti. "Are they recruiting you? Jaish al-Mahdi? Hezbollah? Al-Qaeda?"

"I could help you," I say. "But I can't seem to make her hold still long enough. She's a million pieces of glass shattered on a kitchen floor. She's here, there, everywhere. She's gone again now. No...no ...there she is!"

Layla appears with an umbrella and a raincoat. She splashes in puddles of ocean and makes mud cakes that she holds up for my inspection. The street would be gray from reflected storm clouds except for the bleeding of her bright raincoat into the puddles, the bleeding of blue-sky colors breaking through cloud. I point to her. The lieutenant and the interpreter both look up and behind them. In the middle distance a low, flat warehouse on the edge of town seems to be exactly in line with the azimuth my finger indicates. The lieutenant motions to one of his Humvees. The turret gunner swivels toward the warehouse and hunkers lower behind his sawtoothed weapon.

"Ask him about the papers," says the lieutenant, more forcefully now. "We need to go. Ask him if he will sign them or not."

"Papers," says the Kuwaiti.

I reach for the papers. The Kuwaiti takes them from me. He sees that I haven't signed them yet. He points to the places where my signature must appear.

Then, as I scribble the fake and crazy name al-Mulawwah on the documents, the Kuwaiti says, "If you want to talk, if you want to tell us about 'her,' as you say, we can arrange for the information to be kept secret. We can reward you for your cooperation. We can maybe make 'her' stand still long enough to capture 'her.' Goldfishes and sharks and puddles of raincoat-color—however you want to talk about it, I will find a way to understand."

"Don't tell them about me," says Layla. "They won't believe you."

"I will tell you," I say to the interpreter. "I will tell you everything I know. Come back with a tape recorder in three days' time. I will tell you everything."

Layla frowns and closes her eyes.

My offer excites the interpreter very greatly. He doesn't translate any of this for his boss. Maybe he will later. I don't know. I see the gleam in his eyes, and I know the idea excites him.

When I finish with the papers, the lieutenant shakes my hand.

"It will be a few months," he says. "I finish here in a week or two. Just trying to get home safe now. I will return for her then. My wife will be so pleased. We can't have children…"

The Kuwaiti doesn't even bother to interpret this flow of enthusiasm. He says an elaborate good-bye to me, long enough so that the lieutenant thinks his words have been relayed. I smile. The lieutenant smiles. We all shake hands again. Stars of glory spangle the Kuwaiti's eyes.

They leave, mounting their Humvees, and I take from its secret spot behind my shack the bottle of whiskey I have stored there. I drink from it, turning my back guiltily away from the street. They've taken her, my girl, my Layla. They've wafted her away from me and I want her back, I want her back, I want her swimming around me. I want her back at least for these last few hours and days and minutes. The burning liquid, the whiskey, works as an anchor for her. I slip away from my concerns with reality and with the scene at my store into more dreams, more dreams, dreams overlaying the images of the market in various filmy veils, until the floating images seem more real than the reality. My consciousness vacillates that way, drink by drink, from moment to moment, though I cling to the dreams and force the drink on myself in order to keep Layla near and enlivened. I want dream, not dust. I want story, not truth. I want magic, not politics. I want Layla.

During these days of my binge, Abd al-Rahim brings my wrapped gifts to the house of Ulayya, or to the house of her father, Ali, while Layla brings her gifts to me. I find them each morning in my store.

For most of the first day after Michele's death I think that there is no fourth gift, no jewelry. Layla's monetary resources or her thievish cunning has been exhausted. It makes sense. How could she afford to purchase a gold necklace? Likewise, the sellers of gold keep much closer watch on their wares. They make it too difficult to steal. In such a way I rationalize the absence of the gift of jewelry. I rationalize it until I see Mahmoud returning with Michele's family from Kufa. Then I kneel to retrieve the Kalashnikov from under my counter. There, from the crossbeam under the sill of my shop window, dangles a golden necklace, the same sort of golden necklace Abd al-Rahim purchased for Ulayya. It isn't boxed or wrapped, as Layla's first gifts to me were. But it has the single orange desert flower tangled in its chain.

The next day it is crystal, a set of six goblets with finely hewed prismatic edges spilling light from within. I find them arrayed on my counter inside the shop. Out of habit, I check the room to ensure that no signs of forced entry or theft are present. Layla has entered, as always, without disturbing my locks, without disturbing my merchandise. I cannot determine her method. I cannot determine her purpose.

The crystal goblets are filled with pennies, American pennies. She must have collected a thousand pennies to fill them all. A fortune for her. Pounds of pennies and one orange flower.

"Pennies?" says Abd al-Rahim when he arrives that day.

"Bombs," I tell him. "Copper for the projectiles."

"Fitting end for capitalists."

"You are a communist?"

"The Great Satan."

He pokes fun at me. He uses his catchphrases, like a good jihadist, but smiles all the time when he speaks. He knows I like the Americans. He knows I like the ribald West with all its flaws and all its heart. He knows that it troubles me to attack them, even if the injuries I might cause serve a different, maybe better, sort of war.

"Communist or Islamist? What are you?" I say.

"How'd she get in?" he asks.

He begins snooping around the building's edges. He checks the floor, the joints in the siding. He checks the ceiling, the places where the roof meets each wall. All is tidy. All is well constructed, just as I have already and repeatedly confirmed.

"If there is a way in, don't you think someone would have already stolen the phones?" I ask.

"I don't understand," he says. "You say the girl brings you these gifts. But how? It doesn't seem possible."

He climbs onto a chair, balances on top of it, tests the strength of the tin ceiling against the strength of his upthrusting arms. The tin warps but does not dislodge. I slip a little flask from beneath my *dishdasha* and drink while he isn't looking.

"We'll use copper for bombs," I say. "Melted copper pierces the armor of the Humvees with very little explosive force compared to a traditional bomb."

"Or we use the copper for making a statue," says Layla. "Maybe a statue of a mermaid or a merman, something more permanent than Safwan's blown-up concrete fountain."

"Shh," I say. "He'll hear."

"Who will hear?" asks Abd al-Rahim, turning quickly to face me.

"The bomb," I say, and I giggle as Layla steals the sunglasses from Abd al-Rahim's pocket. She puts them on and strikes a bored, nonchalant pose of exactly the sort Abd al-Rahim often assumes.

The next day it is the clothing Layla brings. Before Abd

al-Rahim arrives in the middle of the morning I have already opened the gift. Out of curiosity I've donned the full ensemble, putting the dress and skirts over my *sirwal* pants, over my *ghalabia*.

"*Ya Allah!*" he says when he sees me.

I look like a fat peacock, I admit. These are clothes meant to be worn under a woman's black *abaya* or inside the house in the kitchen among a gathering of lady friends, fine patterned blue silk and green silk, flowing sleeves, deep neck. They are clothes meant never to appear in the light of day, especially not on the body of a middle-aged man. They are clothes that would be *haraam,* subject to a lashing from Hussein's moral police, should a woman—not to mention a man—be caught wearing them in the market. They are clothes meant for Ulayya, not for me, but Layla stays true to form by bringing for me exactly, exactly, the gifts I bade Abd al-Rahim purchase for Ulayya. I don't want to seem as though I do not honor her gifts, even if they are a bit strange.

I am very drunk at this moment, wearing the women's robes. I don't bother to stand up as Abd al-Rahim enters and looks at me and frowns. I don't think I can stand up, not without holding on to something.

With the voice of a sea captain I say to him: "I didn't know the little experiment with the jack-in-the-box would disturb you so badly. Look at yourself, Gilligan! Getting drunk in public. Wearing women's clothes. You should be ashamed!"

My giggle turns into a laugh. Abd al-Rahim in women's clothes! I have to flatten both hands on the counter in order to hold my body upright.

Outside, in the street, Layla pretends to dance with a trash can. The movements she makes are as lewd as anything Britney Spears ever did in her dances. The movements are unseemly in the extreme. She must think I am laughing at her, rather than at Abd al-Rahim. She is mistaken, though. I don't find her funny at all. I tell myself I should speak to her mother and find a way to discipline her. We will be embarrassed when we move back to America...nobody dances with trash cans in Chicago...little American girls don't ...

I stop giggling.

Abd al-Rahim thinks he has tamed me. He doesn't know that I am mad at Layla. He doesn't know that I am mad at Baghdad. He doesn't know why I brush my hands through the air, wiping at the air, trying to make the dream of Layla dissolve and disappear and leave me alone. I send him away, Abd al-Rahim, so that I don't have to sneak the whiskey when he isn't looking. After he leaves I drink enough so that he finds me asleep when he returns, the blue and green silk clothing cocooned around me. He does not take advantage of me. He is a gentleman. He helps me take off the layers of silk. He helps me walk home. He puts me in my bed, my mattress dusty and oriented diagonally on the cold empty floor. There is no four-poster frame to hold the mattress up, no carved European fantasy of ivy on the headboard. I haven't used the bed in weeks, preferring the flat stillness of my kitchen table, preferring to sit against the wall.

Abd al-Rahim raises the covers and tucks me in as though I were a child. He flicks the light off when he leaves. I'm hungry. I haven't eaten dinner. I try to call to Abd al-

Rahim. I try to tell him I need food. I try to tell him I need to go to Bashar's café.

I say, "I need to tell Bashar that you raped his wife."

I try to say this aloud but I can't because when I roll over and pull the covers up to my face I find Annie Dillon in bed next to me. She puts her finger to my mouth, stops any words I might speak. She places the flat of her palm on my eyes, closing them as a mother would close the eyes of a dead baby. I look through my eyelids and through her palm and I stare unspeakingly for a handful of delicate moments into the abyss of her gaze. Her eyes are blue, ice blue, staring at me through the mirage of her face as though they have a life, liquid and fleeting, all their own.

She whispers, "Father Truth."

Even after the silk clothing, Layla's gifts continue.

The last day it is henna, the gift of henna from me to Ulayya and from Layla to me. I haven't decided what to do with it. I keep the box Layla delivers, just a little box, but with a very fragile glass-stoppered bottle wrapped in several layers of tissue. The bottle is dark, the red darkness of the henna impenetrable in its mass. What use is henna to me? What use is it for a man to make marks of celebration, mystic preparation, joy, before his betrothal? Should I draw patterns of hieroglyphics on my wrists before I go to Ali ash-Shareefi's house for the engagement feast? What will the people think? What will the talkative cousin think, dwelling on his gore, dwelling on such details of death, to see me openly showing my secret languages of celebration? I look at the bottle of henna for a long while, pondering the shapes its liquid might form on Ulayya's wrists and feet.

I excuse myself from my store around noontime. I trust

Abd al-Rahim to take charge of the business for the better part of this day.

"Tonight we do another bombing," I say as I am leaving.

"Okay," he says.

"You watch the store now," I say.

"You already told me to watch it."

"Well, you just watch it. Watch it. I'm going now."

I go but I only make it a few steps before I sneak around the corner, through Ibrahim and Maney'a Shareefi's used-car lot and into the space between our stores. I go to Layla's little lean-to door, slip under it, and take the whiskey bottle from a hole beneath a masonry block where I often hide it, my secret storage place.

"I have to check for thieves," I say to Abd al-Rahim, a little loudly, as a way to mask the noise I make when I bump into the back wall of my shack.

"My uncle is growing concerned about you," Abd al-Rahim says with a measure of patience and a measure of annoyance. He doesn't come around to my side of the store. He waits in front. "My uncle says a little craziness is okay. A little craziness is holy. A little craziness is to be expected in such circumstances as yours."

"It is just a little craziness," I say. "Don't worry."

An idea occurs to me.

"Invite him," I say. "Tell him it's tonight. Invite Uncle Seyyed. I'm inviting everyone, really. Ali al-Hajj ash-Shareefi will come. Hussein from the Hezbollah will come along with all his minions. Why not Sheikh Seyyed Abdullah?"

I say this to Abd al-Rahim even though I have already, myself, personally invited his uncle. Why not? Let the young man, my jihadist apprentice, feel important. Let him feel as though his shined shoes are worth something more than a busboy's smile. Abd al-Rahim doesn't have to know that Seyyed Abdullah is already committed to attending our practice event. Abd al-Rahim doesn't have to know. He thinks I'm a little crazy. They all think I'm a little crazy.

I don't know if Abd al-Rahim is laughing or if he is shaking his head in wonder and fear, but he doesn't answer me. He doesn't answer my command to invite his uncle.

I sip from my bottle, once, twice, enough to keep the dreams coming. When I lower the bottle from the last of those three drinks, Abd al-Rahim stands in front of me. He slaps me on the face. Shocked, I drop the bottle. I reach down to retrieve it but he kicks it away. I try to shove him. I try to steal the pistol from his belt, but I stagger against the lean-to door. I knock my head as I stand up and my shoulder thumps against the inside slope of the lean-to, a bruising thump from which echoes of numbness spread, shivering, down the left side of my body. The door lifts. Its base slides away from my shack, slides in the dust so that the top of it slams to the earth. Abd al-Rahim grabs me and pulls me toward him. Dust puffs around us. Abd al-Rahim holds me, not exactly with a hugging embrace, but close enough.

I start to giggle and I can't stop.

"Rhett Butler, you've saved me," I say, pretending to swoon.

He slaps me again.

"That was last night, you fool," he says.

"You're supposed to say, 'Frankly, my dear, I don't give a——'"

"It was last night. Real bomb but still a practice," says Abd al-Rahim. "And it would have worked."

"What?"

"It was all set up. Every damn dignitary in town invited by you and your loudmouth friend Bashar. A whole line of old men crouching in the quarry and peering over the slag heaps with their watches in hand so they could help you confirm, after the chaos of a real explosion, that it would still take your same precious thirty-eight seconds for the response."

"Did they like our jack-in-the-box?"

"No," he says. "It wasn't the jack. It was the real bomb last night with your melted copper charge and IR trigger beam and remote activation."

"Did we kill some infidels?"

Abd al-Rahim shakes his head at me in disbelief.

"You mumbled something about how Winston and Philip and David shouldn't come to Hollywood. We all know you're crazy. We know. You live all alone in a half-finished house. You pretend to talk to this market girl Layla, even when she isn't around. We know you're crazy—"

"Layla?"

He ignores me. His face is flushed red. I look down at his feet, where my whiskey bottle, unbroken, still sloshes a few fingers of liquid in it. I think about reaching for the bottle but Abd al-Rahim grips me too tightly.

"We know you're a little crazy," he says. "But that bomb cost my uncle ten thousand U.S. dollars. Everything was perfect with it until you strolled out into the road in front of the convoy, waving your arms to stop them."

At that, he slaps me again, one more time.

"Go home," he says. "Sleep it off. We will start again tomorrow."

Abd al-Rahim returns to the front of my shop and I hear him begin to close up, to put the mobile phones back into their boxes from the display cases on the counter, to stack and organize brochures on the various shelves.

I reach down for the bottle. The liquid has stopped moving. I think about drinking from it but instead I push the fallen lean-to door aside and I kick the masonry block with my toe. The block shifts just enough to reveal my hiding spot. I put the bottle into the hole and cover it again with the block.

I am sweating. The evening sun cuts a wedge between the tents and the buildings on the far side of the road. Its light drenches me without the protection of Layla's lean-to door. I feel the heat multiplied inside me, the combined warmths of sun and whiskey.

A smell comes from me, an unwashed dirtiness. I am upset with myself, upset with my lack of hygiene. I resolve to bathe. I resolve to drink no more whiskey before my engagement party tonight, tomorrow night, yesterday night, whichever night. I must keep myself sober. I must be ready and fast and fluid. Maybe I don't have enough time to get sober. Maybe I shouldn't even try. Maybe everything will be easier if I continue to float a little, skim a little, come with a load of story and myth hanging over my head while the dancers at Ali's party dance and the singers at the party sing and my bride, Ulayya, and I agree, formally, to wed.

Maybe I should drink!

I scrounge in the dust at the side of the shack. I remove

my carefully placed cinder block from its position over my bottle's hidey-hole. On my knees in the dirt, I raise the whiskey to my lips so that I might once again toast the vortices. I swallow and joust with the ecstasies, the darknesses, that ease and flood and swirl in comfort around me. I fight them and gulp against them. The burning furrow of the liquid soothes me, woos me, defuses me until I can open my eyes again. Then I see, through the distortion of the thick mottled glass at the bottle's upturned end, Layla standing in front of me. We are at eye level with each other, me kneeling.

"Go away," I say. "Go swimming or something. Go become a goldfish. I know you aren't real."

She doesn't go anywhere.

I think of telling her that the American lieutenant plans to adopt her. I think of slapping her, as Abd al-Rahim slapped me, to knock some sense into her, to make her stop staring at me, to make her disappear again, drift away, away, float away.

She says, "You're going to get married."

"Yes," I say.

"We can't be friends anymore?"

"We shouldn't."

"That makes me sad," she says.

"Me, too," I say.

I should tell her about the lieutenant. I should tell her about the adoption. I summon up the words, the courage. But as I am about to speak, she extends a clenched hand.

"Here," she says. "Thank you for letting me wear it, but I think you should keep it now."

I put my hand up to hers. She opens her fist and the anklet of bird bones and dollhouse keys falls from her hand into mine.

"I will miss you," she says.

She steps forward, stands on the fallen lean-to door, and puts her small hands on my shoulders.

"Stand up," she says.

I obey, rising to one foot, then the other. I'm unsteady. I lean against the wall of my shack. All of me is dun-colored from the dust. I wipe at my knees and leave patches of relatively white cloth showing on them where the dust falls away.

When I am upright, Layla stands back, plugging her nose. She sizes me up and says, "Now you're too tall. Bend down a little."

Again, I obey.

She adjusts me a little more, getting me to the right height, squaring my shoulders in just the right way, straightening my back, lifting my chin. When all is as she wants it to be, she kisses me, once, twice—one kiss on each cheek. Then she pulls away and looks at me to judge the effect of her kisses. I don't know what I'm doing. I might be smiling. I might be laughing. I might be crying. Yes, I think I'm crying. If there are rules for a conversation between an old man like me and a young girl like Layla, I have broken them. She pulls me closer, closer again, and holds me as a mother holds a newborn child. Her arms wrap around the outside of my arms. I feel her hands between my shoulder blades, rubbing small reassuring circles. This embrace lasts until the last light from the sunset lifts above us. Then only the tops of the market tents and the telephone poles shine.

The rest is night.

* * *

It seemed like it lasted an eternity, my inability to pray as I knelt beside the jack-in-the-box in Zawra Park. But it must have only been a moment, for—after I rose from the ground and sprinted back across the bridge—I arrived at my house in time to beat even the Americans. What few neighbors remained in that diplomatic community looked at me from their windows or peered at me from behind the pillars of their front porches. As at the scene of Hezbollah's punishment of Michele, none of the bystanders approached too closely, none offered me help.

Heedless of them, heedless of the heat from the burning wreckage of my home, I rushed forward, vaulting one of the collapsed walls. I kicked at rubble, threw aside burning beams and window frames and melted sections of sofa cushion. I didn't know what, exactly, I was doing. I didn't know what I was looking for. I picked up little things from the cinders, shiny things: bits of glass, bits of bird bone, bird beak, maybe teeth. I picked up dollhouse keys. I secreted these things away in my pockets. I picked up flotsam, tokens from the rubble until I found one of the bigger things I had hoped, without ever forming the thought of such a terrible desire, never, never, ever to find.

By the time the Americans arrived at my house I had emerged from the rubble and the smoke to stand on my front lawn, preciously lush grass scorched black on its tips and littered with burned and burning pieces of whitewashed stucco, shattered brick, smoldering clumps of deep purple bougainvillea. I was dirty and bloody and sweating and exhausted already. Soldiers stormed past me to surround the building. One of them pointed his weapon into my chest but did not shoot. I held myself very still and observed the jerky slowness of everything that happened for the next few minutes: Iraqi paramedics milling about on the street, arranging white sheets on hospital gurneys and spreading plastic tarps over my front sidewalk, teams of soldiers talking on radios, inspecting the home, the damage, a helicopter circling overhead.

At last the American soldier guarding me lowered his weapon at the command of his sergeant. Two Iraqi policemen hurried to take his place guarding me.

The first of them removed from my halfhearted grip the arm I had found inside my house, limp at the joints of elbow and wrist. He took it from me and put it into a big blue translucent plastic bag. Then he labeled the bag with a black Magic Marker and sealed it with a zip tie.

The second of the two policemen took me by the hand and led me behind one of the ambulances, saying to me: "Come, Doctor, we must talk with you for a minute."

32

الخميس حتى فجر الإثنين

Thursday Until Monday's Dawn

IN MY HOME I sit completely naked at my kitchen table for a long while. In front of me I have placed my whiskey bottle. It is empty. Behind the whiskey bottle, I have placed the bomb, the next bomb, the second and, I hope, last of those bombs bought with Sheikh Seyyed Abdullah's money, smuggled across the border in pieces behind the disguise of the whiskey bottles. The thick and rounded glass of the bottle distorts the shape of the bomb. The facets of the bottle reflect the image of my haggard face, superimposed on the curving shape of the detonation charge, so that the bomb seems to have my rough whiskers, my black tumble of hair, my untrimmed mustache, my depthless, reddened eyes.

I sit there for a long while, an hour, maybe two hours. *Father Truth.*

I say it at last, very quietly, admitting the thing that lies at the center of the void.

I say, "My daughter."

The house is very still then. I hear the pulse of my heart as it beats through the veins of my head. No thoughts come to me. I say the truth once, there in my house, and then I stand, don my new suit, the suit tailored for my engagement feast with Ulayya. It is a black double-breasted affair, faintly striped in silver, complete with silken handkerchief folded in the breast pocket. I put on stiff leather shoes over socks with matching faded stripes of the same thin silver thread. I run a comb through my hair, each side, pulling it straight back and holding the mass flat against my scalp with a liberal application of cream.

I sweat profusely as I put on the clothes. The beads of sweat drip from my forehead. They soak the pits of my arms. They drool down my back and down the backs of my legs. I wipe my forehead but I cannot dry my body once the clothes are on me, sticking to me.

I will go to Ali ash-Shareefi's house. But first I will visit each of my friends' homes in town, to admit to them what I have done.

"I have killed my daughter," I say when I reach Bashar's gate. "I brought her to Iraq and she's dead now."

I stand on tiptoe, trying to see over the wall of Bashar's courtyard. I peer between chinks in the scrollwork of the iron exterior door. I can see his house, dim in the evening light, but no life stirs within.

"Are you there?" I yell.

I get no response.

"Maybe he's hiding. Maybe he thinks you're coming to take Nadia from him," Layla whispers.

I look down. I look around me. I see Layla nowhere near me, but I find, there in the dirt at the side of Bashar's gate, a foot. It is hardly noticeable, covered in dust, the flesh dried and textured like jerky. A plain cloth shoe, decorated with pink glitter, clings to the flesh below the jutting, shattered ankle bone. It looks like it has been carried here and gnawed by some roving dog.

I pick up the foot and take it with me.

I proceed to the house of Sheikh Seyyed Abdullah to make my confession there. All the lights are off. The front gate is locked. I walk around to the back, to the shack in the alley where Seyyed Abdullah's servant parks his black bulletproof Yukon. I try the gate there. It, too, is locked. I shake it.

"I want to say something," I yell. "Abd al-Rahim, are you there? Sheikh Seyyed Abdullah? Anyone?"

I wait a moment. I hear nothing.

"I'm responsible," I yell. "She'd be alive and happy and with me if we had stayed in America!"

"But I'm here," Layla says. "I'm here."

"No, you're not," I say.

I look around me again, certain I have heard her voice. I reach to touch her, my eyes closed, thinking that if I just imagine her strongly and precisely enough, I will be able to find her again, hold her again, comfort her again.

Yet where I expect her, I find only the sliced torso of a child, hung from the wall of Seyyed Abdullah's house like a cut of lamb in a butcher shop. I untie the blasted-apart body and lower it to the ground. It does not fit in my pocket as the foot does, so I carry it under one arm as I continue through town.

Always Layla is whispering to me.

I stumble as I walk. I tear a hole in the knee of my engagement suit.

"Where are you, Layla? Where are you? I want you here to guide me. I want you to approve before I marry this daughter of Ali al-Hajj ash-Shareefi."

Staggering, I grasp Layla by the shoulder, gently by the shoulder. The next moment she is gone and the streets are dark and each time I grope in the wasteland of this town, I find near me some additional shard of her: sinew and blood, bone and earth, and waste, such waste, such horror. I have her hands in my pockets and am intertwining my fingers with hers and stroking the cold and mangled joints for reassurance. I walk upright, dapper, hands hidden. Then the next moment I grasp a rusted signpost that warns the unsuspecting passerby of the presence of the antitank ditch. I grasp it as though I have fallen against it. I grasp it as though I am holding it upright, using it to prevent the world from spinning. Dangling from the sign is the crusted mass of her hair, scalped, bloodied, tangled, but still with matching pink bows gracing the locks. Maybe I touch her cheek one moment, but the next moment it is stone under my hand, a worn stair step in some forgotten alley, a lintel, a colonnade column desecrated by graffiti and gunfire. And a face, stripped clean from the skull, disfigured, flattened by the absence of supporting bone, supporting cartilage. Such horrors, such whispers, accompany me as I walk across Safwan in my engagement suit, shouting to all the houses, all the people: "It is my fault that she has died."

At last I arrive at Ali ash-Shareefi's house through the back alley. I find my engagement tent crumpled against Ali's back courtyard wall. I kick it. It is a dusty thing, stinking of mildew. I try Ali's back courtyard door. It, too, is locked. I yell the announcement of my guilt. I hear no reply. I stand on the mildewed engagement tent. I yell again. I mumble. I drop the pieces of the little body, turning my pockets inside out, tearing my shirt and the front of my jacket as I try to rid myself of the accumulated guilt, the dismembered bits of her.

I look into Ali's courtyard through a gap between the courtyard door and the garage. In contrast to the rest of the town, the rest of the houses of my friends, I find this house lit, the windows filled with solemn-looking people milling about. A line of people extends into the street in front of the house, shielded from me, shielded from the empty back-alleyway courtyard.

Again I yell, trying to get someone's attention. "Can anyone hear me? It's me, Abu Saheeh. I've come to marry Ulayya. I'm ready!"

No one acknowledges me. No one can hear me over the noise of the party going on inside Ali ash-Shareefi's house. I think about walking around to the front, but instead I climb Ali's fence and slide over its top, landing awkwardly and then rolling in the dust. No one expects me to enter from the alley—the guest of honor, the groom-to-be.

The only person I find in the courtyard is Ali's guard, the man who never speaks. He stands in front of me, above me, where I have fallen in the dust. He has not drawn his gun. For a moment he merely looks at me. Then he extends a hand to help lift me to my feet.

"Don't go in there," he says, tilting his head toward the main section of my father-in-law's house.

He points to the line of people queued at the entrance of the *diwaniya*. The line stretches away around the corner of the road.

I think, *What a popular groom I am!*

"It's my engagement feast," I tell the silent guard.

I grab his arm for support as I try to stand. He pushes me away, but gently.

"No," he says. "Don't go."

"Ulayya and I will be married," I say.

I look around for Layla. She is nowhere to be seen. She has abandoned me again, like Abd al-Rahim, like everyone I have ever loved.

"Ali is dead," the guard says. "The Americans shot him at your little bombing. He was the slowest, the last to run into the quarry."

Through the window at the back of the house I see Hussein. He doesn't notice me for a minute, not until I take the silken handkerchief from my front pocket and snap it in the air in front of me to shake the dust of my daughter's blood from it. The sudden motion attracts Hussein's attention. Or maybe he hears the sound. Or maybe the dust of blood glitters in the air like snowflakes. I watch him, hoping he will beckon to me. And, indeed, after a moment he waves his mobile phone at me.

"That's my signal," I say to the gate guard. "Time to go into the party now."

Hussein dials the phone. He calls me. He rings directly to my line, the phone in the inside pocket of my suit jacket. I don't use the phone often. All its numbers connect to Baghdad, to ministries there, to ministers there, to great men. I don't know how Hussein got the number. From Bashar? From Seyyed Abdullah? I feel the vibration of the phone like an electric current against my chest.

I let it ring.

I watch Hussein as the call goes to my voice mail. But instead of speaking into his phone, he hands it to a man standing to his side, a man standing just where I cannot see him, beyond the frame of the window in the back of Ali's house.

A few more people gather at the window around Hussein. They are backlit by the orange glow of candles within the room, candles on tables, candles on the lid of a coffin, which, I imagine, must hold Ali's body. Hussein points to me. Then he makes a sweeping motion with his arm, leading the gathering of men toward a descending set of stairs at the side of the house, leading them toward me.

"Go now," the guard says. "Go."

The guard helps me through the gate. On the way out, he pushes apart two trash cans behind Ali's garage and rummages between them.

"Take this," he says, handing me a big brown cardboard box. "The things inside are yours."

He locks the back gate and then steps into the shadows of the courtyard as I leave. Seconds later the group of men with Hussein, ten or twelve of them, bump against the locked gate, rattle it in frustration, caught behind it for precious moments. They don't see me but they know I am near.

"We're coming for you," Hussein says. "You can't go far."

I crawl across the alley, pushing the box with my head. I

call for Layla. I tell her, "I shouldn't have ever brought you here."

But Layla doesn't respond. There are no more pieces of her for me to find.

I am alone, alone.

I hear Hussein gathering more men in the street, calling to them on a megaphone, his voice ungodly loud, crackling, full of static and interference. Some of the men on the far side of the house light torches, oil-soaked rags wrapped on the ends of broomsticks and baseball bats. The light from the torches makes the shadows of the men leap across the alley as if they have suddenly discovered the place where I crouch and cower, waiting for Layla to come carry me away to one of her dreamlands.

But Layla doesn't come.

I hear the crowd stirring. I hear Hussein exhorting them. They are ready to chase me. They have the necessary numbers, the necessary fury, the necessary incitement.

"Rocks," Hussein bellows into his megaphone. "Stones. We'll do this like the *hajj*. We'll stone Iblees, stone the Devil. We'll cast him away from us."

I picture them coming for me. I picture the rain of stones, the inglorious end, trying to keep myself upright, trying to shield my head, my face, as the fist-size rocks pelt me and bloody me.

I gather my strength and, lifting the big brown box in my arms, I dart from the shadows, recrossing the street and dashing into the maze of alleyways. Hussein's mob pursues me, light from their torches flickering off the corners of the passageways behind me, off the roofs and walls of the houses that loom over me. I manage to stay a street or two ahead of them, turning at random, striding down straight-aways, doubling back. Spittle flies from the corners of my mouth. I haven't run so hard in ages. My chest feels as if it has been split open, sawed open, butchered, burning on a line of slashed sutures where my brother has ripped me in half.

Still I call for Layla: "Save me. Save me. Bring me a horse or an airplane or a Jet Ski."

And still she does not reply. She has abandoned me. Without my whiskey, without a moment to stop, to wet my tongue, to loosen my mind and my imagination, I know she will not come. She isn't here.

After a few blocks the light of the torches fades. I have lost them. I slow to a trot and then to a walk. In the distance I hear the rumble of the mob and, by listening to it, I can tell the direction toward which they head: west, toward my house. I know I will not return there. Like the pristine white diplomatic house in Umm al-Khanzeer, it is a place to which I know I will never return. There will soon be no house left. So I head north into the quiet closed shops in the market, my market in the cloverleaf intersection, my van-tage point for watching the American convoys. It is the only safe place left for me.

When I reach the door of my shop, the first ray of the morning sun just barely crests the eastern oil fields, out be-yond the quarry and the overpass.

33

فجر الإثنين
واستدعاء الهاتف

Dawn Monday, a Phone Call

At last I sit safely inside my store. I dial my voice mail so that I can hear the message.

"Hello?" I say. "Hello?"

"Press one for menu. Press two for voice mail."

"Hello?" I say again.

I press two.

After a moment I hear the voice on the message. I expect to hear the voice of Hussein or one of Hussein's cronies, one of the men continually surrounding him. But the voice I hear, the voice of the man to whom Hussein handed his mobile phone, is that of Abd al-Rahim. He says, simply: "My uncle withdraws his protection from you. He says to tell you, to remind you, that you are half dead."

That is all Abd al-Rahim says. He clicks the phone shut,

audibly, midway through a raspy little laugh I hear from Hussein in the background.

I play the message again: "You are half dead."

"You are half dead."

Again and again, Abd al-Rahim's voice instructs me: "You are half dead."

It is the sign, our sign, the sign Sheikh Seyyed Abdullah has all along promised to give me when he determines for certain that the convoy comes. The sheikh has launched Abd al-Rahim into the final phase of our plan. Seyyed Abdullah and Abd al-Rahim easily enough convince Hussein to do their dirty work, getting rid of me. And, if I pull off the bombing of the American convoy, I'm sure Seyyed Abdullah will direct the Americans' fury against Hezbollah, ridding him of that problem, too—a double victory, a masterstroke.

"Seyyed Abdullah withdraws his protection from you. You are half dead," says the voice of Seyyed Abdullah's messenger.

I play it again.

You are half dead: a sign from long ago, a hieroglyph in my Cracker Jack language. A reference similar in its depth and obscurity to my very favorite word of all: *bowling*.

* * *

I didn't sleep for days after the bombing. I never went back to the Americans in the Green Zone. I started drinking and I lived as a homeless man, unkempt, a scarecrow, similar in appearance to the way Saddam Hussein looked, unshaven and wildly filthy, when the American forces pulled him from the hole where he had hidden himself in Tikrit.

Sheikh Seyyed Abdullah came up to Baghdad on some errand of business and it was he who found me, he who rescued me from the life I lived at that time.

If it weren't for the quality of the suit I wore, the fine tailoring, if it weren't for the wingtip shoes, a man of his sort would never have deigned to speak with me, so covered in dust, so ragged had I become.

"Allahu Akbar, God is great," said he. "But you, sir, you look horrible. You look half dead."

I turned, then, to face him, for I recognized his voice from the medical briefings in the American headquarters. I turned to face him, and, despite my hollow eyes, my harrowed face, he recognized me.

"Ya Allah," he said. "Is that you, good Dr. ash-Shumari? What has happened to you?"

The void had opened in me already, blown open. I could not look into it. I could not admit that my daughter was dead, so I said to him: "I thought I was an American. I lived there fifteen years. I thought it would be okay for me to return here and help. I thought I was one of them."

"Certainly you looked the part," the sheikh said, not without a little disapproval.

"Now I want to kill my brother," I told him. "And the Americans, their justice, their life-in-prison, such a thing isn't justice enough for me."

The sheikh recited from the Sura of the Feast for me then, saying, "And we decreed for them that it is a life for a life, an eye for an eye, a nose for a nose, an ear for an ear, a tooth for a tooth, and for wounds retaliation."

"Yes," I said. "That is what I have decided. I tried to bribe my way into Abu Ghraib so I could do the job myself. But that doesn't work with the Americans. He's safe from me. I have no recourse. I have no honor."

Seyyed Abdullah grew silent for a moment as I told him this. When I finished he said, "Abu Ghraib?"

"Yes."

"They are shutting Abu Ghraib, you know."

"No. I didn't know this," I said.

The fact only increased my despair. I had guessed, the moment the bombing occurred, that Yasin was responsible. I knew it in my heart. It was the only explanation. My work was for the good of the ummah, the community. No one else had threatened me. No one else had reason to threaten me. I told the Americans of my suspicion. I led them to Yasin and he confessed. But instead of allowing me to kill him, as I expected, they put him in their prison—just close enough to tempt me, just far enough to be shielded from the justice I wanted, I needed, to deliver.

"Where will they take him?" I asked. "Guantánamo?"

A light flickered in Seyyed Abdullah's eyes.

He said, "They are building a new prison in Basra Province, very near my town of Safwan. A new prison into which they will transfer the Abu Ghraib detainees."

"Impregnable, I'm sure."

"Yes," he said. "Three perimeters. One far out in the desert, with no walls but with remote sensors. Then the fences: a perimeter facing outward, barbed wire, guard towers, machine guns leveled at our goats and oil derricks. The last perimeter, facing inward—more fences, more towers, more machine guns—to keep the prisoners in."

"So?" I asked. I could see that he was thinking.

He offered me his hand, helping me to my feet. We walked to-gether across the street to where his pistol-carrying servant held open the door to a black bulletproof Yukon.

"He will be most vulnerable along the way," Seyyed Abdul-lah said after a moment. "All we will need to know is when the Americans transport him. That will be a piece of information we can purchase from any of the translators who work at Abu Ghraib."

"Then what?" I asked.

34

فجر الإثنين
والعد التنازلي

Dawn Monday, Countdown

THIRTY-EIGHT SECONDS.

The sun breaks free of the eastern desert, lifting above the low haze on the flat horizon.

I am safe, at least for the next necessary moments, while Hussein focuses on my house. Calmly I go out the side door of my store and watch from curbside as the underbelly of the cloudy morning reflects the fire that burns on the far side of Safwan. It didn't take Hussein's mob long to reach my house, a five-minute walk across town, no more. Even from the market I could hear their voices, the chanting. I could hear the shattering of my windows. Now I hear the fire itself, the lapping of flames, the sucking sound, the crackling.

I wonder if the fire might slow or scare the American convoys coming around the bypass. I decide it will not slow them at all. They'll regard it as a civilian matter. Nothing for them to care about as long as the crowd itself, the bulk of them streaming across the road, doesn't affect the transport of supplies north and south, south and north, one thousand semis a day. Even if it does affect the convoys going to and from Kuwait, it will not affect my special convoy, the bus convoy, the prisoner convoy. That group of vehicles never turns onto the bypass. It always continues south, passing Safwan, passing over my overpass on its way to Camp Bucca, just a few kilometers down the road.

I watch the fire and the column of smoke that rises in the west. I watch it for a long moment before I take a small bottle of acid from a shelf in my store—a covered can, nothing more—then gather under my other arm the box given to me by Ali ash-Shareefi's guard. Still calm, I walk up the nearer on-ramp to first wake and then speak with Mahmoud in his tent.

Thirty-eight seconds.

I don't mention my ripped engagement suit, my dirty, unshaven face, my sweaty skin, or red eyes to Mahmoud. His own eyes are still red, his own clothes dirty, his own face unshaven and unkempt. Mahmoud is too deep in his grief to notice mine. It does not take me long to convince him to switch places with me.

"Hussein will come to my shop," I tell him. "He and his mob even now are burning my house. He will come to burn my shop next. He will seek me there."

"You are sure?"

"An eye for an eye," I say.

I hand Mahmoud the can of acid. I unscrew the cap of it, cautious not to let the clear liquid slop over the edges.

The fumes do more than burn my eyes as they escape. They sicken my stomach. I see Michele's body, still kneeling upright in the street, hands repetitively scratching scabbed skin from his face. I see my brother, the blank black look in his eyes when I brought the police to the door of his house and watched them arrest him. I see gore. I see horror. I see bits of Layla in the rubble of my house. Quickly, to protect myself from these visions, to protect myself from lapsing into hallucination, I screw the cap on the acid bottle once again. The smell, the burning scent of it, dissipates. So, too, the upwelling, insistent images disappear—at least temporarily.

"An eye for an eye," I say to Mahmoud for a second time.

He agrees with my plan. He takes the bottle with him to my store. After he enters, he shuts the side door but does not lock it. It remains slightly ajar, an inviting sort of openness, a temptation. I imagine him waiting on the edge of the stool, poised with the bottle of acid for Hussein's arrival.

I set the big brown box in front of me on Mahmoud's cot. I open the box and unpack it. As I suspect, it contains all the gifts I gave to Ulayya.

I take them out and arrange them, one at a time, along the curb in front of Mahmoud's tent, spacing them at three-meter intervals: pretty wrapping paper ripped open, pretty bows wrecked and askew, pretty tissue paper torn and wrinkled, pretty like Michele's face. When I finish the arrangement, the packages blend with the strange debris on the periphery of the road. Nothing out of place, I think, to see unwrapped gift boxes amid such refuse. Nothing out of place to see a big man with brilliantined hair in an expensive but dirty and sweaty pin-striped suit instead of the normal scrubby little overpass guard.

I scan the packages as I sit, just as Mahmoud normally sits, leaning on the three-legged stool.

Farthest down the road, the box that held the blue length of silk and, resting in front of it, the gift that I substituted, the gift Ulayya actually received: a rock the size of a baseball, still with little shards of glass clinging to it from two passages through my upstairs window.

Then the box that held the length of cotton cloth and, resting in front of it, the gift I substituted, the gift Ulayya actually received: a mobile phone, nothing too modern or too fancy, not an iPhone or BlackBerry or whatever the Americans now use.

Next closest to me: the box that held the linen sheets for our wedding bed. Resting in front of it, the gift I substituted for Ulayya: a little microcassette tape containing a song of alien voices.

Then, directly in front of me, the biggest box, the one that held several faceted crystal goblets. Resting in front of it is the gift I substituted, the gift Ulayya received: a Chicago Cubs baseball cap.

Closer to the overpass bridge, I've positioned the box that held the green and blue women's clothes and, in front of it, the gift for Ulayya: a single arm from a toy jack-in-the-box, dwarfed without its body.

Then, even closer to the bridge: a bottle. It originally contained henna, but the bottle now resting in front of the unwrapped box isn't henna at all. It is blood, blood I substituted for henna. If my new bride was to be marked in celebration on her hands and feet, if patterns were to be painted there, I wished it to be with blood from my own veins. And so I had opened the flesh on the palm of my right hand after drinking enough whiskey to dull the pain. I had opened the flesh and filled for Ulayya a bottle of my own living blood.

Last, the final box, the box that had at one time held the golden necklace I purchased for Ulayya. It is a small box. In front of it I have placed the gift furthest removed from its context, furthest removed from any possible understanding that could ever have dawned on Ulayya. It is a single dirty length of yarn adorned with bird bones and dollhouse keys strung into the form of an anklet. What business had I in trying to bequeath this item to Ulayya? How could she possibly have understood it without knowing what had happened to my daughter? How could she possibly have understood it without the context of that first sight of Layla, two or three weeks ago, when her dirty foot jangled in the evening sunlight, bones and trinket-keys tinkling?

The box behind the bird-bone anklet hides the bomb. I intend the anklet to be delivered by the blast, by the speeding melted-copper projectile. I intend for it to be delivered to the exact epicenter of the crisis I am about to create. I want it to be consumed in flames, to be oxidized into infinitesimal nothingness, to be removed from my presence forever.

35

الصمت

Pause

I PAUSE WHILE THE cacophony catches up to me, while the spinning of my head, the last of the noxious, blaspheming whiskey, leaves me. I pause while I sit comfortably on Mahmoud's three-legged chair, waiting for the convoy to approach along the northern road from Baghdad, hoping it arrives before Hussein and his mob.

36

A Fiction

I'VE FIGURED IT OUT.

I've come to a realization.

It might sound crazy, crazier than anything else I've said or done, but I think that I at last understand or can admit what has happened. I understand where Layla has gone, why she hasn't visited me these last few days in the same fashion as she did during the first few weeks of our regular contact.

I've suspected that Layla isn't real for a long time, but I didn't know why.

I didn't know. I don't know. Not with any certainty.

But the anklet: it tells me something. At that first sight of Layla wearing the anklet, I should have known that she was nothing more than a ghost, a genie, a haunting, but I couldn't admit to myself that the anklet was mine. I had strung together the bits of debris from my bombed house and had hidden the little loop of yarn under the counter of my shop, wrapped around the windowsill support beam. I had placed it there, stored it there, when first I opened the mobile-phone business. It was like a talisman for me, a touchstone during my first days of work in Safwan. I would reach under the counter, wrap my fingers around the anklet, and feel reassured, reminded of my purpose. I endured the miseries of starting life anew simply by remembering that collection of trinkets: bird bones, dollhouse keys, little bits of salvaged debris from the burned remains of my life in Baghdad, little bits of my daughter.

Layla isn't real. I know that for certain.

She is a fiction, my fiction.

When I opened the box of gifts Ulayya rejected, here on the overpass, I saw again my Cubs hat, my heart-size rock, the clipped-off arm of the jack-in-the-box. These items confused me. But the anklet in the last box confused me even more. I was sure that I had seen her wearing it, this girl named Layla who haunted me in the market, this girl named Layla who reminds me of my daughter. I am sure that she wore it. But she couldn't have been in possession of it before I met her. She must have been a dream. Likewise, she couldn't have known the things she seems to have known. She couldn't have guessed about America, about Chicago, about home. She is the last flaring, false as fox fire, of the spark that once filled my heart.

No more will I give credence to her seemingly solid apparition as it manifests itself before me. No more will I believe her when she whispers "I am here" to me, only to leave me clenching some blown-apart portion of her poor little figure. I will ignore this girl Layla and I will push forward into cold stark reality without her. I've constructed her from the best bits of my memory, the brightest moments from within my thirteen-year void, pieces of life that floated up to the surface and that I channeled into the dream of Layla's presence around me here in Safwan. I will not carry pieces of my daughter around in my pockets anymore. Because I am burying my daughter, I know I also am burying Layla.

Am I more pitiable without her, without her as a crutch? When she is absent, I am staid, solemn, cold, and quiet, a man without humor, a man toward the end of his life who spends his remaining days counting convoys, watching a weak, heartbroken guard pace to and fro on a deserted highway overpass. Without these dreams and apparitions, I am drunkenly stupid, troubled, and not nearly as mystic or blessed as I have pretended to be. But with these hallucinations, I am only partially real. I've decided, just as I have given up the bottle, to give up my daughter's ghost. I've decided to become real once more, no matter what pain it brings.

The realization of this helps, at least a little. The admission of this helps. It has taken me a long while to get here, but everything is clear to me now, not perfectly clear, but clear enough. Everything is quieter now, too.

I can endure these last moments without my hallucinations. I can, perhaps I must, complete my work in the real light of day.

My daughter is dead.

I'm only just a little bit crazy.

My daughter is dead and the admission proves, proves beyond doubt, that I have chased a phantom here in Safwan, a child as insubstantial as the wind.

Praise be to Allah, the All-Knowing, for His mysteries and for His majesty.

37

قنبلة

A Bomb

THIRTY-EIGHT SECONDS.

Abd al-Rahim arrives at my store just a moment too late.

I think it is he, first, who approaches, striding up the road from the center of town. I find it strange that he comes alone; Seyyed Abdullah would certainly task him with bringing Hussein and the whole gang of Hezbollah to the scene of the accident I am ready to create. I worry that Abd al-Rahim will surprise Mahmoud. I worry that he will be the one upon whom Mahmoud mistakenly dumps the bottle of acid, executing his well-deserved revenge. I had counted on Hussein to be the first to find me, the first to think of me hiding in my shop when I never came rushing, hair on fire and lungs filled with smoke, flushed like a hen from the bush, out one of the doors or windows of my burning house.

I should have thought that, as well trained as Abd al-Rahim is, he might be a step or two ahead of Hussein. I should have thought that he might reach my shop ahead of Hussein. I am about to stand, about to shout a warning to Abd al-Rahim, something like: "Don't open the door!" But something prevents me. I do not shout. I hear the voice of the approaching man, sounding from the direction of my shack, but closer to town, still too distant for me to see him clearly.

I strain to hear the words the voice says, and at last I pick them out above the hundred other noises of the early-morning market. The man screams: "You raped her!"

Over and over the voice screams: "You raped her. You raped her! I beat the truth out of her. You took her honor, you bastard."

I can't discern the meaning of this. I think, Abd al-Rahim. But it isn't Abd al-Rahim. I think, Hussein. But of course it isn't Hussein. I hear the screaming of the voice grow louder as it approaches. I see the silhouette of the man in the dim morning light. It moves behind the frame of my shack, out of view. I hear the side door of my shack swing open, violently, smashing on its hinges against the opposite wall. I have run out of time to stand, to intervene. I hear a scream, then a gunshot, then a second gunshot—pistol fire, higher-pitched and quicker than the tearing recoil of a rifle.

After a moment, just long enough for me to let out my breath, I hear the pistol fall to the floor of my shack, making a dull thump on the wooden-plank flooring. The voice that had accused me of rape, the voice of Bashar, suddenly screams, continues screaming as a wild flailing and flapping, a tearing and cursing, fills my little store. Bashar runs from the shop, from the market, limping and brushing at his left leg where Mahmoud's acid burns through his pants. He runs through the blue-tiled arch and away into Safwan.

I want to call to him. I want to run after him. I think of Mahmoud, who must be dying on the floor of the shack from the two pistol shots. I think of Bashar, fleeing, probably confused, certainly ashamed, certainly in terrible pain—the flesh of his leg eaten through and through. I decide to run after him. I decide I must help him, but as I stand, I see in the northern distance the convoy of prison buses finally approaching. Already it nears the off-ramp of the American bypass along the western edge of Safwan, not far, not far from me at all. The bus convoy won't take the off-ramp. The buses are fated to continue toward me. Repeated observation confirms for me their route. They'll maintain their speed and trajectory southeast toward Umm Qasr, toward the American prison camp at Bucca.

I sit once again on Mahmoud's stool. My hands sweat. I wipe them on the front of my pin-striped, torn-open pant legs.

The lead vehicles of the convoy stream toward me. The noise of their engines overwhelms any last moaning, any calls for my help that Mahmoud might make as he dies. I reach into his tent and pick up his Kalashnikov with my bandaged right hand, the hand I bled to fill Ulayya's bottle.

No need to stand.

No need to look nervous.

No need to be nervous.

Nothing out of place here.

Quickly I glance at the bridge, where I have positioned the last of Ulayya's presents and the infrared sensor beam through which the convoy must pass. The beam triggers the bomb. Most such bombs hit the passenger-side door. They are targeted to kill the commander of the vehicle, who sits in the passenger seat, operating the vehicle's navigation equipment and radios. Maybe the bomb also kills the driver, passing first through the armored door and the body of the vehicle commander, ricocheting within, splintering, setting off boxes of ammunition stored inside the Humvee so that the whole vehicle ignites.

My bomb, though, I've timed to strike in a different way, not allowing that last tenth of a second to deliver the charge exactly against the door of a vehicle moving one hundred, maybe one hundred and twenty kilometers per hour. I want the charge to hit the front wheel of the vehicle. I want it to detonate early, to disable the chassis, nothing more. No need to kill Americans. I'm a friendly guard, dressed up in my engagement clothes. I'm a friendly guard, leaving presents along the roadway. Maybe I'm a little bigger than the guard who is normally on the bridge here—maybe I'm the uncle of that guard, older, taller, more confident in myself.

"My nephew is at a religious celebration," I will say if they ask me, if they interrogate me.

Or perhaps, "My nephew is at an engagement party. A friend of his. I'm here in his place. What? Yes, of course I'll be happy to keep an eye on the prison bus for you while you investigate the bomb that mistakenly struck the wheel of your buddy's vehicle. Lucky for you that no one has been injured, no Patricks, no Davids. All things are as Allah wills...No, I didn't see anyone place the bomb here on the bridge. I was paid to look the other way. We're all paid to look the other way. No need to get involved in someone else's war."

The convoy speeds toward me.

Not much time remains.

I'd like to think that Abd al-Rahim arrives only after he hears the blast from the bomb, but that isn't the way it happens. He arrives with the mob. He is too late to help me but he is just in time to execute his master's true orders. He has brought Hussein. He has implicated Hussein. He has fulfilled his mission.

Together, he and Hussein open the door to my shack. They hope to find me but instead they find Mahmoud. Hussein rushes into the shack to prod at Mahmoud's slumped little body while Abd al-Rahim, more savvy by far, looks up at the place where I sit on Mahmoud's stool. He looks at me but he looks past me, too. He looks past me into the road, where the convoy cruises forward.

His mouth forms the word *No!*

I follow his gaze.

He looks at Layla.

She stands there, there in the middle of the road. She stands with both hands open before her and her bare feet planted wide. She signals for the convoy to stop. She warns them. She waves her arms. She jumps up and down and does everything she can to make them stop, even putting her body between the convoy and the bomb. But it is too late.

I don't believe in her.

I've decided she isn't real.

It is impossible for her to be standing there with her hands outstretched and her teeth clenched and her eyes fixed forward on the grille of the onrushing Humvee. It is impossible: what I see of her is a mirage, nothing more. If

I blink, she will be gone. If I concentrate more precisely on reality—on sunlight above, shadows below, the speeding vehicles, the heated sticky tar on the pavement, the trash blowing across the desert in the dry wind, the plan, my plan, my Greater Purpose—if I concentrate on reality, Layla will be gone. She is a figment of my imagination, my regret, my sadness. She is my dead daughter come back to haunt me or to bring my soul some semblance of life and laughter. She isn't real. I signed no adoption papers for her. What was I signing in those moments of swimming, sharklike interrogation?

The convoy doesn't strike her. It can't strike her.

She isn't real.

I don't believe in her.

I don't hear her body wetly collapse against the front bumper of the Humvee. The noise I hear, the gentle thump, the screech of the Humvee's wheels, I must be creating in my torn-apart mind. The part of her that I see with my own eyes—as it turns, in a blink of infinitesimal time, from living thing to bloody dust—is a trick. Perhaps I hesitate, I dwell on Layla, because I am afraid of this moment of reckoning, afraid of the pledge I have sworn to myself to take my brother's life. Perhaps, in this moment of heightened awareness, my mind replays and recasts the memories of a lifetime of pain and bloodshed and aloneness so that I am fooled into thinking that I see the body of a child standing in the road to block a two-ton Humvee.

Layla isn't real. She can't stop a convoy. She might dance like Britney Spears, but that isn't real. It's movie magic. It's laser lights and light shows and liposuction. Britney Spears doesn't exist any more truly than the tongue of the blind boy in front of the mosque. Abd al-Rahim has joined Hezbollah at his uncle's command. And Layla isn't real.

The first vehicle, that lead Humvee, swerves after it hits the apparition of her. It veers sharply to the right and smashes into the railing at the exact spot where I positioned the bird-bone anklet and the infrared laser. The vehicle cuts diagonally across the beam. The bomb explodes. The front end of the Humvee plants itself into the railing of the bridge. The back end jacks up like a bucking horse as the bomb blast lifts it over its pinioned front.

The Humvee vaults the railing, hurdles upside down over the roadway embankment. The gunner in the turret comes free of his harness. He tumbles with the vehicle. The objects, the huge Humvee and the body of the gunner, are like a falcon and a sparrow in an aerial maneuver, the sparrow doomed, clumsy, beating its wings against uncaring air. The Humvee falls to earth and drives a long ditch through the center of the tents and shacks that comprise the stores in the southwest leaf of the cloverleaf interchange. It skids across the ground and up onto the roadway that passes under the bridge, coming finally to rest just where I chose to locate my mobile-phone shop, the place Sheikh Seyyed Abdullah and I together chose because of its excellent view of the highway.

The Humvee teeters. Metal scrapes against asphalt and whines as it compresses from the heat of the friction and of the blast. Near it, Hussein emerges from the door of my shop. He stands motionless and erect as a bird that has caught its prey. When the Humvee stops rocking and screeching, I see him bend down to the pavement. For a long second he squats and then he picks up an object that has rolled to a stop at his feet. He lifts it by the hair and holds it in front of him. Blood drools down his forearms.

Layla?

Layla isn't real.

She is a figment of my imagination.

I look for Abd al-Rahim, who had stood in just the same spot where Hussein now holds a little girl's head. I look for Abd al-Rahim and find him, oddly, as if he has dodged the falling giant missile of the wrecked Humvee, juking and jiving and slipping past certain death, running bravely forward toward me, running bravely forward past me, running bravely forward into the middle of the roadway, where smoke boils from the bomb crater and draws a veil around the scene like a curtain falling at the end of a theater show. Abd al-Rahim moves offstage. The smoke wraps around him. I wait for a moment, expecting to see him emerge, maybe doing the backstroke, maybe now finally feeling confident enough to swim in the deep end of my dark Lake Michigan nightmare.

Maybe he isn't real, either.

Maybe he will dissolve into goldfish.

Maybe he will plug his nose, dive, and come up from the mucky depths of the lake with a handful of Layla. Maybe he will return for a curtain call, for a tossed bouquet, for headlines in the daily gossip column and comments on his nice shoes.

The buses in the convoy can't turn as sharply as the Humvee. They are spared the fate of vaulting over the railing of the overpass. They continue down the highway for a short distance through the crater of my exploded bomb, each of them veering to the edge of the road, magically avoiding the place where Abd al-Rahim's imaginary body kneels over the imaginary body of dead Layla. I see them, Abd al-Rahim and Layla, wafting in and out of the broken bank of clouds. They are nothing more than two apparitions in a passing illusion.

They are unreal.

I do not believe in them.

The buses come to rest. They skid to a halt. The nearest of them is only three or four meters from the place where I wait on Mahmoud's stool.

The deafening explosion rings in my ears. Everything except the most urgent of movements fades from my mind. I begin, aloud, to count.

"Thirty-eight, thirty-seven, thirty-six..." Whether I run toward the place where I think Layla's imaginary flattened body lies, the place where imaginary Abd al-Rahim kneels, or whether I merely run toward the first of the buses, I do not know. It is one and the same thing.

"Thirty-five, thirty-four, thirty-three..." Whether I board the buses in an orderly fashion, each in turn, unobserved by the panicked and scattering security guards, who tumble, coughing and dizzy, into the roadway, or whether I run from place to place, half mad, I do not know. It is one and the same thing.

"Thirty-two, thirty-one, thirty..." Whether the smoke increases, something on fire, a vehicle, a store, the tents in the market, or whether my eyes cloud with tears, I do not know. It is one and the same thing.

"Twenty-nine, twenty-eight, twenty-seven..." Whether it will take the middle and the rear Humvees as long to sort out the proper response as it would in a normal convoy with thirty-odd vehicles, or whether the response will come more quickly, I do not know. I will reach the buses before the Americans or after the Americans, as Allah wills, one and the same thing.

"Twenty-six, twenty-five, twenty-four..." Whether the safety lever on Mahmoud's Kalashnikov flips itself into the hot position of its own accord, or whether my years in Saddam's army, years of forced operation, training, taught me to do the thing instinctively, I do not know. Either way, it is one and the same thing.

"Twenty-three, twenty-two, twenty-one..." Whether each face I see as I step up into the first bus really is distinguishable from every other face, there in the chaos, there in the smoke and noise, or whether they all, by assuming such looks of doubt and wonder and dismay, blend into one another, I do not know. I scan them on the first bus and I am certain, despite their sameness, that none of the faces is the face of my brother. I would know. I am certain he is not there and I am certain that it is *not* one and the same thing. It is a particular thing. His death is nothing I want to leave to chance.

"Twenty, nineteen, eighteen..." Whether the body of a little girl lies flat beneath this bus, or if by miracle it has been lifted and thrown from the onrushing vehicles—angelic interference, robot psychosis—I do not know. I am crazy. I am crazy to think such things. She is imaginary. She is mine and imaginary and I care only to think of her in the way I will always see her in my memory, before I picked the pieces of her from the rubble of my house, thinking forward already at that moment to the time when I might avenge her.

"Seventeen, sixteen, fifteen..." I do care. I care. An eye for an eye. I will exact my revenge upon my brother, even if the long tortures and deprivations of the American prisons, and the longer decisions of its courts, will not give me Yasin's life. I will have it. I will, may Allah allow. I testified against Yasin in the American courts, and I will have his life.

"Fourteen, thirteen, twelve..." I board the second bus and find no sign of my brother. I do not worry. It is too late for worry. Sheikh Seyyed Abdullah assured me Yasin would be among them this time. Seyyed Abdullah will have his town cleared of interference from Hezbollah after he pins the blame on Hussein's gang. "Hezbollah triggered it," he will tell the Americans. "My nephew Abd al-Rahim witnessed them at the scene. He was standing there in the market next to this very man, this man Hussein, who lifted up the head of one of the victims." The Americans will arrest Hussein. Seyyed Abdullah will have his uncontested authority in Safwan. And I will have my brother's blood.

"Eleven, ten, nine..." The third, the third bus, there in the third, midway down the left aisle of seats, I see him, my brother, Yasin, and he recognizes me as his brother, just as I want him to do. He recognizes me and stands to accept me as his rescuer. All the old hurts will be sewn up, like a kitten's belly, and he will forgive me. He will forgive me for not joining his cause. He will forgive me for being smarter than him. He will forgive me even though Father liked me best. He might go so far as to apologize for my daughter's death, for Layla's death. I see him. I see my brother. He plans his words of reconciliation.

"Eight, seven, six..." He plans his words. They form on his trembling lips. He purses those lips, sputters syllables of thankfulness until he sees my bandaged hand, the hand from which I have drawn the blood I used to swear myself indelibly to follow this path, to board the prison buses, to track him, to find him, to take him at a time when he would be exposed, the blanket of American protection forcibly removed. My brother plans his sweetened words until he sees my finger firm and sure on the trigger of Mahmoud's rifle.

"Five, four, three…" I raise the barrel of the Kalashnikov. I sight it upon my brother's chest. He turns to the side, an instinctive reaction to minimize his exposure. But the shackles of the Americans hold him fast to his seat. They hold him facing forward. I have long expected his flinching reaction. I have long dwelled upon the sweetness of seeing him cower. It is exactly as I pictured it in my dreams: his refusal to take the death I bring him as a man should take it, full in the chest with eyes upturned toward Allah, or gazing directly into the face that faces him down.

No man should die like a coward, like a running dog.

Yet he turns from me. He flinches from me even as I pull the trigger of the weapon to bring his fate unto him. Cowardliness or bravery, they are one and the same thing. They are nothing.

"Three, two, one…" The hammer falls, yet that familiar, comforting stench of sulfur doesn't reach me. I smell no scent at all. The hammer falls and the trigger clicks, but the bullet, the bullet, the bullet has been taken from my gun.

Acknowledgments

I owe a debt of gratitude to many people for helping me process and understand the strange experience of almost-war, slow-war, during the bloody rebuilding of Iraq that I was privileged to help undertake—however successfully or unsuccessfully—in 2005 and 2006. First, to the men who lost their lives in that war, our soldiers, whom none of us will forget. Second, to my military chain of command and to the British troops—Brigadier General Charles Barr, Lieutenant Colonel Todd Taves, Captain Roddy Christie—who supported my work with the Safwan town council. Third, to my interpreters, especially Bashar al-Masri, who not only provided the vital link of language between me and the Iraqis but who also served as a veritable textbook on Islam, local culture, and the recent history of Basra Province. Fourth, to my teachers at the Defense Language Institute, especially Guitta Nader, Loris Ibrahim, Salah Kamal, and Fawzi Khowshaba, who opened up the beautiful Arabic language to me and who read and provided valuable commentary on the various drafts of this book. To the several other people who read the manuscript and commented—my wife, Angie, her friend Deborah Hawkins, my friend Aflah al-Harrasi, and especially Jon Sternfeld and Vanessa Kehren, who each read and reread the book numerous times. Finally, I would like to thank the Safwan town council and the people of Safwan itself. They have endured three wars and the presence of our coalition troops, not to mention the corruption and ineffectiveness of the upper echelons of their own government. Yet somehow, by the grace of God, life there continues.

Benjamin Buchholz is the author of *Private Soldiers,* a book about his Wisconsin National Guard unit's year-long deployment to southern Iraq. He was stationed with his family in Oman from 2010 to 2011 and currently lives in Princeton, New Jersey, where he is pursuing a graduate degree in Middle East Security Studies. *One Hundred and One Nights* is his first novel.

BACK BAY · READERS' PICK

One Hundred and One Nights

A novel

by

Benjamin Buchholz

A conversation with
Benjamin Buchholz

How did the idea for One Hundred and One Nights *come to you?*

In the same way much of Tim O'Brien's work aims to help
him, and perhaps others, find a catharsis for the experience
of Vietnam, I found that even while I was still in Iraq, the
events I experienced began to pour into and (sometimes unintentionally) fill the writing I was doing. Two events in
particular—the death of a young Iraqi girl and the bombing of one of our American convoys—really affected me.
Abu Saheeh's story is an attempt, on one hand, to understand and empathize with the types of personalized hatred
and personalized loss and personalized dementia that I believe to be at the core of the mind-set required for someone
to perpetrate a bombing or kill another human being. And,
on the other hand, Layla's character demanded to be written, maybe in memorial to the dead little girl. So those
two characters conspired. They gripped me. Writing about
them allowed me to think more clearly about them, about
their problems and the ways they might have interacted
during the war that consumed them. It took me a while,

a couple of years, actually, to really put Abu Saheeh and Layla into their current form as characters. They appear, the Layla character especially, in a lot of the shorter, more fragmentary work I was writing and publishing as short fiction before beginning *One Hundred and One Nights* in earnest.

How does your career with the U.S. military overlap with your identity as a writer?

Of course the army has given me a base of subject matter that I can draw on and that, often, seems to demand (of its own accord!) that I process, churn, think about, and eventually clarify into the structure of a story the quirks, shocks, joys, horrors, and moments of close comradeship such experience contains. So that is the big, overarching impact the military has on my writing. But also my day job affects my writing in more subtle ways. For instance, the required format for military writing frowns on any use of passive voice because of the nonattributive nature of passive verbs. I like the fact that the active voice has been ingrained in me, almost brainwashed into me. I think it has had a positive effect on the pace and quality of my fiction. Maintaining a military career makes me think very hard about drawing a line between fiction and nonfiction. Being influenced by and processing real-life events through fictionalization is one thing, but actually reporting them, in a nonfictional way, can strike too close to home, either with regard to the work itself or to the people around me who have experienced war and military life. In a larger way this is something with which all writers contend, drawing a line between fiction and fact. Because military work focuses on fact and present-day circumstances, I find it sort of freeing and necessary, actually, to have an outlet for hypothesizing, a place that allows me to give structure to ideas and concepts that seem in the real world important but also ephemeral, shifty, unquantifiable, nonlinear. I hope that the opposite may also happen, that my writing will someday contribute to and benefit my work for the military, perhaps giving voice and depth to discussions on the Middle East that otherwise remain in the purview of mass media and politics.

Why did you decide to write from an Iraqi perspective rather than a more familiar, American one?

I think it is an issue of empathy, of trying to understand other people. Writing from my own point of view or from the point of view of someone culturally similar to me would have been boring. A novel is a long, painful, intrusive thing to produce. Having some separation between the narrative voice and the voice of "myself" was important during the writing process. Abu Saheeh's voice kept the writing fresh and interesting for me. Additionally, I find the Iraqi man to be prototypical. He dances. He sings. He makes war without flinching from his adversaries, without hiding behind bulletproof glass. He is loyal, temperamental, sentimental, strong. The language of Iraq, the Arabic dialect used in the region, is gruff, thick, and poetic. I knew that the portrayal of an Iraqi man long exposed to the comfort of America and its somewhat emasculating tendencies would automatically exhibit certain types of internal conflict. I hope that Abu Saheeh captures some of this conflict, some of the way in which I think a man's inherent rationality falters when experiencing major, soul-shaking events. Abu Saheeh is offered a softer, less definite spirituality (through Layla's dreams and Layla's haunting) that might help him live a sane life. Whether he chooses to accept that offering is the crux of his internal struggle and the most immediate reason I was compelled to write from his perspective.

Is there a reason you chose to write fiction rather than nonfiction?

As I mentioned earlier, fictionalizing my military experience has allowed me simultaneously to process and to keep a certain amount of emotional distance between actuality and creativity. Also, I've seen a lot of movies and read a number of nonfiction books (some of them very good, like *We Were Soldiers Once ... and Young* and *Black Hawk Down*) told from the perspective of the American soldier. But I have not seen very many efforts at telling the flip side of war. While such stories do exist—like *Slaughterhouse Five, Doctor Zhivago,* and Bao Ninh's *The Sorrow of War*—I don't think an attempt has been made for the current age.

What are you working on now?

I'm really interested in how American culture continues to influence the Middle East, how it affects the traditional lives of people there, sometimes producing moments of beauty, sometimes moments of confrontation or even calamity. This was a theme in *One Hundred and One Nights,* and it is a theme that continues in several projects I'm currently working on. First, I've started a blog called Not Quite Right, which provides small insights and observations on the plethora of things in the Middle East that seem a little weird. But, more than just condemning Middle Eastern oddities, the blog tries to probe past the obvious into the reasons our American perspective finds such things weird. I've covered topics that range pretty widely, both geographically and in terms of subject matter, from Morocco to India, from strangely shaped pyramids to escargots.

I've also got another novel in the works. It, too, deals with the confluence of American and Middle Eastern cultures, but it takes a bit of a different (and perhaps even more explosive) angle. This new novel, which I'm calling *Taxi to Queen Alia,* revolves around the assassination of an American diplomat and his wife outside the U.S. Embassy in Amman, Jordan. The diplomat's two children, boys of similar age to my own two children, who are now eight and eleven, have been seatbelted into the backseat of a taxi when their parents are killed. Somewhat oblivious to the noise of the shooting (like all boys their age, they've got their video games shielding their eyes), they are startled when the taxi driver panics, hits the accelerator, and flees the scene. This scenario provides the novel with the opportunity to explore how two American children, marooned in a foreign culture, react. It also lets me rejoin the idea of writing from the perspective of "the other"—this time telling the story from a point of view where the reader must empathize with several people who are arrested and blamed for the conspiracy behind the assassination.

Questions and topics for discussion

1. What images come to mind when you think of the Middle East, and Iraq in particular? To what extent has your knowledge about the region been informed by the media's coverage of the current conflict? Does *One Hundred and One Nights* change the ways you think about Iraq and the people living there? If so, how?

2. Abu Saheeh is a man caught between two worlds, strongly tied to his birth country, Iraq, but also greatly influenced by the time he spent in America. What actions does Abu Saheeh take that seem to be based on the Iraqi side of his personality? What actions are more in line with the American side?

3. Discuss the relationship between Abu Saheeh and his brother, Yasin. What drives their competition and their hatred of each other? Do you think their behavior goes beyond sibling rivalry?

4. Life in the town of Safwan, Iraq—both in *One Hundred and One Nights* and, for the most part, in reality—continues relatively normally, despite the toll taken by three major wars in three decades. How do you think your community would react to war if it were similarly unlucky?

5. Layla's fascination with America is shared by many young people in the Middle East, yet there is also a

backlash against Western cultural, economic, and military imperialism. How does this tension play out in *One Hundred and One Nights*?

6. Many of Abu Saheeh's actions have unintended consequences. Do you think he could have foreseen them? Do you hold him responsible? Why or why not?

7. Against his will, Abu Saheeh takes on Abd al-Rahim as an apprentice. In what ways does Abd al-Rahim support and even save Abu Saheeh, and in what ways does he work against him? Discuss how their relationship progresses over the course of the novel.

8. Has anyone close to you experienced the tragic loss of a family member? If so, what similarities or differences did you notice between this person's reactions and the ways Abu Saheeh deals with his grief?

9. Abu Saheeh says that there is "an older and more respected reason for war than blind jihad" (page 275). Do you agree with him? Do you think that war is ever justifiable? Why or why not?

10. Benjamin Buchholz served as a liaison for the U.S. Army in Safwan. How do you think his experiences shaped the novel? Does the story have more authority because of his time there?

11. The novel's title is an allusion to *The Arabian Nights*. What are the similarities and differences between the two texts? How is Layla like Scheherazade?

JAN 11 2012